Highland Shift

Highland Destiny I

Laura Harner

Highland Shift is a work of fiction. Names, characters, places, and incidents are the product of the author's imagination or are used fictitiously. Any resemblance to actual persons, living or dead, events, or locales is entirely coincidental.

Third Edition.
Published in the United States by Hot Corner Press

ISBN: 978-1-937252-76-2

Contact the publisher for further information:
Hotcornerpress@gmail.com

Dedication

Virgie, you have touched every word…in so very many ways.

Diane, you are a wonderful sounding board and advocate for the characters. Robyn, Sadye, Kara, Gail, Julie, Dani, and the members, past and present, of HD…thank you for your unwavering support.

Liz, you are my hero. Thank you.

Dan, you have helped to bring the Highland Destiny series to life with your brilliant photography and patient attention to every detail. I can't wait to see where we go from here.

Last, and certainly not least…to my family. On December 26, 2008, I woke up with a dream. Jake, you especially listened to my stories, got to know Faolan and Elena, and never failed to tell me how proud you were of me. That goes both ways, son. Always take the time and put in the effort to follow your dreams. I believe in you.

Prologue

"Scatter," said the queen, imperiously, and then she'd thought no more about the powerfully magickal Druids.

The queen of the immortal race of the Tuatha Dé Danann, or Fae, was annoyed at her royal court for the games they were playing with the humans. With a gentle twitch of her finger and a word whispered on the wind, she'd banished the Druids to the four corners of the world and destroyed their libraries. She believed that once they were unable to pass on their magick, their power would die within a few generations.

The ancient members of the Druid Council, who were wise in the ways of both gods and humans, survived and cast wards around an island known only to them. There they continued to practice their arts despite their banishment, maintaining the veil between worlds, keeping humankind safe from otherworldly harm.

It was from this island that the Druid leaders cast powerful spells to direct certain futures. If you were inclined to believe in fairy tales, then you might believe this island sank into the sea thousands of years ago, taking the last of the ancient

Druids and their magick with it. You might also believe such spells had no place in today's world. You would be wrong on both counts.

Chapter One

Elena MacFarland stood motionless at the airline counter, temporarily lost in the earthy, spicy scent of the man behind her. Tired from the long flight and ready to get on with her fresh start, she resented the musky mixture that made her want to bury her face in his chest. Briefly closing her eyes, she sought inner strength, only to experience a mental vision of naked arms and legs tangled beneath satin sheets instead. With one last shaky breath of the intoxicating aroma, Elena retrieved her passport and ticket from the attendant and turned toward the seating area.

"Excuse me," the man said to the harried attendant, his Scottish burr deep and sexy, "can you tell me if there are any more seats available on that flight? 'Tis a matter of life and death."

Shaking off the additional brain fog his voice induced, Elena pushed forward to the boarding area and placed her backpack by her feet. With a deep breath, she reluctantly raised her eyes just enough to see what had smelled and sounded so enticing.

No doubt about it, there had been a god behind her in line.

Her mouth went dry at the expanse of golden skin and light dusting of hair on display between the top of his sturdy hiking boots and the bottom of his navy and green tartan. A thick cream-colored sweater clung to his broad shoulders, giving him a look of Old World style meets modern rustic. He was six and half feet of barely suppressed power, and her fingers curled as she thought about removing the leather thong that restrained his long sun-kissed hair. Blushing at her thoughts, Elena wondered if anything restrained him underneath his kilt. He looked as though he'd stepped off the cover of a romance novel. She barely resisted the urge to fan herself. She hadn't thought men still wore kilts, but she definitely liked the look.

When Elena had stood at the counter, she'd noticed that the perky attendant's nametag identified her as Shelly, and right now she looked ready to cry as she shook her head. There were no remaining seats available. The man continued to speak softly, and it was plain that he was using his considerable charm to find a way onto the flight. Whatever he said caused Shelly to look directly at Elena, whisper, and nod. He followed Shelly's gaze and raised a sardonic brow when he caught Elena watching him.

His gaze slowly raked Elena's body before he finally raised his gaze to meet her green eyes. Her spine stiffened, and nipples rose to pert attention in a confused and involuntary response. He stirred an ancient hunger deep within her belly, and lower still, as though she had a primal knowledge of his rock-hard body, steely arms, and crushing lips. Twenty feet apart and total strangers, Elena felt scorched by the heat that radiated between them.

Elena extinguished the fire quickly as her mind filled with memories of another egotistical jerk who had oozed such an overload of self-confidence. Over the past few months, Elena

MacFarland graduated from law school, became engaged, passed the bar exam, and landed her dream job. She'd also been dumped on her ass, fired, served with a restraining order, and evicted by Martin J. Worthington, III, who was both her former boss and ex-future-father-in-law. Arrogance did not impress her.

With a sniff, Elena turned away from the drama. She thought about the circumstances that had brought her halfway around the world, ready to start a new life on the outskirts of Inverness. As soon as she realized that she'd been used to advance the Worthington's agenda and unwilling to quit when she was so far behind, Elena had cleverly negotiated a very comfortable settlement with the elder Worthington in exchange for her silence. The only real drawback was that she needed to live in Scotland for two years. It didn't seem such a bad bargain.

Impatiently, Elena pushed the memories away and once more observed the ruckus on the other side of the airport lounge. Shelly had taken the arrogant Scotsman to speak with an older woman who was apparently traveling alone. The woman was listening attentively to Shelly, while never taking her eyes off the man's face. He took up the tale, presented his case, and then waited for her decision. Elena pitied her and expected it was a done deal; the man would get the woman's seat. It would be hard to resist his smoldering gaze.

****

The flight attendant's pampering made Elena glad that she had splurged on a first-class ticket. As she enjoyed her complimentary beverage, Elena watched the other travelers trudge past on their way to economy. The stream of passengers stopped, directions for buckling seatbelts announced, yet the cabin door was still open and the seat next to her still empty.

The senior flight attendant came through the door at the last possible minute, fawning over the gorgeous man from the terminal. He was completely oblivious to her attentions as he scanned the cabin, his gaze settling on Elena. He folded and squeezed himself into the remaining seat and brushed the flight attendant's hands away as she tried to help him fasten his seatbelt.

Elena leaned closer to the window and feigned an interest in the hustle and bustle of London's Heathrow Airport. She hadn't been nearly this close to him in the terminal, and his scent alone had practically given her an orgasm. Now her heart pounded uncomfortably fast as she concentrated on making herself as small as possible. Elena didn't understand her reaction to this manipulative man. She chalked it up to the strain of moving and tried to push her errant thoughts away.

As the plane began to taxi, he surprised her by introducing himself. "Hello, lass," he said seriously, "my name is Faolan." He pronounced it as FULL-an, the words rolling out of his mouth in a low and devastatingly sexy brogue.

Elena longed to wrap her tongue around his name, unsure of her ability to do it justice. She knew he was waiting for her to offer her name in return, but she had apparently gone mute as she stared at his face up close. His eyes were stunning. The golden-amber irises were edged with a dark ring, and his lashes were long enough to make a woman weep with envy. They were eyes Elena could stare into for hours. His nose was strong and straight, with slightly flared nostrils. His lips parted in a half-mocking smile that showed even, white teeth.

She was just thinking she would like to nibble that full lower lip when he caught his teeth on it in a small bite.

Fortunately, the flight attendant provided a timely distraction by asking Faolan what he would like to drink, giving Elena a chance to check herself for drool. With a quick mental inventory, she knew her emerald green eyes must look tired, and her long black curls were tangled into a clip on the back of her head. At least her blue V-necked sweater still clung flatteringly. There was comfort in that small positive. Elena was slightly more composed when Faolan looked back, so she gave introducing herself a whirl.

"I'm Elena MacFarland. Nice to meet you." Oh God, that sounded so lame!

For the next hour, Elena was going to be stuck next to Faolan in a strangely intimate public place. She reminded herself that she wasn't trying to make an impression, just trying to keep from touching the man. Even in the extra roomy seats of the first-class cabin, Faolan's knee managed to bump against hers, and Elena gasped. It was as though a bolt of electricity shot straight up her leg. She thought she heard him laugh softly. Elena stared out the window, more disturbed by her reactions than she cared to admit.

Faolan was a powerfully sexual man. Everything about him set her hormones on fire. Her body and mind had disengaged from each other, and her body wanted to touch him, pet him, taste him. Elena had learned that lesson the hard way, and it wasn't going to happen again. Good-looking, arrogant men like Faolan were never interested in the real Elena, there would always be a catch. Her body would just have to back the hell down; her head was in control now.

Determined to prove just *how* in control she was, Elena decided to risk some small talk. She took a deep breath to relieve the tension, turned toward Faolan, and was surprised to find him staring intently at her. Elena had always wondered why people needed to gather their wits about them, but now she knew. Wits could indeed be scattered. She spent a moment gathering hers and wondering why he watched her so closely.

In her hesitation, Faolan made the first conversational strike. "What brings you to Scotland, lass? Where are you headed?"

"Uhm." That was clever. Try again. She cleared her throat. "I'm moving here. I just purchased a home, north of Inverness, and I'm on my way there." She was relieved to notice that she sounded better, more like the confident woman she knew herself to be.

Faolan seemed politely interested, "How did you decide on Inverness? Do you have family here? Or is your man from here?"

Elena sighed. "It's a long story, but no, I have no family or a *man*." She might have sounded a little sarcastic. "I haven't seen the house yet. It's supposed to be a small farmhouse on the outskirts of a tiny village north of Inverness. It was part of a legal settlement."

"A legal settlement?" Elena ignored the opportunity to explain; she wasn't reliving that story with this man. As she searched for a safer topic, she belatedly remembered his comments to the attendant. He'd said it was a matter of life or death. Maybe it hadn't all been arrogance; he could have a loved one seriously hurt somewhere. She wondered if he wanted to talk about it.

"I don't mean to pry, but I heard you at the counter. You seemed adamant about getting on this flight. I hope everything is all right with your family?"

His jaw tightened, and he turned his head away. He looked livid for a minute, and Elena was glad that she wasn't the focus of his anger. Then as suddenly as the fury appeared, it left him with a sigh. "Nay, lass, nothing will ever be right again. I have no family," he said with a voice full of sadness.

"I'm sorry," Elena offered, not sure of how else to respond. She returned to looking out the window in order to give him some privacy. She knew what it was like to be alone in this world, to have your dreams ripped out from under you, to feel as though nothing would ever be right again.

After a moment, Faolan changed the subject. "How are you planning on getting to the Highlands?"

Elena jumped at the chance to ease away from topics that were more personal in nature. "I leased a Land Rover," Elena continued, trying to keep the subject light, "I made a reservation at the Hilton in Inverness for tonight. Tomorrow I'll drive to Fairth."

They continued to chat about inconsequential things and discovered they had very little in common. She told him she was an attorney; he said he dabbled in investments. She liked sports; he didn't. This was her first trip abroad; he was well-traveled. Soon the flight attendant returned to tell them to prepare for landing. Although Elena had enjoyed their brief conversation, she would be relieved to get away from him. From his sheer physical size to his long brooding glances, everything about him was too intense. It had only been a few short months since her break up with Marty, and Faolan was exactly the type of man she had sworn off for life: great looking, seriously confident with a tangible air of entitlement. Definitely not her cup of tea.

"I'm a little curious," said Elena as they stood in the aisle waiting to exit the plane. "How did you manage to get on the flight? I thought it was full."

She looked up and stifled a gasp. Despite being a foot taller than she was, he towered over her; his face much closer than she expected because of the cabin's low ceiling. His look was positively dangerous, and his tawny eyes turned dark as he scowled. Their gazes locked for a minute, the air doing that strange burning thing around them again, just as it had done in the terminal. He bared his teeth in a tight, wolfish imitation of a smile that didn't reach his eyes. "I always get what I want. *Eventually.*"

Chapter Two

Elena spent a few minutes familiarizing herself with the controls and getting used to sitting on the wrong side of her new SUV. She expected the already dismal driving conditions would only worsen before she reached the Highlands. After turning on the wipers and lights against the persistent mist, she reviewed her route, then struggled to refold the map, wishing she'd gotten a GPS instead.

Lost in her preparations, she nearly screamed when the passenger door was suddenly wrenched open, and Faolan climbed inside. His hand rested lightly on the hilt of a sheathed dagger hanging at his waist. His hair had come loose, and he dripped rainwater and danger in equal measure. "Drive," he growled, his voice rougher than in the terminal.

"Get out of my car," Elena instinctively snapped back, not thinking of the possible consequences. "Get. Out. Now."

Faolan roared, much like an injured wild animal. Through clenched teeth he gritted, "Drive now! Pull out and turn right. You will be safe enough, if you will only just shut up and start driving now!"

Remembering his size and thinking of the knife, Elena

stomped on the gas pedal a bit harder than she intended. "You bastard," she spat out between clenched teeth. She was just building toward a blistering tirade against all arrogant men when she noticed he was clutching his right side. Blood seeped between his fingers.

"You've been hurt. What happened?" Steering with one hand, she reached to get the map from the console, "Where's the closest hospital? You can get out there!"

Faolan grabbed her, his hand a steel vice around her wrist. "I will heal. 'Tis not too serious. But tell me, lass, who is trying to kill you?"

"Kill me? No one is trying to kill me," Elena said, hating that her voice shook with rage. "The only danger I'm in is from the lunatic who jumped into my car and kidnapped me."

"As long as you drive where I tell you, you are in no danger from me," Faolan said, but his eyes and his knife gave lie to his statement.

With as few words as possible, he directed her out of Edinburgh and toward Inverness. Once on the main road, she watched while he used a clean shirt and rain from the lowered window to clean his hands and dress his wound. It looked as though the worst of the bleeding was over; in fact, he seemed to be healing remarkably quickly.

Elena had no idea where he was really taking her, but at least they were headed in the general direction she wanted to go. With a quick mental inventory, she realized she wasn't particularly afraid. No sweating palms, no racing pulse. In a weird way, the fact that she wasn't cowering behind the wheel was comforting. She didn't know why he'd kidnapped her or what he hoped to gain, but she was somehow confident he wouldn't hurt her. It was something in the way he looked at her, as though he knew her already.

As she thought over the circumstances, she realized her options were limited. She certainly wasn't going to overpower or outrun him. They'd seemed to get on well enough on the plane, maybe she could convince him to let her go. If she could just be nice enough, get him talking about himself, she might learn something to use as leverage.

"Why the hell are you doing this? You barged your way onto the plane and now into my car. What do you want?" Then Elena sighed. So much for being nice. Her brain-to-mouth syndrome was in overdrive.

Faolan inhaled sharply but continued his stony silence.

She knew she'd better try that bonding conversation again, so Elena searched for a safer topic. Deciding that talking about the weather was too mundane, she pelted him with questions. His taciturn responses did nothing to curb her growing enthusiasm for the landscape. After a while, she'd nearly forgotten the precariousness of her situation.

Faolan finally said, "Och, lass, do you never be still? Enough with your constant havering!"

"Fine I won't say another word," Elena said. She maintained a ridiculous sort of silence, starting and stopping herself from speaking countless times.

After several minutes, it seemed Faolan had enough of her version of quiet. "What is the real reason you came to Scotland, Elena MacFarland?" he said, his voice a throaty growl.

Elena hesitated, but realized he might have more sympathy for her if she told him something. "It's not a story I usually share," she haltingly began. "My mother was killed crossing the street when I was four, so I went to live with my Grandda MacFarland. I was thirteen when he died, and we didn't have anyone else. There was no chance of adoption as a teenager.

Everyone wants the babies. Instead, I bounced between foster homes, moving every few months until I was old enough to live on my own."

There was a long pause while he appeared to think over what she'd told him. Then he thrust directly at the heart of things, "You still didna answer my question. Why are you here? Why are you not in Phoenix practicing law?"

"I didn't tell you I was from Phoenix. I said Arizona," Elena said sharply.

"Och, lass, doona' be so prickly. I merely said Phoenix because 'tis the only city I know in Arizona. Why not answer my question? Why would you move to Scotia?"

Scotia, he'd said, just like her Grandda. Elena's eyes misted, and her throat tightened. "It's a long story," she said tensely. That really was something she didn't plan to share with anyone. Over was over.

"Why not tell me why you're here?" he asked gently, as though he cared. "We still have a ways yet to go together."

Surprisingly, Elena found herself sharing a story she'd never wanted to think about again.

****

Elena opened her door to the last person she expected to see on a Saturday morning: her boss and future father-in-law. Mr. Martin J. Worthington, III. If Marty was gold on sunshine, his father was silver on ice. He brushed past her and went straight to the dining room to set his briefcase on the table. He turned to look at her, disapproval for the casual way she was dressed was all over his face.

"I wish to offer my congratulations on your successful passing of the bar exam." He handed her a thick envelope that had clearly already been opened.

Her thoughts were whirling, but she kept her head down and quickly scanned the letter. She mentally skipped the happy dance, wondering at the real purpose of his visit.

Worthington reached into his briefcase and removed a sheaf of papers with a light blue outer cover. He examined Elena's face before referring to the document in his hand. "Martin J. Worthington, IV, declares he no longer wishes to maintain any relationship with you. As of today's date, he dissolves any formal or informal agreement with Elena MacFarland, to be engaged to be married, to wed, or to be considered as partners in any form of the word. You are to cease and desist any attempt to contact Martin J. Worthington, IV, any of his family members, or acquaintances. He thanks you for all of the assistance you provided in helping him to accomplish his goal of becoming an attorney. He hopes that the relationship was mutually beneficial and reminds you that you were allowed to live rent free and of the clothes and jewelry that you received."

She felt the slow burn of humiliation as it crept up from the center of her being. There was no doubt in her mind that Marty's father was telling the truth. Like father, like son, the arrogant bastards. She was surprised to realize there was a large part of her relieved to have the fairy tale over. That didn't mean she was going to make it painless for either of them. To hurt a Worthington, you just needed to know what was most important and take it away.

Money!

"I see. Thank you, Martin, for making Marty's position perfectly clear. I wonder if you would speak as to your position in all of this," Elena said coolly.

Martin glanced up at her, then deliberately dropped his eyes to her bare feet and raked them slowly up her body. His steely gaze lingering on her breasts, he asked, "What did you have in mind Ms. MacFarland?"

"Oh dear, Martin. You seemed to have misunderstood my question." Elena smiled, a feral cat on the hunt. "I am under contract for the next two years with Worthington, Tyler, and Walters. Aren't you concerned

with any awkwardness in the office?"

*"You dare presume, Ms. MacFarland, that you are still employed?"
Worthington gave a delicate snort, "Allow me to present you with an order
of eviction and a restraining order preventing you from contacting my son,
any member of our family, or any member of the law firm ever again. If
you have any personal belongings at the office, you may call my assistant to
have them delivered to your new place of residence. You have twenty-four
hours to vacate these premises, and I no longer expect to see you anywhere,
especially not in the office."*

*With that, he handed her the documents, closed his case, and prepared
to leave.*

*"That's an interesting opening argument, Martin. Let's think this
through a minute, shall we? I have a perfectly valid contract, which
guarantees my employment for a period of two years, providing I
successfully pass the bar, which I did.*

*"I work for the firm, not for you personally, and the policies of the
firm, as well as all Equal Opportunity laws apply to my situation. This
leaves me entitled to my full two years of pay, plus the signing bonuses.*

*"I believe a case could be made that I provided certain services to
Marty in the form of tutoring and study aids, which were necessary to help
him become an attorney. Marty offered me this townhouse as partial
compensation for my work as his tutor. He obviously passed the bar or you
wouldn't be here; therefore, I expect to receive the deed." She took the sheaf
of legal documents and threw them on the table.*

*"Although you have far more legal resources at your disposal, I have
right on my side. I won't go quietly. Marty's academic records will become
public as will your role in this unpleasant situation. I will subpoena every
person at every event I attended with Marty, every client, and every
opposing counsel with whom I have come into contact while working for the
firm.*

*"Make no mistake, Martin. This will not merely be a personal
disagreement between us. I will seek compensation from Marty, from you,*

and from the firm for breach of contract, pain and suffering, and defamation of character. Perhaps you should speak with your partners before we proceed any further with our negotiations."

For one long minute, Martin and Elena stared at each other—then a slow smile formed on his lips but never reached his cold eyes.

"Name your terms, Miss MacFarland."

****

Elena was physically exhausted from the travel and emotionally drained from the humiliation of her story. After talking for what seemed like hours, she'd certainly told Faolan enough to make a personal connection. Would that be enough for him to let her go? Elena kept her eyes on the road, but she sensed his gaze on her. They didn't speak again except for his terse directions once they arrived in Inverness.

Elena tried to sort through her muddled thoughts. Somewhere along the way, she'd forgotten to think of him as a kidnapper. After all, he now knew more about her than anyone else in Scotland. More than anyone, anywhere, really. When she saw the Hilton right in front of them, she realized he'd seen her safely to her destination. She pulled to the curb, but Faolan stared into the rain, his expression unfathomable.

She watched her traitorous hand as it reached up to gently touch his face, "Are you okay?" The moment Elena touched him, a bolt of electricity shot up her arm and coursed through her body, straight to her core. Her breath caught in her throat, and her gaze lingered on his firm, luscious lips. If he kissed her she knew she'd be lost forever. At that thought, Elena's lips parted and she unconsciously wet them with the tip of her tongue, an invitation as old as the ages.

Faolan turned to face her, a fierce, haunted look in his eyes.

Then his expression changed to something hungrier and need seemed to smolder between them. "Elena," he whispered hoarsely. Then his mouth was on hers, and she thought no more.

His kiss was gentle. He reached to cup her face in both of his hands, caressing her cheek with his thumbs. Her mouth parted on an exclamation of surprise, and his tongue darted past her lips as he deepened the kiss. Faolan loosened her hair, and her raven curls spilled down her back. Threading his fingers through the silken strands, his kiss turned urgent as he pulled her even closer, and the console pressed into her side.

He kissed her with such suddenness that her brain was ten steps behind her body. His tongue thrust in, then retreated, gliding in an intimate rhythm. Elena leaned toward Faolan, getting as close as possible to his broad, warm chest and moaned softly into his mouth. Her fingers splayed across his stomach, and she slid her hands over powerful muscles that rippled under her touch.

Elena's body sparked to life, heedless of the circumstances that brought them together. A reckless abandon fueled her kisses. She laced her fingers behind his neck and pulled him closer. He groaned, and Elena felt the heady power of a woman who knows she's desired. She was being devoured and had no will to stop him. His kisses claimed her, and she wanted him to keep kissing her until her last breath.

Breathing heavily, he pulled back slightly and nibbled on Elena's lower lip before running kisses along her jaw to her neck. With his face buried in her hair, he whispered her name once more, "Elena."

Then he pulled away from the embrace, opened the door, and walked away without a backward glance. Faolan disappeared into the mist as though he were nothing more than a figment of her imagination.

Chapter Three

When Elena had presented her counteroffer to the elder Worthington, she'd expected to get half of what she asked for. However, since Martin wanted her gone from Phoenix more than he cared about the money, Elena had a bigger bargaining chip than she'd realized. In their final agreement, she'd received five years' worth of salary plus the performance bonuses. It turned out that the townhouse had actually belonged to the firm, not Worthington, so it couldn't be part of the settlement. In an effort to end the unpleasant situation quickly, Martin had offered a small bungalow on a hundred acres of land in Scotland as an alternative.

Moving to Scotland had seemed like a big step until she realized she'd been the only one really surprised Marty was just using her to get his license. When Martin sweetened the pot by offering to pay off her student loans, Elena decided leaving Phoenix for a while was a good idea. An isolated farm in the land of Grandda seemed a great place to escape her embarrassment.

As promised, the house had three bedrooms, fireplaces, and oak floors throughout. Unfortunately, the house looked long abandoned, and there was no way to tell what damage lay hidden under the years of dirt. Elena's new local solicitor, the ancient and frail Mr. Burns, dryly informed Elena of her right to refuse the settlement. The house was clearly not in the condition advertised by Worthington.

Her solicitor's advice notwithstanding, she wanted nothing more than to have this final connection to the Worthington family over. Elena signed the documents with a flourish. Mr. Burns would continue as her accounts manager and promised he would send a handyman for repairs. Less than an hour after arriving, the farm provisionally belonged to Elena MacFarland. She need only complete the six-month waiting period as stipulated in the agreement and the house was hers.

Once alone, Elena surveyed her first home with a mixture of pride and purpose. Surrounded by frozen grass and patches of snow, Elena turned slowly around, letting the atmosphere of the old farm wash over her. The farmhouse was nestled into gently rolling snow-covered hills and canopied by a sky so blue it made her throat tight with the beauty.

Her house was over three hundred years old, made of stone, and retrofitted somewhere along the way with large picture windows on all sides. There was a barn-like structure that was listed in the particulars as a 'steading.' Similar to a large modern horse barn, the outbuilding was U-shaped and opened into a fenced paddock. The south side of the steading was two floors tall, probably to accommodate storing hay. The north end butted up against a hillock, and looked as if it disappeared into the land.

After a quick inventory, Elena drove back to Inverness to get the items most necessary to her survival. She couldn't imagine staying another night at a hotel. This place already felt like home, even if it meant roughing it for a while.

****

Elena tackled the master bedroom first. The windows faced the east and had an expansive view that stretched for miles. Perhaps in the spring and summer it would include a stream or loch, but for now, large patches of snow blanketed enough of the landscape to leave her wondering. She built a roaring fire and began to clean.

By bedtime, the rest of the house was still cold and dark, but Elena's room was cozy, warm, and mostly clean. She looked around with satisfaction. Her back might ache from the hours spent scrubbing, dusting, and sweeping, but now she'd reclaimed the space from decades of neglect. A warm glow built in her chest as she imagined a new bed, a dresser, maybe even a rocking chair to place by the hearth. She marveled at how far she'd come to get here. She was in Scotland; she was home.

She stepped outside into a spectacular night. Her breath frosted on the air. Stars dominated the heavy black velvet sky, but Elena knew they would soon cede their supremacy to the rising moon. As she stood, surrounded by darkness and a silence so complete it pressed against her ears, she watched a wolf cross a field in the distance. When a howl echoed over the land, Elena wondered if the wolf was lonely. She realized that she had been lonely for much of her life. Now she was alone in the truest sense of the word, in a new country, in a completely new life.

She had never felt more at peace.

****

"How do you do? Mr. Burns sent us. Said you could use some

help out here. I'm Lilly, and this is my husband, Red," said the short, soft-looking woman with white curly hair. She looked like Elena's idea of a real mother, full of hugs and laughter, spun sugar with a steel core. Elena suspected summer followed her wherever she went.

Red was tall, lean, with a ruddy complexion and, appropriately enough, a full head of red hair that faded to gray around the temples. He wore denim and flannel and heavy work boots. With his easy smile and gentle manner, he reminded Elena of the Scarecrow in the *Wizard of Oz.*

Elena invited them into the recently cleaned kitchen, and they looked around with interest.

"Aye, looks as though you have your hands busy. We'd like to help, if you've a mind to hire both of us," Lilly said. They suggested a reasonable salary and were happy to start right away. With her settlement from Worthington filling her bank account, she was pleased to accept the terms and get the business of renovation underway.

Elena left them to work in the house while she went to explore the steading. Beginning on the south side, she discovered a workshop and a garage-type storage area. Although Elena longed to build her own garden, the thought of using even a small tractor was intimidating. The rest of the space contained an assortment of tools, sawhorses, and feed.

The main part of the barn was set up with stalls, each with a two-part stable door that opened into the fenced paddock. As she continued through to the north side, she noticed it was definitely warmer than the other two sections. This wing was also deeper and darker than the others. When her eyes adjusted to the dim light, her jaw dropped as she saw the jumble of contents.

Elena had shopped in second-hand stores all her life; there

had simply been no money to shop elsewhere. She loved the challenge of the hunt and the excitement when she unearthed a treasure that had been someone else's trash. The day had just turned into Christmas and her birthday all rolled into one. The entire back part of the wing was one giant rummage sale, and everything was free.

Sleeves rolled up and hair tied back, Elena dragged an iron headboard, three dressers, and two brass lamps with filthy leaded glass shades that made her heart beat fast, to a corner of the room she mentally labeled the 'Save' pile. A sled without runners, a box of broken dishes, and three rusted bicycle frames went into the 'Toss' pile. She'd even started an 'Unsure' pile in a third spot, so she could delay making a decision on an old bookcase and some rusted farming tools.

Several hours later, most of the junk was sorted into her three separate stacks. The boxes at the very back of the barn would have to wait until she had more light, so she could see the contents. She stretched her back, then twisted from side-to-side in order to relieve the ache she'd begun to think might be permanent. Just as she decided she'd done enough for one morning, Lilly called out that lunch was ready.

Lilly ladled homemade chicken soup into bowls and ordered Elena to wash up in the kitchen sink. Elena moaned with her first taste; it was like heaven, rich and loaded with vegetables. Served with thick slices of fresh baked bread with butter, she swore it was the most delicious meal she'd eaten in her whole life. Lilly beamed, and Red's eyes sparkled.

Red and Lilly took turns telling Elena stories of the previous owners and tenants. Then they shared a quick glance, and Elena suspected there was more to the story. Lilly admitted as much and said, "I hope you aren't the superstitious type?"

"Not at all," Elena replied quickly.

"Good, 'cause there's them that think this place is haunted," Lilly said, with a wink.

Elena laughed delightedly, "Even if it *is* haunted, it won't scare me away. This place feels like home deep down in my bones. I don't know how else to describe it. It calls to me." This time the glance Red and Lilly exchanged was longer, but they were not inclined to share.

****

Saturday morning found Elena working in the north wing. She'd decided to spend the weekend cleaning out the corner where the junk pile had started. All week trucks had hauled in appliances and furniture and carried away the unwanted items from the steading, so she had much more room to spread out.

The week had passed in a flurry of activity. Elena worked with Lilly to clean the remaining rooms, and Red had the floor polisher going non-stop, bringing the oak floors to a gleaming shine. The house was still sparsely furnished but she wasn't sure which of the other pieces of furniture she'd found could, or should, be salvaged. There was plenty of time to decide, and she thought she might like to fill any gaps with pieces from local antique shops. With Red and Lilly away until Monday, she could work on the items she wanted to restore.

Late that afternoon, she'd moved enough boxes and furniture to notice that the rear wall of the north wing had a slight downhill slant. It was very dark, but she discovered a dirty metal plate against the rear wall, tucked into the corner. Elena examined it as best she could in the dim light. It looked like two pieces of metal, attached somehow to a boulder that formed the back wall.

Realizing she'd found the source of the warmer air, Elena placed her hand on the metal and felt a slight vibration beneath her hand. It was almost as though there was a breeze blowing behind it. The air wasn't exactly warm, but it was certainly warmer than the frigid outdoor temperatures. She wondered just what secrets those panels were hiding.

Elena wanted to pry the metal panels apart, but her meager flashlight just wasn't bright enough to illuminate the dark corner. She was ready for a little field trip anyway. She locked up the house, grabbed her shopping bags, and a few minutes later, she was on her way to the Village of Fairth.

****

All conversation stopped the second Elena walked through the door, and every person turned to stare. The barkeep broke the silence first with a hearty, "Welcome to Fairth, Miss MacFarland!"

"It's Elena." She grinned as she approached the bar. Several voices called back, "Elena," and she experienced an absurd moment of feeling like Norm on *Cheers*. Apparently, there were no secrets in small Scottish villages, she thought.

Conversations resumed, and Elena pulled up a stool. The pub was small and dark with three booths on each of the long walls. It was split down the middle by a classic bar, complete with a brass foot rail and heavy stools of burgundy leather and oak. Glasses and copper pots hung above the bar, and the barkeep stood at the front end of its horseshoe shape, grinning at Elena as though they were old friends.

"Lovely to meet you, Elena. We've been wondering when you might show up and bend yer elbow with the likes of us. Name's Michael, but you can call me Mike. Everyone does."

Mike was a little taller than she was, with broad shoulders and massive forearms, covered in ink. A trident on one arm and a sea serpent on the other, she noted and hazarded a guess.

"Nice tats. Were you in the Navy?"

"Aye, I was, but it didn't stick. Missed my Highlands." Then, without asking Elena's preference, he shouted, "Bar wench, bring me a special!" and then roared with laughter a moment later as his wife backed through the door carrying a tray laden with a crock of bean soup, homemade bread, and an enormous salad.

The woman snapped Mike on the butt with her bar towel, looked at Elena, and said, "Never you mind him, darlin'. He's as full of blow as the Nor'wind. Name's Kate. Welcome to the Lone Wolf. It's our pub and none finer in these parts or others. We saw you arrive last week. And of course, our Mr. Burns told us of meeting you. I see you hired Red and Lilly. No one better to take care of you. Will your family be joining you?"

Nearly as round as she was tall, Kate had curly brown hair surrounding her rosy cheeks. When she finally paused to take a breath and wait for an answer, her bright light blue gaze seemed to be taking inventory and Elena had no doubt that by tomorrow morning the rest of the village would know every detail of what she'd been wearing.

Elena decided to answer the last question first, and then figure out if anything else needed a response. "I have no family; it's just me."

"Good golly, lass. Are you not lonely out there by yourself? I have just the thing for you." She bustled from the room without waiting for an answer, leaving Elena to wonder at the whirlwind of action. When she reappeared a few minutes later she carried a cloth-lined covered picnic basket on her arm. She thrust it at Elena and turned back toward the kitchen. Just before she disappeared behind the swinging doors again, she shouted out, "Leave them here until you're ready to leave. Mike, doona' forget the first meal is on us. Doona' worry, dear. We'll get our money out of you later."

Mike roared again, as did most of the regulars in the pub. It seemed everyone was in on the joke but Elena. After quickly scooping the last spoonful of the soup into her mouth, she lifted the edge of the cloth so she could be part of the inside scoop. She peeked cautiously inside and instantly her heart melted. Curled up together were two tiny kittens, one black and the other an orange tabby.

Elena looked up to find Mike's eyes twinkling. "My Katy girl likes you," he declared.

Elena laughed. "How can you tell?"

"Och, lass, ye'd be payin' for your meal if she didn't!"

With a promise to return for her kittens, Elena stepped out into the cold to find the hardware store. Outside the air was freezing, and a damp fog had settled in, shrouding everything in the mist. There were rapid footsteps behind her as she crossed the alley behind the pub. The fog was so thick, Elena couldn't see anyone, but she could hear muffled voices. Probably other pub-goers calling it a night, she thought. She turned the corner and pulled up short. Two men stood in front of her, wearing dark sweats and hoodies pulled tight around their faces.

"Excuse me," Elena said, as she tried to step around them. They blocked her path while two others came up quickly behind her, all apparently with bad intentions. The men surrounded her, clearly herding her toward the open door of the brown panel van next to the sidewalk.

Girls who grow up moving from one foster home to

another have two choices: become a victim or become a survivor. Elena was a survivor. She didn't wait to see what they had in mind. Screaming like a wild woman, she ran straight at the smallest guy and jammed her knee hard into his groin. She put every unproductive ounce of fear into generating enough force to drop an elephant. She was rewarded by his soft "Oomph," and then he fell like a stone to the ground, hands clutching his privates.

Elena knew that taking one male out with a good swift knee to the groin made every other male in the vicinity lose momentum and bend slightly forward. *Yet another form of male bonding. Go figure.*

Still screaming like a banshee, she charged one of the other men, aiming her backpack at his head and connected solidly. She grinned as another of her would-be attackers fell to the ground. Elena turned to look at the two remaining men, and her heart sank. Although the third man was on the small side, the fourth was a monster of a man. She couldn't see their faces, but she sensed from the way they were inching forward, retreat was not on either of their minds.

Elena let loose another war cry, surprised and definitely pleased to hear another female voice join hers. Kate entered the mix with a broom in her hands, swinging and yelling to wake the dead.

"You lousy, chicken-hearted bastards. Get out of here. Back off, before I send Mike out here to kick some more arses!" She connected with the backside of the one who seemed to be the leader.

Suddenly in full retreat mode, the big man began yelling orders. "Grab Reggie, and let's get out of here!" Then he turned to face Elena directly, "You'll pay for this, bitch!" He jumped into the driver's seat, and the van sped away.

Suddenly the street was busy with patrons from the pub spilling out, looking for a fight. Kate pulled Elena into a victory dance, whooping and hollering, "Doona' be messin' with these badass babes! Mike, you shoulda seen this young one. She was kickin' ass and takin' names. Where'd you learn to fight like that? Who were those punks anyway? I've never seen any of them 'round here afore. Did anyone get the registration number? Has anyone called Officer Davy yet? Darlin' Elena, you need to come back inside and have a cuppa."

Kate finally took a breath, and others had a chance to be heard. Everyone spoke at once, and no one knew anything. Not who the men were, why they'd attacked, or where they'd gone. The consensus was they'd come from a bigger city and randomly targeted Elena because she was a young woman walking alone. No one believed they'd be back.

Mike personally walked Elena to Murphy's Hardware to get her lanterns and flashlights, and of course, kitten food. When they returned, everyone came out to wave good-bye and see Elena and the kittens safely on their way.

****

"What do you mean, you didn't get her?" the voice asked over the phone.

Liam stammered, trying to make it sound reasonable that four men hadn't managed to throw one woman into the back of a van. "Master, she charged Reggie, and her screaming brought half the town. We only just got away. If only you would let me use—"

"I want her tonight. She lives alone. Get to the farm before she returns. Don't bring her to headquarters; this is personal.

Call me when you have her, and remember to make it look random. Whatever you do, don't get caught."

****

Elena took the kittens in first so they wouldn't get cold. When she came back out, she went to the far side of the Rover to get the lantern and flashlights. She shifted a fraction of a second before she was hit. The bat caught a bit more shoulder than her attacker probably intended. One moment Elena was bent over the back seat picking up a lantern; the next she was falling to the ground, trying to remain conscious.

A stabbing pain shot through her shoulder, and Elena's right arm went numb. It hung uselessly by her side as she tried to catch herself. It was a testament to her jumbled brain that her first thought was that she hoped her arm wasn't broken. Men were talking as though from a great distance, and although she couldn't swear to it, she had a sneaking suspicion there were four. She pushed back against the wave of unconsciousness trying to pull her under. She was half inside the Rover but still on her knees in the snow, aware of a presence behind her, but unable to turn to face her assailant.

Elena grunted with pain when a booted foot kicked her hip. Then, using her hair as a handle, the one behind her lifted her to her feet and laid a cold blade of steel against the tender skin of her throat. Elena was face-to-face with the monster from the alley.

"Remember us, sweetheart?" he asked, his voice cold as the night air.

"Get away from me," Elena said, trying for fierce, getting feeble, instead. Fear threatened to overwhelm her, and she pushed it ruthlessly aside.

The hand in her hair tightened painfully as he lifted her off her feet, forcing her to balance on her toes. He pushed Elena back against the frame of the Rover and pressed himself hard against her.

There was laughter as he caressed her cheek with the knife, and then slowly stroked the blade down the column of her exposed neck, then down the front of her shirt to her waistband. "Thought you were too good for me, did you?" he asked silkily.

One of them said, "Go on, Liam, get a move; I want me some, too."

He had a name, Elena thought. *Liam*. She wouldn't forget. She struggled to catalog identifying characteristics, such as his cultured speech pattern, the smell of tobacco, and sound of his voice. Belatedly, their words penetrated and she realized these men intended to rape her. There would be no help this time. Her farm was several miles from the village, and her closest neighbors would never hear her, even if she could scream.

"Shut up, or you'll be going last." Then Liam whispered something only Elena could hear, "Maybe I'll keep you for myself." He slipped the knife under Elena's sweater and laid the blade flat against her bare skin, terrifyingly close to her breasts. His breath was hot and moist on her neck. "There are depths to you, lass."

The smallest one—Reggie, she thought—yelled out, "You ain't too good for us; we'll make you forget any man you ever had. You willna be wantin' no other man neither. You'll be beggin' me for more before I'm done with you." The other two men were laughing at Reggie's boldness, making excited sounds. None of them seemed to realize their leader had gone quite still at their remarks.

"Don't worry, Elena," Liam whispered, as intimate as any

lover. "If you please me, I won't share you with them. Convince me it should be just the two of us."

He ran a tongue along her neck, then squeezed her breast painfully, before moving his hand to grip her face. He kissed her brutally, and Elena kept her eyes and mouth tightly closed.

She'd never been moved enough by a relationship to make love with any man, and now these bastards were going to take that first moment from her, rip it away as if it were nothing. To them it *was* nothing. This was about power. If they knew she was a virgin, it would give them that much more control over her. She would keep that secret to herself.

When she refused to yield to his kiss, Liam pulled the knife back savagely, splitting her sweater from waist to neckline. She gasped but wouldn't give him the satisfaction of hearing her scream. Liam grabbed her roughly by the hair again and then kicked her legs out from under her.

"I see you would rather share with everybody, you fucking bitch." Liam shoved Elena face first into the back seat of the Rover, and slid the knife into the waistband of her jeans. With a jerky yank of the handle, he cut her jeans open from waist to crotch.

A feral growl rent the night air, raising hair on the back of Elena's neck. It was impossible to tell from which direction the growl came; it echoed throughout the yard and bounced off the walls. Everyone froze, and Liam's grip on Elena's hair loosened. She took advantage of his momentary distraction and kicked out with her boot, catching him in the shin.

The growl reverberated around the yard again, and then a disembodied voice said, "Leave!" Elena tried to twist and aim a kick at Liam's groin, but he recovered quickly and slammed her head into the Rover's door with a resounding *thunk*. It was the last thing Elena remembered.

Chapter Four

When Elena regained consciousness, she was in her own bed, and a fire was roaring in the grate. She reached with her mind to find the last thing she remembered...her hand went to her forehead. There was a huge knot there. With a moan, she touched the back of her head, and found another knot, and her scalp was sore from having her hair pulled so hard. Her right arm felt dead from the shoulder on down. The palms of her hands were raw, as if she had fallen and tried to catch herself.

Questions whirled in her mind. Who were those men, and why had they attacked her? How did they get to her house before she did? Her quick inventory had revealed she was naked underneath her fluffy robe, and she had no recollection of how she'd gotten undressed or in her bed. Who'd put her to bed? More importantly, who'd taken off her clothes?

With sudden panic, Elena realized it was likely that Liam and his thugs were still here. They'd probably brought her inside where it was warmer and there would be no one to find her until Monday when Red and Lilly returned.

Footsteps sounded in the hall. Someone was walking toward her room. There was nowhere to hide; they'd find her easily if she tried to escape through the window. She grabbed the fireplace poker and stood behind the door, ready to bring it down on whichever of them came in first. Heart pounding erratically in, she stared in horrified fascination at the doorknob as it turned and the door slowly opened.

"Elena?"

"Faolan?" She'd never expected to hear that unforgettable voice anywhere again, but especially not in her own bedroom. She stepped out from behind the door, but she didn't drop the poker. "What the hell are you doing here?"

"Apparently, saving your life again, lass," he said softly. He approached her slowly, as if she were a skittish animal ready to bolt. He moved closer, and held both of his hands palms up, as if inviting her to put her hands in his. Elena couldn't quite bring herself to trust him that far, and after a moment he dropped his gaze and his hands.

"You shouldna be up and about yet. You had a rough experience. Who were your friends out there?" he asked, his tone casual.

"Those weren't my friends! They tried to attack me outside the pub, and I fought them off. They must have followed..." Her voice trailed off, as she realized they'd been waiting for her. *They knew where she lived.* Then to her horror, she began to cry. Crying was something best done alone, if at all, but she couldn't help it. Great, racking sobs shook through her, leaving her feeling vulnerable and exposed.

Closing the gap between them, Faolan took the poker and dropped it to the floor. He swept Elena into his arms and cradled her like a baby. "Shhh, lass. Doona' cry," Faolan crooned repeatedly, holding her tight against his chest and rocking her gently. He held her until, with enormous shudders, her crying subsided into occasional hiccups. Faolan sat Elena on the bed and pulled the covers over her legs. He sat down next to her and stroked her hair once before settling his hands in his lap.

"Why doona' you tell me what is happening, so I can help you?" he asked. His whisky-rich voice sent shivers through her, and apparently, misunderstanding, he pulled her covers up higher.

Elena thought about his question. She had very nearly been raped and hadn't escaped being badly beaten. Now, a man she'd met only once before, under less than trust-inspiring circumstances, showed up, claiming to have saved her life for a second time. She couldn't think of any reason for Faolan to be at her home. Unless, of course, he was somehow connected to those punks. She hadn't told any of them where she lived.

Elena countered, "Why don't you tell me why *you're* here, Faolan?"

He seemed to consider either her question or his answer for a minute. Then he met her gaze levelly and shrugged his massive shoulders, "I was worried about you, lass. There was a man following you at the airport. I wondered what he was up to, so I followed, too. When you went inside to get your car, I walked up behind him and asked what he was doing." Faolan stopped for a moment, likely envisioning the scene in his mind, before he continued, "At first, I was only slightly suspicious, and I didna think he posed a physical threat. I wasna expecting him to turn swinging a knife."

Faolan looked chagrined to admit he'd been caught off guard. He continued his story, but with short pauses here and there. She was sure she was getting an edited version. "I took his knife from him, waited for you to come out, and rode with you to Inverness. I thought I would check on you from time to time, since I needed to be around here for my..." he paused, as if searching for a word, "business. Last night, I happened to be driving by, when I saw a van pull off the road near here, and four men got out. Since the only thing this far out of town is your farm, I followed to see what they were doing. You drove up before I got a chance to find out."

He reached his hand up tentatively to her face and touched her gently. "I am sorry, lass. I should have been closer. Lie down and try to rest. We can talk more on the morrow. I'll be in the other room should you need anything."

"Who undressed me?" Elena blurted, embarrassment making her voice sharp.

Again, he carefully considered his words before he answered. "I did, lass. You were wet, cold, and I didna' know how badly you were hurt. I took your clothes off and put you in your robe. You will have some bad bruises, and your shoulder will be very sore tomorrow, but I doona' think you need a doctor." His manner was matter-of-fact and his voice carefully neutral.

Without waiting to hear if she had any more questions, Faolan pulled the covers up to Elena's shoulders then leaned down and gently kissed her on the forehead. He turned out the light and pulled the door partway closed. It was a testament to her mental fragility and physical exhaustion that she closed her eyes and slept, feeling safe in the knowledge Faolan was here.

****

The next morning was another matter altogether. All the unanswered questions from the night before came rushing back, demanding answers. Foremost in her mind was how Faolan came to be here, supposedly just in time, once again. Elena was about to go in search of him and ask, when she heard the sound of mewling from the kitchen.

The kittens! In all the chaos last night, she'd forgotten about the kittens. She went into the kitchen and found Faolan sitting at her table. The kittens were in a basket at his feet and his hand was dangling within reach of their paws. The orange kitten was climbing over the back of the black kitten, trying to chew on his hand. When he wiggled his fingers, the orange kitten lost his footing and rolled over on his head. The black kitten rolled over too, and started chewing on the orange kitten's tail.

Elena swallowed a laugh, and Faolan turned to see her standing in the doorway. He was wearing blue jeans with a long-sleeved tan t-shirt that clung tightly to his shoulders and hugged his chest. His boots were by the back door, and it felt uncomfortably intimate to see him in his stocking feet, drinking his coffee at her kitchen table. To keep from staring at the domestic picture he presented, Elena turned to the stove to start water for her tea. "Why are you here, Faolan?"

Last night he was concerned and gentle. Today, the more self-assured and mocking Faolan was back. He grinned and said, "T'was a good thing that I was."

Elena couldn't argue with that, unless of course, he was in league with the thugs. She didn't want to think Faolan had anything to do with the attack. Her lawyerly mind tried to apply a logical solution to fit the facts, but she was at a loss for a reasonable explanation for his presence.

What she really wanted to know but was afraid to ask was what he'd been thinking when he undressed her last night. She was confident he hadn't touched her anywhere inappropriate; that was just about the *only* place she wasn't sore. However, the idea that Faolan had undressed her while she was unconscious left her warm and fuzzy in places she had no business being warm and fuzzy.

Elena gasped with pain as she tried to lift the teakettle when the water boiled. Faolan was at her side in an instant.

"Sit down, let me look at you." He examined her with the detached thoroughness of any physician. When he pulled the front of her robe open, he was careful not to pull it too far, and kept his hand on her shoulder. "Now, let me see your hip," he asked. Faolan knelt down in front of her, before carefully opening the bottom just far enough to look at the hip Liam had kicked the night before.

Elena was horrified to see a deep purple imprint of a shoe marring the fleshy part of her hip. "Oh, God!"

"Aye, you're bruised badly." His amber eyes gazed up at her somberly. "Would you like to visit the doctor or the police?"

She had watched him carefully as he folded back her robe, looking for any sign of duplicity, any indication that he might somehow have been involved with Liam. His jaw had clenched and unclenched, he'd swallowed convulsively, and his eyes had narrowed as he gently probed the edges of the bruise.

Her track record wasn't the best when it came to reading men, but she would have sworn what she saw on Faolan's face when he'd looked at her injuries was pure, unadulterated rage. With a sigh, she thanked Faolan sincerely, then answered, "I'll be fine. Maybe just some ibuprofen after breakfast. Speaking of that, what would you like for breakfast?" She started to rise from her chair but with a firm hand and a roll of his eyes, Faolan gently pushed her back into her seat.

"Sit," he ordered. Elena watched him as he moved comfortably around her kitchen. He seemed to know more about where things were stored than she did. He made her a cup of tea, and then put together a light breakfast of toast, yogurt, and peeled an orange. "What else would you be likin', lass?"

"This is fine, thanks. Why don't you get your own breakfast before you head out?" His question just stoked a fire that did not need any more heat. She hoped that if she fed him, he would see that she was all right and leave. She didn't want to think too long about the way he'd kissed her the last time he left her.

Faolan laughed easily and shook his head. "I'm not going anywhere, lass. Which bedroom would you like me in—yours?" he teased, with a raised eyebrow and lazy grin.

"Wh-what?" she stammered. *Had he read her mind?* She felt her face burn in embarrassment and no small amount of lust.

"I am going to be stayin' here 'til I make sure you're safe, so where would you be likin' me?"

Okay, that was a trick question right? "Well, you're not staying in *my* bedroom," Elena said indignantly, pushing back the immediate image of tangled sheets and naked limbs.

"Right, 'tis the next room to it then." He grabbed a black duffle bag near the kitchen door and stalked down the hall.

Stupid Scott! What was his business here, anyway? She couldn't decide if he had some ancient sense of chivalry at work, or if there was something else he wanted. She would explain to him why it was so inappropriate for him to stay at her house. The situation reminded her of that old adage: keep your friends close and your enemies closer. *And which one is Faolan?*

Chapter Five

After breakfast, Elena forced her bruised and battered body into jeans and a flannel shirt to keep warm so she could work in the barn. Although there was still plenty to do in the farmhouse, she was anxious to put a bit of distance between herself and Faolan. Throwing on her jacket and donning her boots, she went to look at her Rover to check for damages and get the lantern and flashlights.

Grabbing the lights, Elena walked through the interior of the barn to the north wing. It felt like a lifetime had passed since she'd decided to go to town, but she hadn't forgotten the reason for her errand. She was still determined to see if the metal panels ever opened. Moving gingerly, she ran her hand around the flat edges that looked fused to the surrounding stone. Heat radiated beneath her hand as soon as she touched the metal.

Elena looked closer. There was a small seam that ran from top to bottom and looked like an opening for a door. She pressed her hands flat against the panels, one on either side of the seam, to see if she could pull them apart. They began to glow noticeably and vibrate under her touch. With a gasp, she pulled her hands away.

Heart pounding uncomfortably fast, she raised a shaky hand and pressed it to the panel. It was warm, but nothing more exciting happened. Taking a big breath and holding it, she put both hands on the panels again. The light and vibration returned. Before she could chicken out, Elena pressed hard and when the panels slid easily apart, she nearly tipped ass over teakettle through the opening.

A secret room!

Picking herself up, she grabbed the lantern and a flashlight, and climbed inside. Not a fan of enclosed spaces, she propped the lantern in the doorway, ensuring an escape route before she went further. The room was narrow, deep, and built right into the mountain.

A small table held what appeared to be ancient treasures, including a jewelry casket, a hand mirror, and a dagger with a stunningly large, deep red jewel embedded in the handle. A thin book that looked like a journal was splayed open on its back. Elena shone the flashlight on the open page, and although she couldn't read the faded writing, the date showed the last entry as 1693. She would need to do some research to find out who had lived here then.

Elena carefully opened the lid of the jewelry casket and saw two large keys nestled on top of a pile of gold and silver coins. Both keys had markings on the top, but nothing she could easily decipher. Other than that, the box was empty.

The mirror was tarnished silver, and she turned it over, admiring the ornate design. The glass was dirty, so she rubbed the surface with the tail of her flannel shirt. Something appeared in the smooth, dark surface and it wasn't Elena's reflection. She gasped as Faolan's unmistakable image appeared in the swirling mist. The distorted figure began to fade and subtly shift until she was watching a wolf stalking through the shadowy glass just before the surface went completely dark.

The sound of her breathing was harsh in the silence of the tomb-like chamber. *What was this place?* Thousands of butterflies took flight in her stomach and she was suddenly frantic to be out, to see the light of the day. She needed reassurance that, despite what she'd seen in this room, the real world still existed.

Tucking the mirror under her shirt, Elena took a final glance around, and then climbed from the chamber. She didn't know the purpose of the room, but she suspected it had remained hidden for a long time behind all that junk. There were deep secrets here, not to mention some kind of magical woo-woo. She would keep these discoveries to herself until she knew more about them. She had to admit, finding the underground chamber pleased her greatly. Her farm held secrets.

Educated as a lawyer, Elena knew how to examine, organize, catalog the facts of a case, and assemble them to tell a story the way she wanted it heard by the jury. She also knew the opposing counsel had the same facts, yet arranged them to tell a different story. The proper interpretation of facts could mean the difference between guilty or innocent, jail or freedom, life or death.

Faolan told her someone had been following her, someone who attacked when questioned. A week later, she was jumped outside a pub, and then again outside her home. These weren't local punks looking for harmless fun. They were serious, they knew where she lived, and had it not been for an inexplicable interference, they would have raped and possibly killed her.

She supposed there was a remote possibility that these were random acts of violence. Just as likely as winning the lottery. It seemed far more reasonable to assume that they were aimed at her. If so, someone wanted her dead, or at the very least, scared away.

It always comes down to the same old question. *Cui bono? Who would benefit by my death?* That was an easy question, for sure. Martin Worthington, III. As a provision of the sale, the house reverted to his ownership if she died in the next six months. *What about Faolan? What did he have to gain? Was seeing him in the mirror just the wishful thinking of an overtaxed and over-imaginative brain?*

She stopped suddenly in the middle of the yard. Something was....missing. She pivoted, looking for Faolan's vehicle. There was no sign of how he'd arrived in time to rescue her the night before. She blew out a frustrated breath; she didn't have enough information. She hurried inside to put away the mirror.

When Elena had been scrubbing the fireplace in her room on her first afternoon at the farm, she'd been startled when one of the stones sprang open to reveal a secret hiding space. She'd been preoccupied at the time, and merely closed the door again, so she could finish cleaning the hearth. It made a perfect hiding place for the mirror. Pushing open the stone once more, Elena added her new treasure, closed the stone front, and went in search of Faolan.

Earlier this morning, she'd intended to tell Faolan over lunch that he couldn't stay. It was just wrong, in so many ways. Now, she was about to make sure he stuck around for a while. She didn't think she was in physical danger from him; he easily could have killed her while she was sleeping last night. However, believing he wasn't trying to kill her wasn't the same thing as trusting him. Although she had theories, she needed to know what he wanted.

Her most *elaborate* theory involved Faolan hiring the punks to scare her, so she would believe he saved her and come to trust him. Then he could take advantage of her and... She shook her head at the foolishness of that fantasy. She didn't own anything worth stealing.

Her *favorite* fantasy theory was that after their kiss in Inverness, Faolan realized he couldn't live without her, and was protecting her because he—

She grinned at the image of Faolan charging in on his white steed before she mentally kicked herself for nearly slipping back into her Cinderella syndrome. She'd once believed Marty was a prince, and she'd discovered he'd had more warts than she cared to count. Thinking of Faolan as her Prince Charming wasn't going to work, either.

All her life, Elena had followed the rules and always tried to do what she believed other's expected. She could have died last night. Maybe it was time to live a little. The attack had knocked something lose inside her, and there was no going back. Elena was starting over, free of emotional entanglements, free to experience life on her terms.

It's way past time to stop believing in fairy tales.

Chapter Six

Elena found Faolan in the library, unpacking boxes and putting books on the shelves. There was a roaring fire in the hearth, and the kittens were snuggled together in their basket. He looked for all the world as though he was the lord of the manor, and that made her more than a little cranky.

"What do you think you're doing?" she asked, sharply.

He smiled and said, "It looked like you could use a bit of help here. I was just putting the books on the shelf so you could arrange them where it suited. How are you feeling?"

He stood and closed the gap between them with his question. Putting his hand under Elena's chin, he tilted her face so he could examine the bruises. Elena tried to pull her head back and step away, but Faolan used size to his advantage and crowded her against the doorframe. She had to tip her head nearly straight back to look up at him; he was a full foot taller than she was. It was a show of pure male dominance, and it pissed her off.

"Tell me, Faolan, just exactly why would that be of any concern to you?"

"Still feisty, lass, even after I twice saved your life? In

Scotia, if you save a man's life, he owes you his. Will you be paying me with your life twice over, Elena?"

Elena's breath caught in her throat. Faolan's beautiful mouth curved in a soft smile, his tone lightly teasing. He was standing so close, too close. She wanted to look away but his tawny gaze held her captive. She could feel the electricity as his body tensed and became aware of hers. The heat between them blazed, became a white-hot fire that threatened to steal all the oxygen from the room. Elena grew embarrassingly wet with desire, and Faolan's nostrils flared, as though he was a predator scenting his prey. His gaze turned dark and went from teasing to hungry in an instant.

Step away, this is definitely a dangerous situation, and after last night...

Elena's body ignored her brain, shutting it down before she could complete that thought. She arched her back and leaned into his chest. He was hot and hard, and everything about him spoke of desire. Her breasts felt swollen, her nipples tight little buds that burned for his touch. Elena instinctively molded her body closer to his and felt the press of his shaft, hard against her stomach. Faolan loosened her hair from its tie, and black curls spilled down her back as she turned her face up for the earth-shattering kiss she knew was coming.

Faolan groaned quietly, laid his cheek against the top of Elena's head, and pulled his hips back slightly, putting an inch or two of space between their bodies. His ragged breath matched her own and her hormones screamed in protest at the separation. She wanted his kisses, she wanted his body next to hers, she wanted him to take her and make her his. *No more thinking. For once, I just want to feel.*

Faolan stepped away. He took a deep shuddering breath, turned to lean his forearms against the fireplace mantle, presenting her with a broad expanse of back. In a tight voice, he growled out, "Nay, lass."

"Wh-what do you m-mean, nay?" Elena stammered, feeling chilled, bereft of his heat.

Faolan turned and looked at her then, and she was shocked to see something akin to real emotion in his eyes. He shook his head and said, "I am not the man for you, lass."

Not the man for me? I thought he wanted me. Did I miss something? Oh God...

The thought hit her like a thunderbolt. "You're married," she practically shouted.

He laughed. A genuine, throw your head back and roar kind of laugh that made his eyes sparkle with amusement. "If I was, would you care? No, 'tis not married I am. There has never been a woman to claim this heart," he said, thumping his fist against his chest.

Then in another quicksilver change of mood, Faolan looked at Elena, his face serious, and said, "Come here."

In a show of maturity mixed with stubbornness, Elena stood her ground; she was not going to throw herself at this man. Nor would she come running like his little pet just because he called. "Say whatever you have to say. I can hear you just fine from here."

He walked over and swept her up as though she weighed nothing, instantly reminding Elena how vulnerable she would be if he really wanted to hurt her. She kept her arms crossed tightly across her chest. He carried her over to the chair near the fireplace. She saw the kittens still curled in a fuzzy little ball inside their basket, right where he'd put them.

The man was a walking contradiction, leaving Elena reeling, never knowing how she felt about him from one minute to the next. In a little over a week, he'd saved her life-twice, tucked her into bed, played nursemaid to kittens. He'd kissed her until she no longer knew who she was, then turned and walked away from her, just when she could have been convinced to go farther than she'd ever gone before. He pushed her away, only to draw her back in, and she didn't like being so off-balance.

"Och, Elena, I scarcely know where to start," he said when he got her settled on his lap. She knew he must find her desirable, since he was still hard inside his jeans, but he shifted her carefully so his erection didn't press against her bottom.

When he didn't immediately continue, Elena spoke up, "I don't understand you, Faolan. Are you trying to hurt me? If so, you're doing a terrific job of it. I came to Scotland for a chance to start over. Instead, bad things are happening, and you seem to turn up at the strangest times, but you won't explain anything.

"Sometimes, I'm grateful to you for saving my life, and other times, I'm half-convinced that you set this whole thing up. Please tell me what's happening. Despite the fact that I'm sitting in your lap at the moment, I'm *not* some fragile little girl who needs to be sheltered. If there's trouble, I can handle it," Elena finished, hoping the direct approach might work with him.

Faolan gave her a long look before finally speaking. "I am sorry, lass. I canna tell you everything you want to know. I am telling you the truth that someone was following you, and he cut me with a knife. I have been out here watching over you because I was worried. There are things about me you canna ever know, but know this, Elena MacFarland, I will not let anything bad happen to you." He caressed her cheek with the pad of his thumb.

Elena sensed he was telling the truth, but it didn't make her feel much better. She knew next to nothing of the man, and it was time to start getting answers to her questions. "Where do you come from, Faolan? And why haven't I seen you, if you've been out here?"

"I come from right around these parts, lass. My family has been here for a thousand years. 'Twas black hearted treachery that lost my family their land more than three hundred years ago, now. 'Tis said the hills and rocks around this land hide the secrets known only to the generations of my clan.

"Your Mr. Worthington and his family have been trying to find these secrets for centuries. I believe he offered you this farm as a diversion, and planned to kill you before you could get here to claim it. He *never* would agree to just give it away."

He thought for a moment before continuing, almost absently, "What I can't figure out is why he is still trying to have you killed. Once his plan failed and you signed the papers, the land was yours. He'd lost his little gamble."

"Worthington made me agree to have the ownership revert to his family should something happen to me in the first six months," Elena said quietly, horrified that Worthington would try to kill her.

Not missing a beat, Faolan smiled, "Och, lass, I guess you are stuck with me here for a while then."

Elena blinked, the shock of someone trying to kill her temporarily leaving her brain while something in the pit of her stomach squirmed with pleasure at the thought of Faolan staying around her house for the next six months. She lost track of the conversation as her mind reviewed what it felt like mere moments before when he pressed up against her, and she was waiting for his kiss.

Giving herself a mental shake, she tried to understand what was happening between them. There was a constant push-pull, a feeling of safety, then danger; steamy hot, then cold as stone.

She felt as shaky as a newborn foal. Turning her gaze to the fire, Elena hesitantly asked, "Why did you walk away after kissing me in Inverness and why turn your back on me just now?"

Faolan wound her hair between his thumb and forefinger, and smiled. "In Inverness," he paused, before slowly continuing, as though considering whether he should tell her the truth, "I kissed you because I wanted to, just to see what it would be like. I didna' know I would like it so verra much." He looked down and then continued softly, "I walked away because I am no good for you, lass."

He looked back up, his tawny eyes locked with hers, and the butterflies in the pit of her stomach started up again, with a vengeance.

"I could make you want me, lass. You wouldna refuse," he whispered.

After all her years of holding out for the right man to share that special first time with, here she was, sitting in his lap. Faolan was correct. Elena wouldn't refuse him. She'd learned an important lesson yesterday; life was too short to wait any longer for some fairy-tale romance. If those punks had raped her last night, all those years of waiting for *Mr. Right* would have meant nothing.

Elena was here with an incredibly sexy man, one who only had to look at her to make her feel more than any other man. This was the stuff of dreams, the curl-your-toes attraction every woman deserved to experience at least once in her life.

She had decided against finding love, but Elena had also decided she would experience sex on her terms, when and where she was ready. She'd vowed to make a fresh start and it was time to make good on that promise.

"You're right," she whispered back, "I wouldn't refuse. I do want you." His gaze smoldered as he digested what she'd said. Elena reached one hand up to his face and placed the other behind his neck. "Please, Faolan, kiss me."

Faolan started to lower his face, pulled back, and said again, "I am no good for you, lass."

Then he brushed his lips gently over hers, and it was as if the ground shifted beneath them, like a small earthquake, and even stronger than the first time they'd kissed. Faolan stiffened, pulled back, and looked at Elena searchingly, then brushed his lips against hers again, as if confirming the primal connection between them.

He ran his tongue over her lower lip, and pulled it gently with his teeth before covering her mouth with his. Elena's lips parted, and he opened them further, his tongue claiming ownership, hot and demanding. Their tongues tangled in deep searching kisses. Elena couldn't tell where he began and she ended. He thrust his tongue in and then slowly withdrew, over and over, a promise of what was to come. She twisted her fingers into his beautiful hair, pulling it loose about his shoulders. Faolan lifted her slightly and repositioned her on his lap so she could feel the hard length of him beneath her. Someone moaned, but Elena didn't know if the sound was his desire or hers. His thumb caressed her jaw line and continued slowly down her neck to the front of her shirt. He deftly worked the buttons to expose her lacy bra. His large hand cupped a breast, kneading gently, before his fingers traced feather light circles around each nipple. Elena's breasts felt tight and swollen in his hands, and she rocked against his hard shaft in response. Without a word, Faolan swept Elena into his arms and never broke the kiss as he carried her down the hall to the bedroom.

****

"Let me look at you, lass," he said when he laid her on the bed. She knew her hair was a tumbled mess around her head and her lips felt swollen from his kisses. Her shirt was completely opened, showing her creamy white bra cupping her full breasts. "Och, lass, you are so verra beautiful, you take my breath away." He sat down next to her and leaned down, his kisses gentle again.

His voice was whisky rich against her ears. "Lay back and relax. Let me make love to you." He ran his tongue over her lips, before moving on to her neck. He climbed fully onto the bed and straddled her legs, then he was back at her mouth again, all heat and passion.

Elena captured his thrusting tongue, holding onto it lightly with a gentle suction. She bit his full lower lip, pushed her tongue into his mouth and out again to taste his lips. She sat up and pushed his shirt up across his chest, and he helped by pulling it impatiently over his head.

Faolan's bare chest was spectacular. His muscles were ripped, the pectorals tight with small copper nipples, and dusted with fine reddish-brown hair. His skin was golden and velvety soft. Elena ran her palms over the ridges of muscles, and then traced the fine trail of hair that disappeared tantalizingly into the waistband of his jeans. She longed to follow that trail with her tongue, to explore every part of this magnificent man.

Pulling her shirt off but leaving her bra in place, his large hands cupped and massaged her breasts, rolled, and pinched her nipples, and she ached to feel his mouth on them. His hands were rough, the calluses heightening the sensations as he touched each breast. He laid her back again and ran his tongue along the lace of her bra, teasing with the promise of his mouth. He pulled the lace down with his teeth and pulled the hot, tight nipple into his mouth. Elena gasped with pleasure.

Faolan pushed her legs apart and lay hard and heavy between her thighs, letting her feel his arousal as he continued to suckle her breasts. "Elena, lass, you have lovely breasts," he said hoarsely, his breath fanning over her sensitive nipples. Then he pulled one nipple deep into his mouth, sucking hard, flicking the nipple with his tongue, before turning his attention to her other breast. He continued to kiss, lick, and bite her until she was in a frenzy.

Oh God! She was hot and wet, ready to have him deep inside her. She was ready to become his woman, in every sense of the word. He was languidly rubbing his hard shaft against her, causing the seam of her jeans to rub against that sensitive spot, promising her pleasure with every stroke. Elena pushed back, meeting him thrust for thrust; she never knew she could feel like this. She tried to move her hands between them, to start taking off his pants, her pants. "Too many clothes," she muttered.

Faolan laughed and pushed her hands away. His mouth moved lower, kissing her stomach, running his tongue down to the top of her jeans. He opened the fly, exposing her lacy panties, and Elena lifted her hips, expecting him to slip her pants down, but he laughed again and pushed her back down. "Not yet, love. My pace."

Elena moaned as he ran his tongue across the lace, rubbing his shadow beard across her lower belly, igniting a fire deep within her like nothing she'd ever felt before. He showered the sensitive skin just above the top of her panties with kisses, gentle nips, and long strokes of his velvet tongue. Elena sucked in air with quick gasps. *Is he going to kiss me there?*

She laced her fingers into his hair, insane with desire and raised her hips again, instinctively directing him to the center of her need. He kept his face there, feeling her heat, nuzzling her, then took in a long slow breath, filling himself with her scent. He put both his hands under her hips and raised her to his mouth, biting gently through her jeans.

Elena's hips bucked wildly, and she exploded, as wave after wave of pleasure coursed through her. *Yes!* She cried out with the intensity of the feeling, nothing in life had prepared her for this. "Faolan, ohhh," she cried, "It feels so good, I... I can't, ahhh…"

Faolan watched her face greedily, "Tis but a small taste of the pleasure I will give you today, Elena. I want to make love to every part of you, to make you forget any man but me."

Elena murmured, tried to say "No other man," but his lips were on hers again. He pressed his hard shaft against her, rubbing it between her thighs, sending residual spasms shuddering through her. Even though they both still wore their jeans, she could feel how huge he was. She wanted him inside, she had never even been close to wanting a man the way she wanted Faolan. She was thrilled to have waited for him and she was completely ready to give herself to him now. *This is how passion is supposed to be, mind numbing, thought robbing, breath-stealing.*

Elena turned her head away from his mouth, kissed along his jaw line, then whispered her secret in his ear, "There's been no other man, Faolan."

He froze for the merest second, then leaned up, to look at her, his eyes smoldering. He kissed her again, his mouth light against her swollen lips. He tenderly cradled her face in his hands, "Am I to be your first, Elena? Are you still a maiden?"

Surprised at his use of the word maiden, and embarrassed by her confession, Elena just nodded. His eyes filled with something unfathomable. He rolled off and sat next to her on the bed. "Why, lass? Why me?"

That was the question, wasn't it? Why had she selected him? There had been no shortage of available and willing men in her life, but she had always held out for more than sex. Even with Marty, when she believed they had a commitment, she'd been unready to take that next step.

So why Faolan?

From the moment she first caught his scent behind her at the airport, she was more than just attracted, she felt some primal connection that called to her soul. Some connection that ran deeper for her than any conscious decision she could make. Quite simply, she knew he was the one for her.

Without knowing why, when, or how it happened, and despite every promise she had made to herself, Elena was losing her heart to this man. She wanted him to feel the same about her, but she knew from experience, letting someone know how you felt gave them a weapon to use against you later. Instead of telling him all of her feelings, she gave him a partial truth.

"Faolan, I waited this long so I could find someone truly special for my first time. Last night I almost lost my virginity to a bunch of street punks. You saved me. You've saved my life twice now, and I don't know why you did, but that makes you pretty special. Life is short, and I don't want to wait any longer to experience this part of it."

He laid her back on the bed and stroked her hair. Brushing it back from her face and kissed the bruise on her forehead. His lips moved along the column of her neck, planting open mouth kisses, sucking gently, biting the tendon that ran the length, and then dragged his tongue across her collarbone.

Then Faolan pushed himself off the bed and stood looking

at her, a small smile playing at the corners of his mouth. Elena could see the tip of him, straining to be free of his jeans, and her mouth went dry at the size. She waited for him to take his pants off; she wanted to see his naked body, to have him now. Then he was talking again.

"You honor me, lass, thinking to bestow such a gift to me. 'Tis one I canna accept. I'll not be takin' your maidenhead." His burr was thick, voice rough.

"I'm not looking for promises, Faolan."

"Nay, lass, but you should be, and I am not the man to give them to you. You deserve to be cherished by one who will love you and who can promise to stay with you. You deserve to be romanced, not given out of gratitude."

He smiled his devastating smile. "Doona' be worrying, lass. I will be here to take care of you. I willna let anything else bad happen, you will be safe."

"Faolan, wait," but he had already turned and walked out of her room. She heard the shower start in the bathroom down the hall.

Elena lay there a long time. Her legs felt like rubber after that earth-shattering orgasm. And she hadn't even taken off her pants! What did it mean? Was she really and truly falling in love with this total stranger? Was she ready to give him what she had always withheld before, both physically and emotionally? She smiled ruefully. She was certainly physically ready.

Was he right? Was sex with him just a form of misplaced gratitude? She didn't think so. But Faolan seemed so sad when he spoke of promises. He'd told her that he wasn't the man for her. Did he think he wasn't good enough?

She could choose to be hurt and angry that he'd walked away again, but he hadn't left her. He had withheld his own physical gratification, out of concern for her. He didn't want her coming to him out of gratitude. His reticence seemed old-fashioned in many ways, a chivalrous act from another time. Elena was too confused to decide how she was feeling, but she'd learned her lesson well, she wasn't going to be sharing her emotions anytime soon. She was willing to enjoy just being around this fascinating man for a while.

She closed her eyes and imagined a wet and naked Faolan. *Whuh!* Elena grinned; she had no doubts about his sudden need for a shower. Faolan wanted her as much as she wanted him. Maybe she wasn't the only one who deserved some romance. *Hang on to your heart, Elena. It's going to be a bumpy ride.*

Chapter Seven

Red and Lilly didn't seem quite sure what to make of Faolan staying at the house when they showed up Monday morning. Elena asked how they all seemed to know each other.

"Everyone knows everyone around here," replied Lilly. "I've been knowin' young Faolan since he was a wee one, and his da before that." She seemed to accept that he was a bodyguard of sorts, after hearing of Elena's attack, and they left it at that. Although Lilly didn't seem to approve whole-heartedly, Red was happy to have another pair of hands to help with the work.

Cleaning the floors and shelves in the library took the entire morning, but the reward was worth it. By lunchtime, Elena had a gleaming, warm, and inviting library in which to work or relax. She loved it.

Lunch consisted of sandwiches on some of Lilly's fresh baked bread, with lively discussion and much laughter. It seemed Red, Lilly, and Faolan were very friendly with each other. *Yet something else to ponder.* When lunch was nearly over, Faolan asked about the condition of the apartment. Elena looked to Red, waiting to hear his answer, and then realized everyone else was looking at her.

"What apartment?" Elena asked, completely flummoxed.

"The flat above the south end of the steading," Faolan replied.

Since Elena had no idea there was a flat or apartment there, she hadn't even looked at it yet. They decided a field trip was in order, put on coats, and crossed the yard to the steading. Red and Faolan went in first, to make sure the stairs and floor were stable, with Lilly and Elena trailing close behind.

Inside was a cute little six-room flat that was in good shape. Apparently, a caretaker had lived here off and on over the years. There was an electric stove, refrigerator, and wall heaters. Elena probably would have spent the first few nights in here had she known about it. After everyone ooh'd and ah'd, Faolan looked at Red and said a little too casually, "It would be great if you and Lilly could move in here. That way there would always be one of the three of us here to keep an eye on things."

Red said quickly, "'Tis a grand idea. We could move in tomorrow."

Lilly and Elena exchanged glances, and although Elena felt the surprise on her own face, Lilly's expression was thunderous.

"Faolan MacGailtry and Red Thomas!" Lilly turned to look at Elena, "I am sorry, dear. Pay no attention to these fools. 'Tis plain as the look on their faces they cooked this scheme up betwixt them."

She was right, one look and Elena knew exactly what Lilly meant. They looked like a couple of naughty boys caught stealing cookies. Elena couldn't help it, she burst out laughing.

Faolan crossed the room, took both of Elena's hands in his and looked deep into her eyes. "Och, I am sorry, lass. I shouldna' have tried to trick you, 'tis only your safety I was worried about. I canna be here all the time. Please think about it, and of course 'tis up to you."

For a moment, the feel of her hands held tight in his overwhelmed her, and she couldn't remember how to talk, let alone what she wanted to say. "Uhm."

She cleared her throat, pulled her hands from his and looked at Lilly before she tried again, "Of course you're welcome to stay here, Lilly, but what about your other job? Will this be too far out of the way?" Elena was only paying them for their help half days, four days a week.

Lilly looked at Faolan, again with that unfathomable expression, and then back to Elena. "Our other work is taking care of some accounts, keeping records, and such. We can do that from anywhere. But you would be havin' a right to more of our time or some rent money for us to live here."

"Let's agree to expenses for the utilities, and draw up an agreement for the other duties you propose to take on. Helping to keep an eye on the place would be considered part of the job, and providing a place to live as partial compensation seems reasonable."

Elena looked over at Faolan and added, "You and I should also draw up an agreement, since it seems I'm also providing you housing in exchange for watching over me." His face darkened and he looked about to argue.

Elena's legal radar went on high alert, and she cut Faolan off. "There is obviously something you all know that I don't. How about the three of you get your stories straight and tell it to me tonight after dinner?" Elena smiled sweetly and left, closing the door on her way out, leaving the three of them standing there looking at each other, dumbfounded.

As she descended, she heard Red's laughter ring out, "She

has your number, lad!"

Since there was not likely to be any danger to her in town in the middle of the day, Elena decided to go shopping as a way to get out of the house to give them time to talk and give herself some time to think. She wasn't sure what to make of the three of them. Clearly, their relationship was much closer than she'd initially thought. The idea of Red and Faolan scheming for an invitation to live onsite pleased her more than it should have. She should have been upset that they were talking behind her back, but it felt like one more proof that Faolan wouldn't hurt her. After all, why would he bring witnesses to the farm if he was planning to do harm?

****

Dinner that night was a lively event. Lilly had outdone herself in the kitchen. She served lamb, roasted potatoes, sweet carrots, homemade rolls, and Caesar salad. Faolan sat very close to Elena, considering how large the table was. When he reached for the salad bowl, his arm brushed against hers, shooting electricity through her arm. Once, their knees met under the table, and she pulled hers back, apologizing. Later, when their knees bumped again, Elena wondered if he was doing it on purpose, just to get a rise out of her.

Two could play at that game.

It was as though they were both playing with fire. He said he wasn't the man for her, yet he couldn't seem to stop touching Elena. She told herself she wasn't going to get emotionally attached, but she couldn't help watching his face, judging his emotions.

The next time his leg bumped hers, Elena left hers where it was and then pushed it over a little more firmly, so there would be no doubt in Faolan's mind that she was doing it on purpose. He didn't pull away, and it got very hot on their side of the table.

After dinner, Lilly said, "You two kids wait for us in the library. Red and I will just clean up. We'll be there in twenty."

The fire blazed cozily, and the bookshelves and floor gleamed in the firelight. Elena started thinking about what furniture she wanted. She would keep the small oak table she was using as a desk, but the spare kitchen chairs and lawn chairs had to go.

Elena knelt in front of a box of books and opened it, intending to put them away. She turned her head to ask Faolan if he would like to help, only to find him standing directly behind her, having approached silently. *Which puts his zipper right in front of my face.* He was aroused, and when she reached to touch, he grabbed her wrist and pulled her to her feet. Instead of the kiss she was expecting, she got an examination, as he looked at the bump on her head, and declared it to be healing.

She stood there, her chest inches away from him, the feel of his fingers lightly touching her forehead, and she ached with desire. "Faolan," she whispered.

He placed his fingers gently on her lips, and then replaced them with his lips, his fingers lingering, and pulling her lips apart. He kissed her deeply, insistently, his hands threaded into her hair. With a shudder, he pulled away from her lips and kissed the top of her head.

Taking a careful step back, he asked in a husky voice, "What are you working on in here?" He wouldn't look directly at her.

So that's how it's going to be. Tease and then stop. He had done it in her bed, at the kitchen table, and now in the library. He might think he wasn't good enough for her, but he couldn't stay away either. He was a moth to her flame. *Good, it gives me something to work with.*

Elena bent over to reach into the box, keeping her butt in the air, just inches from where he stood. "I thought I would unpack some of these boxes," she said innocently. "Want to help?"

"Uhh," he replied, his eyes glued to her backside. Elena handed him a stack of books and went right back to unpacking, hiding a feline smile of satisfaction. He stood where he was, inches from her backside for a long minute before he slowly stepped away.

"Elena, we need to talk."

Uh oh, it was never good news for the woman when a man said that.

Elena turned and looked at him with dismay. "You're leaving again." A statement, not a question.

He read her face and was quick to reassure her, "Nay, love, I told you I would take care of you until this was sorted out."

Oh my God! He just called me love.

He took her hand and led her to the seat where he had held her in his lap the day before. This time he grabbed a second kitchen chair and straddled it backward. Elena sat down, worried about what was coming next.

"You were right. There is more between Red, Lilly, and me than just casual acquaintances. I have known them all my life. They raised me after my family died. There is much to this story, and some of which I am not proud of. Will you just let me finish, before you judge me guilty?"

"Faolan, whatever it is, you can tell me. I won't judge you."

"Och, lass, you will, and I wouldna be blamin' you if you never wanted to see me again. But a promise is a promise, and I swore to care for you 'til this mess was over, so 'tis about time you know some of what this is about.

"I know now the story of how you got involved with the Worthingtons, but I didna know at first. I told you the other night the Worthingtons have been trying to take certain things from my family and have gone so far to commit murder to get them. They are all pure evil. Your Marty's ancestor killed my whole family: my parents, my two sisters, and younger brother."

Elena gasped in horror and put her hand on Faolan's arm. His gaze focused on some unseen distant horizon. He didn't seem to know she was there.

"I was in the steading, in a stall asleep on some hay. I heard men shouting. I saw my family shot down by crossbow in the paddock. I was but twelve, but I wanted to go kill the bastard with my bare hands." His eyes were dark with the memory.

"Oh my God, Faolan." Elena could think of no words of comfort, she knew firsthand the pain of being an orphan. But to watch your family be murdered!

"Red was near enough to me to see what happened. He grabbed me and held me, with his hand tight over my mouth until Worthington and his men left. Red saved my life that day. He and Lilly were the caretakers for my family, and they took me then and raised me." He smiled toward Red and Lilly who had just joined them.

"Some of this we heard the day he killed my family, the rest we discovered long after. The killer said he would let them live if my father would break a sacred vow, sign over ownership of the farm, and forever leave the land of our ancestors. My father was desperate to save his family. He broke an eternal oath when he revealed the..." he paused, searching for the right word, "artifact."

Faolan's voice was bitter as he continued. "I think my father knew they would all be killed, but he tried to save them, anyway. Instead of saving them, he sold my soul." Faolan, took a deep breath, and said, "I need a drink."

Red went to the kitchen and brought back a bottle of Macallan, a fine, single malt whisky, and poured four glasses. Both Faolan and Red shot the first glass back and poured a second. Lilly sipped, so Elena followed suit. She had never tasted whisky before, but the taste was smooth and warmed her all the way down.

"Faolan, did you think I would hate you for this? Because you didn't tell me you knew Red and Lilly?" Elena asked.

"Nay lass, 'tis only the beginning of this story. You will have to trust me. There are things in the world that you shouldna' ken. Things not of this world. Worthington is a bastard for exposing you to this, because once you know, you can never completely go back.

"Although my father hid the items the killer was seeking, he did admit they existed, thereby breaking the trust with the otherworld. He gave away sacred knowledge that was unearned to someone not worthy. The wards that protected my family were broken."

Elena felt her grip on reality slipping. *Crossbows? Protective wards? Other worlds?* Elena looked to Lilly and Red, expecting to see some subtle sign that she should go along with Faolan's story, should humor him. Instead, she saw two people looking at Faolan with the love of parents shining in their eyes. Whatever this was, they believed it too.

Faolan continued, "After the Worthington gained possession of the farm, they spent a small fortune searching for the things my father revealed. He also looked for other relatives, believing the secrets he sought were clan knowledge. He was right, in a sense because they would have been handed down to me had my father lived long enough.

"Recently, when Worthington contacted the solicitor to have the property sold, I knew something was wrong. He would never sell it without first finding...what he has been looking for. I went to Phoenix to find out who you were and how you were connected to the Worthingtons. I followed you. I searched your home when you were away," he said softly, avoiding Elena's eyes.

"When I found out you were engaged to the youngest Worthington, I was positive you were part of the plan. I followed you to London and paid that woman to let me have her seat on the flight to Edinburgh. You told me on the plane where you were getting your car, so I waited there in order to send the description ahead to Red. The plan was, I would follow behind, and Red would wait in Inverness. We didna' intend to let you out of our sight.

"Then I noticed someone else was watching you. He was hiding, waiting for you to come out to your car. I wanted to know who hired him, so I tapped him on the shoulder, and he swung around fast with a knife in his hand. I was careless, and he caught me in the side and ran away. You came out of the office just then, and without thinking it through, I jumped in your car and told you to drive."

He finally looked at Elena and said, "I am sorry I scared you, lass." Then he smiled at the memory, "Och, you are a feisty one! When you finally shared your story with me, I realized you were a victim in this, too. I still thought there was something wrong with Worthington selling you the farm, so I stayed close, trying to figure out what he was planning."

His head went down again, and his voice was just above a whisper, "I was away the night you went to town. By the time I got here, you were in the yard with those...and he smashed your head...and I thought I would kill him." His voice, which had started to shake with anger, faded away, and he just looked at her.

Bleakly, he said, "I am sorry, Elena. I should have protected you better. I should have believed you were really in danger. It's just that the first time, I thought it still might just be a coincidence or that Worthington had somehow found out something. Now that we know the property will revert to him if something happens to you in the next six months, we must be extra vigilant. He never intended you to own this farm."

Elena looked at all of them and waited. They all watched her, as if waiting to be told she believed them. She thought through what he had said. She was convinced of the evidence of the recent attacks. It made sense that Martin wanted her out of the way. She certainly hadn't gone as quietly as he'd initially expected. It also made sense that if this were Faolan's family home, he would track the new owner, especially if the family lost it under coercion. Elena could also make a convincing case that Faolan would initially be suspicious of her, and track her movements. That was all evidence that told a story she could believe in.

However, an apparently unreported murder, ancient weapons and artifacts, and what sounded suspiciously like magic were stretching Elena's credulity to the limit. Faolan hadn't spoken very much about any of them, yet they were integral to understanding the whole story.

They were at an impasse. Faolan was finished telling the story he *wanted* Elena to hear, but not the one she *needed* to hear. She knew she hadn't heard the whole truth yet, certainly not enough of it to explain everything. Most importantly, Elena still had no idea why Faolan was pushing her away.

"Faolan," Lilly said gently, "you must tell her all of it."

He looked back at her, his face stricken, and then roared,

"No!" He stormed from the room, and the front door slammed behind him.

Elena looked at Red and Lilly in the deafening silence that followed. Both of them were looking towards the door where Faolan had just left, their eyes full of love and concern.

"Lilly, tell me the rest, tell me how to help him."

"Nay, lass. 'Tis his story, and he must tell it in his own time and in his own way. Just as you must find the way to tell him of your feelings for him."

Elena started to speak, but Lilly cut her off, "'Tis plain as the look on your face, dear."

Red finally spoke, "We need to be goin' now, but we will be back on the morrow, and if it pleases you, we will arrange the flat in the morning and bring our things back after lunch. Doona' fash yourself about being alone. Faolan is out there watchin' over you, lass. He willna' let anything happen tonight."

Lilly hugged Elena, then she and Red said good night, leaving her alone in the house. Elena stirred the fire and turned out the light in the library. She walked to the window and stood staring out at the snowy landscape. The new moon did not diminish the brightness of the stars.

Elena thought about all she had heard and all that she'd *not* heard, and realized none of it changed her growing feelings for Faolan. She already trusted him with her life. She needed to show him he could trust her, as well.

Out on the hill a lone wolf howled. The sound echoed around the house, and it reminded her of the dog growling the night of her attack. Then another, smaller wolf joined the first wolf, and they turned and ran together into the night. Elena picked up her kittens and went to bed.

Chapter Eight

When Elena was in foster care, she hated that transitory feeling of not belonging. You could never be sure when your caseworker, a judge, or the foster parents would send you packing. As soon as morning came, she presented Lilly, Red, and Faolan with written agreements indicating she would provide them room and board for the next year in exchange for them living on the property. No other strings attached. They could break the contract with verbal notice. Since she already had a work agreement with Lilly and Red, Elena was comfortable with the arrangement if they were.

Red and Lilly took their copies with many assurances that it wasn't necessary. "Truth be told, lass, me and the missus are just grateful to have the old place back," Red added gruffly. As the family's caretakers, they would have lived here when Faolan's father was alive, but Elena was positive they had forgotten to mention that little detail.

Faolan kept his face carefully neutral but didn't move to take the agreement from her, so she set it on the table to give him time to think about it. His strong jaw clenched and unclenched, the only trace of his deep emotions. His tawny eyes were deep and full of secrets.

Lilly suggested this would be a good day for Elena to visit the furniture stores in a nearby town, "Perhaps even Inverness for the harder to find items, dear."

Faolan turned his flat gaze on Lilly, and with a look that would cause grown men to crumble, growled through clenched teeth, "I will go with the lass."

Lilly smiled imperturbably.

****

Elena wanted to buy a larger bed for Faolan's room; she knew the current twin-sized bed was too small for him. Not that Faolan would ever complain. In fact, she was sure he would object if he thought she was buying anything especially for him. Elena risked his towering rage and sent him across the furniture warehouse on an urgent mission to check the measurements of a couch she didn't want.

Once Faolan was finally away from her side for a few minutes, she bought the largest bed available to put in his room, hoping it would accommodate the six and a half foot Highlander. She enlisted the sales clerk in her conspiracy and swore him to secrecy. The clerk was more than happy to add it to her already impressive list of purchases, and he assured Elena that her husband would love it. *Yikes, husband!*

Faolan's black mood was in full force, rating a category four on the hurricane scale when he returned from his errand. Perversely, he wouldn't leave her side, even though she seemed to have gotten on his very last nerve. He glowered while Elena arranged delivery for her purchases, and they walked back outside to the Rover.

Outside, Faolan surprised her when he took her arm and

directed her to a small café. They ordered lunch, and Elena prattled on about her purchases. It was a totally novel experience to have enough money to buy what she needed without giving up something else. Like food. She still wanted to buy rugs for all the rooms, and Faolan suggested a small specialty shop back in Fairth.

Faolan seemed distracted by something over Elena's left shoulder, and she turned and saw a beautiful woman leaving the café. The tall blonde was everything Elena wasn't: elegantly thin and dressed like a fashion model. She couldn't compete with a woman like that.

"Would you like me to wait here while you go introduce yourself," she asked dryly.

"Yes, doona' move," he ordered and stood up.

Elena's jaw dropped. "Don't you recognize sarcasm when you hear it, you big Neanderthal?"

Faolan looked down at Elena, back up at the door, scanned the room and street, and pulled her to her feet. He threw some bills on the table and rushed Elena out of there so fast her feet barely hit the floor. They practically ran to the Rover, where he tucked her in on the passenger side, ran around to the driver's side, and told Elena to buckle up.

He started driving, cutting in and out of traffic, keeping one eye on the rearview mirror. He stopped at a petrol station, and got out to examine the Rover. Finally, he found what he was looking for, got back in, and drove away. He still hadn't spoken to her, and Elena wasn't going to break the silence. She realized he was angry that she'd made a fuss when he wanted to go meet Blondie, and this silent treatment was part of the payback. What a complete and total ass!

Elena risked a glance in his direction, and his clenched jaw confirmed he was royally pissed off. She stared out her window again and blinked hard against the sting of tears. She was angry and hurt with no one to blame but herself. If she'd kept her big mouth shut, he wouldn't have known she was a virgin until it was too late to stop and they would have had terrific sex, even if they both couldn't call it making love. Now she realized he would keep her at arm's length because she wasn't the type of woman he wanted.

One of the tears spilled over and ran down her cheek. She kept her head turned so he wouldn't notice. So she wasn't his type. He probably considered her obvious fascination with him as nothing more than a schoolgirl crush. No wonder he didn't want to tell her the rest of his story. Faolan didn't want to furnish a room because he didn't want to stay. He was only staying because he wanted his revenge on Worthington. Elena finally had a story that fit the facts. How could I have been so blind?

"Take me home, Faolan," she said in a small, choked voice.

Without a glance or another word between them, he did.

****

As soon as they arrived back at the farm, Faolan went to find Red, and Elena went to go check on her kitties. She needed some unconditional love. Their personalities were very different. The orange tabby rarely needed attention, he would love on her for a few minutes when it suited him, and the rest of the time, he was nothing but trouble. She'd named him Rascal. The black kitten was much more needy. With his white boots and a wisp of white on his chest, he followed her wherever she went, earning the name Shadow. As predicted, Rascal came over, gave a quick head bump, and then went in search of something to stalk. Shadow howled for her to pick him up, licked her chin, and began to purr loudly.

Her mood restored by the kitty loving, Elena began to plan the arrangement of the new furniture. She realized, good intentions aside, the bed she bought for Faolan was too big for his room. She would have to switch and put her current bed in his room and put the new king in hers. With such a large mattress, if Faolan changed his mind and wanted to make love with her, there would be plenty of room for both of them. Holy show! She blushed at her thoughts and for what Faolan might think about her getting such a large mattress.

Faolan didn't show up for dinner that night, but the rest of them ate together in the kitchen. Elena described the new furniture, but left out the details of the tall, leggy blonde. She accepted an invitation to Red and Lilly's flat the next evening for dinner and a little house-warming party. They all worked together on the dinner clean up before the older couple left for their own apartment, and then Elena got to work.

She went to the library and finished pulling all of the books out of boxes, dusting them as she went, and stacked them on shelves or on the floor. There had to have been nearly three hundred books and still more left in the steading. She wanted to categorize them so she could put them on the shelves in a logical order. For now, she ran her hands lovingly over the fine leather covers, randomly picking up one book after another, thumbing through it before moving on to the next.

She flattened the boxes and carried the stack out to the steading. Elena grabbed another box of books to bring inside and started for the back door. Midway between the house and the barn, caught in a proverbial no-man's land, she froze in her tracks. No more than fifteen feet away, a giant wolf watched her progress. His lips drew back in a feral grin and his yellow-brown eyes locked on her in silent appraisal. His reddish fur was a lighter mask around his eyes and muzzle, and gold on his chest. He was a magnificent animal, bigger than anything she'd ever seen.

Elena's heart pounded, and the adrenaline was rushing with the need for fight or flight. She had no weapon, even if she had been willing to use one, so fight was out. That left flight, but with a quick glance in both directions, Elena knew she could never outrun the beast. She did the only thing she could think of, inhaled sharply and began to speak, "Hi there, big fellow. Why don't you run along now? I need to get back in my house."

He looked for a minute longer, shook his head, as if to clear it, then turned and loped easily into the night. Elena's heart was still racing when she finally convinced her feet to cross the yard.

****

The next morning Faolan was at breakfast and as usual said nothing about where he'd been the previous night. Conversation turned to the various projects each of them was working on, but Faolan appeared not to be listening.

Elena told Lilly about the hundreds of books she'd found, and her plan to start sorting them by topic, maybe after dinner tonight. Faolan looked up and asked, "Do you mind if I help with that?"

Without looking at him, Elena said, "Of course not but don't feel obligated. You don't work for me." It was the first comment he had directed at her since the café, and her response was sharp with pent-up hurt. Faolan stood and left the kitchen, letting the back door close with a bang. Saying nothing further, she helped Lilly clear the table before getting ready for the furniture deliveries.

Elena dressed in jeans and a sweater, so she could push up the sleeves when she got too warm. She pulled her black curls into a ponytail, all the while thinking about what a jerk Faolan was being. When she came out, someone had already laid fires in all of the rooms, and Lilly had started sweeping and mopping the lounge.

"Why don't you wait until after they deliver? I'm sure they'll be tracking in mud from the yard."

"I will be laying down somethin' for them to walk on to reduce the tracking, and this way I know 'tis clean underneath. I will most likely be doing all the rooms twice today. Mebbe you would like to go talk to Faolan while you wait for the truck," Lilly added, slyly.

Elena sighed. Clearly, Lilly wanted more for Faolan and Elena than she was going to get.

"Lilly, he doesn't need me to go chase after him to try to cheer him up or anything else."

"Och, but you were a bit sharp with him this morning lass, I thought perhaps you might be wanting to apologize."

Elena was stung. "Maybe I was a bit sharp with him, but you weren't there yesterday when he asked to be excused to go talk to a beautiful woman. He's made it clear; I'm not his type."

"Is that what you think? That he had eyes for another? I doona' believe it."

"Lilly, you want to believe that I have feelings for Faolan and that he has them for me, but it just isn't like that. He wants his revenge on Worthington, and believes I'm the key to making that happen. Once he gets his vengeance, he'll leave, and I'll be left alone. I've been there, done that, and gotten the badge."

"Doona' be an idiot, girl. Go to him, say you're sorry," Lilly said, sounding cranky, then stormed out of the room, leaving Elena alone with her thoughts.

I'm not going to chase after that man!

She did decide to get Rascal and Shadow and take them to the barn while she worked on her piles. There might be mice or other adventures for a couple of rambunctious kittens. She told herself she was not going out there in hopes of seeing Faolan.

With one kitten in each arm, Elena struggled out the kitchen door and into the center part of the barn, closing the door behind her, to keep the kittens and the warmth inside. Someone had started a fire in the wood stove and it was warm inside. Both kittens crouched low to the floor, tails puffy, looking around to see if it was safe. Of course, Rascal was the first to recover, and he charged off in search of adventure. Shadow stayed by her feet a little while longer; just to be sure it was safe.

Thunk, crash, clunk.

It was coming from the south wing. "Bloody hell," then *thunk, crash, clunk* again. Soon it was a smooth rhythm, interspersed occasionally with a salty word. Elena walked over to the corner where the east part of the steading joined to the south wing.

Faolan had his back to her, and his shirt off. He glistened with sweat, and his muscles rippled as he swung a heavy axe. *Good Gawd! Was there a finer specimen of man anywhere on the planet?* He was splitting and stacking firewood, and he looked angry. He didn't just look angry; he *sounded* angry. He muttered to himself between swings. Elena couldn't quite make out most of the words, but then one phrase sounded clearly, "I will bloody well kill her myself."

Elena turned and left without saying a word.

Leaving Rascal out in the barn since he was stalking across the beams in the open ceiling, Elena took Shadow back to the house. Lilly looked at her expectantly, but Elena just shook her head and stormed into the library. *Kill me himself? I can take care of myself, and if he thinks he can use me for his own benefit, well, I'm nobody's fool anymore.* Worthington hadn't gotten the best of her, and Faolan MacGailtry wasn't going to hurt her either.

The furniture truck arrived to interrupt her gloomy mood, and soon she'd forgotten all about anything making her unhappy. *There is nothing like a truck full of brand new stuff to warm a woman's heart. Shallow, maybe. Therapeutic, definitely.*

The deliverymen were only too happy to take a bit more money to move the furniture Elena restored from the barn into the house. Once everything was sorted into its proper room, and the truck departed, Lilly, Red, and Elena moved the furniture from one spot to another, trying out different floor plans. Eventually even Faolan came in to help, and soon they were all bossing each other around, pushing and pulling, and generally having a good time.

Elena had the lounge and library situated and was ready to move on to the bedrooms. Lilly went to move the sheets from the washer to the dryer so they could make the beds. Red went to bring in some firewood, and suddenly Faolan and she were alone in his bedroom. "Elena, I…" he started.

Her anger flared instantly. She did not want to hear him tell her she shouldn't have bought furniture for his room. She raised a hand to interrupt, "Don't. I will see to my own room. You can set yours up however you want it. Or not. Sleep on the damn floor for all I care."

She stormed to her room and shut the door firmly, then

pushed the dressers to where she wanted them. Then she pulled the ironwork headboard and attached the legs to the bed frame. She moved the rocking chair in front of the fireplace and pulled the nightstands to either side of the bed. It was only then she saw what she had done. In her anger at Faolan, she had dragged all the furniture around the room by herself, leaving long scratches in the waxed finish.

In dismay, she dropped to her hands and knees and began to rub frantically at the marred surface. As she rubbed, everything she'd been through since coming to Scotland crashed down on her. Someone she hated was trying to kill her. She'd been badly beaten and nearly raped. She'd nearly made love, too. Now the man who spoke to her soul had dismissed her. He said he wanted to kill her, too.

She started to cry. Some part of her recognized this was not her usual behavior; she didn't cry and she never fell apart. Above all else, she was a survivor. She just couldn't seem to stop herself. Shadow crawled out from under the bed and climbed into her lap, purring. Elena heard the door to her bedroom open, then close, but no one was there when she turned to look. Elena took a deep breath and decided it was time to pull herself together.

Chapter Nine

They ate dinner that night in Red and Lilly's flat, and the design of the unit fit the two of them perfectly. The small table in the kitchen was set for dinner. The little windows had cheery café curtains, and the kitchen counter had a small washer and dryer under the kitchen counter. In the lounge, they had set up a television in one corner and had a love seat and two easy chairs in a semi-circle. Elena noticed two recent-looking pictures of Faolan on the end table. The little radiators hanging on the walls seemed to be working just fine, and the flat was warm and cozy.

Everyone was already inside the flat by the time Elena had arrived. She'd taken extra time to get ready, sending Faolan on ahead when he'd knocked on her door. She'd used every trick the stylist back in Phoenix had taught her to make sure she looked the confident, sexy woman she wanted to be tonight. *So what if I'm not exactly Faolan's type?*

Elena was feeling more like her old self. She'd given herself a stern talking to while she'd been dressing, and she was more than ready to declare herself over her recent moodiness.

Rascal had still been in the barn when Elena came over,

hunting some imaginary creature or another. He raced her up the stairs and shot through the door as soon as Lilly opened it, as if he owned the place.

Elena laughed and said, "I didn't get you a housewarming gift, but it looks like one showed up anyway. Would you like him, Lilly?" Lilly's smile was lovely as she picked Rascal up and crooned softly. He bumped her chin with his head, purring loudly.

In the kitchen, Elena offered to help, while Faolan and Red poured drinks. Of course Lilly shooed her out of the kitchen with a laugh, saying everything was nearly ready. They all sat together in the lounge, enjoying small talk. Elena was determined not to let the tension between Faolan and her carry over into the evening.

Apparently, Faolan was too, because he was behaving like a different man. He was funny, engaging, and flirted shamelessly with both Elena and Lilly. He wore the faded jeans that he'd worn the night they almost made love and a steel-blue cable knit sweater. His hair was unbound, the mahogany mane falling to the middle of his back, the red and gold highlights more visible with it loose.

He laughed easily, and the tension that had been making his face and voice tight for days was gone. His electric mood made her happy she had dressed up for dinner, but she still wasn't sure how she felt about him. He'd made it clear yesterday that she wasn't his type. *What was he up to now?*

Elena wore a short black cocktail dress, shirred in the front to display her cleavage. She also wore her black hair loose, and it fell in waves to her waist. She'd even put on high heels, just to walk across the yard, but the added height lengthened her legs, and showed her calves to their advantage. She was feeling sexy in her low-cut dress and made a point of leaning over in front of Faolan a few times, just to see if she had his attention. It appeared from the bulge on the right side of his jeans that she did. *Mercy!*

Red poured Macallan freely before dinner, and Lilly followed up with wine at dinner to accompany a delicious pasta and salad. The meal was a lively affair, with a lot of laughter, mostly at stories told by Red and then topped by Faolan. Lilly and Red would hear none of it when Elena offered to help clean up. In fact, they seemed anxious to have their guests leave as soon as dinner was finished.

Everyone shared one after dinner drink, and then with a sincere thank you, Elena and Faolan took their leave. Lilly hugged her, and then kissed Faolan on the cheek, saying something in his ear that Elena couldn't hear.

Elena wasn't used to drinking and she was decidedly tipsy. Faolan took her arm to steady her as they crossed the yard. Again, Elena felt the fire that shot through her at his touch. They went straight to the library because Elena insisted she was ready to begin the job of sorting the books by category. Faolan poured them each a nightcap of Macallan, while Elena sat on the new leather sofa. He joined her, raised his glass to her, and said, "Cheers," in his sexy brogue.

For some unknown reason, Elena found that hysterically funny, and she began to giggle. *Are you kidding me? Swear to God, I never giggle. Of course, I never drink, either. Here I am sitting on a deliciously soft couch with the sexiest man on the planet, and the best I can do is giggle. What I really want to do is rip his clothes off, but no, I giggle.* Her inner dialog made her laugh, a deep belly laugh that left her gasping for air.

Then something remarkable happened. Faolan snorted, then he chuckled, and finally, he started to laugh, too. His laughter was deep and rich and only made Elena laugh harder.

Her laughter fed his, and it became a vicious cycle. Stomachs aching, and trying to breathe, they looked at each other, and laughed so hard tears filled their eyes.

Elena tried to stop, really she did. She held her stomach and tried not looking at Faolan, then he snorted and it was all over. She erupted into another fit of laughter. Faolan took a deep breath and tried to gain control. He straightened his face, looked serious, and Elena couldn't help herself, she sniggered. Then they both lost it all over again. After what seemed like a very long time, they both finally pulled it together and managed to take a couple of deep breaths without fresh bouts of hysteria erupting.

"Och, lass, you are good for me. I canna remember the last time I laughed like that. Maybe never."

His arms stretched out along the back of the couch, and he started to play idly with Elena's curls. She smiled, a wicked idea forming in her drink-addled brain. *He's happy, I'm happy; I'm a virgin, and he's a man.* She threw back the rest of her drink and poured them each one more. His head was back, his eyes closed, and still he twirled strands of her hair between his fingers. The situation was perfect, they were alone, relaxed, and Elena was just drunk enough to lose her normal inhibitions. *It was now or never.*

Elena climbed onto his lap, her knees straddling him and she kissed him. She took his face in her hands, the way he had done before, and she stroked his jaw, first with her fingers, and then with her lips and tongue. He stayed very still, keeping his arms on the back of the couch, head thrown back, and eyes closed. Elena could tell she had his attention by the press of his erection between her legs. Her lips lingered over his neck, paying special attention to his collarbone, she ran her tongue up to his ear, and whispered, "Faolan." His cock twitched beneath her.

Elena returned her mouth to his. She was hungry for him, she wanted him, and she wanted him to want her. Smiling lightly, Faolan let her kiss him. His lips parted, inviting her tongue, tasting it, sucking on it. Still his arms didn't move from the back of the couch. Encouraged that he hadn't stopped her and challenged that he hadn't moved, Elena raised herself on her knees, putting her breasts at a height even with his mouth and leaned into him, daring him to keep ignoring her. She pulled her fingers through his hair, lightly scraping her nails against his scalp. Then she pulled his head forward, so that his face was buried between her breasts.

Faolan capitulated with a moan, and reached to pull the front of Elena's dress down, revealing a lacy black bra that barely contained her lust-swollen breasts. He massaged her breasts and licked and kissed her nipples. He lifted one breast and put the nipple in his mouth and sucked hard, shooting waves of pleasure straight through her that connected to the achy need between her legs. When he pulled her other nipple into his mouth, Elena reached down and unbuttoned the fly on his jeans. She pulled away the material as best she could, then pulled her dress up over her waist and settled her hot, wet center against his swollen shaft.

She began to move up and down against him, as he had done the night he pleasured her, but withheld his own release. His hands cupped her ass, and he pulled her closer still so that the fabric of her thong pulled tight into her womanly folds, rubbing her clitoris with every stroke. Again and again, she slid against him, hotter and wetter, until they were both nearly insane with desire.

Elena knew finding her release was a point of danger, it was when he'd chosen to walk away the last time. Tonight she was determined he would find his pleasure; she would wind him up so much he would have to make love to her. She ached to see him, touch him, so she slowed, carefully watching his face.

Faolan's head was thrown back again, his eyes half closed. His breath was ragged as his hands gripped her hips, trying to guide her back to that quick pace. The passion and desire on his face told her what he refused to say.

He wants me. He wants this.

Elena slid off his lap, kneeling between his legs and pulled at his jeans. She wanted them all the way off. He lifted his hips off the couch to help, staring at Elena, apparently mesmerized by what she was doing. She tentatively stroked him, fascinated by his size, unable to reach her fingers all the way around his shaft. This part of him was such a contradiction, hard as steel with a velvet soft covering.

As she slid her hand up and down the length of him, his hand covered hers, and they rubbed his shaft together. They started slowly, then going faster and faster. A small drop formed on his tip, and Elena savored the taste of him. His hand froze at the touch of her tongue. Elena had never done anything like this before, yet tasting and stroking him felt natural, and she couldn't get her fill.

Faolan's breath was coming fast and shallow. His hand gripped hers once more and together their strokes became faster. He moaned, and Elena felt his body becoming increasingly taut. He thrust back, grabbed her shoulders, lifting her slightly, to spill his seed between her breasts. Spasm after spasm rocked his body, and Elena was thrilled with her newfound power.

Elena held him close and pressed her face to his sculpted stomach, and his hands tangled in her hair. Elena's head was spinning, with too much alcohol, or too much Faolan, she wasn't sure.

Breath coming in hard gasps, Faolan leaned back against the couch looking stunned. "Elena," he whispered. "Och, Elena, what spell is it that you have woven around me? I am determined to resist, and yet you break me as easily as a twig. Are you some witch come to further torment my life?"

Elena looked at up at him, worried he really was angry, but he was smiling tenderly. He pulled her up beside him on the couch, and kissed her. Gentle fingers stroked her cheek, and down to her jaw, opening her mouth, he kissed her deeply, stealing her breath and giving her his in return.

"Wait here, love," and then she heard water running in the big slipper tub. *Was this real or fantasy? It was all so surreal.*

Faolan returned holding a warm, damp washcloth with which he tenderly wiped her breasts. He pulled up the top of her dress, covering her, and then carried her to the bathroom. Faolan undressed her with infinite care, caressing and kissing each part of her body. He pulled her dress over her head, revealing her black lace bra and matching thong.

He kissed her breasts through the bra, before unfastening it and caressing her breasts with his tongue. He knelt before her and pulled the thong tight against her folds, kissing and tasting her. Then catching the lace in his teeth, he pulled the thong away, down toward her hips, where his hands finished removing it completely.

When she stood naked before him, exposed in all of her insecurities, Faolan looked at her and said, "Och, you are so verra' beautiful, Elena MacFarland."

Elena caught sight of herself in the mirror over Faolan's shoulder, and stared in wonder at the vision they presented. Her hair was wild, spilling over her shoulders and down her back, in tangled masses of raven curls. Her green eyes slanted in contentment, her lips were swollen, and the skin on her full breasts was rosy from his raspy shadow beard. The man at her feet was looking up at her, as a mortal worshiping his goddess, and in that moment, Elena felt beautiful.

When the tub was full, Faolan picked her up, and lowered her gently into the water, draping her hair over the side so it wouldn't get wet. The tub had tall slipper sides, and Elena leaned back to let the water spill over her shoulders and breasts.

"I will be right back, doona' go anywhere," he smiled.

Elena luxuriated in the hot bath, her eyes closed, sure she was dreaming. *He let me make love to him. He doesn't hate me. He's going to make love to me.* The words were a mantra to her soul.

When he returned, Elena opened her eyes in wonder. He had brought candles, freshly poured drinks, and a bottle for refills. He handed Elena her drink and made a toast, "My little enchantress," and they both drank, before he kissed her deeply. She should stop drinking, but the whisky made everything so smooth, just one more drink wouldn't hurt, and she held her glass out for a refill.

Faolan removed his sweater, and now stood before her in all his glory. He was huge, and ready for her. Elena sucked in her breath as she imagined trying to take all of him inside of her. *What a beautiful man!* She reached out to touch him, and he smiled and stepped back to grab a stack of towels and laid them on the floor. Faolan knelt next to the tub, picked up a sponge, and began washing her body with exquisite care.

Faolan leaned in to lick and then nip at her neck. He gently washed her neck then squeezed the sponge sending rivulets of water running down her breasts. His eyes followed the water, locked on her breasts and then his velvet tongue licked the droplets from her sensitive skin.

His rough hands created a gentle friction against her swollen breasts and he rolled her nipples between his fingers, lightly pinching and squeezing, before he pulled the puckered peak into his mouth. The combination of the warm water and his hot mouth sent signals directly to her most private of female places, telling her to prepare for invasion. She shuddered; her muscles contracted in anticipation, leaving her achy with need, waiting to be filled.

Faolan draped her leg over the edge of the tub and rubbed the sponge slowly up the inside of her thigh. Brushing lightly over her mound, he started on her other leg, draping it over the opposite side of the tub, opening her to him. He continued to rub back and forth with the sponge as the heat between her legs built. She felt weighted by desire, her muscles heavy with the heat of the water and his touch.

When his hand replaced the sponge, a moan of pure pleasure escaped Elena. He cupped her mound in his hand and rubbed up and down, applying pressure. His fingers pulled gently at the folds of flesh, revealing the core of her most sensitive female parts. He pinched and rubbed, until she was moaning and gasping, still she couldn't move. His fingers tenderly opened her, and he gently inserted one finger, exploring, in and out, careful never to go too deep. First just one finger, then another, taking up a rhythm, stretching her. Elena sucked in air at the feel of his fingers inside of her.

Oh, how I want him.

Elena opened her eyes and looked up at his face. His eyes were hungry as he watched his fingers touching, spreading, entering her. He turned his head, his gaze locked on hers, watching her pleasure when he touched his thumb to her lust-swollen nub. She nearly came out of the tub with the intensity of the feeling. Slowly he began to rub, never stopping his fingers, he brought her to the edge of orgasm, and then he stilled his hand, releasing the pressure an instant before she came. Elena could barely open her eyes. Her limbs floated on the water. She wanted him to take her over the edge, but all she could do was gasp and moan.

Faolan lifted her with a hand beneath her hips, letting the water buoy her, her legs still draped over the edge of the tub, spreading her. With his fingers still pumping rhythmically, he lowered his mouth and touched her with his tongue, kissing, sucking, nipping, and stroking. Elena's inner muscles locked down tight around his fingers, and the world around her shifted. The edges of her vision became wavy as though the entire room was losing its shape with the strength of her climax. Somewhere stars exploded, showering her with thousands of fiery sparks that singed her, leaving their marks imprinted on her forever. Sounds of ecstasy filled the room, and Elena nearly blacked out as he finally carried her over the edge.

Faolan stopped stroking and just held his mouth there, letting the extra sensitivity pass, tasting her pleasure while her body continued to shudder with the force of her orgasm. When she could breathe again, he lifted her out of the tub and stood her on shaky legs while he dried her. He paused to lick the water off her breasts and to taste the sweetness between her legs. Gently, he pressed her back until she was leaning against the sink. He fell to his knees in front of her and began to lick her again with long slow strokes of his tongue. He pulled her into his mouth, and kissed and licked, faster and harder, until she had to hang on to his shoulders as another orgasm rocked her body.

Wrapped in the towel, Faolan carried Elena to the bed, and then returned to the bathroom to retrieve their drinks and the candles. Elena's hands were shaking as she sipped her drink, savoring all the emotions she was feeling. She watched as Faolan stirred the fire and added another log, before he joined her.

"Faolan" Elena murmured.

"Aye, lass?"

Elena sipped more of her drink, while she thought about what she wanted to say. They had just shared the most intimate of acts, save one, and she knew that despite his initial reservations, he would make love with her tonight. Faolan had made this night the most special of her life, and no matter what happened tomorrow, she would always treasure this memory. "This has been the best night of my life. I'm still not asking for promises."

"I know, love, I know." He gave her an inscrutable look, before kissing her tenderly. "No talking now. There's plenty of time to talk tomorrow. Now turn over." He rolled her over onto her stomach. His voice roughened with unsuppressed desire, "Elena, lass, you are a vision. Your hair is wild, your ass so lovely. You make a man crazy with desire."

Elena's breath hitched and she shivered in anticipation. He was going to take her from behind, and soon he would fill her. She would be a virgin no more. He straddled her hips, and poured something warm and slippery on her back. Then he began to rub. It was body oil, and it smelled of the earth and the wind and of him. He rubbed her back and her shoulders, his firm hands kneading away any remaining tension. Big hands stroked down her back, then up along her sides, fingers trailing over her breasts each time his hands returned to her back. She could feel his erection, hard and heavy, nestled in the cleft of her behind, a promise of what was to come.

He moved his hands to her legs, rubbing the oil into each

leg, working his way from her thighs to her feet and back again. She couldn't imagine anything more seductive.

Somewhere along the way, while he was working his way back up her legs toward her ass, Elena fell into a relaxed, deep sleep and didn't wake until morning.

Chapter Ten

When Elena awoke, she was alone in her bed, but she could still smell Faolan. *Faolan, oh God, what did I do?* Everything was so wonderful. They'd made love in every way without actually consummating it. How could she have fallen asleep? She hoped he wasn't angry with her. How ridiculous. Of course he would be angry. What man wouldn't be?

Elena threw the covers back and jumped up quickly to go find him and nearly cried. Before she could think too much about the pain in her head, she doubled over and ran to the bathroom and vomited. *Kill me now.* There was a knock on the door, and Faolan said, "Elena? Are you all right?"

"Go away," she managed, just before the vomiting turned into dry heaves.

Faolan laughed. She tried to rejoice at the sound, but all she managed to mumble was, "Jerk."

"Come on, love, splash some water on your face, and drag yourself to the kitchen, Lilly has the cure."

Twenty minutes later, Elena finally made it to the kitchen. She dressed in jeans and a button front long sleeved shirt. She couldn't stand the thought of brushing her hair, so she pulled it back into a sloppy ponytail. *Ugh, I think my eyes are bleeding.* Faolan was grinning at her. *Well, at least he wasn't angry.*

He handed her some coffee, which she normally didn't drink, but he was brooking no resistance this morning, "Drink," he ordered. She sipped and shuddered. The coffee was strong with a definite shot of something in it. She looked a question at Faolan, and he answered, "A bit of the dog, lass. You'll feel better soon."

"Where are Lilly and Red?" she managed to croak out.

"They thought we might need some privacy." He grinned.

"Oh my God, Faolan. I'm so sorry about last night, I can't believe I fell asleep." She started to say more, but he stopped her with a kiss. "Last night 'twas a gift, lass. No apologies, no regrets." He kissed her aching head.

Not long after that, Lilly and Red came into the kitchen, all bustle and noise. Elena went red to the roots of her hair when Lilly gave her an appraising look, then said, "Well, now."

Faolan picked Lilly up, twirled her around the kitchen and said, "None of that, Lilly."

Faolan was still in his cheery mood from the night before, entertaining them with stories and laughing easily, mostly at Elena's expense. They all found it amazing that this was her first hangover. They were also chagrined that a lass with the name of MacFarland couldn't hold her whisky, something they vowed to remedy as a matter of national pride.

Lilly bullied Elena into eating some toast and drinking a second cup of coffee. After a while, Elena realized she felt almost human and considered living a reasonable possibility. However, she vowed to stay out of the bright sunlight and away from hammering for now. It seemed like a good day to try again with the categorizing of the books.

Faolan followed Elena into the library, swept her into his

arms, and said, "Ah, returning to the scene of the crime," before setting her back on her feet.

Then he kissed her so thoroughly that her knees buckled and he had to support her weight. Faolan carried Elena to the couch, sat her on his lap, and kissed her some more. Her lips felt swollen and bruised. He moved on to her neck, his lips burning, teeth biting. Elena ground her hips against his erection. *Hmm, maybe going back to bed wasn't out of the question.* Then he whispered, "I have to leave today, Elena."

Elena jerked her head back to look at him. "Leave? What are you talking about? Why?"

"Do you remember when I made us leave the café so swiftly?"

"Yes," Elena said tightly. *Here it comes; he's finally going to tell me about the blonde.*

"There was a man there I recognized. I had seen him around you before, only I didna know he was following you then. When I realized he was tracking you, I drove 'til I was certain he wasna' behind us before I stopped. I searched the car for a bug when we pulled over. I found it near the rear bumper. Someone was following your movements by placing a tracer on your Rover. Now I need to follow it backwards, and find the men behind these attacks, prove it's related to Worthington and stop this once and for all. Although we are using an investigator in London with operatives in Phoenix, he willna report to us over the phone. Lilly and I must go, Elena."

"I thought you wanted that woman. The tall blonde? You remember her," Elena asked sweetly.

His blank look told her just how wrong she'd been. Then a wolfish smile crossed his face, "Were you jealous, Elena? Would you mind it so verra' much if I were interested in another woman?"

"Not really," she affected a bored look. *Not once I'd killed her. And if he says verra' one more time like that, I will come right here.*

He laughed. Elena loved this laughing Faolan. He brought his hand up to caress her face, and ran his finger across her lips. She caught his finger with her teeth and pulled it into her mouth and sucked it. His breath caught, and his eyes turned dark and heavy. He was so very hard beneath her.

"I don't want you to go," she whispered.

"I know," he whispered back. He slipped his hand under her shirt, cupped a breast and pinched her nipple.

"Are you almost ready?" Lilly called from the hall.

Elena tried to jump off Faolan's lap, but he held her tightly to him, his only concession to decorum was removing his hand from her breast. He grinned at Lilly as she entered the room, and said, "Be right there."

He stood up and swept Elena into another long, hard kiss. "Don't lose faith in me, lass. I will explain it all when I return. This I promise you." Then he tucked his hand under her chin and pushed it up until she was looking directly in his eyes, and she saw it.

They were the eyes of the wolf.

****

She was too restless to work on the books, so she decided to go back and search out the secret room in the north wing of the steading. She closed the panels behind her and then quickly opened them again, from the inside, just to make sure she could. In her backpack, she'd brought additional lighting, a pad of paper and pencils, and her digital camera.

Elena examined the walls carefully. As she'd noticed on the first visit, some of the stones had carvings, and she'd done a little Internet research in the subject. She'd discovered these were likely Pict in origin. After taking a few pictures, Elena mapped each stone, taking note that the entryway to the room was on the south wall of the vestibule and one carved stone was on each of the remaining walls.

Starting with the west wall, she ran her hand lightly over the first carved stone. She immediately noticed it was warmer than the surrounding stones. With a deep breath, Elena tried placing her hands on the stone, as she had with the panels, and pushed. The stone moved, and then the other stones around it seemed to ripple, disappearing to reveal a small closet. The closet had a dozen or more shelves, each laden with books, drawings, and other artifacts.

Elena photographed the treasures on each shelf, then moved to the north wall. Again, the carved stone opened easily when pushed. This time the opening revealed a passageway that ran slightly downhill, disappearing straight into the mountain. Elena shivered. She wasn't sure she was ready to walk down that dark passageway yet, so she decided to try to open the remaining wall in the entry chamber first.

This closet was slightly larger than the first one, filled with more books, some folded plaids, daggers, and rolls of parchment. *This place is fantastic! I wonder if anyone knows about it?*

Returning to the long passageway made her palms sweaty and her heart thump uncomfortably. It led deep into the hill behind the farm, and there was no way to tell what might be down there. With a deep breath, Elena forged ahead. The walls were a mixture of stones and boulders, with sconces holding unlit torches protruding every ten feet. The passageway sloped downhill, and after walking for at least fifteen minutes underground, she finally reached the end. Or more accurately, the end of this journey, since she was facing two massive oak doors with iron hinges and locks. She made a half-hearted attempt to open them and then realized the keys in the jewelry casket probably opened the locks.

Her stomach started to swirl and a sense of vertigo threatened to overtake her as she looked back up the passageway. As her panic started to rise, Elena felt an overwhelming need to escape. With a faked indifference, she walked quickly back to the entrance chamber, picked up after herself, and left, once again hiding the entryway behind her pile of junk. She would come back another day. *Maybe a day without a hangover would be a good idea.*

****

After a bath, Elena nibbled on cheese and bread in the library while she sorted, first grouping the books by language. If she could read it, it went in one stack, and if she couldn't, it went in the other. Since this didn't take much brainpower, her mind drifted to other things.

To Faolan.

When he'd discovered she was still a virgin, he told her that she honored him, and then left, making it clear they would go no further. He'd told her once there were things she couldn't know, yet today, before he'd left, he said he would tell her everything when he returned. What had changed? Had she caught him off guard last night with her boldness in the library? *He's as confused as I am!*

Something just wasn't making sense. As wonderful as last night had been, Faolan still had been careful not to go too far with his fingers. She spent a few minutes side-tracked, thinking about those fingers. With a jerk back to reality, she tried to think dispassionately about last night. Faolan had brought her to pleasure once again without actually consummating the loving. He had plied her with drink and given her a bath, topped by a long massage. She would need to think more about that.

Faolan had asked her to trust him and promised to tell her the truth when he returned. She wondered which truth he would tell her: the one she wanted to hear, or the one he wanted to tell her. She was sure they weren't one and the same.

Elena turned at a soft noise near the window. Suddenly, Shadow was there, fur on end, tail enormous, and his back arched. "Good grief, Shadow. You startled me." *The old fight or flight syndrome really kicks in when you're out here on your own.*

Shadow was up on his toes, turned toward the window, his eyes narrowed to slits. His hissing and spitting turned into a menacing growl. Elena laughed as Shadow stared at his reflection in the window. Then the laughter died in her throat, and her blood ran cold.

The growl grew louder, reverberated through the glass pane, into the house, and out into the night. Elena ran to pick up the kitten and looked out. There was another wolf right outside the window. He wasn't quite as large as the one she'd encountered in the yard, and his fur was lighter. His teeth bared, his hackles rose, and he crouched, leaning forward, prepared to attack, growling low and menacingly. He was facing *away* from the window, looking out into the fields surrounding the house. He was guarding her.

****

Elena asked Red about the wolf the next morning, but he hadn't heard anything from his flat. She got the impression he didn't think much of her story but was too polite to say so.

Elena waited until he'd gone back to the barn before donning her boots and jacket and going outside to confirm her own story. Sure enough, right in front of the library window there were several large paw prints.

She walked straight out and back from the window, each time in a slightly different direction, creating spokes. Confirmation came on her fifth or sixth attempt when she found the spot where someone had stood and watched her house. Someone with high-powered binoculars could have seen right into her windows at night, and she never would have known. Elena followed the footprints until she found the spot where a car had been parked. There were fresh cigarette butts in the snow, so presumably whoever it was had waited there for a while, probably until after dark, before hiking out to spy on her.

Elena walked slowly back to the house, thinking about the wolf. Or more accurately about the wolves. She had seen at least two, but she thought it was probably three different wolves since she'd had been at the farm. The one in the yard had only been a few feet away from her, yet hadn't tried to harm her in any way. Last night a wolf had stood guard at the window. She'd heard a wolf howling on more than one night. The night of her attack, she'd thought that she'd heard a dog growling. Could that have been a wolf too?

Was there some connection between this place and the wolves, something that caused them to stay close to it and protect it? *Maybe I should be feeding them.* She went to the library, logged on to her laptop, and searched for wolves in Scotland.

Color me flabbergasted. The wolves in Scotland had been extinct for nearly two hundred and fifty years! Plans to reintroduce wolves here were on hold, due to pressure from farmers protecting their herds. Yet she'd seen two of them up close and personal. Elena decided to ask the others about the wolves at dinner.

She spent the rest of the day measuring windows for window treatments. It seemed absurd that, although she had no visible neighbors, she would have to cover her windows for privacy, but she didn't want to feel so exposed again. She would also ask Red to start repairing the shutters.

Chapter Eleven

Elena heard Lilly's truck in the yard and peeked out. She watched as Lilly emerged and Red pulled her into a passionate embrace that left her feeling as though she was intruding on a private moment. Faolan studiously ignored them and busied himself with unloading their bags and some boxes of supplies at the rear of the truck.

Faolan turned as if sensing Elena, and their gazes locked through the window. He reached the back door in three long strides, threw it open, and took her in his arms, lifting her high off the floor. She wrapped her legs around his waist so he couldn't let her go. She didn't know what this was or where it was going, but she was going to hang on for all she was worth. He kissed her, but it was with a sense of desperation that made Elena uneasy.

Faolan only set her down when Red and Lilly came in the back door, and Red cleared his throat and said, "Sommat smells good in here."

"Oh, I better get the cornbread, before it burns," Elena exclaimed. She made dinner American style: fried chicken with mashed potatoes and gravy.

She busied herself putting the food on the table, running into Faolan constantly, since he didn't seem inclined to leave her side. Finally, Elena tasked him with serving the beer in the frosted mugs while she finished mashing the potatoes and Lilly whisked the gravy. Red put new logs on the fires throughout the house.

When they sat to eat, Faolan again sat so close to Elena their legs touched, keeping her unsettled and anxious. Based on his reaction to seeing her, she had high hopes for how this night might end. She couldn't seem to track the conversation. At one point, Elena asked if they had found what they were looking for, but Lilly derailed any talk of business—as she called it—at the table. When dinner was over, Red pulled Faolan aside for an intense conversation before they helped with the cleanup.

Once again, everyone met in the library after dinner, and Elena noticed a change in all three of them. *This really was going to be business.* Lilly and Red sat together on the couch before Red popped up to pour drinks. Faolan stood by the fireplace and stared into the fire. He had one hand propped against the mantle with the other fisted by his side.

Red declared the American beer they'd had with dinner suitable only for lightweights. When Elena demurred from taking a whisky, Faolan insisted, saying through a tight jaw, "It will make this conversation easier, lass."

Elena watched the firelight flicker on Faolan's face and waited for him to begin. Instead, it was Lilly that got things started.

"We traced the transmitter back to a small surveillance company in Phoenix before the trail went cold. The investigator working for us in Phoenix said the man who operates the company is an ex-con who is represented by

Worthington, Tyler, and Walters, so we know who is behind having you followed."

Elena's face felt incapable of expression. She sat motionless, staring at Lilly, as if waiting for the punch line to a very bad joke. Somehow, the situation had all become more real, more deadly with that bit of information. It really *was* Worthington that tried to have her killed.

"What now?" Elena managed to stammer out after a minute.

Faolan growled.

Red looked at Faolan's back, then turned to Lilly, "'Tis not quite all. There was someone here last night; I got the license number before I scared him off." He faced Elena. "The car was rented to a fellow that we already know works for Worthington."

Her mouth fell open to hear Red admit someone had been out there after all. He'd been lying when he let her believe he'd dismissed her concerns this morning. Faolan bowed his head, dragged his fingers through his hair, and then held on to his head, as if to keep it from splitting open. He still hadn't looked at Elena.

Lilly took up the tale again. "Worthington knows about us, about all of us now. He knows we are connected to the farmhouse. We doona' think he knows Faolan is the Gailtry, else he would have been here long before now. Perhaps he thinks we are treasure hunters, trying to find the same secrets he is looking for. The Worthingtons thought they had killed the last of the Gailtry and his family years ago, so the longer Faolan stays out of his sights, the better.

"Our job, Red's and mine, is to protect the MacGailtry. His job—" she thrust her chin at Faolan "—is to preserve the family legacy."

Elena wasn't quite clear on what the Gailtry was, but she knew from her grandfather, adding "Mac" in front of a name meant "from the clan of," and names were sometimes used with or without "Mac." Lilly spoke as though Faolan was some kind of clan chief, which was an outdated notion in this day and age. Wasn't it?

Faolan groaned quietly but did not turn around or lift his head.

"I am sorry, lass," said Red, "but there is no choice. We have a flat near Beauly that is secure. Worthington does not know us there. You can go tomorrow and be safe. Once the land passes to you permanently, you will sell it to us. You'll be safe enough then, as long as Worthington does not believe there is any other connection between us."

Lilly and Red both looked at Elena expectantly, clearly waiting for her to agree. Try as she might, Elena couldn't think of anything to say. She shot back her drink and rose to pour another. Still no one spoke. Only the crackling of the fire marked the passage of time. Elena leaned against the doorway and looked back at them all, her mind rapidly trying to sort through this confusing moment.

Red and Lilly exchanged uneasy glances, then both turned back to look at Elena. Faolan stood with both hands resting on the mantle, his head down between his outstretched arms, apparently staring into the fire, his long hair hiding his face.

There was something unusual about this place, about all of them. People had died to protect the secrets of her farm, and Worthington was willing to kill to get it back. What kind of secrets could stir such passion? Elena sifted the evidence of underground tunnels, ancient artifacts, and animals long extinct. She tried to sort fact from fantasy. If she took a rather large leap of faith, she thought she could weave a story from the facts she knew and those she now suspected.

Faolan had planned to tell Elena his secret, but now she was sure he'd decided she'd be safer not knowing. She hated the idea that he would sacrifice his own happiness and hers in order to keep her safe. He was having Red and Lilly send Elena away because he couldn't bring himself to do it.

If Elena tried to argue with them, they would only become more convinced they were correct. She had to think of a way to get them to tell her the truth about Faolan, about all of them. She drank a second glass and poured a third.

"Faolan," she said, looking directly at him. His back stiffened slightly, but he didn't turn. "Faolan, tell me about the wolves."

When Elena was practicing to be a lawyer, she'd taken a lot of sworn statements. Unsurprisingly, there would often come a time during the questioning when she'd known she'd caught the witness in the lie. She would go on the hunt then, change her questions slightly, a little bit at a time, hemming him in, leaving no way out but the truth. Once the witness finally realized he was trapped, he would sigh.

A sigh swept around the room now, and Elena knew she had them. Faolan turned slowly and locked gazes, first with Lilly and Red, and then finally, with Elena.

Faolan said, "Och, lass, you shouldna be involved in this—" Then he changed tactics mid-sentence. "Why do you ask about wolves?"

"Oh, please," Elena said, as if insulted. *It was a technique.* When no response was forthcoming, she took a giant mental leap from the high dive and gave them her most outlandish theory. Because if she was wrong about the secret they were sharing, then she was wrong about all of it, and all hope for love was lost.

"Okay, I'll go first," Elena said, in her most detached voice. "I've seen three different wolves since I've been here." She looked at Lilly first. "The first one I saw was out on the hill, howling in the night. She made me think of the coyotes back home. It was comforting."

Elena shifted her gaze to Red. "A different wolf saved me from the men who tried to rape me, and last night stood outside the window guarding me."

Then Elena turned to look directly at Faolan and waited until he raised his tawny gaze. "The third wolf has looked me in the eyes from only a few feet away. And I do know those eyes. The funny thing is, according to all government sources, wolves are extinct in Scotland."

Faolan smiled a sad smile and looked at Red and Lilly. "I will tell her," he said with a sigh. "'Tis a long story, lass. Why doona' you sit down."

Elena returned to her chair and sat, waiting for the shock to hit when she finally realized that her wild theory was somehow true. "Go ahead. I'm ready."

"I told you what Worthington did to my family. When my father broke his sacred vow, everyone in our clan was damned. The only blood relative left living was me, but apparently Red and Lilly are either some kind of distant relatives or so close to us the curse affected them too.

"Aye, you are right, lass. We are the wolves, but we are human. We are shape shifters. There are other shape shifters out there, but few like us. We have been changing...a long time and have learned to protect others from our curse. We can turn to wolves when we want to, but there are still times we are forced to our wolf form against our will. 'Tis only those times that we are dangerous, true to the nature of wolves. I told you there were things not of your world, and you shouldna' know of them. We are some of those things."

Lilly looked as though she was about to add something, looked at Faolan, and then forged ahead. "This doesn't change anything, Faolan. She needs to go to Beauly. We must protect you, and she makes you vulnerable. Once we figure out how to break the curse, you can see her again."

Elena answered, even though Lilly was addressing Faolan. "I won't go, Lilly. This is my house. You may all stay here or you may leave, but I won't be put out of the first home I've ever owned." She'd always been a fighter, a scrapper, and she wasn't going to run now, but neither would she bury her head in the sand. She stood and looked at Faolan, put on her best business face, and continued in her professional attorney manner, "I'll ask Mr. Burns to draw up my will tomorrow leaving the entire estate to you should something happen to me. That should tie Worthington up in court long enough for you to prove the estate was yours to begin with. If nothing happens to me, we can work out the ownership after the provisional period has passed.

"And I believe Lilly when she says she must keep you safe. If you leave, you'll be safe. Go stay in Beauly. I'll do everything in my power to help you bring down Worthington. Whether through natural or more…*supernatural* means. Meanwhile, if the resources you need to break the curse are here, they are at your disposal. I am an excellent researcher. Let me help."

The room was silent for a long time. Red, Lilly, and Faolan exchanged looks, and again, Elena sensed that something more passed between them before Faolan finally spoke.

"Nay, lass, I won't be leavin' either." He looked at Red and Lilly. "We can talk more about this on the morrow, but I'll not be changin' my mind."

Red and Lilly stood to go, clearly recognizing the

determination and dismissal in his voice. Lilly paused to hug Faolan before they left. Her face was creased with worry. "We'll be out there," she said as they walked to the door.

"I know," he answered.

When they were finally alone, Elena turned to look at Faolan, "There's still more, isn't there?"

"Aye, lass."

"Will you tell me what it is?"

"'Tis nothing to be worrying yourself about. I'll not hurt you, you know. Are you afraid?"

"Will you make love to me, Faolan?"

"Nay, lass. I told you I wouldna be takin' your maidenhead. That you must save for the now."

Elena felt the tears well in her eyes, but she wouldn't let them fall. She sat back down, feeling defeated. "Then yes, Faolan, I'm afraid of you, because you have the power to hurt me. It was all an act the other night, wasn't it? You meant for me to pass out!"

Faolan crossed the floor in two quick strides and knelt between her knees. He reached his arms around her waist and looked deep into her eyes. "Elena, if it were only a matter of desire, know that I would be yours. If it was only *my* soul in question, I would forsake it, just to have one night with you." His hands slid up her arms to her shoulders as if to shake her. "Elena, doona' ask for what is not mine to give."

Coming to her feet, Elena yelled, "I never asked for your heart. I never asked for promises. All I wanted was sex! A lousy stupid night in your bed. My first time and it could have been with someone I cared about and who I thought cared for me. Instead, you used me!" Her voice dropped to a whisper, "You let me do things to you... you did things to me, but you knew you were never going to make love to me." Her face twisted into a mask of pain and bitterness. "No, you wouldn't make love to me, but you made me love you."

Elena turned and walked to the fireplace. This was more than she could handle. She wasn't even freaking out that he was a shape shifter. She was having a much harder time accepting that he had gotten her drunk so he wouldn't have to have sex with her. *I will not crumble; people's lives are at stake here. Worthington will try to kill me and maybe Red and Lilly, too. I don't want to think what he'll do to Faolan.*

Faolan grabbed Elena from behind and turned her roughly around. His face was fierce, and the eyes of the wolf looked out at her. He clamped her face between his hands and kissed her, hard. His lips pressed against her unyielding mouth, crushing her with the force of his kiss. Bruising her, punishing her.

Elena jerked her head back. "I will not be used," she said through clenched teeth.

The fight went out of him as quickly as it had come, "Nay, Elena. I would not use you. 'Tis why I won't take your maidenhead. I am promised to another."

Elena's head snapped back, the pain as intense as if he actually had struck her. Her stomach roiled and she thought her knees would buckle. She forced back the sob that wanted to escape. "You're engaged? You said your heart belonged to no one."

"I doona' know what it is I am supposed to do," he yelled. "My father died too soon, he didna pass on the knowledge, and I am left to search for answers, forced by the full moon to hunt like a wolf, forsaking my true love to find another with the true heart!

"I am cursed, Elena, and I must break it," he said in a choked voice. "The spell is somewhere, maybe in these books." He waved his hand toward the stacks around the room. "We also know from legend I must mate the one with the true heart. I doona even know how I am supposed to find her, but that answer may also be in here."

His confession stunned her to silence. Compassion filled her heart, for the boy who'd lost his family, for the man who'd lost his way. It wasn't fair. She wanted to raise her fist to the fates, to throttle those long-dead ancestors. Instead, she fought to push away every selfish feeling she had. "I'll help you, Faolan; we'll find the answers," Elena said, softly.

Faolan looked at Elena, an expression on his face that she didn't recognize. "I willna have sex with you, Elena, but believe this, if you believe naught else. I did make love to you. I made love *with* you."

A wolf howled in the distance. They stared at each other for another long minute, and then Faolan turned and left the house.

Chapter Twelve

Elena was alone at breakfast the next morning. The coffee and teakettle were both hot, and there was fresh bread on the table, but the house was deserted. She steeped a cup of green tea and cut a thick slice of bread, contemplating her plan for the day. She was dressed for industry, not romance, in jeans and a blue sweater, her hair hanging down her back in a long plait.

Faolan needed to find information that would help him break the curse, so she planned to try to organize the books in the library to make it easier for him to look through them. She could also do research on the Internet, if she could only figure out what to look for. That would be her first avenue of attack: identifying search terms, either digital or paper-based.

She carried her breakfast into the library and started to Google. She would need to ask Faolan if his father was a Druid, since much of his story seemed to coincide with what little she knew about the ancient practice. As long as she was online, she ordered a couple of Gaelic, Celtic, and Scots reference books to help with the search.

She took all the English language books to one wall of shelves and began the slow process of sorting them according to topic. There were hundreds to sort through. She picked up one book after the other, trying to give it a one or two word subject and then placed it in the corresponding stack. She had loosely arranged all of the books by lunchtime. After lunch, she would see what she could do with the ones she couldn't read.

When she turned from the shelves, she was surprised to find Faolan standing in the doorway watching her. Her focus had been so intense that she had no idea how long he had been there.

"Good morning," she smiled.

He seemed surprised by her pleasant tone but smiled and returned her greeting. "Good morrow, lass."

"I was just going to have some lunch. Will you join me?" she asked.

"May I take you to lunch instead?" he replied rather formally.

That surprised her. "Why? Shouldn't we be looking for answers?"

"Aye, lass, we will be looking for different answers."

Elena agreed to go, curious as to what they might be seeking outside these walls. She begged a few minutes to change her clothes, but Faolan again surprised her.

"Nay, lass, wear what you have on. 'Tis how I first saw you."

He remembered this blue sweater? She didn't know he'd paid such close attention. The thought pleased her more than it should have. She realized her days with Faolan were numbered. Unlike most budding relationships, this one had a definite expiration date and strict parameters. She knew his code of honor would not allow him to commit to her. And without a commitment, he was unwilling to take their relationship any further.

With a heavy heart, she acknowledged, if only to herself, that he was her one true love. She couldn't say which exact moment she became sure of her feelings, but she was. She could choose to protect her heart and leave today, but she would stay for the six months. If all he had to give was friendship, then she would be his friend.

Elena had thought a lot about her position last night and again this morning while she was sorting books. Sometimes in practicing law, you faced impossible situations with two divergent solutions. Following one path would lead to a legal resolution, and it was the remedy that almost always applied. Unfortunately, though, the legal solution didn't always equate to an ethical solution. An ethical solution required the courage to do what was morally right. At the conclusion of the six-month provision, Worthington would no longer have any claim to this land; it would legally belong to Elena.

There was only one moral outcome for this dilemma. In six months, she would return the land to Faolan. She'd already called Mr. Burns and given instructions to draw up her will. Mr. Burns was also researching the best ways to protect this land under Scottish land laws and restore the rights to Faolan and his future family.

****

They had lunch at a small café in Fairth where they drew many speculative glances and became the subject of much gossip, no doubt. There was nothing to indicate they were a couple, just a man and a woman sharing a meal. Yet, she was sure anyone who knew human nature would take one look at her face and know she was in love.

Elena had a large salad, and Faolan opted for a bowl of

thick chowder. They kept the talk casual since anything they said might be overheard. They spoke of repairs to the house and plans for a garden. Faolan asked if she would raise farm animals, but Elena demurred. She was hesitant to agree to anything that would require a long-term commitment. She asked about places to purchase drapes and rugs, and he promised to take her there after their errand. Overall, a completely normal and casual lunch between friends, and Elena treasured every minute of it.

It turned out their errand was just on the outskirts of Fairth, or rather *around* Fairth. Faolan believed he had located and removed another tracking device on her Rover and wanted to take a ride to see if anyone followed them. As they drove around, he told her stories of the area, how it had changed over time, and more importantly how it had stayed the same.

Their last stop was at a small sandstone building near the town square. There were no signs, save a small note taped to the door that invited them to enter. They did, and a little bell announced their arrival. The shop's watchdog raced out, barking ferociously, letting them know this store was hers.

"Ooh, hi, beautiful," Elena said as she squatted down to pay homage to the Yorkshire Terrier, who was not much bigger than a tea pot. The little dog sniffed regally and was mollified since Elena obviously recognized who was in charge. She then pranced over to Faolan, clearly swooning and rolled over onto her back, paws in the air, baring her chest for him to pet. *I know how she feels.*

"Hello, Hussy," Faolan said, laughing.

"Faolan—" Elena gasped on a laugh "—that's not nice!"

"Aye, lass, that's her nature, and that's her name," said a soft burr from the doorway leading to the back of the shop. Elena smiled at the tiny, wizened woman who continued,

"Faolan knows her nature, just as she knows his."

Faolan picked the old woman up in a bear hug. "Brigid, it's good to see you! Still as ornery as the divil, I see!"

"Aye, and I see you finally found your light," she replied completely apropos of nothing.

She looked like a child's toy in his arms, and Elena was afraid Faolan might break her.

Setting the old woman carefully on her feet, Faolan bowed grandly, and said, "Let me introduce you to your new neighbor. This is Miss Elena MacFarland, recently of America, and now Mistress of the Gailtry Farm.

"Elena, this is Brigid. She will provide you with the rugs you need and window coverings too, if you still desire."

"Come, dear. We will have tea," Brigid declared, grabbing Elena's wrist in a surprisingly strong grip and ushering them into a sitting room filled with wool rugs. She seated them in large wing backed chairs covered in tweed and set about making tea. Hussy followed and splayed herself across Faolan's foot, content to be touching him. *Lucky dog.*

When the tea was ready, Brigid handed Elena the cup and directed her to twirl the contents three times in a clockwise direction before drinking, "And mind you drink it all, lass," she admonished.

Faolan started to say something, but Brigid cut across him, using words Elena couldn't understand. Whatever it was, it caused him to look at Elena thoughtfully, before shaking his head and answering Brigid in the same language. They argued back and forth for a while, switching interchangeably between what she assumed was Scots and Gaelic. She could understand neither.

Elena diligently drank her tea while she looked around the overcrowded shop. The assortment of rugs displayed around the room was impressive. There were hundreds from which to choose. Some were simple throw rugs while others were enormous and suitable for an entire room. Tapestries hung from the walls and rafters, in case your castle was drafty. Since she didn't own a castle, Elena narrowed her choices to the smaller rugs and hurried to finish her tea so she could start looking through the shop.

Faolan was listening intently to whatever it was Brigid was telling him, but he didn't seem to share her opinion; his scowl deepened. As Elena took her final swallow, Brigid snatched the cup from her hands before she even lowered it from her lips. She stared into it, moving her lips, tilting her head like a bird, contemplating her worm.

Then Brigid's nimble face stretched into a grin. She stood, thanked them for coming, and walked briskly toward the front door. Belatedly, Faolan and Elena jumped to their feet and followed. Elena looked a question at Faolan, but he just shrugged and hurried to catch up.

At the open door, Brigid grabbed Faolan's arm and whispered something Elena couldn't understand. Then speaking slowly, and with far less of a brogue than she'd previously used, said to him, "You will pick me up two mornings hence. Bring Lilly's truck. Faolan, hear me now, and do not stray from my direction. Follow your light." Then she stepped back and closed the door on their startled faces.

Back in the Rover, Elena looked at Faolan and asked, "What was that all about?"

Faolan didn't answer her; he seemed lost in thought. Elena kept the rest of her questions to herself, and they drove home in a companionable silence. The house was dark and the yard empty when they arrived, and Faolan swore lightly under his breath.

"Och, lass, I am sorry, I was supposed to bring home something for your dinner tonight; Red and Lilly will be out for the evening. Let me take you back to town."

"Nay, lad," Elena said seriously in her best imitation of a Scottish brogue. "I'll be makin' us omelets and such for dinner then." Her attempt was so poor that Faolan just looked at her for a second before he roared with laughter, his eyes sparkling. Elena started laughing too, and they just barely contained themselves, avoiding breaking into that near hysteria that had consumed them previously.

As Elena thought of that night, she thought about what had followed their laughter. She turned away, simultaneously embarrassed by her behavior and saddened at her loss. Faolan seemed to know what she was thinking. He wrapped his arms around her and held her close. He kissed the top of her head and then stepped away, saying, "I'll get the fires going."

Elena wasn't offended when he stepped away so quickly. She'd felt his reaction to her as he'd held her. After dinner, they started on the books together, and he'd shown her how to distinguish between the different languages. Once she'd looked at a few examples, she was accurate with her sorting. The evening passed companionably, if quietly; they were both preoccupied. He'd been distracted ever since their visit to Brigid. Elena was thinking about his reaction to her, knowing that no matter what he said to her, he wasn't indifferent. She worried about the complicated situation.

Elena yawned and stretched. It was time for bed, but she hesitated, knowing that as soon as she left the room, Faolan would go into the night. He stood with her.

"Elena, let me hold you," he asked in a pleading voice. His face was bleak, as if there was no hope left in the world.

She wrapped her arms around his waist and held him close,

savoring his spicy male scent, yearning to feel his skin against hers.

"You know I canna be with you the way you want, but 'tis not in my power to be away from you. You have captured my heart. You are the keeper of my soul. Whatever is mine is yours, but for the one thing for which you have asked. I canna live with myself and I canna live without you." He reached for her plait of hair and loosened it, letting cascades of black curls spill over his hands and her shoulders.

Elena looked up into his eyes and saw a tormented man. "Come lay with me, Faolan. I won't ask for more. Come lay beside me and hold me. Let me fall asleep in your arms." He swept her up into his arms and carried her to her room. Elena laughed and told him she needed a few personal moments, and suggested he pour drinks and stir the fire.

She went into the bathroom and prepared for bed as usual. She wore her soft flannel drawstring pajama bottoms and a loose sleep t-shirt. She was determined she would not try to tempt him in any way tonight. He truly was a man torn between desire and duty. She would not torment him further.

Once she was washed and pajama'd, she came back out with her brush. She always brushed her hair each night before sleep or else she would never get it untangled in the morning. She sat on the bed and began brushing while Faolan stared into the fire. He came to sit beside her and took the brush from her hand. Lifting her heavy hair in his hand, he brushed back from her face, and then he swept it up from underneath. She let him brush far longer than she would have herself, just to enjoy the intimacy. *Heavenly*.

When he finished, he kissed her softly on the top of her head. She got under the covers and slid over to the opposite side of the big mattress, giving him all the space he needed.

Elena longed to hold him, kiss him, and tell him everything was going to be all right. Instead, she curled onto her side, facing away from him, and waited to follow his lead. Faolan sighed deeply and lay down beside her, on top of the covers. He buried his face in her hair, his hand rested lightly on her hip, and he whispered, "Sleep well, my love."

Chapter Thirteen

When Elena woke the next morning, Faolan was still asleep, still holding her, only now he was holding her in a much more possessive and intimate position. The covers were kicked off, and there was nothing between them except their pajamas. They were spooned together; his chest was hard against her back, his erection pressed between the cheeks of her bottom, knees tucked tightly against the backs of her legs. With his arm draped over her waist and his big hand inside her shirt cupping her breast, Elena never wanted to move again.

Of course, her body immediately betrayed her. Her breathing quickened, and her nipples budded. Her hips relaxed, pressing his erection even harder against her backside. Faolan began to move, too. His hand massaged her breast. His fingers found her nipple, and he rolled and pinched it. Faolan pressed his lips to her neck, and she knew for certain he was no longer sleeping.

Elena wanted to be good and help him keep his promise; she knew how much his honor meant to him. She might believe his sense of chivalry was misguided, but she didn't want him to do something he would regret. Even if it was something her body craved as much as breathing. She wanted him to choose to be with her and not just out of convenience.

Elena rolled onto her back, and hoping talk would distract him, whispered, "Good morning."

His hand found her other breast under her shirt. Faolan leaned up on one elbow, "You are so beautiful when you sleep, I love waking this way, with the scent of you in my nose. The feel of you pressing agin' me is more than any man can take." He covered her mouth with his. Hungry and demanding. She answered with a hunger of her own, reaching up weaving her fingers into his hair and pulling his head even closer.

They kissed for what felt like forever. She sucked greedily at his tongue, and he pulled it back then slid into her mouth ounce more. He traced her lips with his tongue, and then bit her lower lip. *Holy smokes, this was one seriously sensual man.* She needed to stop this before it went too far.

"Faolan?"

"Mmmm," he murmured as he lifted her shirt to expose her breasts. He began flicking her nipple with his tongue.

"Faolan?" she tried again. He sucked her nipple into his mouth and squeezed her breast, his other hand wrapped into her hair. *Oh God!* Her legs fell back of their own accord, opening wider, inviting him in. She was on fire with her need for him. Her body demanded she surrender, give in to the physical connection they shared. She craved him with an all-consuming desire. But she knew she must try one more time.

"Faolan, please look at me," Elena asked with her very last bit of self-restraint.

Faolan shivered, pulled his hand and mouth from her breasts, and leaned on his arm to look at her. "Elena, love. What did I do? Och, Elena, I am so sorry. You *are* my temptress. I have told you before, you enchant me."

"Waking next to you is a dream come true, Faolan. You don't need to apologize. However, I don't want this to be about lust in the morning. If you want to make love with me, I need it to be because you've decided that's what you want to do. No regrets."

He brushed her hair back and stroked her face. "Twas almost the most beautiful of mornings." He bent to kiss her, slow and sweet, once, twice, then a third time with more heat. Then he pulled her shirt down over her breasts, smiled, and said, "Let's go get breakfast."

****

Elena curled up on one end of the couch, and Faolan sat at the other. There were two stacks of books on the floor near her, and a small pile on the couch between them. Elena briefly scanned each one, looking for references to anything on her keyword list. Faolan had looked at her list, mostly without comment, although he corrected her spelling, explaining, "*magic*" was a trick, whereas, "*magick*" altered reality. Elena put that thought away to contemplate later and continued her search. If a book looked promising, it went on the couch between them; otherwise, she put it in the stack to return to the shelves. They had been at it all day, and her eyes were getting tired.

The room glowed brightly with every lamp lighted and a roaring fire in the hearth. Through the window, the scene was surreal. The wind whipped, snow swirled, and it felt as if the house was inside a cocoon. Nothing existed beyond the close confines of their walls. Red and Lilly had decided to wait out the weather at the flat in Beauly.

Shadow was in her lap, and a visiting Rascal stalked the

perimeter of the room before climbing onto the bookshelves in search of danger. It made her think of what Brigid had told Faolan about knowing the nature, know the name. It was certainly how she had chosen names for her cats. She wondered idly at the meaning of Faolan's name.

She snuck another peek at him. In profile, he was magnificent. His eyes were hidden from her as he read, his nose straight, jaw strong, and his hair was pulled back in its usual fashion. He wore a brown long sleeved V-neck sweater that emphasized his broad shoulders and sculpted chest. With a small sigh, Elena shifted the cat on her lap so she could stretch her legs out on the couch and went back to work.

Several of the books had information about the history of Druids or stories of legend and the supernatural, but so far, none of the English language books had any actual spells, curses, or magick. Neither of them really expected they would find the exact spell they were looking for in these particular books, but Elena hoped that having the background would help.

Faolan put his hand on her leg and was absently rubbing, sending bolts of electricity straight up her thighs. She tried to keep her breathing normal. Her hormones had been in overdrive since waking that morning. She thought of the way he had kissed her and how easy it would have been to let nature take her course. *Stopping him had been the better part of valor, definitely in his best interest, not mine.*

Elena placed the book she was reviewing on the stack to return and grabbed another, displacing Shadow from her lap in the process. "Finally, my turn," Faolan said, as he put one hand on each of her outstretched legs, his thumbs pressed firmly on her inner thighs as he slid his hands slowly up.

She thought he intended to slide his hands to her waist, to

lean over and give her a kiss. Instead, when his hands reached the junction between her thighs, his thumbs rubbed over her inseam, pressing against her nub.

"Faolan," she cried as her hips bucked in an instantaneous, shuddering orgasm. Faolan quickly pressed his face to her crotch, rubbing his mouth against the seam of her jeans, increasing the pressure against her most sensitive spot, wringing every last spasm from her. Elena moaned, her breath coming in short gasps. Faolan laid his head in her lap and put his hands under her bottom, holding her close against his face.

Elena covered her face with her arms, trying to figure out how to disappear. Tears welled up and spilled over, running into her hair as she leaned back against the couch. She needed to get away.

Faolan raised his head to look at her, but she kept her face hidden under her arms. "Elena," he whispered. He lifted himself off her, and she jumped up and ran from the room. He caught her before she had taken three steps. "Elena, what's wrong? Did I hurt you?"

"Oh God, Faolan, I'm so sorry." She kept her tear-streaked face down, letting her hair hide her face, not meeting his eyes. Wrenching herself free from his grip, she ran to her room, closed the door, fell on her bed, and cried.

Elena felt sick to her stomach over what just happened. She'd been wound up tight ever since she wakened with his erection pressed against her backside. She knew it was dangerous to tempt fate again. It had felt so good to be close, to feel his hand on her leg. She'd just wanted the comfort of his touch. God help her, she'd not been strong enough to keep the distance between them that she knew he needed. *That they both needed.*

Faolan needed her to help him find the spell that would

free him and his family from the curse of the wolf. He was struggling to remain true to his purpose, and lives depended on him lifting the curse. It was his destiny to be with his true heart, and it was her destiny to love him, and let him go.

With a deep shuddering breath, she pulled herself together and went to wash her face and brush her hair. Pulling her hair back into a ponytail, she took a good look at the red-rimmed and tear-swollen eyes of her reflection. Elena sighed. She needed to get back to the research, not lay around feeling sorry for herself. With one final talking to about proper decorum, she went back to work.

When she entered the library, Faolan was staring out into the darkness of the late afternoon. He shifted to look at her in the reflection before he turned around. "Elena?"

"I think we're nearly finished with all the books in that stack," she said brightly. "The ones on the couch and in this stack are the last of the English language books. I'll try to do some research on the Internet while you look at the Gaelic ones." She was busy picking up books and placing them on the shelves, refusing to meet his gaze. "What time are you going to pick up Brigid tomorrow?"

Faolan looked at her for a long minute before slowly answering, "I will be leaving at nine if the roads are clear."

"I'll put some food on plates in the refrigerator in case she stays for lunch. Do you know why she's coming?"

"She said she needed to talk with Red, Lilly, and me, but she wouldna tell me why, other than to say 'twas time. I expect she will also have your rugs ready," he grinned mischievously.

"Rugs? I didn't even have a chance to look at them, I didn't pick any out."

"Aye, lass, that's the way it is with Brigid. She will bring them, and you will put them where she tells you."

"Oh really? And will I like them, too?" Elena asked, light sarcasm hidden in a smile.

"Undoubtedly," he laughed.

She laughed, too. Somehow, it wasn't hard to imagine such outrageous behavior from Brigid; she was of an age that she could get away with just about anything.

They smiled at each other, and he tried again, "Elena?"

She shook her head and asked if he was ready to keep working on the books. He sighed and started on his pile, while she finished putting the rest of the books away that they had already reviewed.

When Elena finally sat back down, she sat in a chair opposite Faolan, rather than next to him, and began on the final small stack of books to review. Near the bottom of her stack, she found one scholarly-looking tome that explained Druidism in great detail. It was fascinating.

Druids had been around since at least 3500, B.C. although there were tales they went back even further. The Druids had served many roles in their time, scholars and judges, healers and bards. They were pioneers in astronomy, cosmology, physics, and theology. Some believed they had the powers of time travel through the ancient standing stones, like Stonehenge.

Rumors regarding the source of Druid knowledge surrounded an ancient race called the Tuatha Dé Danann, and many believed the Druids served as gatekeepers between the Fae realm and humans. Flipping back to the glossary, Elena learned that the Tuatha Dé Danann were the Fae, also known as fairies. *Fairies? Would any of this ever make sense?* She needed to come back to that idea later.

Few scholars believe that written examples of any original Druid practices still existed. It was the author's opinion, that if there were detailed records, it was likely they would exist in private, personal collections, and be recorded by hand, since they would predate the printing press by hundreds of years. Modern sects of Druids might exist, but again it was unclear what, if any, relation these modern-day versions had to their ancient ancestors.

Elena tried not to let her disappointment show, and she slid the book into the pile to put away. She needed to think about this before she shared it with Faolan. What if he could never be released from this curse? Would it change how she felt about him? *No, I love him the way he is.* Would he change how he felt about her? Would he be willing to someday stop looking for a cure and grow old with her? She didn't know, but she'd be willing to wait.

Before they could think about a possible future, they needed to make every effort to find a way to break the curse. Assuming the author was correct, they wouldn't be finding a cure in a mainstream published book. They needed to look for a less traditional source of spells and magick. She might be able to locate alternate sources on the Internet. What else could she try?

Elena looked around the room, and wondered exactly where all the books had come from? She'd found them in the north wing of the steading, in boxes stacked in the piles of junk. The house had belonged to Worthington. What did he know about spells and curses? Were these his books? Or had they belonged to Faolan's father?

Mental smack to the forehead. This is where I should have started, not with a generic search, but with one based on the known evidence. The key wasn't Worthington or even Faolan, but Faolan's father. He was the one with the spells. He knew the secrets. He was the caretaker of something sacred, something that an older

Worthington wanted so badly he would kill for it. He had revealed a secret to his murderer, causing Faolan to become a shape shifter, a wolf. Yet, he held something back, and a Worthington continued to search for it to this day. Worthington was willing to kill for it. Whatever the secret, it had something to do with this farm and the MacGailtry line. It was valuable enough for the search to carry on for at least two generations.

Elena would have to speculate a little here, so she could formulate a theory. Faolan's father was a Druid or sorcerer of some type. He was responsible for caring for something, but she didn't know exactly what. He must have had artifacts, a place to perform his ceremonies, and possibly hand written books or records.

Elena had seen evidence that such books and records existed. She believed she knew where some of those ceremonies and training sessions must have occurred. *The secret chamber in the north wing of the steading!*

It had taken days for her to clear the front of those panels and figure out how they opened. Was it possible that the secrets the elder Worthington sought when he murdered Faolan's family had been buried there all along? Was it possible that Faolan himself didn't even know of the chamber's existence?

Tomorrow, while everyone else was meeting with Brigid, Elena would go back down into the chamber to see if her theory held up. She needed to keep this idea to herself until she was more confident the answers they needed could be found there. She couldn't bear to disappoint Faolan if she was wrong.

****

Elena dominated the dinner conversation over their soup and salad in an effort to keep Faolan from mentioning her humiliating behavior that afternoon. After dinner, Faolan asked if she would be okay by herself for a while. He wanted to go out and look around. He assured her she would be safe, and she believed him. She welcomed the time alone; she needed some space between them. She washed up, changed into her pajamas, and went to bed before he returned.

When she woke the next morning, Faolan was again on her bed with his arm around her. He had fallen asleep on top of the covers with a little throw blanket covering a ridiculously small part of him, but he felt toasty warm to her. He had on pajama bottoms and nothing else. Elena tried to sneak out from under his arm without waking him, but his arm banded around her as soon as she moved, pulling her close.

"Good morrow, lass." He kissed her neck and then rolled on his back and stretched his arms high above his head.

Elena sat up as soon as he released her and asked, "Was everything okay out there last night?"

"Aye, the snow stopped around ten. No one was about."

They never mentioned the fact he shifted to his wolf form to patrol the grounds. *Some things are better left unsaid.*

When she glanced down, she saw Faolan's pajama bottoms had ridden low across his hips. So low that his persistent erection peaked out from the waistband. Elena fought to keep from licking her lips.

Reluctantly, she dragged her gaze away and caught Faolan watching her with laughing eyes. "Can we talk about yesterday afternoon yet?"

"I don't want to talk about it. Ever," she said, trying to get up from the bed.

Faolan wrapped his arms around her waist and sat her on

his lap, his erection an obvious indication of his desire. Elena kept her eyes determinedly away from his face. Faolan pulled her chin around, so she was forced to look at him. She sat stiffly, trying to figure out what he was up to this time.

"Have you changed your mind, Faolan?" she asked with a hint of sarcasm.

"Nay, Elena," he said softly, "I have not changed my mind. *Yet.*"

A thrill of desire ran through her at the promise in his words.

"Look at me, love. You need feel no shame about what happened yesterday. Feel me, underneath you," and he pressed himself against her. "Every time I look at you or smell the scent of you or think of you, the desire to take you roars within me. I am always on the ready for you, and yesterday—" he shifted his hips slightly, rocking against her backside before he continued, his voice a husky growl "—yesterday, you showed me that you are ready for me, too.

"We doona' know what tomorrow may bring, so I canna be sayin' never to you. I feel we are close to answers, Brigid says the time is here. We will be knowin' something soon, I just know it. Then you and I will have to make some decisions. We canna go back as if we never knew each other. I told you. You have touched my soul. I doona' know how there can be a true heart when you already own mine."

He pulled her hand to his lips and kissed it. "Aye, I want you, lass. The day is coming when I may no longer be able to resist your enchantments." He stood them both up, gave her a kiss that curled her toes, and then left to dress for the day. *Whooh.*

Chapter Fourteen

Elena threw on a pair of jeans and a flannel shirt to ward against the chill in the chamber. She planned to leave the house once Brigid had Red, Lilly, and Faolan in her meeting. With any luck, she would be able to give Faolan some hopeful news by dinnertime.

Elena assembled small sandwiches and placed the tray in the refrigerator, in case their meeting lasted through the lunch hour. Then she went to the library to build up the fire and arrange the chairs for the meeting. She wanted everyone on the opposite side of the house from the steading. She needed to come and go without attracting their notice. She wasn't going to tell anyone what she was up to before she had something positive to share.

She loaded her backpack with the book on Druids, her camera, and two flashlights, and stowed it by the door so she could grab it on the way out. Just as Elena completed her preparations, Faolan returned with Brigid and a truck bed full of rugs. Faolan and Elena exchanged conspiratorial grins, as everyone helped to carry the rugs into the house. Brigid directed the placement, and hard as it was to believe, each rug fit its room as though designed especially for the space. They were beautiful and perfect. Elena thanked Brigid profusely.

Once the business with the rugs was completed, Elena suggested they all go to the library to talk, and then excused herself. She was anxious to get started. She stopped long enough to arm herself with the lantern, and walked through the interior to the north wing. She squeezed behind her piles, entered the chamber, and got to work.

First, she checked both of the closets to see if the tomes were handwritten or mass-produced. *Bingo!* These were ancient beyond belief. These were genuine illuminated manuscripts on thick, sepia-toned vellum with leather covers and silk bookmarks. Some of the colors of the illumination were faded with age, but the gold and silver were bright, creating strangely vivid paintings. Someone had added personal notes to many of the pages, much as Elena added explanatory notes to her law books during class. In a cursory examination, she could see illustrations depicting ceremonies, maps of the night skies, and numerous illustrations of the four seasons.

She struggled to make out the words. She recognized names of ancient gods, but most of the language was indecipherable. She also found a small number of books in English grouped together on one of the shelves. Elena slipped one of the books carefully into her pack to take back to show Faolan. These had to be the sacred books used by his father and generations of Druid priests before him. *Holy cow! Could this be the bulk of the Druid library?*

Faolan and Red had spent years researching where they could, but since Worthington stole the land, they must have been unaware of this secret chamber. There wasn't anything she could do to decipher the texts herself, but she would give this gift to Faolan. She would help free him from his curse and find his true heart. *While losing mine.*

Elena took the keys from the jewelry casket by the door, and steeled her nerves as she walked the long passage to the rooms at the end. Randomly selecting the room on the right to explore first, Elena inserted the key, and the door glided open, a surprise, since it looked as though no one had been in there since Faolan's father.

Starkly furnished, the room held a narrow table and two large wooden chairs that looked like simple thrones. One shelf on the back wall held an assortment of daggers, a gold plate, a chalice, and beeswax candles in a golden candelabrum. In the center of the table, displayed in a place of prominence, there was a leather-bound volume at least twelve inches thick. It had several silk ribbons marking pages in different sections of the book.

Elena's breath caught in her throat. *Could this be what they were looking for?* She carefully examined the book, to make sure it was sturdy enough to touch, let alone open. The cover was in excellent shape as was everything within the chamber and she wondered at how it was all so well preserved. She began to examine the tome under the light from her lantern, and dug out two pencils from her backpack, so she could use the erasers to turn the pages. Well-preserved or not, she was not about to mar the pages with oils or dirt from her fingers.

As soon as Elena opened the cover, the similarity to large, ancient Bibles was obvious. She looked at the room again and wondered if this was a room for religious ceremonies. The table could easily have served as an altar, and she had seen similarly built chairs at the front of churches that her various foster parents had dragged her to.

It was another illuminated manuscript, with gold and silver leaf, brilliant colors, and intricate details. As she examined the pages, she realized some of them looked more recent as though added over the years. Each page was elegantly lettered and in a language Elena couldn't read. *That's okay, there are lots of pictures.*

She started to look at each of the illustrations, searching for wolves.

****

In the library, Brigid faced Lilly, Red, and Faolan, and said, "I have read the signs. 'Tis no mistake. 'Tis a change in times a comin'. Tell me, how is your search progressing?"

Faolan made a sound of disgust. "We doona' have anything so far. We doona' believe Worthington found the collection, but neither has it been revealed to us. I too have seen signs. The stars are in motion, and dreams are as visions, showing the ancient ones coming closer. I doona' yet know what it is they demand of me, only that I must control the wolf."

Brigid replied, "Aye, the visions have beset me as well. You must be very careful this moon. All depends on you."

Faolan made a sound not unlike a growl.

Brigid sighed, placed a hand on Faolan's arm, and added gently, "You were nigh on thirteen when you were changed, the time you would have been invited. You were to wear the mantle. You have done well, Faolan, but there is more you must do."

"What more must he do? 'Tis time for him to be free and have his own life," cried Lilly.

"The lad has been destined for this life in the stars. One is come who will complete you, one who will bring you to destiny. Follow your light, Faolan of Gailtry."

Lilly rose, saying, "I will serve lunch in the kitchen. Red, come and help."

Red, who appeared to be deep in thought, hopped to his feet, startled to be called, then followed his wife from the room.

Faolan looked at Brigid, and she stared back for a long time, neither speaking. Finally, Faolan, with a great sigh, asked Brigid, "'Tis all you have foretold come now?"

"Och, lad, you still listen with your ears. Listen with your heart. I have told of your one true heart. You must follow your light. 'Tis a time of change, the time you will bring forth the ancestors, the time of eternal renewal. I canna say more until you have completed your sacrament. You must follow your light."

"Och, old woman! My light! My light! Canna you say anything I understand?" Faolan shouted.

Brigid laughed, then turned serious. "Follow your light, Faolan. 'Tis here, this is the time, 'twill be clear, but danger is close. This moon all could be lost. Think on all I have told you." She rose and left the room to follow Lilly and Red.

Faolan stayed, committing her words to memory, as was his duty. Later, he would meditate on them until the meaning was clear in his heart.

*

The four of them enjoyed the lunch Elena had prepared before Faolan drove Brigid home. He had looked for Elena, so she could either join them or say good-bye, but he hadn't found her. Her car wasn't in the yard—he couldna remember...had it been there earlier? He realized she must have gone to town unescorted. Still, she would be safe enough in the daylight.

When Faolan returned from taking Brigid home, he sat at

the table with Red and Lilly, talking over all they had heard. Brigid was wise in the old ways, and although she had never shared her story with him, he suspected she had been the life mate of a Druid. Nay, maybe she herself was a Druid Priestess or even a witch, he thought. Her knowledge was vast, but she spoke in riddles, guided through divination to share only certain knowledge with him.

Brigid had been particularly insistent this time, and there was a sense of urgency that hadn't been there in all the years he'd known her. He felt a pivotal event was on the horizon. He dared hope 'twas the lifting of the curse, yet feared it would mean he would lose Elena forever.

Faolan went back to the library to work further on the Gaelic books, hoping to find something useful for Elena's sake. She had pinned such hope on finding a clue in these books, but most of them were relatively recent, many less than a hundred years old. He doubted there would be any of the old ways included, especially not in a publicly available book.

He sensed an old and noble soul within Elena, and he mourned her loss already, but leave him she must. From what Brigid had said, his heart was near, but so was danger. He needed to protect Elena from his life. He must know that she was safe, even if it meant she was safe with someone else, someone she would grow to love in time. The thought saddened him. He would have a few more months near her, not that a few months would be enough. One lifetime would not be enough. Never had another touched his soul, yet Brigid had said his heart was coming. How could he love another? There was no more room in his heart; Elena had taken it.

Follow his light, Brigid had said. For many years, Brigid had been telling him his true heart must be found in order to lift the curse, now she spoke of light. What did it mean? What was she trying to tell him? Faolan found the reference books on the shelf and began to look at the various ways to translate light, to use light, to have a light. Nothing there seemed helpful.

Elena's computer was next, but too many search results made it futile. If only Brigid would be more specific about which light. He blew out a frustrated breath, Faolan stood and restlessly began pacing.

He knew Brigid set great store in names. She was named for Brigit, the Celtic goddess of inspiration and healing, daughter of Dagda, and a Tuatha Dé Danann. Faolan knew his own name meant 'Little Wolf,' which seemed a strange irony to be named for that which you would become. Could Brigid mean for him to follow his light, with light referring to a person's name?

Again, he turned to Elena's computer and searched for sites that would help him find names that meant light, or some variation of light. The first search revealed more than two million entries, most of them web sites devoted to finding the perfect name for a baby. He randomly selected one and began.

Faolan sucked in a sharp breath, and his heart raced. It had taken him a long time, because he had been looking for Gaelic names. This was a name more associated with Spain than Scotland, but he was sure. He now knew what Brigid meant. It was the name of his destiny, his true love, and his true heart.

Elena, form of Helene. Torch, light.

Chapter Fifteen

Hunched over the book for hours, Elena finally stood and stretched. What started as a cursory inspection of the large volume had evolved into an obsessive search for truth. It was a comprehensive description of Druid life through the ages, from the mundane to the fantastic. There were hundreds of illustrations, each followed by explanatory text. Or at least she assumed it was an explanation, just as she assumed the next part was the actual spell associated with the picture. *Too bad, I missed out on taking Gaelic as a foreign language.*

About halfway through she discovered the actual spell they needed to free Faolan. A man was drawn in a series that showed his transformation from full man to full wolf. There was no one with him, he didn't appear in pain, and it was daylight. Nothing about the illustration indicated he was suffering in any way.

By contrast, the next set of pictures showed one man acting as spell caster, another as victim. The victim wore an expression of terrible agony, and he was more than half formed into a wolf. The full moon was clear in the night sky, and a woman cowered in the background, as though afraid the wolf would eat her. Elena shivered before something about the picture made her take a closer look. The spell caster was holding a mirror in his hand and below the picture of the wolf was another illustration of a mirror. It looked exactly like the mirror that she'd hidden in her room.

This really was it, Elena was sure of it. She held the secret in her hands that would free Faolan, Red, and Lilly! They needed the mirror in the picture, and she knew where to find it. The spell was in the book; the cure was so close. It didn't matter that she would lose Faolan completely once he was cured. Nothing else mattered at this moment, not now that she knew he could be freed from his terrible curse.

Elena put the book carefully in her pack; she would not let it out of her sight. She wanted to wait to tell him until they were alone, so after dinner would be best. *Dinner!* Elena had been so busy all morning that she'd missed breakfast completely. Lunch must be long over, and she was thirsty and hungry. Hopefully, there was a nice big roast or something similarly filling for dinner.

Elena hefted her pack onto her back and opened the door. Or rather, she tried to open the door…the handle wouldn't turn. She yanked and pulled, twisted, and kicked, but the door wouldn't budge. Panic set in immediately and she was no longer the intrepid explorer of all things magick. As memories of the worst of the foster homes flooded her, she started banging on the door, yelling and screaming for someone to let her out.

Finally, forcing herself to calm, she remembered how she'd opened the panels to the chamber. She laid her hands on the door, concentrated very hard, and prayed for it to open as she pushed. Nothing happened. Breathing fast, Elena pressed her hands against every surface, including the doorknob, hinges, and the keyhole, anything she could think of. Still nothing worked.

Oh God, no…not this, please, not this. Elena carefully examined each of the walls, looking for markings, looseness, or warmth. Anything to indicate there might be more than meets the eye. There was nothing to show there was another way out. The floor and ceiling were similarly disappointing.

Please let me out, I'll be good, I'll be good. The familiar childhood plea came back to her now, and her throat closed on a scream. She returned to the door, fighting against her captivity until her throat was raw and her fingers bled. When she could no longer claw at the door, she sank to the floor with her back against the solid piece of wood holding her captive. Wrapping her arms around her knees, she rocked, lost somewhere in her past. *Someone always comes home to let me out eventually.*

When Elena came back to herself, she was hungry and very thirsty, but she was also exhausted. She knew she'd reacted foolishly. It was imperative that she conserve her strength. She needed some rest before she tried anything new. Pulling the two chairs from either side of the altar, she pushed them together so they were facing each other and lay down.

It felt as though she'd been in the chamber for many hours. Faolan would look for her. *Right, and where would he look?* She fought against the rising panic that threatened to overtake her, once again. With deep, slow breaths, she forced herself to calm down and eventually she slept.

While she slept, she had nightmares. She was four, and her mother left her; she was thirteen, and her Grandda died. She'd been teen, on the cusp of woman, and her foster father kept her locked in the closet for tempting him. The panic she felt became part of the fabric of the dream.

Then, in the disjointed way of dreams, women in long

flowing robes of the softest white surrounded her, soothing her, calming her fears. They chanted quietly, a melodic, haunting sound that left her comforted.

When Elena woke, disoriented and sore, she had no idea how long she'd been asleep or how long she'd been in the room. This morning, she was the calm, analytical Elena. She knew she was in danger of shock and dehydration, and keeping her panic controlled was crucial.

She examined the door. The hinges were on the outside, so she couldn't get at them. The lock was like nothing she'd ever seen before. Picking locks wasn't in her skill set, but maybe if she could remove the doorplate, she could access the locking mechanism.

She looked for a useful tool; no stones were loose. The chairs were too heavy to lift, and too sturdy to break pieces off. She couldn't use the gold candelabrum because the gold would be too soft. *Damn! The dagger!* Why hadn't she thought of using the dagger sooner?

With eight inches of blade and a jeweled handle, the dagger should be sturdy enough to dig at the wood surrounding the iron plate. If she loosened it enough she could knock the locking mechanism out or shift it so it would release. She worked on it for a long time, and managed to carve a groove into the wood around two sides of the doorplate. It didn't look as though she was making much progress, but what else was she going to do?

Her arms and hands hurt from the exertion, and no amount of shifting her hold on the knife was providing any relief. With a flutter of yesterday's panic she realized the light was growing dim. *Crap, the batteries in the lantern are wearing out. Just how much time has passed?* Conserving batteries and strength were top priorities. Switching from lantern to flashlight, Elena climbed back onto her impromptu bed again, and in a very few minutes was sound asleep.

The chanting started shortly after she dozed off. When she opened her eyes, the room glowed softly, bathed in candlelight, and again the white-robed women surrounded her. Elena knew she was safe as long as they were with her, so she closed her eyes to wait for the end of their ceremony.

The women were gone when she next woke, but Elena knew they'd be back later. She must have slept well; her limbs were heavy and relaxed. She turned the lantern back on and went back to work on the door. Her muscles ached from all the pushing and cutting she'd done on it yesterday. *Yesterday, all my troubles…* Something about that seemed familiar. She was beginning to lose track of what was happening, of when she was awake and when she was asleep.

This must be a very magic room, she thought. *Oh, wait… magick.* Faolan told her it was spelled m-a-g-i-c-k, so you could tell the difference between real magick and a magic trick. *What was I talking about?*

"Elena? You stay right here. I just need to run to the store for some more medicine. I'll be right back. I'm locking the door. Don't open it." Her mother's voice was soft and blurry, like it always was when she drank her medicine. Elena sat up straight on the couch, hoping Mommy wouldn't notice she wasn't in her room.

Okay, this isn't right. Her mother had been dead for twenty years. In a lucid moment, Elena realized she must be hallucinating and started pacing the room, trying to keep the blood circulating. Surprised that images of her mother had come to haunt her, Elena used thoughts of her family to stay focused and went back to work on the lock.

Elena was four when her mother went out one night, never

to return. She remembered telling her Grandda about Mommy's blurry voice, and Grandda sighed and shook his head. When she was older, she realized a blurry voice was what a four-year-old might think a voice sounded like when someone had been drinking. Her mother was usually drinking.

Grandda had taken her into his house, but he'd also been blurry. The social workers came and said they would take her away if he didn't stop drinking. He had been a widower and a drunk for nearly ten years before Elena came to live with him, but to his credit, he pulled himself most of the way out of the bottle so he could care for Elena.

Although Grandda had given up the booze, it hadn't given up on him, and he died of liver failure when she was thirteen. All the money went to pay for his medical bills. The state buried him for free and placed his granddaughter in foster care.

Why in the world am I thinking about this?

Elena was very tired again, and a dim part of her mind acknowledged that she must be dangerously dehydrated. She was no longer hungry, and beyond thirsty. She just felt tired all the time; maybe she had iron-poor blood. *Stop, stay strong.*

The women returned, and they brought Brigid with them. "Lass, these are the sisterhood. They are here to take you on a journey now. They will keep you safe, but this journey 'tis important. There are things you will need to know. Some you willna remember until you need to, others you will remember for Faolan. May the gods and goddesses smile upon your light."

The robed figures stood around a circle drawn on the floor, and Elena was in the center. The women took turns reciting lines and Elena wondered if she was supposed to have something to say.

"Oh Earth beneath us, you are the sustainer of all life."

"Air surrounding us, lifting us, you inspire all life."

"Stars of Fire above us, you empower our lives."

"Water within us, you refresh our lives."

The women of the Sisterhood gently bathed Elena's face and trickled water from the gold chalice into her parched mouth.

A voice that could have belonged to an angel said, "Elena, on this journey, the water will be your guide and will give you life at journey's end."

Then Elena stepped onto a small boat, and they sailed to the western coast of Scotland where a small island emerged from the clouds, which confused Elena for a minute because she thought they were in the ocean. A wren appeared from the clouds and lighted on the branch of a nearby tree.

"I don't understand what's happening," Elena told the wren, which in her dream seemed a perfectly reasonable thing to do.

"Reflect. You will be seen and you will see. Then without hesitation, you must follow the path of learning, 'tis important to our world. You will be sought as one who is wise, so begin your journey. There is a time coming, all your skills and all the true disciples may still not be enough. It is coming."

When Elena stepped from the boat, she was back in the chamber, and the robed women were waiting to care for her as though she were their precious child. They laid her back on her makeshift bed, brushed her hair from her forehead, and dribbled more water between her dry lips.

"Faolan is looking for you; he will find you," Brigid whispered. "You must give him the mirror so all can be saved. Faolan will find you on the morrow. Rest now, Elena, Light of Faolan."

Elena slept.

Chapter Sixteen

For three long nights and two full days, Faolan searched every part of the farm. He would never forgive himself if something happened to Elena. She has to be here somewhere, he thought. Was it possible Elena had shifted time, even now trapped in a century that wasna her own? Faolan didn't know much about time shift, but he knew that many believed the ancient Druids had that ability.

The MacGailtry land had an ancient stone circle hidden deep in the woods that was nearly 10,000 years old. It was protected by strong wards, and as far as he knew, Elena wouldna be able to see it because of the spells hiding it from view. Faolan had spent nearly half his life researching Druid use of the stones to no avail. Yesterday, he'd examined every inch of the circle and found nothing to indicate anyone had been near the area recently.

Could Elena have found the circle? Had she been ensorcelled? There was one person he knew who could read the signs. Why had he not thought of going to Brigid sooner? He ran through the kitchen yelling at Lilly that he was going to get the old seer.

Even though he'd not called ahead, he wasn't surprised to find Brigid waiting by the street, a large carpetbag in her hands. Faolan started to ask her a question, but she cut him off.

"Go. Och, you left it late, lad." Brigid climbed into the truck and said again, more urgently, "Go, go fast."

Faolan peppered her with questions, but Brigid sat still, her eyes closed, listening to something only she could hear. When they arrived at the farm, Brigid climbed out of the truck and went straight to Elena's bedroom to look around. She stopped near the fireplace and sighed, "Ah, 'tis true."

"What is it? Do you know where she is, has she shifted time?" Faolan asked desperately.

"Nay, lad, she is near, but you must find her."

Faolan ran his hand through his hair, dark circles under his eyes, looking half-mad. "How? How do I find her?"

"Is there something you and she have both touched, something personal?"

Faolan's eyes scanned Elena's room, "Her hairbrush," he said.

"Get it, lad, bring it along," demanded Brigid, already heading for the kitchen.

Red and Lilly were hovering, desperate to help, but unsure where to start.

"Where does the lass go when she is by herself?" Brigid asked.

Red answered right away, "The north steading. She is always mucking about in there, messing with her stacks."

"I looked there," insisted Faolan.

"Och, of course you did, but which eyes did you use, lad?" Brigid issued orders, "Red, go build up the fire in Elena's room. We will bring her there. Lilly, make tea, add sugar, and let it begin to cool. Start a broth as well. Faolan, come, we will bring her home."

They went directly to the north wing of the steading where Brigid grabbed Faolan's hands, looking ridiculously small next to his giant frame. "Faolan, 'tis time for you to draw on your magick. It sleeps deep within you. We must draw it forward and call on the gods and goddesses to awaken it in you. 'Tis time," she repeated.

"Tell me what to do, Brigid," Faolan pleaded.

Brigid drew a candle, bottle of water, a bowl, incense, and four stones from her bag. She handed the stones to Faolan. "Place them one each on the points of the compass." She put the unlit candle in the center of his circle and put the bowl filled with water next to it. She lit the incense, then turned to Faolan.

"This must be your magick, not mine," she said. "I will guide you as best I can, but beware. This all depends on you. I canna do it. When it comes time to close your mind to all but the spirits, you maintain your absolute focus. You will receive your answer only if you let nothing else intrude."

Faolan entered the circle from the East and lit the candle, clutching Elena's hairbrush. Following the path of the sun, he offered a greeting of peace to each of the four points. He sat near the center of the circle and focused on opening himself. It filled him with awe to know after all these years he was saying the words of his father, his ancestors. He felt the mantle of his ancestry settle onto his shoulders, filling him with a sense of destiny.

At first, Elena's name entered his brain every few seconds, but he pushed thoughts of her back and closed his eyes, straining to hear. The sound began as a distant whisper, the chanting soon filled him. In his mind's eye, he watched as the flame left the candle, made a sun-wise circle around the room testing his resolve, and then beckoned him to follow. Faolan floated behind the flame as it passed through a pile of furniture stacked against the wall, through the wall, and into a long, dark passageway. At the end of the passageway were two large doors, and Faolan floated after the candle's flame, through the door on the right.

He entered a chamber that was very cool, the only light was that which he'd brought with him. White-robed figures lined the room, yet disappeared as soon as he was fully through the door. Two chairs faced each other against the far wall, and he could see Elena cradled between the arms. He could not see her breathing.

The scent of freshly turned earth signaled a renewal of the seasons. Then the roar in his head reached a crescendo and filled Faolan with sounds of nature: wind rushing through the trees, water tumbling over river rock, the roar of fire wiping a landscape clean. A voice, ringing clear and pure as a bell, spoke from within his soul, "Welcome home, Faolan of Gailtry, Faolan of the Light."

He came slowly back to himself as if returning from a long journey. Brigid was there, but silent, careful not to intrude too soon. When he was ready, he looked up at her, his eyes full of uncertainty.

Brigid said, "Hurry, lad. There's not much time left."

He stood a bit unsteadily, shook his head, and asked Brigid, "What do I do now?"

"Did they not show you?" she asked her voice pitched higher than usual, filled with tension.

"There was a candle," he said, walking to the junk pile. "I followed it through walls. It started over here." When he walked around the pile, he saw what he had missed before. There was an opening in the far corner, not visible unless you squeezed around the back. He pushed boxes and a dresser aside to make a clear pathway. He put a hand on the metal plates; they felt warm to his touch. He wanted to scream with frustration. How was he supposed to know what to do?

He looked over his shoulder at Brigid, who nodded encouragement. Faolan placed one hand on each plate. The doors glowed, and in his aggravation, he pushed. They opened easily.

Faolan entered a vestibule that he recognized. It was the room from his vision. He raced through the opening, heedless of any danger ahead, desperate to find Elena. Brigid followed behind whispering strange phrases.

The small candle flame flickered in the breeze he created in his haste as he ran down the long passageway. He was dimly aware of the unlit torches hanging on the wall, and that he was heading downhill as he raced toward the doors. He must be deep inside the land. He was relieved to see the oak door on the right had a key in the lock. Brigid took the candle from him as he turned the key, his hands shaking.

He flung the door open, calling, "Elena?" As soon as he stepped into the room, something white fluttered just beyond his peripheral vision. He raced across the room and found Elena, asleep or unconscious, looking peaceful. "Elena," he cried, his voice breaking. He tried waking her, shaking her gently, calling, "Elena, love, wake up, I am here. Wake, Elena."

Brigid's voice was tight, full of tension as she said, "Pick her up. We must get water into her and get her warm. Hurry, 'tis near too late." She picked up Elena's backpack and held the door open.

Faolan picked Elena up and ran back up the long passageway. His heart thundered but not from the exertion. Nay, his heart was pounding too hard from the thought that she might even now be lost to him. How could life be so cruel to show him his true heart, the light of his life, only to steal her away? Elena must be all right; she must live. "Please wake up, Elena."

Faolan pleaded to any god that might listen with favor upon his request. "I canna live without her. If you must take a life today, take my life for hers." He'd no sooner completed that thought, than the entire passageway rocked, the walls seemed to shift, and Faolan struggled to maintain his footing. The world righted itself, and Faolan ran faster.

As soon as they entered the house, Faolan carried Elena to her bed, and Brigid barked out orders. "Faolan, remove her boots, socks, and pants. Rub her legs. Get the blood circulating. Lilly, bring the sweetened tea. Make sure 'tis warm but not hot."

Brigid reached into her bag and pulled out incense and a jar of paste. She unbuttoned Elena's shirt and started slathering the paste on her chest, and Faolan inhaled deeply of the warm, earthy smell. "Rub faster, lad."

Lilly returned with a mug, lifted Elena's head, and spooned the tea into Elena's unresponsive mouth. Brigid would not let Lilly stop until the whole cup was gone. "Give it another fifteen minutes, and do it again."

Brigid felt Elena's legs and ordered Faolan to take off his shoes and pants and to climb under the covers with Elena. "Press every bit of skin agin hers. We must make her warm." Faolan undressed and pressed his legs tightly against Elena and wrapped her in his arms. Elena was completely unresponsive, cold and limp to his touch.

"Should we take her to hospital?" he asked Brigid, fear making his voice harsh.

"Nay, lad, she wouldna make the trip. There's no time to

lose. You must use your magick to heal her. 'Tis the only way. Close your eyes and call to fire to warm her and to water to restore her. 'Tis not supposed to be her time. Heal her with me."

Brigid laid one hand on the center of Elena's chest and the other on her forehead, and began whispering under her breath. Faolan, still holding her close and pressing his warmth against her, closed his eyes. He blocked everything from his mind, spoke with his heart, and called upon the spirits to feed his light, fire to heat her, and water to her veins.

A sensation of fullness took him. The roar of an internal wind howled, battering him with its intensity. Then, as the wind began to still, he heard a very faint and thready heartbeat. He willed his heartbeat to match it, to strengthen it, to carry it on wings until Elena was strong enough to sustain it herself. The beating grew stronger, and Elena's breath came more evenly. He slowly opened his eyes to meet Brigid's steady gaze.

With Elena's heart beating strongly on its own, Faolan wanted her to wake, but Brigid insisted she needed to heal, and sleep was the best medicine. Once she warmed to a normal temperature, Faolan reluctantly slipped out of her bed and dressed. He took over sole responsibility for giving her tea and broth when Lilly brought them in.

As nightfall approached, it scared him that she hadn't wakened yet. So many things could have gone wrong. Why hadn't he taken her to the hospital? He could still call a doctor. "Brigid, I doona' know what else to do. Why hasn't she opened her eyes yet? What if something is going wrong?"

Brigid was packing her bag to leave. "Doona' worry, lad. She will wake for a time tomorrow, more the next day. You must just be patient and be there for her. Doona' leave her. Give her time."

"Thank you, Brigid," he said hugging her tightly.

"Och, be on with you, Faolan," and she patted him lightly on the arm.

When everyone left, Faolan sat on the bed next to Elena. He felt her forehead, her arms, and reached under the covers to touch her legs, She felt perfectly warm, neither too hot nor too cool. It hurt him to see the dark circles under her eyes, the dirt smudges on her face. He took her hand in his, and kissed the ragged tips of her fingers. Faolan still had Elena's brush and he began to brush small sections of her hair, gently removing the tangles. He tenderly washed her face and hands. Elena slept unmoving through all his ministrations.

He lay down on top of the covers, cradled Elena tightly against his chest, and whispered, "Come back to me, love. I need you."

Chapter Seventeen

When Faolan woke the next morning, Elena was staring at him, her luminous green eyes filled with uncertainty. He quickly touched her forehead and Elena flinched. "Elena?" He sat up, pulling his arm back, and tried again, "Elena, love, 'tis me, Faolan."

Her eyes filled with tears, "Oh, Faolan, tell me you're real," she whispered in a scratchy voice.

"Aye, lass, 'tis me. You're safe now," he said in a voice tight with unshed tears of relief. He touched her face, stroked and kissed her hair. "Drink up, lass." He handed her the glass of water by the bed. He lifted her head, and Elena winced when she moved. He laid her back down, went to the door, and called for Lilly to bring some oatmeal and toast.

When he returned to the bed, Elena was drifting off again. "Elena, love, doona' sleep quite yet, you need to eat something." Faolan helped her to a sitting position, just as Lilly walked in with a tray.

"Faolan, go freshen yourself, I will stay with her for a few minutes," Lilly said.

He started to argue, but when Elena croakily assured him

she would be all right, he went, saying, "I will be but a minute, love."

Elena was so weak that she could barely lift the spoon of oatmeal to her mouth. Lilly fed her three full spoons, a bite of toast, and Elena drank as much of the water as she could stand. The water made her realize another bit of business she needed to take care of, so Lilly helped her to the bathroom. A bath was more than she was capable of, but a washcloth and fresh pajamas felt good. Leaning heavily on the older woman, they returned to the bedroom. Faolan returned, took one look at her, swept her off her feet, and carried her to the bed.

"Doona' be tryin' that again, lass. I will carry you wherever you want to go."

Lilly chided, "Doona' be daft, man. A lass needs her privacy sometimes." Faolan flushed.

Elena lay down and was asleep as soon as her head hit the pillow. They woke her every hour, to take a sip or two of tea or water, but she never really came fully awake. Faolan had a bath ready when he woke her for dinner. She let him carry her to the bathroom but smacked his hand away when he tried to help her undress.

"I'm going to take this bath by myself, Faolan." Although the bath was heavenly, the warm water brought back the lethargy and she pulled herself from the tub before she needed to call for help. In fresh pajamas, she wobbled her way back to the bedroom, where Faolan was waiting, with a tray of food. Tomato soup and a grilled cheese sandwich never tasted so good, and she ate every bite.

"Faolan, how long was I gone? What day is this?"

"Och, love, you were gone for three nights. Then you slept through another once we found you. Today is Friday."

"Friday?" she gasped. "What happened to me? How did

you find me?"

"Doona' worry about that now. You need to rest. You could barely walk across the room just now. I promise I will tell you what happened, but not tonight."

She really was tired, but she couldn't shake the feeling there was something she was supposed to do; she just couldn't quite remember what it was. She drifted back to sleep, secure in Faolan's arms.

With the morning came the dream of a small, familiar-looking mirror. The glass was cloudy, and filled with an image not unlike the great mist that rolled in over the hills. A wolf's face appeared in the fog. The scene changed, and Elena was on the small hill outside the farm with the wolf. His sharp teeth bared, his maw dripping, wet with blood, and he slowly turned and looked at Elena with familiar tawny eyes.

The dream Elena was frozen in place, unable to turn away, unable to run. The wolf crouched, stalking slowly toward her, coming closer with each step. With a growl deep in his throat that raised the hair on her neck, Elena watched, mesmerized, horrified. He was coming for her. Elena screamed as the wolf sprang.

Faolan was there to wake her from her nightmare. He cradled her against his broad chest, murmured into her hair, and rocked her until her heart stopped pounding so frantically.

It was early in the morning, and further sleep was elusive, so she told Faolan she was going to the library to read. What she really wanted was to get on her laptop and conduct some research. She insisted that she could walk and she was correct. Her legs were still shaky, but she suspected that was due to lack of use during the six days since she'd been lost. Faolan tucked a blanket around her legs, and then brought her a cup of tea, and a coffee for himself. They sat companionably on opposite ends of the couch, in front of a cozy fire.

"Faolan?"

"Hmmm," he answered, dragging his eyes up from the book he was studying.

"What happened? How did you find me?"

Faolan, stirred uncomfortably in his seat, and said, "Are you sure you're ready, lass?"

Elena sighed, "Yes, Faolan, I'm ready. What happened?"

****

Faolan hadn't yet decided exactly what he would and would not tell Elena. Between what Brigid and the ancestors told him, he knew he needed Elena in order to be released from his curse and claim his heritage. She was his light, his heart.

Och, but she was so much more than just the key to his transformation. She was his life now, his life for hers he had vowed to the gods. Elena was already in mortal danger from Worthington. How much worse would it be if Worthington knew for sure who Faolan was and that Elena was his mate? He couldna risk losing her.

He looked at her a long time before beginning. He took a deep breath and began his edited version of the story. "Brigid wanted to meet with us to tell us that the time to end the curse is coming. We still have to find the spell and true heart, but she said the signs are ripe, the time is nigh. She wanted me to search for my true heart. We discussed some details of how I could search. When I took her home, I thought you must have gone somewhere in the Rover.

"It wasn't until dinner we realized your car was parked in the barn. By then it was dark, and I was in a panic. Red and Lilly tried to track you to town or nearby hotels in case you had decided to leave. We also spent a long time tracking the known associates of Worthington. I looked everywhere I could think of, lass. For three days and nights, I couldna find you anywhere," his voice lowered to just above a whisper on the last sentence.

Without looking at her he continued, "Brigid came to the house on the last day and spoke to her spirits. Och, I didna believe in her spells at first, but they brought you back. I found the path behind the pile in the steading, and we found you lying on two chairs." He stopped then. Up until that point in the story, he had been all business, but now his throat worked, and he struggled to continue.

"I carried you to your bed. Brigid again called on her spirits, and I held you to warm you. Lilly gave you tea and broth. You wouldna wake, I thought—

He swallowed hard. "I am grateful to have you back," he said, resting his hand lightly on her leg.

Faolan thought about what he hadn't told her, of the things that had happened while she was lost. He had run to find her, to share the news that she was his true heart, to make love with her. He'd had much time to think while he was looking for her, and he now realized he couldna tell her the truth, couldna give her false hope for a future that wasna his to give.

****

"What were you doing, Elena? How did you find that place?"

Elena thought about her response for a minute. "I don't remember too much about it, to tell you the truth. I found that room while I was cleaning the steading, but I wanted to know more before I told you.

"I remember trying to find something that might help lift

the curse. I thought I would look for it while you had your meeting with Brigid. When I tried to leave, the door was locked." In a very small voice, Elena added in a whisper, "I don't like enclosed spaces."

Shuddering, she continued, "I kept trying to get out. I didn't have a watch, and I lost track of the days. I remember I tried to use a dagger to pry off the doorplate.

"Then, um, then these women," her voice rose at the end, like a question. She knew how crazy this was going to sound. "These women came to me and cared for me, they gave me water. I know I must have been hallucinating. I know they didn't actually give me water, but it seemed so real, and that gave me hope. I thought about my mother, my Grandda, but mostly about you. Brigid said you would come find me." Tears threatened and in a thick voice, Elena said, "I don't remember any more."

Her talk with Faolan had taken its toll, and she was ready for a nap. Faolan brought her a fresh glass of water, stroked the hair back from her face, and kissed her forehead. Then he picked up a book to read while she stretched out on the couch and slept.

Chapter Eighteen

Elena thought someone was shouting as she surfaced slowly from sleep. Her unfocused eyes settled on two men pointing cross bows at her, and Faolan was nowhere in sight. Their outfits seemed vaguely familiar, black sweats with hoodies and ski masks. Elena stared at the ridiculous dream characters, willing herself to wake, when one of them slapped her with a gloved hand so hard her ears rang. *Not a dream.*

Elena sat up quickly, her head spinning, and clutched the side of her face. While it was the taller man who hit her, the shorter, stockier one might be the more dangerous. The arrow of his crossbow pointed straight at Elena's heart, and his finger was on the trigger. His hand didn't waiver.

The tall one said, "Give it up, bitch. We know the mirror is here somewhere. Give it to us now, and you can still walk away." Then for emphasis, in case she wasn't taking him seriously enough, he raised his cross bow so the tip of the arrow rested next to her ear.

"What mirror? I don't know what you're talking about," Elena asked confusedly. She wasn't even lying at first, mostly because she'd forgotten about the mirror she'd found when she first entered the chamber. It was commanding her attention now, through dreams, visions, and now thieves. There must be something important about it. Apparently, her blank look and stupid question hadn't been convincing because they didn't go away.

"Don't lie to us, you stupid bitch. We will kill you! Get us the mirror now!"

"What mirror? What's it look like? What kind of mirror?" Elena stammered, firing questions at them, stalling while she tried to figure out where Faolan had gone.

"It's a mirror. It looks old. Now quit wasting time, and get it." Again, from the taller man, which she took to mean he was the one in charge. He didn't sound as though he knew what the mirror looked like, so he must be working for someone else. She wasn't going to underestimate them though; they were serious about their crossbows.

A wolf howled outside—and she knew what she needed to do.

"Listen, I'm not sure about any mirror. None of the mirrors in the house are old," Elena said, "but there's a large pile of antiques out in the steading. Maybe what you're looking for is there," she added helpfully.

"Show us," the taller one ordered. He grabbed her roughly by the arm and jerked her to her feet, then shoved her toward the door. He seized a handful of her hair, twisted it painfully tight, and forced her to walk ahead of him. *I know who this is; I kicked him in the shin. It's that bastard, Liam.*

Elena tried not to whimper. She walked slowly, partly because she was terrified, but mostly because she was still unsteady on her feet. Outside it had grown dark; Elena realized she must have slept longer than she thought. She had a good idea of what was going to happen next, but she couldn't be sure. *Just get them through the door...*

As soon as both punks stepped into the barn the wolves were on them. Three snarling wolves surrounding you can be a terrifying sight when experienced up close and personal.

They're the most beautiful sight in the world.

The wolf she knew was Faolan leapt at Liam, knocking him off his feet. Then Liam was on his back swinging his arm up to try to push Faolan back. *Snap.* Elena heard Liam's wrist break in the maw of the massive animal.

Red was standing on the chest of the other man, snarling and baring his teeth. Liam screamed as Faolan shook the arm in his mouth. Lilly pushed the crossbows away from the two men with her snout. Then as one, all three wolves looked at Elena, as if waiting for something.

Oh, right. I have to be the spokesperson.

"All right, assholes," Elena growled, trying for fierce, "who hired you and what's this mirror you're looking for?" Liam's face was ashen with pain, but he wasn't going to talk, so she looked to the short one. "Tell me now, or you'll be next."

"You stupid bitch, he's going to kill you," said the one she thought was called Steve.

"How much is Worthington paying you?" she fished, hoping to reel in a big answer. What she got stunned her.

"He doesn't need to be paying me. He is the next *Master*. You have no idea what you're fucking with. There are powers here beyond your ken. You canna possibly hope to defeat him. He knows you, knows the only thing here is a novice, a sapling. Get out while you can."

"Shut the fuck up," Liam roared.

Faolan shook the arm he was holding again, causing Liam to scream in agony, but he had nothing more to say. The other one just smirked. "You can kill us. More will come."

"Hold them," Elena said, and she ran to the house for her digital camera. When she came back outside, she pulled off their hoods and took pictures. They both had the same tattoos on the insides of their left wrists, the letter 'Z' tilted at an angle. She'd been learning a lot conducting all this research lately, and she knew this was called a Z-rod, and it was an ancient Celt or Pict symbol. This particular Z-rod had a hissing serpent wound through it. A symbol of afterlife.

Elena searched them and found a long dagger sheathed in Liam's boot. She piled all their weapons to the side and then looked to Faolan. He seemed to leave the next decision up to her. "Get out of here now and don't come back. Next time, they'll kill you."

The punks ran for the door, and the wolves stalked them down the road. Elena assumed they followed them until they were off the property. She heard a car start and drive away. Shortly after, Faolan was running back, this time in his human form, calling her name.

****

After looking at scores of web pages, Elena decided there was a lot of crap out there in cyber space. However, not all of it was wild imaginings. She was beginning to put together a picture of what was happening, and it wasn't something she had prepared for in law school. What she was learning about required a leap of faith so large, it couldn't be held within the realm of the world as she understood it.

Faolan was right; there were things not of this world. Or rather not of this world as she knew it before she came to Scotland. Was there really an otherworld? According to many of the sites she visited online there was. Druids existed in ancient times, but there were modern-day versions as well. Druids, Wiccans, and others actively practiced magick. Werewolves, vampires, banshees, and all manner of heretofore-fictional characters, walked beside her, she just couldn't see them. And Fairies? Apparently, the Fae had walked the world for thousands of years as immortal and powerful beings. *Who knew Tinker Bell had so much hidden potential?*

None of the others had known anything about a mirror, and Elena wanted to understand a bit more before she told them what she'd found. She thought she could place the one she'd found in the 15th or 16th century. This made sense, considering all the other items in the chamber. She couldn't say why it was so important to her to figure out the approximate age, except maybe because there were so many unanswered questions surrounding everything else.

Several of the websites theorized that Druids could project powerful spells into inanimate objects, imbuing the object with magickal power. Could this be related to the spell needed to remove the curse of the wolf? Something about that idea tickled her brain, but she couldn't place what she knew about it.

Again, she examined the evidence, but this time she included the evidence of her heart, and began to weave her own theory. Whatever Faolan's father was—probably a Druid Priest, he must have been extraordinarily powerful. The secrets he protected were valuable beyond her understanding. A spellcaster...or something, had placed a protective curse on that knowledge. This had to be old magick. It couldn't have come from one of the start-up or revival groups she read about on the Internet.

Something hidden on this land held secrets that were

valuable to Druids. Worthington's ancestor murdered an entire family, and stole this farm to get it. Could it be the mirror? Obviously, Worthington knew about the mirror and he wanted it badly enough to kill for it. The mirror was at least three hundred years old. *Was it possible?*

Elena looked up at Faolan. So proud, like a true Highland warrior, doing everything in his power to take care of his clan. He carried the burden of his father's duty. He lived to do the right thing for Lilly, for Red, for the future of his bloodline, and for her. She needed to help him, and she thought she had some of the answers within her reach. She just needed a few more pieces of information.

She decided to trust her head with her heart, Elena asked, "Faolan, how old are you?"

Faolan closed the book he'd been reading and set it on the ground, and stared into the fire for a long moment. Then he turned and looked at Elena, with eyes as old and lonely as his years, "I was born over three hundred years ago, lass. 'Tis part of the curse that we not age in the normal way."

"I see," Elena said carefully, as though this were a common event in her experience. "Did you know about the mirror, Faolan?" she asked. "Did you know that Worthington was looking for a mirror?"

"Aye, lass."

"And to lift this curse, we need to find the mirror, the spell, *and* your true heart? All three before you can be free?"

"Aye, 'tis what we believe, Elena."

"Worthington believes the mirror is here, so if we find the mirror and the spell, do you know your true heart yet, Faolan?"

Faolan turned to stare out the window. When he answered, his voice seemed heavy. "Nay, lass."

Elena's heart was breaking. She paused, not sure she

wanted the answer to this last question. "When you get all three, the mirror, the spell, and your true heart, then what? What will happen then, Faolan? What will happen to you?"

"I doona' know, lass," he groaned, his voice a rough whisper against her heart. "I doona' know if I will stay in this time or return to the past. I doona' know if I will resume my normal aging process or age suddenly and die, a very old man, in the blink of an eye."

Elena moved across the couch to climb into his lap, put her arms around his neck, and laid her head on his chest. Sometimes there just weren't any words.

Chapter Nineteen

The next morning, Elena knew she had some decisions to make. After telling everyone she needed some time alone, she locked herself in her room after breakfast. She crawled on top of her bed with her laptop, backpack, and cat, and got to work. She pulled the books out of her pack first. Elena hated feeling fuzzy about what happened to her in the chamber, but she was sure she remembered finding what she thought was a spell.

As she looked through the largest volume, more of the missing three days came back to her. She found the page with the pictures of the wolves and opened the secret hiding place in her fireplace. Sure enough, the mirror the spellcaster was holding in the illustration looked just like the one that she now held in her hand. *Was this it? Could we be this close to finding Faolan's cure?*

What had those women said to her in her vision? Had Brigid really been there too? She said something about being Faolan's light. That was it! She was supposed to be Faolan's light and guide his way. Somehow, fate had led her here to find the spell and the mirror, and guide Faolan to find his true heart. She would ease the suffering she saw on Faolan's face when he thought no one watched. The robed women said she needed to reflect and follow the path of learning. She was convinced that on this path of learning, she would find the last piece Faolan needed. Elena had it in her power to save him. *And lose my own heart forever.*

Before she gave Faolan the treasures he needed, she was determined to give him something else, something they *both* needed. Tonight would be the first and last time for them. He might try to be noble and spare her heart, but it was way too late for that. She would lose her virginity to him tonight in one last evening of romance. In the morning, she would give him the spell and the mirror, and they would devise a plan to find the last piece he needed to lift the curse. Then, Elena would leave, because as long as she was still here, Faolan would never seek his true heart.

****

Elena took Lilly into her confidence about her plans for the evening, and told her she wanted tonight to be very special for Faolan. They needed a special dinner, special wine, special everything. Lilly enthusiastically agreed and promptly shooed Elena out of the house to go to get new "everythings," in Inverness.

Elena treated herself to an indulgent afternoon of pampering; she got her hair washed and trimmed and a manicure. She bought a low-cut, deep emerald-green silk dress that clung to her curves and highlighted her eyes. She also bought sexy new lingerie and even a lacy new nightgown, just in case she had to go to extra innings to get him to play.

She knew how careful Faolan was being not to cross the imaginary line he drew in their relationship, but he was still sleeping on top of her bed. He said he was keeping her safe. Elena knew he couldn't stand to be away from her, any more than she could be away from him. So if he rebuffed her initial advances...well, heaven help him when she came out dressed for bed in this little bit of nothing. *Not playing fair? You better believe it.*

Hurrying home to check on Lilly's progress and to start getting ready, Elena knew she had to be careful. She didn't want Faolan to catch on, to realize until the very last minute that this night was going to be different. She would leave him no room for excuses.

At Elena's request, Lilly was preparing lobster tails with melted butter, twice-baked potatoes, and a salad. Lilly added chocolate dipped strawberries and thick cream, should they need dessert. She had selected a bottle of wine and a bottle of champagne, and both were chilling. Red had taken it upon himself to lay a fire in every room and build them up—she supposed so that clothing could be optional in any of them. If Elena wasn't so determined, she probably would have been embarrassed.

Everything was almost perfect; they just had the tricky part of having it all ready, before Lilly and Red snuck out. Faolan had been in the library all afternoon, oblivious to the preparations going on around him. Red had set up a small table for two in the lounge, not too near the fireplace, so they wouldn't be having their romantic dinner at a table for ten. They had two wine buckets, champagne flutes, wineglasses, the best dinnerware they owned, a linen tablecloth and napkins. It was an elegant setting.

The plan was simple. Elena would go into the library, dressed in her slinky new dress, carrying Faolan's favorite, Macallan single malt whisky. Lilly and Red would sneak off and have a lovely evening of their own at the pub in Fairth. The food was plated and waiting in the warm oven, all Elena had to do was bring it to the table.

Once Elena was ready, she came to the kitchen and twirled around the room in her new dress. Lilly made the appropriate noises to let her know she looked good. Elena left her hair down, with soft black curls cascading down her back. She'd added a necklace of a solitaire diamond nestled just barely above her cleavage at the perfect length to draw his eyes to her breasts.

Lilly and Red both hugged her and said their good-nights. Lilly called over her shoulder as they left through the back door, "We'll be over around lunch time, dear," and she and Red both laughed.

Red added, "Maybe we'll take a couple of days away."

Elena did blush at that; she was starting to get a serious case of nerves. She didn't know how to seduce someone, what if she screwed this up? Would he laugh at her? Hate her? Leave? *Yikes, I need to get this started before I talk myself out of it.*

She took the two crystal rocks glasses, with the finest whisky into the library. Faolan, looked up and smiled distractedly for a moment, and then did a double take, *"Wow!"*

Elena laughed, that was such an unexpected saying from her ancient Highlander. She spun for him, handed him his glass and sat next to him on the couch. His eyes roved appreciatively, starting at the bottom and slowly working his way up. When he got to her breasts, he paused for a long time before finally raising his eyes and finding her face. "Elena?"

"No questions, no promises. Let's just enjoy this night together."

"I'll not be beddin' you, lass."

"I'm not asking you to," she told him. *Not yet.* They sat

together on the couch, although Faolan squeezed himself against the arm and away from contact with Elena.

She raised her glass to him, said, "Cheers," which made them both smile warmly with the memory. Then Faolan tossed his drink back, and stood quickly to refill his glass. He raised an eyebrow at her and asked, "Another?"

Elena declined, remembering all too well another night that she had fallen asleep at a very crucial moment. They each stared into the fire, the silence deafening. Elena was thinking of how to bring seductive suggestions into the conversation, and Faolan was probably thinking of how to deflect them. Either way, they were both quiet for a long time.

"Are you hungry? Lilly made us a lovely dinner." *Oh God, could I get any more cliché?*

"I suppose Lilly and Red are in on this, too?" Faolan smiled, and she felt the power of it deep in her stomach. Their gazes locked, beginning a slow simmering burn. He sucked in a ragged breath, and took two long steps, then wrapped her in his arms. "Elena."

She turned her face up for the kiss she'd been waiting for, the kiss she needed to know she was alive. He mashed his lips against her, possessing her, punishing her. She opened her mouth in a small gasp at the fierceness of the kiss and he immediately thrust in his tongue claiming her mouth as his. Her knees buckled and he held her weight with the arm he had around her back crushing her to him.

The small voice in the back of her head, kept trying to get her attention, this was not right, not yet, he was angry, this was not right. *Not. Right.*

When she pulled her head back trying to catch her breath, he switched to her neck, kissing and biting, scratching her with his stubble. There was desperation in his kisses. She didn't want him to take her in this mood. "Faolan?"

He groaned.

She tried again. "Faolan?"

"Elena, you almost died. Nothing since I met you is right in your life. I am a curse upon you."

Elena pulled slightly back from him, and he turned his head from her. She cradled his face and turned him to look at her. "Faolan, I'm okay. I told you, I'm tough," she smiled. Seeking to relieve the tension, she added, "Let's go eat dinner, come on."

He took a deep shuddering breath and released her from his bone-crushing hug. Not looking at her, he started to turn away. She placed her hand on his arm, "Faolan, please. I really am okay, let's relax, and enjoy tonight."

He looked at her, and she could almost see the mental shake he gave himself. He smiled his killer smile. "Your wish is my command." *If only!*

He started to walk toward the kitchen, but stopped when he caught sight of the small table in the lounge. Grinning, he said, "You went all out, lass!" Laughing softly, he went to the wine buckets and examined the contents. "Champagne or wine?"

"How about we have the wine with dinner. We can save the champagne for later," she suggested.

"We'll not be celebrating any big events tonight," he said, putting on a stern look.

"I'm sure you're right, Faolan," she smiled innocently, causing Faolan to roar with laughter.

The evening went much better after that; they were both able to relax. They got their plates from the kitchen and poured the wine. The lobster tails were cooked to perfection, and Elena enjoyed watching him watching her, as she used her fingers to dip a morsel into the melted butter before slipping it into her mouth. She licked her fingers, looking deep in his eyes, making promises she intended to keep. When she dipped her last piece of lobster in butter, she leaned across to feed it to Faolan. He grasped her wrist and guided her hand to his mouth, his tongue savoring the butter on her fingertips. She nearly purred with pleasure.

He poured another glass of wine, and they worked together to clear the table and wash the dishes. They were laughing and having a good time together, which was exactly the evening Elena had wanted. Of course, it wasn't the only thing she had in mind, but the night was young.

****

Och, Elena was so beautiful, she took his breath away. She had orchestrated this entire evening, clearly with the idea of giving her maidenhead to him. He didn't think he could convince her to drink enough to pass out this time, he thought wryly. When she had first walked into the room, and he had seen the intention in her eyes, his heart swelled with love. For one so wee to have faced so much in the last month and yet keep fighting for what she believed was right.

She had the heart of a lion, nay, of a Highlander. He knew it would hurt her when he bade her good night before consummating their love, but he had no choice. How could he make love to her until he knew how to break this curse and what would happen once it was broken?

He had lost control of himself at the enormity of her love and the trust plain on her face. His rage knew no bounds when he thought of how he had almost lost her twice this past week. He had been holding himself tightly, reining his emotions back, lest they consume him. Yet when Elena called his name, touched him, the beast within him was loosed, and he wanted to claim her for all time.

Elena was his true heart, his light. Consummating their love would bind their hearts together forever. It was all he had ever wanted, to know this eternal love. Yet, he couldn't bind her to him if he would be dragged back to another time or die once his curse was lifted.

Faolan would love her with his heart and soul for this evening but not his body. In the morning, he must send her away for her safety and his sanity. He felt he was on the verge of finding the spell, and Worthington must sense the mirror was closer than ever. Brigid said the time was at hand, and he must be especially careful this moon.

The full moon was on the morrow, and Elena must be far away. He must know she was safe. He had to make her understand. Once he knew the outcome of the spell, he could better prepare both of them to accept what the fates would bring. Above all else, he must keep Elena safe. If that meant this evening would end on a bittersweet note, so be it.

****

Elena was thrilled with the way the evening was going. At first, when Faolan had been so fierce, she was afraid she had screwed things up somehow. Had she not stopped him, they would be in bed right now. However, it would have been a union born of fear and desperation. Elena wanted him to know that her heart was at peace with his decision. Tonight she wanted to be with him in celebration. Tomorrow, she would gift him with the mirror and the spell and then she would leave so that he would be free to find his true heart.

Faolan took the champagne, the crystal flutes, and strawberries into the library, and she felt her heart in her throat. This was it; the seduction would begin in earnest. He popped the cork and poured them each a glass. They clinked flutes, and drank. The bubbles tickled her nose and danced on her tongue. She watched his lips on the rim of his glass.

Mesmerized by his mouth, Elena imagined the two of them naked on the rug in front of the fire. He knelt between her thighs, took his champagne, and slowly drizzled it over her white-hot womanhood, the bubbles tickling and teasing, and then Faolan's clever tongue began to lick, to lap up the champagne slowly, lovingly…

"Elena, what are you thinking of? You look so far away."

She dragged her eyes from his mouth to meet his gaze. In her mind, she still held the image of Faolan buried between her legs, lapping champagne. His eyes widened and he inhaled sharply. Suddenly she knew he could see the image, too. *Holy show! Did I do that?*

They both swallowed hard. *Wow.*

Without speaking, Faolan refilled their glasses of champagne, took Elena's hand, and led her to the couch. Neither of them was quite ready to talk about what had just happened. After a few minutes, he sighed deeply, put his arm around her, and pulled her against his side. Elena leaned her head on his shoulder, feeling content for the moment just to be close to him.

Chapter Twenty

Elena woke with a blinding headache, but none of the nausea she experienced the last time she passed out. *Damndamndamn! How could I have fallen asleep again?* She tried to sit up, but couldn't move. Faolan was draped across her, sprawled sideways, and dead weight. Something was wrong. Very wrong. She squinted her eyes open, trying to make sense of what she was seeing.

She was on the hard ground in a stone room. *Oh, please no, God no!* She felt the panic start to rise and began to struggle under Faolan's weight. He moaned, and started to move.

"Faolan, Faolan, wake up. Faolan, are you all right? Wake up, please, Faolan, wake up."

Faolan came awake in one smooth motion, jumping to his feet, his stance ready to fight. His eyes glowed and his nostrils flared, as though his wolf senses were at work in his human body. "Elena? Are you all right? Where are we? What happened?"

"I don't know what happened or where we are. I have a terrible headache, but I don't think I'm hurt anywhere else. Are you okay?"

"Aye, I also have a headache. We were drugged. Where has he put us?" He spoke to himself and started pacing the room, examining it from every angle.

It was more cell than room. It was a circular stone structure, and unlike like the one in which Elena had been trapped, this one had a small, barred window at the top of the wall near the ceiling that let in light. There was a tapestry hanging on the wall, and a threadbare rug on the floor. The door was heavy oak, the same as the other underground rooms. It wasn't going to yield to force, no matter how strong the shoulder.

"Faolan, lift me up. Let me look out the window." Elena stood a bit shakily, and he lifted her high enough to peer outside. She'd thought they were in a tower of some sort; instead Elena saw the ground at eye level. The cell was sunk into the ground. There was not a single building in sight. She was looking into a small clearing, surrounded by trees. It looked familiar, yet she knew she'd never been there before. Elena could hear the sound of water nearby, maybe a brook or stream. She described everything to Faolan.

"Worthington. The bastard. He drugged us and has us somewhere. It must have been in the champagne. He wants that damned mirror or something else. Och, Elena," he cried, his voice pure anguish. "I should have protected you better. I was prepared for a fight. I never considered such a cowardly attack as poison. This is all my fault!"

"Faolan, stop it. You didn't do this. If this was Worthington, it's *his* fault, not yours or mine. He is the one we need to blame, the one we need to fight."

"Aye, lass, fight him we will." He smiled. "There is more to you than meets the eye, Elena MacFarland." They shared a smile, each willing to give anything to save the other one's life.

They held each other, taking comfort.

"Isn't that just too sweet?" The voice came from outside the small window, and Elena jumped and started to pull away, but Faolan's arms were steel bands. "I see it didn't take the little slut very long to move on, did it? From one Laird to another, whatever pays the most. Whore."

His voice struck Elena with the force of a slap. Worthington! *What the hell was he talking about?* She opened her mouth to respond, but Faolan gave a little squeeze and shook his head.

"Worthington, the girl is nothing, leave her out of this. It's me you want. Let her go." This time, Faolan put his hand over Elena's mouth as she fought to protest.

Worthington laughed. "What are you willing to deal for her life, wolf? Does she know who you are? *What* you are? What will you give me if I let her go?"

So, Worthington did know who Faolan was. "What do you want?" Faolan ground out through clenched teeth.

"The mirror. It's the price for her life. Give me the mirror and I will let her go." Then Worthington squatted down in front of the window to look at Faolan. Faolan growled. "Careful, wolf, you wouldn't want that nasty habit to get out of control. Give me the mirror, and this can all be over. I'll even let your servants go free."

Elena gasped. He had Lilly and Red somewhere, too.

Faolan's gaze was fierce, and he spit out, "You stupid fool. Do you think if I had the mirror I would still be here? Do you think this little girl has enough charm to hold the likes of me? I doona' take Worthington hand-me-downs." Faolan squeezed Elena's hand behind her back, giving lie to the words he spoke. "I was using her to find out what you knew. It appears my time was wasted, you never told her of your interest here. Let her go, and we will get to business. I doona' want her knowing any more about this."

"Tell me where the mirror is," Worthington said flatly. He was watching Faolan and had a gun pointed at Elena. Faolan started toward the window, and then stopped in his tracks, trying to keep her behind him. "I'll shoot her right through you. I can keep you alive and still kill her. Where is the mirror?"

"I doona' know where the mirror is, dammit, Worthington!" shouted Faolan. "Let her go, and I will swear an oath to give you the mirror when I find it."

Worthington said in a quiet, deadly voice. "I am not wrong! I know the mirror has surfaced. I can feel it. Now where is it?"

Elena was standing there listening to them, and a picture of the mirror hidden in her room flashed in her mind. *That must be the same mirror Worthington is looking for.*

Both men whipped their gazes to look at her, both wearing nearly identical faces of disbelief. She had an instant to realize that they both had seen the mirror she'd pictured. Somehow the things she pictured in her mind were being transmitted.

Quick as a flash, Faolan jumped in front of her, and Worthington fired. Faolan crashed to the floor. One moment he was tall and strong, trying to save her; the next his body slapped hard against the stone floor, blood leaking from his chest.

Elena didn't know if he was unconscious or dead. She screamed, and tried to turn Faolan, to find the source of bleeding and stop it. "You bastard, you killed him!"

"He's not dead yet, Miss MacFarland. I must say, your cunning surprises even me. It is clear the wolf had no idea you knew where the mirror was. So tell me, were you planning to keep it for yourself, to find all your desires? Tell me now, where is my mirror?" His voice was black silk, sliding over her, raising gooseflesh.

"Save him. Save Faolan and I'll tell you." Elena was still struggling to turn him over, with her hand pressed against his chest, trying to stop the bleeding.

"Tsk, tsk, Miss MacFarland. Deals with you seem to have a way of working in your favor. Not this time. You tell me where it is. I'll let you both go if I find it, and you can get him help. If you don't tell me, I'll leave you locked in this cell with his dead body, until you give up your secret. You will tell me now or tell me later, you won't be able to defy me for long."

Elena's bones chilled at his tone. She knew she couldn't trust him, but it was the only chance Faolan had. Faolan was still breathing, but how bad was his wound?

"You bastard. If I tell you, I want your oath you will come to let us go. Faolan must be saved."

"My word as a gentleman?" he mocked her. "Very well, you have it. Is it at the farm?" Elena nodded. Worthington continued, "Then you have my word I will have you released, providing I find the mirror."

Elena gritted her teeth. "Not good enough. If the mirror is where I say it is, you will return within an hour from right now to let us go."

"Agreed, my oath. Now where is my mirror?" he shouted.

Worthington left as soon as she told him how to find the hiding place. She knew Faolan would be devastated. She might be condemning him to an eternity cursed as a wolf, but he could not die. They would find a way to get the mirror back from Worthington. First, Faolan had to live.

When she finally got him turned over, she was relieved to see the wound looked much closer to his collarbone than his heart. She removed his shirt and tore it in half, folded one part into a bandage and pressed it tightly. She rolled the other half into a rope and tied it awkwardly against his shoulder. It would have to do for now.

It was cool in the cell, with the window opening at the top, but not nearly as cold as the outside temperature. The underground position of the room offered protection from the weather. She needed to keep Faolan from going into shock, so she grabbed him by the ankles, twisted and pulled, until she had him all the way onto the edge of the rug. Once there, she folded the other end of the rug over Faolan, making him into a giant burrito. It still wasn't warm enough, but the only other covering in the room was the tapestry. It would be next.

Elena grabbed the bottom of the tapestry and pulled for all she was worth. *No effect.* She grabbed it again and swung, twisted, tugged, and pulled before it finally came loose. It fell like a ton of bricks, landing on her and sending a flurry of dust motes around the room. She dragged it over next to Faolan.

"Faolan, Faolan wake up. I need you, Faolan. Please come back to me." Elena's voice was choked with unshed tears. She cradled his head and checked on his wound. The bleeding had nearly stopped, but he was still unconscious. She gently felt around his head, feeling for any bumps or lumps. "Faolan, can you hear me? Faolan?"

He started to moan. "Elena?"

"Shh, I'm here, Faolan. Don't try to move."

"What happened?" he asked hoarsely.

"Oh Faolan, I'm so sorry. Stay still. That bastard shot you. I thought you were dead." Elena went on like that for a while until he reached up with his good hand and pulled her to him by the front of her dress and kissed her into silence. She was so stunned, she kissed him back before she got a hold of herself and sat back.

"Lie still while I check." She pulled back the makeshift bandage, watching his face for any signs of extreme duress. Seeing none, she continued and probed gently at the edges of his wound. "Okay, I don't know how, but you've stopped bleeding. Worthington will be back to let us out soon, and I'll get you to the doctor as soon as I can. Are you in much pain?"

He tried to sit up, and winced. Elena pushed him back, "Wait a minute," and she moved the tapestry against the cell wall. "I want to try to move you onto the tapestry. Do you think you can move if I help?" She knew the added thickness would help keep him warmer.

"What do you mean, Worthington is coming back? Elena, what happened? How did I see the mirror?"

"Oh Faolan, this is all my fault. I didn't know about the mirror until I figured it all out yesterday. Then I thought we could have a romantic evening and then I would give you the mirror. I didn't know he would come, I didn't know he could sense it."

"Listen to me, Elena. This is very important. Doona' explain anymore right now," he said urgently, placing his fingers over her lips. "You can tell me later. There are some things I have to ken before he returns." Dropping his voice even lower, he whispered, "Did you find the mirror in the chamber? Does it have the spell?"

"I found it in the first secret room, a long time ago, but forgot all about it. I found a spell book when I was locked in the chamber. The spell is hidden someplace else, not with the mirror." Elena matched his whisper, in case Worthington came back unannounced and was trying to listen.

"And you told him where to find the mirror?"

She nodded miserably.

"I have many more questions for later," he said, "but this is really important. Since you were locked in the chamber, twice now your thoughts have been projected into my mind, and I think into Worthington's mind today too when he asked about the mirror. When he comes back, you must block him from your thoughts. He will not let us out, so we must try to get him to come in."

Faolan lay back down and pulled the covers up high, then continued to whisper, "You must pretend I am hurt much worse than I am. Try for any boon that makes him come inside with us. If you canna get him to come inside you must go out. Doona' stay in here with me. You must get out. He comes." With that, Faolan closed his eyes, and moaned.

"Faolan," Elena cried, he opened his eyes and winked, then closed them and moaned again. "Oh, my God, Faolan, wake up. Please wake up." Elena went over near the window and yelled for help. Not because she expected any to come, but because she wanted Worthington to believe she was desperate. *Who am I kidding? I am desperate.*

"Miss MacFarland, stop your yowling. No one can hear you. Is he dead yet?"

Elena shook her head. "Let us out! You promised you would let us go when you got the mirror. I know you have the mirror now, so let us out! I must get him to the doctor. He may be dying."

"Wake him," he commanded.

"I can't. He's unconscious. He's lost a lot of blood."

"I have my gun pointed at Miss MacFarland, wolf, shall I shoot her?" Worthington asked silkily.

Faolan groaned weakly. "No," he moaned. "Let her go," he said, sounding feeble.

Elena looked up at Worthington. He was peering in through the window, his eyes fixed on Faolan. "You have the mirror, I can see it. You gave your oath, now let us go," she demanded.

Worthington ignored Elena and spoke to Faolan, "What is the spell? You will tell me. You cannot hope to win this battle, wolf."

Elena went to Faolan and added a gasp for effect, "He's still bleeding. Damn it—you promised. He's going into shock. It's freezing, and we have nothing to keep us warm, no food or water and he needs a doctor."

Worthington turned, said "Shut up," and fired his gun over Elena's head. She screamed, and Faolan pulled her down and covered her with his body. Worthington began to laugh. "Never show an enemy your weakness, wolf. You will give me the spell."

"I doona' know the spell. I never even saw the mirror," Faolan said, still speaking weakly. "Let the girl go. I gave you my oath to help find the spell. A boon for a boon, the girl for my help."

"Come to the window, wolf. Look at the mirror," said Worthington.

"Help me, lass." Faolan struggled to his feet, leaning heavily on her, barely able to lift his head. Only Elena knew he wasn't putting any weight on her shoulders. They slowly crossed the cell.

"Hand me the mirror," Elena reached up expectantly.

"Do I look stupid?" Worthington roared. "The mirror is mine. I will have my true desires! We have sought this mirror for hundreds of years, as have you. I will never let you have it, Wolf; I will see you in hell first."

Faolan stumbled, coughed, and moaned. Elena thought he might be playing it a bit thick, but Worthington seemed to buy it. Worthington held the mirror toward Faolan but kept it carefully back from the window, and only showed Faolan the silver plating of the mirror, not the glass. Elena focused, picturing the mirror on her dresser, imagining her reflection from last night, when she'd first put on her new dress. She didn't want to reveal anything she'd seen in the mirror.

Faolan slumped down against the wall, and Elena went back to work. "You're going to keep us in here, aren't you? We need blankets. We need food and water, light. We're freezing; we'll die by morning if you don't help."

"An excellent suggestion, Miss MacFarland. You have one hour to tell me the secret to the mirror, wolf." Without another word, Worthington walked away.

They spent the time waiting for him to return looking around the cell while there was still a little light. Elena focused on the stones in the wall, looking for one that was loose, warm, or any other indication that something wasn't what it seemed. Faolan walked around slowly and looked at the ceiling, the floor, and the window bars. The bars fastened on the outside; there was no surface to try to pry loose. The door was solid oak, with iron fastenings, and hung from the outside. There was no obvious way to escape.

Worthington returned when the hour was up. Ordering them to sit against the far wall with their hands flat on the floor, he unlocked the hasp; then he propped open the iron grating that served as their prison bars. He threw in blankets, a flashlight, and a bag with food and drink. With a long, triumphant look at Faolan, he locked the grate.

"I will keep you alive until you tell me, wolf. Tonight, however, you will solve a surprisingly persistent problem for me. Tonight, in this cell, that which you hate the most will destroy what you most desire."

Worthington walked away.

Chapter Twenty-one

Faolan paced. He walked in circles muttering under his breath, the power of his words resonating in her soul. He came to a stop and sat heavily on the tapestry, his eyes closed. Elena left him alone for a few minutes, while she examined the contents of the bag: bottled water, crackers, cheese, apples, and a bottle of whisky.

She took one of the blankets over to Faolan and wrapped it around his shoulders. Sitting down next to him, Elena untied the bandage and carefully checked his wound. It looked like it was several days old already. All the bleeding stopped, and the healing was well underway. She didn't replace the bandage. She used some of the water to dampen an unsoiled part of the cloth and washed the blood from his shoulder, and then cleaned her hands.

Faolan never said a word.

"Faolan, I'm sorry." *No response.* "Yesterday when I realized that I probably had found the mirror and spell, I was so happy. I knew I had it in my power to give you nearly everything you needed to break your curse. I kept thinking the only thing you still needed was your true heart. I knew you needed to focus on finding her, to not be distracted by me. I just wanted one night with you before I left. I didn't think it could hurt," Elena finished lamely, her heart breaking.

Faolan still didn't speak, so she stumbled on, "Now I realize my stupidity. My selfishness could cost you your life. I don't blame you for hating me; I put my own pleasure before your well-being. I'm sorry. Oh God, I am so sorry." Then the tears she'd fought so hard started to spill. She didn't cry heart-wrenching sobs, just quiet tears, slipping down her cheeks.

Faolan pulled her onto his lap and held her, while she cried for every lost opportunity, for the love they would never have. Elena cried for herself, for being such a terrible person, and mostly she cried for Faolan, because she was afraid Worthington would kill him in the morning. Faolan kissed her hair, rocked her, and cradled her in his arms.

Eventually, Elena began to be aware of things besides her tears: his broad chest, naked and warm against her face, his strong arms surrounding her, and there seemed to be something pressing against her underside.

She looked up at Faolan; his face was etched in pain. He brushed his lips so very lightly against hers that she might have imagined it. She had to look away. *I betrayed this beautiful man.*

"Elena, love, 'tis my lie that I canna live with. Look at me, lass." He cupped her face in his hands and the look he gave her seared her heart.

"When Brigid came to the farm to meet with us, she told me the time to find my light, my true heart was here. I didna ken just what she meant, but I have a duty to listen to her. Her spirits have provided guidance much of my life. Names have e'er been important to Brigid, and I wondered if she was referring to a name. I used your computer." And finally he smiled. "I told you once you had claimed my soul. Do you remember, lass?"

Elena nodded, her heart happy to see a hint of her smiling Faolan.

"So, there I was, looking at names and their meanings and I found my light. Elena means light. Brigid said I had finally found my light, and my light was my true heart."

"What are you saying, Faolan?" she asked, breathless, her own heart beating erratically.

"I am saying you are my light, my true heart. You are all I have ever wanted, someone to love and someone to love me. I could spend eternity looking into your eyes, feeling your skin, listening to you laugh. I love you, Elena."

Elena's heart rejoiced at his words. The breath she'd been holding was released on a sigh. That this man, tormented by a terrible secret for so long, could still love was amazing. That he loved her, nothing less than a miracle. She reached up to pull his face to hers, but he resisted with a little shake of his head.

"Nay, love, there's more I must tell you." He looked away. "I went to find you as soon as I knew, to explain that you were my light, but instead you were lost. Find your light Brigid had said, and I lost you before you even knew. When Brigid returned to help me locate you, she gave me a Druid ceremony to perform.

"Our family was supposed to carry on the ancient traditions, and you know my father died before I was trained. In all the years since my father passed, the ancestors have never once spoken to me. This time the ancestors welcomed me.

"I went into a trance, and they guided me to you. They filled me with power when you were in bed almost dying. They helped me save you. I wanted to tell you what I was, that somehow, although I am untrained, I am still Druid.

"At first, when you were so sick, I couldna tell you, and by the time you were well, I decided not to tell you. I didna ken how long it would take me to find the spell nor if I would be able to be with you once the curse was lifted. I decided to send you away while I looked for the cure in order to keep you safe."

Elena started to speak but again Faolan stopped her, placing his fingers on her lips and shaking his head.

He continued, his voice nearly a whisper, "I knew what you wanted last night, but I was determined that we would wait. Once true hearts mate, each will never know another. If I died when the curse was lifted...you would be alone for the rest of this life. I couldna do that to you."

He stopped then, and they just looked at each other. *Last night, we could have lifted the curse, if only we'd talked to each other.*

Despite the dire circumstances in which they found themselves, Elena realized that they had each acted out of love. They had each been trying to protect the other. Seated on his lap, locked in the cell, Elena was happier than she ever thought she could be.

Twice now, Elena had pictured something in her mind, something that affected her profoundly, and somehow Faolan had been able to see what she was imagining. It was as though she were a human projector. She wondered if she could do it intentionally. Faolan was still looking deep in her eyes, so Elena imagined loving him, that he was the owner of her heart and soul. His eyes changed, and she knew he was seeing into her, that she was successful in projecting her thoughts.

Now for something a bit more complicated. She visualized the two of them, on the couch. She was telegraphing the images from when she slid between his legs in the library, their hands together, stroking, tasting. She shifted the image yet again, and thought of the tub, her legs draped over the side, Faolan lifting her to his mouth.

Faolan's breathing was fast and ragged. Still he said nothing.

Elena shifted from memory to a mental request. *Make love to me, Faolan. Right here, right now.*

"Och, love, I doona' know how you are doing that," he said in a strangled whisper, "but there is more I must tell you. Worthington never plans to let us go. Apparently, that mirror is what he has been looking for all these years. Or at least a big part of it. He thinks it will show him how to get all his desires. He thinks I can show him how to make it work, but I doona' know how."

Elena realized she might have the answer, but it was not going to be one Worthington liked. "When I looked in the spell book, I think there were two different spells. I couldn't read them, but they're illustrated, so I have a pretty good idea about the two of them. In one, the man turned into the wolf on his own, I expect he was a shape shifter.

"In the other spell, the man was forced to a wolf shape. The background included a full moon and the spell caster was pointing to the mirror. The mirror reflected the spell onto the wolf. The mirror won't show anyone who looks at it how to get what he desires. It will only show the cursed man his true desire, his true heart, so that the curse can be lifted. The mirror will never show Worthington anything," Elena finished triumphantly.

Faolan looked at her in surprise, and after thinking about it for a minute, he agreed. It felt right to both of them. Elena expected Faolan to feel happiness, but she could still sense his feelings and he was despondent. "What's wrong, Faolan? Worthington can't force you to do his bidding. You'll soon be free of your curse."

"It's too late, Elena," Faolan cried. "You have not realized the day, but Worthington did. 'Tis why he left us in here tonight. 'Tis the full moon." He looked at her, horror for what he would soon become, what he soon would do, filled his eyes.

Chapter Twenty-two

Elena climbed out of Faolan's lap, kissed his head to show she wasn't afraid and to reassure him that she just needed to move around in order to think. She had forgotten how cold it was; sitting on Faolan's lap was like having her own private furnace. She wrapped a blanket around her shoulders.

She took a bottle of water and handed one to Faolan, then ate a few crackers and some cheese. Faolan declined when she offered to share. He was alternately watching her pace and staring out at the darkening sky. Elena wondered how long until moonrise.

"About two hours," Faolan answered her thought.

Hmm…I'll have to be careful with my new power. He smiled in response. *Still not careful enough, apparently.*

Elena reorganized the cell and asked Faolan to help her move the tapestry so that it laid completely flat, providing a luxurious floor covering in their otherwise barren cell. She brought over the blankets and the bottle of whisky and piled everything else off to the side. Faolan was watching, but Elena was keeping her mind a blank for now.

Faolan was looking at the bottle of whisky, and suddenly

she could hear *his* thoughts. He considered then dismissed the idea of trying to get himself drunk enough to pass out, maybe sleep through the moon. Then he considered asking her to drink the whisky so she would pass out before he changed, before he killed her.

There it is. He will kill me. Not because he wanted to but because an enchantment hundreds of years ago changed his essential nature. Elena had roughly two hours to live. Two scant hours to think about her life, to remember all the loved ones, all the good times.

Except there hasn't been much happiness in my life, not until now.

Faolan needed to know about her, to understand her life. She'd made him see the champagne, she'd made a body appear on the floor, surely she could make him see what her life had been like before him. Elena knelt in front of Faolan, making sure she had his attention. She focused on bringing her memories to life for Faolan to see. She showed him the lonely little girl she'd been, The days alone in the apartment, the night her mother left her forever for a bottle of vodka. She pictured Grandda, who loved her in his gruff silent way but left too, dying after only a few short years. Then there was a series of foster parents, before she broke free with the help of college loans and two jobs. The scenes flashed by, Elena didn't want to spend much time thinking about them, just long enough for Faolan to see, to get a sense of her life.

She showed him Marty, who seemingly rode in on his white horse to give the poor little girl a happily-ever-after ending. When she remembered the scenes of Marty asking if she was ready to, "Give it up," as he'd liked to say about her virginity, Faolan growled. Then Elena showed Faolan that humiliating scene when Worthington had come to tell her it had all been a lie.

Finally, Elena showed Faolan how the real happiness in her life started the moment he had stepped behind her in line at the airport. His earthy scent played to her soul, their first earth-shattering kiss, and their most intimate moments. Elena smiled and looked at him, making sure he followed it all.

Cupping his face in her hands, Elena pressed her forehead to his, needing him to understand this most important point. *When I was lost, your magick awoke, and you saved me. I know you love me, and I love you. If my life is to end this night in this room, then I want to go with your loving arms around me, with you inside of me, finally a woman.* Your *woman.*

"No, I'll not take you here," Faolan roared, jumping to his feet and moving to the far side of the chamber. "Doona' you understand? I will kill you, and that will kill me. At least it will kill my soul."

He desperately looked around the room. "I will wrap you in the tapestry, roll you up to hide you, and maybe I can fight it. Maybe we could use the blankets to tie my hands to the bars, or bind my mouth. 'Tis not enough whisky to knock me out, love, I'm sorry. If you drank it, you wouldna know what was happening. Damn it, I canna do it, Elena."

Elena waited patiently for him to finish, then tried something different. He'd said she was his light, so she concentrated on projecting her love in the form of a pure white light, flowing into him. She focused on controlling that light, that feeling, on filling every part of him with her light, just as his love filled every part of her.

She crossed the floor to stand directly in front of him, nose to pecs, considering the difference in their heights, and placed her hands on his chest. They could both feel it. A wave of pure energy poured from Elena, from her hands, into Faolan, bringing peace to his troubled mind. She felt strong and full of purpose. *Tomorrow might never be. This night is our destiny.*

Faolan placed his hand on top of Elena's, and the energy began to flow both ways. He filled her with his love. They stared into each other's eyes, and Elena wondered at the connection. Something was changing; something spiritual was happening.

"Love me, Faolan."

"Elena, you know I do."

With a groan, he swept her up into his arms, and she wrapped her legs around his waist and put her hands on his face. Still looking into his eyes, she kissed him, and the world shifted once again. The movement was more than just their own personal earthquake; everything around them shimmered in Elena's peripheral vision.

Faolan staggered under the motion of the shift, then held Elena tighter and deepened the kiss. His mouth covered hers, pressing gently, molding her lips to his. He rained kisses on her face and neck, lightly touching, teasing. His kisses claimed her. She felt light-headed at the passion flowing between them.

As though unable to stand the barest of separation, Faolan unzipped the back of her dress, slipped it over her head while Elena squeezed her legs even tighter around his waist. His hands returned to cup the bare cheeks of her ass. Elena loosened Faolan's hair, raking her nails through silky strands. The fine cover of hair on his chest brushed against Elena's breasts, raising chill bumps.

Lowering them to the floor, Faolan settled Elena on the blanket-covered tapestry. He kissed her, tongue thrusting, promising her infinite pleasure. She captured his tongue before releasing it, traced his lips, and pulled gently on his lower lip with her mouth. He rested his weight on one side and slid a hand from her hip along her waist and continued upward to cup her breast. The lacy bra was dark against her skin, her breasts were full and tight with desire.

Faolan traced the scalloped-edged lace with his tongue and rubbed the pads of his thumbs against the soft undersides of her breasts until she cried out with pleasure. When he finally unfastened her bra and drew a nipple fully into his mouth, Elena arched her back and pulled his head tighter against her breast. Faolan massaged, alternately licking, suckling, and nipping, and just when she thought she couldn't take any more, he switched to the other breast and started over.

Elena pushed at him and he rolled onto his back to let her slip out from under him. She straddled his hips, feeling his erection between her legs. Her mouth and tongue explored every chiseled ridge of his stomach and chest. She rose on her hands and knees so she could reach his mouth, she kissed him deeply.

Faolan cupped her face, gently, before running his long fingers down her cheek, along her jawline, and feather-light over her lips. When she sucked his finger into her mouth, her eyes locked on his, they both saw what she planned to do next.

Then Elena was suddenly on her back again and her breath left her in a whoosh.

"Not this time, love. This time is for you, from start to finish."

His words flamed the fire deep within, and Elena reached to pull him closer, but he smiled and caught both of her hands in one of his, pinning them above her head. With his free hand, he unbuttoned his jeans and pushed them down to his hips, taking his underwear with them. With a little more effort, he got them down around his knees, then kicked them the rest of the way off. The only thing separating them now was her lacy thong.

He moved both of his knees between her thighs and pushed her legs wide apart. Faolan kept her hands pinned, covered her body with his, then ravaged her face and neck with his kisses. His hair brushed silkily against her skin, caressing a thousand places at once. He traced a path to her breast with his tongue while his unrestrained manhood traced a lower path, velvety smooth, hot as a brand.

He lingered for a few minutes at her breasts, before tasting every part of her stomach. When he reached the thong, he caught it with his teeth and pulled it tight between her folds. He kissed the spot where the thong disappeared. He pulled himself back up, covering her mouth with kisses, and the press of his erection against her mound brought her close to the edge.

"Oh God, Faolan, please, I'm ready, I want you," she panted.

"Where do you want me, love?" he purred. He pressed against her, pumping languidly, teasing her.

"Please now. I want you in me." She gasped, and he stopped moving, leaving her breathless, begging for release from this exquisite torture.

He let go of her hands and ever so slowly kissed his way back down her stomach and kept going all the way to her ankles. Then he started a long, slow journey back up, one leg at a time, kissing his way to the spot they joined, and then back, never coming quite close enough. Her hips began moving, seeking his lips, his tongue.

Every strand of his hair, every touch of his hand, every bite, kiss, and lick, sent a thousand signals at once. Elena's nerves were on fire. *Oh God, I can't breathe without him.* When his mouth finally found her clitoris, Elena moaned with pleasure. "I'm so ready, Faolan," *I might just,* "Oh," *might just,* "I can't, ah, ah, ah..." She came with the slightest touch of his lips through the cloth.

"I love that you are so ready for me, lass," Faolan laughed. Laying his cheek against her pubic bone, he let her recover slightly before starting again.

Elena lay there panting, shuddering, wanting more. "If you stop now," she gasped out, "I will hurt you!"

Faolan laughed again, even as he pulled off her thong and ran his hand up the insides of her thighs. This time, he pushed her legs up, knees bent and apart, exposing her entire womanhood to him. He positioned her knees over his shoulders and lowered his mouth. Again and again, he kissed and licked, his tongue making long slow strokes.

Opening her folds, he inserted one finger, then two, slowly pumping, spreading her wetness. His mouth began to tease, first tracing slow circles, flicking and kissing. He added a third finger, and Elena moaned at the feeling of fullness. Faolan slid his fingers in and out, increasing the pressure against her muscles, encouraging them to loosen, "Relax, lass. We are made for each other."

Faolan brought her close to the edge again. Her breath was coming faster, punctuated by little gasps of pleasure. Elena wanted him deep within her, and told him so, "I can't wait, Faolan. Please. I want you now."

Faolan rose to his knees and looked at her for a long moment. It was such a powerfully loving look, that she knew she never wanted to turn away. He didn't need to ask if she was sure, her answer was plain on her face. He raised her hips and brought his erection to her hot, wet opening. He rubbed the tip of his cock in the creamy wetness of her desire, and gently pushed it between the folds of her flesh.

Despite her desperation to have him inside, Elena's muscles

fought against this invasion. She didn't think he would fit. Faolan took his time. He inserted one slow inch at a time, letting her adjust. After each inch gained, he pulled back, just a little before going another inch deeper. *Oh God, he's so big.*

"Relax, Elena, I will fit. We are meant for this," he assured her. He continued slowly, giving her plenty of time to adjust to him. He watched her face, measuring her readiness, seeing her desire. They both knew when he reached the barrier, and he hesitated, just for a moment, afraid to hurt her more. With her legs wrapped around him, she thrust her hips at the same time she pulled him closer, taking him deeper into her, gasping at the slight tug.

Faolan lowered himself, covering her with his body, staying very still, waiting for her pain to subside. It passed quickly, and Elena started moving, encouraging him to go on. He wasn't even halfway in yet. He continued his gentle progress until, stretched to the limit, she finally had him fully sheathed.

"I am inside you, love. You have all of me," Faolan growled. Then he pulled out slowly, almost leaving her completely before gradually filling her again. Elena pushed her hips to meet his, trying to quicken the pace, but he was deliberate, seemingly enjoying her hunger for him.

Faolan raised himself up on his knees again, lifting her hips, and wrapped her legs around his waist. He quickened his stroke a little, he rubbed his finger against her clit. Her breath came in ragged gasps, and her muscles sensed release coming from somewhere deep inside her own body.

The world as she knew it drew down on itself, pulling into a tightly closed ball. Waves of sensation passed through her, ripples just under the surface of her skin and deep within her bones. His body called to her, claimed her, owned her. There was nothing she would withhold from him, nothing she could.

Then in a sudden reversal, all the energy that flowed toward her core exploded outward, shooting off sparks in all directions. A crazy kaleidoscope of color and heat.

I will never be the same.

He pushed in as deep as he could go, gently moving his hips, wrenching every last shudder from her orgasm. Then Faolan was kissing her, moaning into her mouth, and he began again. Reason passed. His strong, hard strokes filled her repeatedly. He was pushing harder now as her muscles contracted and relaxed around him, fitting him to her. The room grew steadily brighter as the moon rose higher in the sky, but they paid no attention.

There were no worries, no regrets, only this moment, filled with their love and the sensation of being bound together for eternity. Their pace increased; faster, harder. Elena felt his leg muscles flex, gripping her tightly. Her hands reached for his hips, driving him faster, her own hips thrusting, meeting his. The sound of their breathing was loud in the night.

"Elena," he whispered.

Faolan shifted his hips slightly, and the angle he entered her changed, rubbing against her clitoris. His thrusts were hard, even deeper in this new position. She felt him thicken inside her, and she looked up to meet his passion-filled gaze. They were the only two people left alive in a vacuum of love, the rest of the world had ceased to exist.

They began to change. The walls around them shimmered, rippling outward. Every nerve, every cell in her body was connected to the spot where their bodies joined; alive, electric. Faolan's stroke was strong and sure. He thrust and a roar filled her ears. He thrust again, deeper still, pressing against the mouth of her womb. All `her feelings pulled in from her edges, gathering in a storm of sensation.

"Now, my love," Faolan whispered.

The earth didn't just shift; it exploded with the power of their union. There was a flash of lightning from outside their window, then a loud crack of thunder rent the night, and the world changed yet again. They both cried out at the magnificence of their coming together, just as the moon crested the window and shone on Faolan's back.

Chapter Twenty-three

Their bodies were still in the throes of pleasure when Faolan's spine arched. His mouth opened wide in a silent scream. Elena wrapped her legs around his hips keeping him tight inside her body while holding herself against his chest to keep as much of their skin-to-skin contact as possible.

Faolan's neck muscles corded as he strained, whether from the pain of transformation or the strain of resisting it, she couldn't tell. An unerring sense of self-preservation warned her to keep silent.

It can't end like this!

With a part of him still buried deep within her, Elena focused all of her newfound power, projecting her light into him, her energy flowing, eyes closed in concentration. The women from her earlier vision returned, and surrounded them. Their power joined Elena's, and their light united with the moonlight, bathing Faolan, caressing him, soothing his pain.

Outside, the sound of chanting joined the bubbling sound of the nearby stream. Another flash of lightning and simultaneous crack of thunder exploded from the clear sky. A tree began to burn, the flames fanned by a sudden gust of wind that swept the clearing.

The earthy smell of nature's compost filled the air. The speed of the wind increased and formed a small whirlwind, picking up leaves and dirt from the clearing, spinning faster until a cyclone formed. It circled the clearing, then dipped in through the open grate and swept into the cell. The sound of chanting grew louder.

As it reached a crescendo, they were pelted by debris from the swirling tempest as it twisted and turned, battering itself against the walls. Elena fought desperately against the scream that formed in her throat as her skin was pelted and her hair whipped wildly. Then as suddenly as the whirlwind had entered the cell, it swept back out into night.

Elena looked at Faolan, still buried inside her, his hands on either side of her shoulders, and his back arched. His head was thrown back, eyes closed, his long hair spilled over his shoulders and down his back, tangled, wild. He was magnificent, and she had never loved him more than at this moment. He began to stiffen and move within her again, the tempo frenzied, and his body clenched with effort. Elena kept her legs wrapped around him, driving her hips up to meet his every thrust. Pounding, primitive, life-affirming.

Faolan's strokes reached a crescendo, his muscles jerked against Elena. With a shudder his seed filled her once again. His neck muscles were tight, the tendons stretched taut like thick cords. A wolf's howl ripped from Faolan's throat, inhuman, terrifying. Then a shadow of a wolf passed from him, racing out of the window carrying the howl with it into the night. Peace descended upon the clearing and they were alone.

Faolan opened his eyes. "Elena?" he asked, eyes confused.

"Faolan, are you okay?" she asked, reaching up to touch his face.

"Aye, lass." He turned them both on their sides, never breaking their bond. They said nothing further for a very long while, just held each other, testing the strength and boundaries of their new world.

When they finally began to talk, Faolan asked Elena to tell him what happened.

"I don't know for sure. What do you remember?"

"Och, lass, the last I remembered we had reached our climax together. Then I was pouring my seed again, and I dinna' know how I got there. I doona' remember what happened. Oh God, Elena, did I hurt you? Rape you?" he asked as his hands frantically began to search her body for injuries.

"No, Faolan, don't worry. I've never been better. Let me show you." Elena said soothingly. Then she used her new powers to play her memories back through her mind, projecting it to him, watching his face as he experienced what she'd seen and felt.

"Is it gone?" she asked, and then quickly rephrasing it, she confirmed what she already sensed. "The curse, it's really gone. You are released."

He looked around the room at all the leaves and debris the wind had left behind. "Aye, lass, I am clear of it. We will have to find Red and Lilly to see if the entire clan is clear." Shaking his head, he said, "Elena, I have called you my enchantress, but the power you have...you saved me. What are you?" He looked at her tenderly, lovingly, reverently.

"I don't know. Before I met you, I was just a woman. I've never had anything special around me at all. When I was little, my Grandda used to tell me stories from Scotia, of the fair folk, of magick. They were wonderful, but I always thought they were fanciful tales of an old man. Knowing you has awakened something deep within me. I don't know if this is me or you making it happen."

Hesitantly, she began to tell him of the things she was beginning to remember about when she was locked in the chamber. "I had visions when I was lost, Faolan. The women I told you about, who cared for me in the chamber, they took me places and told me things. I still don't remember all of it, but they changed me. They said I was supposed to do things in my life; they welcomed me to their sisterhood. Tonight, those same women came to help me pour light into you. They saved my life then, and I believe they helped to save my life tonight. I just know it. I'm supposed to start on something they called a learning path. What does all this mean?"

"Och Elena, I doona' know. When Brigid told me that it was time and gave me the words to say, I performed an ancient Druid spell, and the cloud of vision took me. I told you before that my clan was Druid. However, I have tried without success for centuries to call the ancestors. I had wondered if the power skipped me. This time, the ancient ones welcomed me to them, they showed me how to find my light, they led me to you. They also told me 'twas time to start on my journey."

Elena's throat became tight with emotion at his words. *A journey…would he leave her, now after all this?* With feigned casualness, she pulled away from his embrace and turned over to reach for a bottle of water. With her back to Faolan, she sipped from her bottle, carefully hiding her thoughts and her face from him. Taking a deep breath, she asked in an offhand manner, "When will you be leaving? On your journey?"

"I doona' think you understand, lass. We have mated for life now. I willna be leaving you, and you willna be leaving me. Not ever."

"You don't think it's a journey that you have to go alone?"

Elena asked, holding her breath, fearing his response.

He answered her with action. He got to his knees behind her and pressed himself tight against her backside. Elena shivered with the feel of him. He was hard again. *Still?* He placed his hands on her waist and began to kiss her shoulders. He pulled her hair aside and nuzzled her neck, alternately biting and kissing. "I willna be letting you go, lass, not ever," he growled low in his throat, sending a shiver of thrill through her at his possessive tone.

Elena leaned back into him, molding herself against him. The feel of him pressed naked to her back, the hard broad chest hot against her skin, made it impossible to think. What was he saying, that he would always be with her? She could feel his powerful thighs tight against hers, his cock nestled between the cheeks of her ass.

Faolan reached around her, and lifted her heavy breasts, massaging, and teasing her nipples into hard little buds. He trailed one hand lazily down her stomach, raising goose bumps, leaving a molten trail wherever he touched. His fingers found her soft curls and began to stroke. He reached between her legs, spreading her, softly exploring, seeking the wetness.

Elena moaned and pressed back against him even harder. Correctly interpreting her sighs, he continued. He took one hand to her chin and tilted her head to the side, allowing him access to her sweet mouth. He held her jaw with his long fingers and kissed her deeply. Her tongue met his, and they took turns sucking, tasting each other's lips, before he began a rhythmic thrust into her mouth.

His other hand traced patterns feather light over her skin, scorching everywhere he touched. From one breast to the other, down to her waist, then lower, dipping to rub her clit before returning to her breasts. "Let me show you, Elena," he murmured in her ear.

Placing one arm around her waist, he murmured instructions, "Bend forward, love. Rest your weight on your forearms." Faolan moaned as Elena's ass was presented. "I have dreamed of taking you like this, your ass in the air, hair wild. My cock buried to the hilt inside you." His fingers spread her and with his other hand, he gently rubbed himself in the wetness between her legs, finding her hot opening.

"I shall go slowly love, even if it kills me." He laughed softly. "You will likely become tender, so I will wait to ravage you later," he teased.

Once she had taken all he had to give, he began to rotate his hips, massaging her internal muscles, easing any lingering soreness. When she started to rock her hips back, showing that she was ready, the moments of discomfort eased for now, he began to teach her.

"Tighten your muscles again, Elena. Squeeze me deep inside of you."

She tightened them as he moved, slowly withdrawing his cock, then pushing deep again. Elena gasped with the pleasure of it. He increased the tempo, and she met his thrusts. The heavy weight of his balls slapped against her as he pumped faster.

He moaned, whispered, "Elena, my love." He traced his fingers down her spine, then back up along her sides, gently touching her breasts. He leaned over her and pressed his fingers to her nub, rubbing faster, pumping harder.

Elena never knew a man could be so deep inside a woman. With each thrust of his hips, his cock went deep, to the lip of her womb. Her breath escaped in a small grunts, with each deep plunge. "Ah, ah, ah…"

He took his hand from between her legs and laughed when

she whimpered with disappointment. He buried his face in her neck and chuckled. "Did that feel good, love? Do you want some more?"

"Touch me, Faolan, please don't stop. So close," she finished on a pant. He slid his hand down her arm, threaded his fingers through hers, and then brought her hand to join his. She was mortified and tried to resist. He never let go, just placed her fingers against her clit, holding them still. He stopped with his cock deep inside and began a different type of seduction. He moved his hips in slow sensuous circles and whispered in her ear "Feel how wet you are Elena." She held her breath, embarrassed by her desire. "Reach farther back, feel where we are joined." He took her hand and placed it between them.

He continued to whisper in her ear, "Open your hand, lay it palm up between us and spread your fingers. Can you feel it? Feel me slide in and out of you. I am so hard and you are so wet."

She could feel his cock, slippery and hard, sliding between her fingers and it sent a thrill through her to know she did that to him. Desire replaced embarrassment, as his shaft slid against their hands.

Then he took her hand and placed her fingers between her folds. Once again, he pushed his cock as deep as it would go and then began to massage her internally with small movements of his hips. He brought her fingers to his lips and licked, sucked them into his mouth, then releasing them with a kiss, he put both their fingers against her clit, and began to rub.

The desire in her flared hotter. The newness of the experience, the intimacy, the raw hunger he felt for her fanned the flames. Her ears were ringing, sensation seemed to be leaving all of her but one spot, filled with him. She pushed herself harder against their fingers, and lost track of which of them was rubbing her.

"Tell me, love, let me hear you," Faolan coaxed, his whisper a velvety growl in her ear, breath hot against her cheek. "Does it feel good?"

"Yes, feels so good," she gasped, then moaned. A few moments later she moaned again, deep in her throat. She exploded in sensation, his name on her lips, squeezing his shaft in spasm after spasm. He stilled their hands and his hips, as she continued to shudder against him. When she quieted, he held her close, and began to kiss her neck, running his tongue down from her ear, and then bit her neck. Elena gasped. He was still hard. *He was insatiable.*

He put his hands on her hips pulling her close against him. Then he began slowly stroking in and out again, his shaft penetrating deeply. Elena continued to shiver and shudder around him. He finally pulled out completely and stretched out on his back next to her and said, "Elena, come, love. You on top this time. I want to watch you."

His words sent a new thrill of desire up her spine. She straddled him and he put her hand on his shaft, so that she could guide it herself. She took him in fast this time, in one single stroke, then holding him deep inside, she began to rotate her hips, pushing him even deeper, squeezing him. With Faolan's hands on her hips, she moved up and down, discovering there were some advantages to being on top. Besides being able to control the pace, she could watch his face as he watched the joining of their bodies. She didn't resist when he again brought her fingers to join his. This time they came together.

Chapter Twenty-four

"Worthington will be back in the morning. We need a plan."

"I know," Elena agreed contentedly.

Faolan was eating an apple and handed her a cracker with a piece of cheese. "Come on, sleepy one. We can rest once we get out of here."

"What if I want to go to bed instead of getting some rest when we get out?"

Faolan laughed, and the sound warmed her heart. She sat up, completely sated from their lovemaking. She ate the cracker and drank water, trying to build up some strength. She slipped her thong back on, as it was the only underwear she had and redressed, moving like an old woman.

"You've ruined me," Elena accused. "I'll never be able have sex again."

Faolan leaned in and kissed her deeply, put his hand to her breast, and she pressed toward him.

"Liar." He laughed again and pulled away. She smiled at his playfulness.

Faolan's face turned serious. "We have no more weapons in here than we had when he left us last night, save one. Us.

When Worthington left, he believed you would be dead by morning, and I would be a broken man. He expects to find your body. I want to see what you can do with your projection powers, lass."

"You want me to think about what happened, show him you're cured?" she asked, and heard the uncertainty in her own voice.

"Nay, lass. I want him to think I am dead. Do you think you can show him something that hasn't actually happened and make him believe it's real?"

It was an intriguing idea and she felt herself surrendering to the thrill of using magick. Elena concentrated very hard and imagined Worthington instead of Faolan. She pictured him lying dead in the middle of the cell, his throat cut, blood oozing from his body. She projected the image to Faolan.

Faolan sucked in his breath. His gazed fixed on the projected image of Worthington's body lying dead on the floor. "You are positively terrifying, love."

Elena grinned. "I am, aren't I?" She was beginning to really enjoy this power. She quit thinking about Worthington, and his image popped from sight. She'd had another idea. "Can you shield yourself, Faolan?"

"What do you mean?" he asked.

"I don't exactly know. The phrase just popped into my head." Elena sat quietly thinking for a minute. "It was something I saw in the spell book. There was an illustration showing a room full of people, it looked like a meeting. There was one person alone in the back of the room watching what was happening. Then the picture was repeated, only this time the person at the back of the room wasn't visible, except his figure had been outlined with a dotted line, to show he was really still there.

He thought about what she said for a minute. "I think you might need to shield your mind. No, maybe 'tis my mind I need to shield? Your mind will be a shield because you will be projecting." Then veering off track he began to worry again. "You canna let it slip, Elena. No matter what he says, doona' respond, doona' listen. He will try to get answers from you any way that he can. We need him to come inside. You will be the bait. I canna think of any way to get him to come in if he thinks I am alive. I will protect you."

Frustrated that she didn't have better words to describe what she meant, Elena tried again. "I think everything you said is right, Faolan, but I still want you to try to shield. I don't even know if you can, but I think Worthington might be able to sense if there are two people in the room. I think what I mean by shielding must be like when I project. Stand over there," She pointed at the wall under the window. "Now examine it minutely. Memorize every brick and blemish. Imagine that's what you look like, or that you're standing behind it," she explained.

Faolan did as Elena directed and then turned to look at her. While she watched, Faolan seemed to fade in and out, becoming nearly invisible before appearing again suddenly.

Elena grinned. "Finally, something I can do better than you! You nearly have it. It's like you told me, don't let any other thoughts in. I couldn't control it at first, either. Heck, I didn't even know I was doing it. I'm getting better at it. Now I can project, and still think about the other things happening, still see the room. You shouldn't try that yet. Block everything out."

He faded from view and stayed that way this time. Elena crossed the room to where she'd last seen him and reached out to grab a free feel. He popped back into view.

"That's fighting dirty," he said before pulling her into a kiss that possessed her and drained her of her will to continue working. Her toes curled, and then Faolan pulled away, laughing.

So he wants to fight dirty?

Elena turned around to pick up her bottle of water on the floor, bending over from the waist, keeping her legs straight, feet apart. She felt the hem of her dress rise, as she knew it would, exposing her thong and the cheeks of her behind. Faolan groaned and stepped forward, pushing his erection against her, pulling her hips back.

Elena laughed and danced away, giving him a bit of his own back. When she looked over her shoulder at him, she sucked in her breath. His eyes had darkened, and he was looking at her full of hunger and desire. Faolan reached her in two long steps, pressed her against the wall, and rubbed his hard cock against her backside.

Elena's pulse raced, her heart pounded, and she shivered with the change she sensed in Faolan. This was the hard, dangerous Faolan she knew he'd kept hidden from her. He pulled her hair aside and bit her neck, all gentleness gone.

"Och, lass, I'm going to fuck you now."

Elena's knees buckled, and all thoughts of preparation were forgotten.

****

It was a couple of hours past sunrise when Faolan raised his hand to indicate he'd heard someone approaching. He faded, chameleon-like to match the wall next to the door. He had to be perfect in his shield or else he would appear directly in Worthington's line-of-sight.

Elena sat on the sat on the floor, staring at the image of Faolan's lifeless and bloody body. Worthington's sharp intake of breath let Elena know her projection was a success.

"Well, well, Miss MacFarland. It seems I have underestimated you, once again. Or did the wolf do it himself to spare you?" Worthington sneered.

Elena continued to stare at Faolan's lifeless body, making no sign that she heard anything. Tears dripped down her face. *Oh, I am getting so good at this.* Worthington continued to badger, harangue, and verbally abuse her. Without warning, there was more than just his words. She could feel darkness, a black power emanating from him. It poked sharply against her mind, reaching out to test what she was seeing, to judge if it was real. *Good God, could he reach into her head?*

She dared not try to thrust back, but she felt violated, dirty from the contact. She kept her mind tightly closed, and kept the focus on the projection on the floor, making sure the image stayed where she wanted it. Worthington finally left the window, and she didn't hear him for a very long time. Finally, she heard him behind her, but it was imperative that he come all the way through the door. With a bit of luck, he wouldn't shoot her before Faolan could get him. They hoped it was enough. The door opened slowly, and before Worthington entered, Elena again felt the insidious black tendrils of Worthington's mind pushed at hers. His mind was devoid of light. It was oily, filled with the foul odor of his soul. Focusing very hard at projecting the image of a dead Faolan on the floor kept Elena's thoughts protected from his mental assault.

Worthington moved cautiously as he entered the cell. She heard a commotion and then Faolan said, "Doona' even think about moving."

Elena turned then to see Faolan's forearm around

Worthington's throat. He stripped the gun away and kicked it toward her.

Faolan said, "Take the gun, Elena, and doona' hesitate to shoot him. He tried to kill you last night." Faolan's rage was palpable.

Elena pointed the gun at Worthington and stepped back against the wall. She had never held a gun before; she was proud her hand didn't shake.

Faolan searched for other weapons', and found a dirk strapped to Worthington's leg. Faolan removed the dirk, cell phone, watch, and wallet. "Take off your clothes, down to your underwear," Faolan ordered. When Worthington hesitated, Faolan added, "If you doona', I will cut them from you, and I willna be too careful."

Worthington removed his jacket and shirt but was reluctant to part with his pants. When Faolan approached with the dirk, Worthington changed his mind and quickly removed his slacks. "Fold all your clothes and put them in a pile with your shoes. Then sit over there with your back to the wall." Faolan indicated the wall opposite Worthington's clothes.

"Elena, wrap a blanket around your shoulders. We'll leave the rest of the blankets for Worthington. There are enough supplies to last 'til the morrow for one man."

Elena did as requested and came to stand near Faolan, wondering what it would be like to shoot a man. Then she wondered what it would be like to let Worthington see her think about shooting him. The thought amused her more than it should, but she kept it to herself for now.

"All right, Worthington. Tell us why we shouldna kill you? Convince us with the details of the mirror. What do you know of it, why did you want it?"

Worthington looked calculatingly at Faolan. "If I tell you,

will you let me go?"

Elena felt his mind reach out again, testing Faolan, and she used her power to push back, to keep them safe from Worthington's invasion.

Worthington's head whipped around, and he glared at Elena. He had recognized the shield had come from her. She wished she could have kept that bit of information to herself, but it was out now.

"No deals," Elena said flatly. "If we let you go, it will be because we choose to. There is no dealing with a liar."

"Surely you're not going to let this stupid little bitch enter into our negotiations," Worthington said with a sneer.

They had already planned that once the negotiations started, Elena would talk, and Faolan would remain quiet. They expected to fail this first round, and they didn't want to give Worthington any clues about Faolan.

"He doesn't know anything, Faolan. He's just a minion," Elena said. "We need the boss if we want to learn anything." *Wow! That got a mental rise!* She could feel the hate emanating from him. Somehow, that shot in the dark was correct. He wasn't the top dog in whatever organization he belonged to, and that bothered him. *A lot.*

"You stupid bitch. I thought you were smarter. There is none more powerful than me," Worthington yelled. He was breathing hard, and his eyes seemed to glow slightly. "You really should be more discriminating, wolf. You'll give Druids a bad name."

Elena was frightened by the hate that rolled off him. She pressed her hand to Faolan, sending the light she knew would give him strength to resist Worthington's provocation.

"Let's go, Faolan, maybe he'll be ready to talk tomorrow, or the next day, or next week. We're in no hurry."

Faolan moved stiffly. White-hot anger rolled off him in waves. They took Worthington's shoes and pants, and they left, locking the door behind them. Once they were outside the cell, they looked around.

Faolan started to say something, but Elena stopped him with her hand on his arm and a shake of her head. Worthington had powers, and she didn't know what they were. She wasn't willing to risk that he could reach into their minds out here.

They were in a small chamber that had two ways out. One was a locked oak door and the other was a stairway leading up. Choosing the stairway, they used caution as they exited, just in case Worthington hadn't come alone. Outside there was a small hill, on the edge of a clearing in a grove of birch trees. The cell was under the hill, the small window hidden from view by an evergreen shrub and rocks. From inside the cell you could see into the clearing, but from the outside, it was invisible.

Quickly glancing around the clearing at signs from the previous night's storm they saw that the bare top of one of the trees still smoldered from the lightning strike. The keys were in the ignition of Worthington's Land Rover, and they got in and drove out the single lane track.

Once they hit the main road, Elena realized the track ran along the back of the farm. They were right around the corner from home.

Chapter Twenty-five

They jumped from the Rover as soon as it rolled to a stop, Faolan bellowed, "Red, Lilly! Lilly are you here? Red!"

Red and Lilly raced from the house. "Faolan! Och, Faolan. Where were you? Are you all right?" Lilly sobbed her questions as she raced to embrace Faolan.

Red was just as relieved, if a bit more taciturn than Lilly. "Lad, 'tis good to see you."

Lilly started to ask, "What's happened? We didna cha—"

Faolan cut her off, "Let's go inside, first."

Elena stayed near the Rover, trailing behind to give them privacy. Tears filled her eyes at Faolan's joy.

The door flew back open, and Faolan raced back out, "Elena?"

Smiling, she said, "It's okay, I was letting you have some time to yourselves."

Sweeping Elena off her feet, Faolan said, "Never leave my side, love." He kissed her tenderly, pouring his heart into hers, scratching her with his beard of three days. "Shall I carry you over the threshold?" he asked teasingly.

Elena's quick intake of breath and widened eyes warned

Faolan not to tease with this one. He knew her history, the promise of belonging to a man, the man belonging to her, building a family. These were not ideas she took lightly; these were her dreams.

Faolan looked at her seriously, his face now solemn. "Elena, lass, I have no words to explain what happened last night. The elements of this world joined our union when we made love. Doona' you know? You canna leave me, even if you wanted. We have been joined for life already."

He sealed his words with a kiss that was possessive, claiming Elena as his. It left her breathless. Then he proceeded to carry her into the house and she caught sight of Lilly and Red watching as they entered. The couple grinned at each other, and then rushed forward to shower Faolan and Elena with hugs and kisses. Elena's throat tightened, and she fought back the tears. She was wanted. *I belong to this family, and they belong to me.*

****

"We have much to share, but it can wait until we've showered and changed," Faolan said, "and Lilly, could you fix us something to eat? It has been a long time since our last meal."

Still holding Elena tight to his chest, he carried her to her room. *Their room.* He set her gently on the bed, pausing often for kisses and touches. He knew he should let her body recover for a few days before making love to her again. He was acutely aware he had taken her too many times last night and that he had been particularly rough that last time. *Christ, that last time…*

Elena had bent over in front of him, baring her ass, legs spread wide, only to dance out of his reach, laughing. His cock had instantly become rock hard. When she had looked over her shoulder at him, her long raven hair tangled down her back, it had been his undoing.

He had slammed against her back, had practically ripped that damned green dress off her, and pushed her against the wall of the cell. Her small grunt as she'd hit the wall was not a protest, but a guttural declaration of desire.

Holding her against the wall, he opened his jeans and pushed them down far enough to release his aching shaft. He licked his fingers, and slid them across his cock, hoping it would be enough. He pushed aside the thong with his cock and entered her, relieved to find her wet and ready. He didn't want to hurt her overmuch, but this was a desire such as he'd never felt before.

He tried to get a modicum of control back, to keep from hurting her. He knew he should lay her down, take his time. Shuddering from the effort of his restraint, he made sure her feet were balanced on the floor, fully intending to pull out and reposition her.

Then his sweet Elena did something that shattered his resolve. She pushed her hips hard against him and bent over. With one hand on the wall and the other braced on her knee, she looked over her shoulder and said one word. "Yes."

He'd grabbed her hips with both hands and slammed into her until they were both grunting with every thrust. His balls slapped against her, until they pulled up tight and hard. "Och, lass, I'm gonna explode!" He bent over further and reached his hand between Elena's legs, to bring her along with him when he came. "God Elena, tell me when."

"Now Faolan, I'm ready now!"

Smiling at the memory, he knew he would pull that one out often and relive every moment. Shaking his head, he brought himself back to the thought that had started the reminiscence. He needed to let Elena recover. She would be sore for several days and nights and probably wouldna appreciate certain types of his attention. Then he got an idea and went into the bedroom to get the small bottle he'd put in the nightstand many weeks ago.

While he was busy with his memories, Faolan had filled the tub for Elena, and she'd brushed her teeth. He grew hungry again as he watched her stand naked before the mirror, brushing her wild tangle of hair. He hugged her to his chest before scooping her up and depositing her, laughing, into the tub. All thoughts of letting her recover were immediately forgotten.

The little hand shower in the tub provided its own enjoyment as Faolan sprayed the water onto Elena, then stopped to soap and shampoo her before spraying her with the water again. When he reached the tender spot between her legs, he let the warm spray of water linger longer than strictly necessary, his nimble fingers gently massaging with the oil to ease her lingering soreness.

Faolan opened the drain while he continued to minister to her. He'd put some of the massage oil from the small bottle into the palm of his hand and carefully worked it into the tender flesh and folds. He watched her face, looking for any signs of discomfort, prepared to stop immediately.

*

Elena laid her head back and draped a leg over the side of the tub, allowing him greater access. The oil had provided relief to her raw labia. She hadn't realized just how sore she would become from all their activities the previous night.

She smiled secretly to herself when she thought of the groan of pleasure wrenched from Faolan when he'd come that last time. That had been wild sex, certainly nothing she had imagined for herself for her first night of lovemaking.

Just thinking about how she had changed last night, the things she had done. Had that really been her? She was so turned on right now, Faolan hand slid back and forth from her mound to her ass, and she was slick from the oil. He was being very careful not to hurt her, but she wasn't sure anything hurt much right now. Except maybe the parts that were aching because they needed release. She moaned and put her other leg over the edge of the tub, opening herself to him, begging his touch.

He poured more oil in his hands and rubbed them together, then began a gentle massage of her thighs, one leg at a time. Every nerve below her waist was screaming for more. His hands caressed the sensitive juncture where her hips joined her body before returning to the soft curls on her mons. She moaned.

"Doona worry, lass. There is plenty of pleasure just in what I am doing now. Relax. If you are too sensitive for more, I'll stop now."

Elena forced a deep breath, sending oxygen to her muscles, and shook her head, meaning don't stop.

Faolan resumed his lazy caress of her inner thighs, then back toward the center, between her ass cheeks and back up. He slipped a gentle finger inside then spread her wetness to her nub, and he began to circle her clit, rubbing harder now. She pushed back against his hands with her hips and held tightly to the backs of his arms, increasing the pressure he was applying. She couldn't find where one sensation began and the other left off. Her orgasm built inside of her, a giant wave moving inexorably toward the shore.

The fingers rubbing her nub moved more quickly, and Elena hung on by a thread.

"Come for me, love. Let me feel you now," Faolan whispered in his sexy brogue.

With a moan, Elena's orgasm began in a slow crescendo

building from inside and rolling outward. As Faolan felt her first shudder, he slipped two fingers deep inside her hot, wet opening.

Elena exploded…shattered into a thousand shards of light, her muscles clamping down on his fingers as they continued to gently pump, and wave after wave crashed over her. When she finally relaxed enough he could reclaim his fingers, he used the hand shower to rinse her one more time.

Faolan lifted her from the tub and wrapped her in a fluffy towel and held her against his chest. Elena cupped his face in her hands and kissed him deeply.

They changed spots, and Elena washed him, touching and loving every part. She washed his hair and used her crème rinse to remove the tangles. Then thinking of another use for the silky conditioner, she squeezed some into her hand and began to stroke his hard shaft, giving it the special attention it deserved.

Faolan lasted exactly three minutes before he grabbed the little hand shower, rinsed himself off, and jumped out of the tub, unable to wait a minute longer. Carrying Elena to the bed, he stripped back the covers and laid her tenderly back against the pillows. "Elena, my love," he said, "you are my life now. Every fiber of my being is tied to every fiber of yours."

"I know," she replied simply. She sat up, and his manhood was majestically displayed at face level. She reached her hand as far around as it would go, and began rubbing, stroking, tasting him. His hips moved against her, his fingers tangled in her hair.

****

When Elena and Faolan finally emerged from the bedroom, they were clean and presentable in fresh jeans, sweaters, and warm socks. Although they had served their purpose well, Elena was glad to be free finally of that thong and green dress.

The smells from the kitchen made her mouth water, and they raced each other to get to the food first, laughing as they entered the kitchen. They needn't have worried; there was enough food to feed the four of them and an army besides. Eggs, potatoes, biscuits, bacon, sausage, all of it delectable. Elena and Faolan piled on the food and dug in, not waiting for Lilly to sit. It had been a long time and a lot had happened since their lobster dinner two nights previous.

Lilly laughed and said, "Looks like the two of you haven't eaten in a while."

Red added dryly, "Or worked up an appetite."

Faolan nodded, mumbled, "Both." Elena blushed.

Red said, "We'll start, so you can eat." Faolan nodded again, and Red continued. "We left after preparing dinner," he nodded at Elena, "and went for a bit of a dinner ourselves. Then we went to the Beauly house to prepare for the full moon."

Faolan, interrupted, quickly explaining to Elena the townhouse in Beauly had a safe room with electronic locks on timers. The door locked at sunset on the eve of the full moon and released at sunrise the next morning, keeping them safe from their base urges. He looked at Red to continue.

"Aye, we completed our preparations and waited for you to join us. Lilly put food in the house expecting the lass would join you for the trip. We knew you wouldna be willing to leave her behind, and we suspected she dinna want to leave town for the night." He smiled dryly.

"When the time drew nigh, we entered and waited for you. Once the door locked, we were near distracted with concern. As the time approached we hoped you were secure, that you didna' harm the lass. We knew neither of you would survive it." Red looked seriously at the two of them. Faolan and Elena exchanged looks.

"The time came, and we felt the pull of the moon entering us as it has for an eternity, and then…" He paused searching for words, then looked to Lilly for help.

Lilly took up the tale. "Then we were filled from within by joy. I doona' know any other word for it. As soon as the door released, we returned here to find you, but all we found was the back door open in the wind."

By then, Faolan and Elena's frenzied need for food abated and they were ready to tell their story. Faolan looked at Elena and asked if she wanted to share. She knew what he meant, and projected the first part of their story directly to Red and Lilly. They gasped, first at her power, then at the cruelty and evil nature of Worthington.

Elena continued in a more traditional story-telling format. "Faolan doesn't remember most of this. I am sorry, some of this is personal and embarrassing, but I think between us, we need to be very frank right now. Her face heated and she knew she had turned beet red as she continued, "It got close to the time of the moon, and we were, uhm…"

Faolan rescued her by inserting, "Making love. She is my true heart. I claim her for all eternity."

Red and Lilly looked at each other and beamed, then turned their smiles on Elena, blithely waiting for her to continue, as though they'd expected him to say something like that.

Stunned, Elena stared at Faolan. His words sent shivers down her spine. For all eternity.

He looked up and smiled, his eyes crinkling at the corners. "I will tell the world, if you like, lass."

Elena smiled back. When she continued, her words came

out quickly, embarrassed. "Well, when we, er, you know, got to the most important part, the earth shifted, like an earthquake. It sounded like an explosion in the clearing. At the same time, the moon touched Faolan's back while he was still... uhm, you know..."

Faolan and Red both laughed aloud at her discomfort.

Lilly patted Elena's hand. "Never you mind those randy lads, go on with you, dear."

After taking a deep breath, Elena continued, "Well, I don't know how to explain this, but when I touch him I can send a light, like a white healing light into him," her voice rose, making it sound like a question. "Only this time, the women I saw in the chamber, when I was lost..." She trailed off. This was really complicated.

Again, Faolan supplied some help, "She's had visions of a sisterhood," and he nodded for her to continue. Apparently, that was sufficient information for Red and Lilly, because they both nodded encouragingly.

Valiantly, Elena continued, "So the sisterhood joined me and the moon. We spread light into Faolan, soothing him. I held him as close as I could, trying to touch him in as many places, to uhm, keep him... uhm, inside."

Faolan started to laugh again, but when Elena raised an eyebrow to look at him, he sobered quickly and gestured for her to continue.

"I heard chanting in the clearing outside our cell. I don't know who that was." Elena described how the previously calm night had turned into a symphony of nature at her wildest. "Then Faolan started to... uhm, you know again and just before he...uhm, got to the important part again—"

Elena had to stop talking. Faolan was laughing so hard no one would be able to hear her.

"Are you quite finished?" she asked archly, when he finally subsided to an occasional chuckle. He nodded contritely.

Determined to be bold, Elena said, "Anyway, just as Faolan reached his—" she paused for effect and looked directly at Faolan "—climax, he threw his head back and a wolf's howl echoed around the stone cell. Then a shadow of a wolf came from Faolan's throat and flew out through the window, taking the howl with him."

"Worthington knows Faolan is a MacGailtry. He knew what would happen to Faolan in the full moon, he calls him wolf. He locked us in the cell, making sure we had enough food and blankets. He wanted us to stay alive long enough for Faolan to transform and kill me. He meant for me to die. He always planned to kill me, but now he's trying to break Faolan." Elena looked directly at Faolan, "I think he wants to control you."

"Control me? Why would he want to control me? It would have killed me if I had hurt you."

"We thought all he wanted was the mirror, but he said he came back for a spell. He knew you didn't have the spell when he left us there. He could have shot us, and no one would ever have known. He could at least have shot me. Instead, he had a plan that would get rid of me and break you. He wants to bring you to whatever it is he's doing. What did Liam's partner call you? A novice and a sapling, and Worthington said you were going to give Druids a bad name.

"I think he is a Druid priest or master or whatever you call it. He senses your power, and he wants it for his own. Faolan, there is much more to him than just a bad man who wants a magick mirror. This isn't about money; it's about power. And though Worthington has far more magickal power than we thought, he wants more."

As Elena finished, her gaze turned inward, as though she wasn't in the room with them but somewhere far away. She saw Worthington standing in the middle of the chamber. He began to chant, turning slowly clockwise, his face turned up, arms stretched out to his sides. The wind began to swirl, twisting, turning, pulling the debris from last night's storm into a black vortex. When the wind and his voice reached their crescendo, a shadow owl flew from the room. Worthington settled onto the ground with the leaves and waited.

Chapter Twenty-six

"Elena? Are you all right?" Lilly's hand was on her arm, and Faolan raced around the table, full of concern.

Elena looked at him. "Worthington sent a message. He has a shadow owl. I think someone will be coming to help him." Elena described what she had seen, then said, "I don't understand how I know these things, how I can see them. Is there something wrong with me?"

"Nay, love, doona be afraid. I think 'tis the magick of this place that speaks to you." Faolan looked at Red, "Let's go."

Lilly and Elena in unison said, "Wait."

"What's wrong?" Faolan asked. "We have his gun. He canna get out. Let us see if we can get him to talk."

"Then I must go with you. I don't know what's wrong, but there is magick at work here, Faolan, and he knows a lot more of it than we do. I felt his mind, and he tried to feel mine when he came to the cell and found me still alive. It was full of darkness, full of dark power. He will try to get inside you."

Faolan thought that they might be able to shake Worthington's confidence and get him to talk. They thought he must be concerned already since they'd managed to disrupt his plan to kill Elena. Now he was their prisoner. If they told Worthington about the owl, he would realize they were far stronger than he'd suspected, and he might reveal something of his plans. Faolan hoped to convince Worthington that he would consider becoming his apprentice, to learn the Druid ways. They would try just about anything in an effort to get him to talk.

Elena wasn't at all happy with the idea of the two men talking to Worthington alone. She'd never intended to wait in the car as Faolan directed; she was going to stay close to the men. Unsure of the extent of Worthington's powers, she did knew he could reach into people's minds. She had felt it. What if Worthington could project images as she did. He could make Faolan see something that wasn't there. She flat out didn't trust Worthington.

Once Red and Faolan left the car to go to the clearing, Elena told Lilly she was going to follow. Lilly started to argue, but Elena overruled her objections. "Lilly, I'm really worried about what Worthington can do. I know he's after more than that mirror or other artifacts. I'm sure he's after Faolan."

With her thoughts carefully shielded, Elena followed a path through the trees and hid on the edge of the clearing, close enough to hear and definitely close enough to project.

"Wolf, you returned. Did you miss me?" Worthington asked in an oily voice. "Where's your strumpet? She seems to have some latent talents of which I was unaware."

"What's your story, Worthington? Tell me about the owl."

Worthington just stared at Faolan, temporarily speechless. Then his eyes narrowed. "Your powers are more advanced than I thought. Who is training you, novice?"

"I have no trainer. *Yet.* All I know I have found on my own. So what are you, Worthington? Druid? Sorcerer?"

"Do you really wish to know?" Worthington asked quietly. Then he did something strange that caused Faolan and Red to take quick steps back. He floated up off the ground, raising his head high enough to look through the window at Faolan. Worthington whispered a command, and Elena felt Faolan try to raise his mental shields to protect himself half a second too late. Then Worthington was inside Faolan's head.

What happened next seemed to unfold in slow motion. Faolan raised the gun and turned toward Red. Elena threw a projection of Red ten feet to the right of where he was actually standing and shouted to Faolan with her mind. Faolan continued to turn until he had the gun pointing at the false image of Red.

Time returned to normal as Faolan spun quickly back, pointed the gun to the side of Worthington, and fired. Worthington dropped to the ground, landing lightly on his feet. Elena kept her shield around Faolan's, adding an extra layer of protection.

In a strange vibrating voice that filled the clearing, Worthington said, "Come train with me, wolf, and I will teach you all of my skills. No one could stop the two of us. Unlimited money and power at your disposal. Come let me out, and I will take you to be with your kind. *Come*."

Faolan shivered as the booming voice rolled through the clearing. "You are not my kind. You are the usurper. There are those who are waiting to stop you. *I* will stop you."

Lightning streaked from the sky, thunder exploded, and the tree that had burned the previous night was burning again. Red and Faolan jerked back, momentarily distracted by the unexpected show of nature. When they turned around, Worthington was gone, the cell completely empty. Nearby, just to the side of the shrub, Elena was laying on the ground.

****

Elena was in the room but wasn't in the room. It was confusing, but she couldn't think of another way to describe it. She could see Worthington, in his boxers, standing with another man who was wearing a gray business suit under a slate cloak. The man had gray hair and a gray complexion. In fact, everything about the room was shades of gray, even Worthington. Maybe she was only seeing in black and white, as if she had an old television receiver that wasn't in sync with modern day standards.

"Master Symington," said Worthington, inclining his head toward the other man.

"What the bloody hell have you done?" the Master growled.

The office was opulent with a slate topped desk large enough to land a plane on, two leather couches, club chairs, a bar, and a flat panel television. The walls were filled with photos of the Master shaking hands with local and national leaders, political, business, and religious. It looked as though everyone wanted a piece of the Master. Or the Master owned a piece of everyone.

Elena could sense that Worthington needed to be careful here. She could hear that he was having two very different levels of thought. Behind the words he was telling the Master were other thoughts. This was a deep game, one he had been playing for years. He would not lose now. He knew he was a dead man if the Master learned of his plans. He lied smoothly, weaving in bits of truth, in case the Master wanted to check up on him.

"Master, I found another person searching for the ancient ways. I do not believe he is part of an organization, but someone who stumbled upon the old rumors. He learned of the farm I own, far north of here, and believed the old stories of a hidden Druid library. We proved that story a myth many years ago, but he was unaware of that fact, which is why I am sure he is not with any organization.

"He'd tracked me to Phoenix and asked me if I had heard of such stories or had found any old books. I told him those were false rumors, that there was nothing there. When he left, I followed. He returned to the area of the farm, and even though I knew the stories to be untrue, I stayed around to watch. I was stupid. I went without back up and he trapped me in the cell by the clearing."

The Master's face was livid, and he said between clenched teeth, "What did he say?"

Worthington continued, "He was foolish. He told me he was looking for some ancient spell books, that he was going to be an author, and he was gathering a history of the ancient Druids. His story was consistent with what he'd said in Phoenix, and with what I stripped from his thoughts.

"I told him the land had been looted by treasure hunters for centuries, and long been proven to be artifact-free. I pointed out that as I was American, I would have no problem shooting him with my hunting rifle, should I catch him trespassing again. Although he left me in the cell, I believe the threat has been handled."

"You did well, Worthington, but he concerns me. I want you to follow up, find where he is, and if he can be safely removed, do it."

"For the good of the order, Master," Worthington agreed.

When he left, Worthington allowed the true nature of his thoughts free reign.

****

"Elenaaaaa!" Faolan ran to where Elena had suddenly appeared on the ground near the trees. He had no idea how she had gotten there or what was wrong with her. Red stayed near the window watching the cell in case Worthington had done that same shielding trick and was just blending in, appearing invisible.

"I smell sulfur, Faolan. I expect Worthington is truly gone," Red said.

Elena was breathing shallowly, her eyes moving rapidly under her lids. Faolan picked her up, and held her close against him, he carried her to the center of the clearing. He crooned to her, begged her to please wake up, told her he loved her, promised everything would be okay. Lilly left the Rover, running up to see what happened. Still Elena didn't wake.

Lilly wanted to take Elena home, but Faolan said they would stay, she would know where to come to if he stayed here. Faolan didn't know if Worthington had taken her, or if she had tried to follow, but he was certain her spirit was not with them right now. He also knew something that none of the others knew, not even Worthington. He alone knew just how magick the clearing was, and that his ancestors were close by.

He directed Red to build a fire, which Red did by knocking a branch from the burning tree and Lilly brought stones and water from the brook. Faolan wished Brigid was here with him, but he knew the four elements needed to be greeted, before he could petition his ancestors for help. He might not have the right words, but he could speak from the heart. He hoped it would be enough.

He sat near the center of the circle, holding Elena, and focused on opening himself to hear. The chanting started almost immediately and filled the small clearing. It was rhythmic, ancient, resonating with power. The fire flared, sending sparks to carry on the wind. One by one, Faolan shut out all external sounds. He focused on hearing his heartbeat, forcing out everything else. He welcomed the visions when they came and was lost in them for a very long time.

Faintly at first, Faolan heard a second heartbeat inside his. It was faster, lighter than his own beat. He focused everything on hearing that second pulse. It became stronger, louder, closer. Faolan's eyes opened on a now dark night. He saw Red and Lilly watching him anxiously, but not interfering.

He sensed Elena was near. Faolan stroked her forehead, "Elena, it's time to come home. Come back to me now." He kissed her hair, smelling her sweetness.

Elena moaned softly and began to move. Her eyes fluttered open, and she screamed.

****

They gathered in the kitchen once again and Elena told her story. "I am sorry I hid my plan from you, but I wasn't sure you could shield by yourself against Worthington. I thought the two of us together would be stronger. I thought you would try to stop me if I told you."

Faolan looked at Elena a long moment before he answered, "Och, you are right. I wouldna have let you, and I would have been wrong. You said the two of us together would be stronger, and that is the new reality for us, lass."

Taking a deep breath, Elena continued, "I saw Worthington direct you to shoot Red, so I projected Red's image to a different spot." She looked back to Lilly and Red, "If Faolan had succumbed to whatever Worthington was doing, I hoped he would shoot the image, not the man. Once Red was safe, I threw my shield around Faolan's to reinforce his protection.

"It was then I felt Worthington drawing in on himself, like a vacuum, as if he was sucking power from the clearing. I tried to sense inside of him, to see what he was planning. I hadn't tried that before."

Elena shuddered and gagged. She barely made it to the bathroom before vomiting. Faolan followed and got a washcloth to bathe her face in cool water. She brushed her teeth and returned to the kitchen, apologizing.

"Touching his mind made me sick. He's pure evil, Faolan. We must be careful. He *does* want to control you; he wants your power."

"I doona' even know I have any kind of real power," Faolan said. "I thought it was all about the artifacts."

"Worthington believes you do, and so do I. I can sense it in you," Elena told him quietly. She continued, "I thought he was preparing to do magick in the clearing or on one of you. I believed I could prevent him from hurting you if I could get inside him. I didn't realize he was leaving. He created a roar in his head, and there was an answer from somewhere farther away. I saw the lightning, and then he was gone, and I was trapped."

Elena told them of watching Worthington and of Master Symington. She didn't know who he was or of over what he presided, but he was one source of Worthington's bitter blackness. She continued, "Worthington put up shields around most of his mind while he was with Symington. He was determined to keep his true feelings hidden. I could hear both the story he was telling and the thoughts he was hiding. He lied about the farm and he kept you hidden, Faolan.

"Once Worthington left Symington, his thoughts lost some of their cohesiveness. He was thinking of finding someone, but I don't know who. He thought about his son, and he thought about murder. It was like being in a room of thick, black smoke. Words and pictures floated on the inky tendrils, and I could sense some of them, while others were unclear."

She looked at Faolan, and said simply, "I wanted to come home and I heard you calling me. I followed your voice with my heart."

It was Faolan's turn to tell Elena what had happened after Worthington left. Faolan said, "I saw you suddenly appear on the ground at the same time Worthington disappeared, and I couldna wake you. I called upon the spirits again, they were very near," he said with an evasive expression.

"Visions overtook me and I was taken by boat to an island, surrounded by clouds. I told the island's keeper you had been taken, and he said you were powerful. You had learned much and would return soon. There was a wren-"

Elena interrupted, "That told you to reflect, and you will be seen; follow the path of learning—"

Faolan finished, "There is a time coming when all your skills and all the true disciples may still not be enough."

They looked at each other for a long minute, wondering what it meant. Both of them had experienced the same vision. Obviously, there was something they must do, somewhere they must go together.

Clearly shaken, Faolan said, "Red, do we have any unopened whisky? I willna take a chance on anything opened previously."

"Aye, lad," and he went to fetch a fresh bottle. Lilly got the glasses. Faolan was not inclined to let Elena move from his lap, and she was not inclined to want to move. Drinks were poured, tossed back, and refilled, in short order.

"'Tis a night's rest we all need. 'Twill be more clear in the morning." Faolan said. Red and Lilly said good night.

Faolan insisted Elena have one more drink, and the warmth finally spread through her. She melted against him, relaxed and sleepy. Faolan held her close, nuzzling her hair, kissing the top of her head. Elena turned her face up for a kiss, and he kissed her eyes, her nose, before finally settling his lips possessively on her mouth. He stood, keeping her close in his arms, and carried Elena to their room. He ran a bath, filling the large tub with warm water and bubbles while she undressed.

"Here you go, love. Climb in and relax. I'll come get you out when you are finished."

Elena stared at him, a bit dumbfounded. "Aren't you coming in with me?"

He swiftly moved to her and cupped her face in his hands. After planting a kiss on the tip of her nose, he said, "Nay, lass. Doona' fash yourself. I will be satisfied to hold you while we sleep. In a few days, I will make love to you every way you can imagine. Maybe in some ways you canna imagine perhaps," he laughed.

Elena snaked her arms around his neck and pulled his lips to hers. She molded her naked body to his fully clothed one, she thrust her tongue in his mouth. Faolan growled and sucked her tongue deep into his mouth. His erection pressed against her stomach.

Faolan buried his face in Elena's neck, breathing hard. He whispered roughly, "Och, Elena, I willna be able to resist if you kiss me like that again."

Elena scraped her fingernails lightly against his scalp before grabbing big handfuls of his hair to pull hard enough to guide his mouth back to hers. She kissed him hungrily. He capitulated with another throaty growl.

Elena smiled the self-satisfied smile of a woman who knows she is desired and watched him quickly undress. When he picked her up and stepped into the tub, soapy water went everywhere. *As big as this tub is, there's not much room when a six and a half foot tall Highlander climbs in with you. Seems the only reasonable course of action is to climb on top.*

After rinsing off the bubbles, they dried each other, and Faolan carried Elena to their bed. He laughed easily and smiled often. His mouth rained kisses upon every inch of her, and instead of quenching her thirst, they created a fire. "Faolan, I need you. I want you inside me, love me now."

He was infinitely patient, filling her slowly, lovingly. He watched her face, responding to her quick intakes of breath, her moans, and sighs. He pleasured her without seeking his own release. As she neared the crest again, she said, "Come with me, Faolan. Fill me now."

With a groan, his restraint snapped and with fast, furious strokes, he pounded against her, possessing her, taking her higher than she'd been before. His yell of release coincided with hers, and they came thundering and shuddering to completion.

Elena was drifting off to sleep when she sensed Faolan pulling back. His arm left her waist, and he started to leave the bed. "Faolan?"

"Shhh, love. Nothing is wrong. I will be but a few minutes." Elena drifted back into a light sleep. When he returned, he smelled of the earth and wind. Again, she sleepily asked, "Faolan?"

He laughed, and said "Go back to sleep, love. I am here." Conversely, that woke her.

"Where did you go?"

"To run the farm. Red was out there too."

Elena sat up, covers dropping to her waist, hair wild, eyes wide with fear. "You were the wolf again? Oh, Faolan, I thought the wolf was gone."

"Nay, lass, 'tis the *curse* of the wolf that is gone. I was always supposed to be a shape shifter with the wolf as my second form. 'Tis part of my heritage. The curse mutated my abilities and bound me cruelly, but the wolf is my strength. I am able to shift at will, but not forced into a cruel mockery of my gift by the moon. Doona worry, love. Now go back to sleep. I will stay here the rest of the night."

Elena couldn't lie back down yet. She looked at him searching for answers, her insecurities returned with a vengeance and were suddenly as awake as she was. *Why me? How long will he stay?*

Either Elena projected or he was getting very good at reading her because she heard his sharp intake of breath, then his low growl.

"Elena, you doona' see yourself very clearly. At this moment, your green eyes have captured the light from the fire. They glow and hold me captive. Your breasts are ripe, and my tongue and mouth long to taste their sweetness. Your hair is wild, calling me to weave my fingers into its tangles. Yet these are all just physical treasures."

He placed her hand on top of his heart, and continued, "I no longer have a heart of my own, for 'tis yours. Were your heart to stop beating, then mine would surely follow. I will be by your side as long as you'll have me. Should you send me away, I would always remain near, keeping you safe. You are mine in every way possible, save one."

Faolan got down on one knee beside the bed and looked into her eyes. "Elena MacFarland, I love you with all of my heart and soul. I doona' ever mean to be separated from you. There is deep magick in us, and I doona' know where it will lead, but I always want you by my side as we journey together.

Will you do me the honor of takin' my name to be going with the heart and soul you have already captured?"

Elena's mouth went dry, and her eyes damp. The breath seemed to catch in her throat, even while her heart raced. She was quite simply stunned. *Has any women ever received such a passionate proposal?*

"Aye, Faolan MacGailtry, I will be your wife. My heart is yours. Do with it what you will. I cannot live without you." Faolan reached into the nightstand, then took her left hand and slipped a slender gold band with a large emerald surrounded by smaller diamonds onto her third finger. He was watching her, his eyes suddenly careful.

Tears welled in Elena's eyes. She could see the love he felt for her on his face. He wanted the ring to mean as much to her as it did to him. Elena began to cry. She was overwhelmed by the elegance of the old-fashioned setting. It was the most beautiful ring, the most beautiful proposal. Her throat was so tight from her tears she couldn't speak.

"We can go pick something out together, love. Doona' worry. 'Tis but a family heirloom and all I have at hand for the now. Och, lass, 'tis all right. Please doona' cry."

She wiped away her tears, she smiled tremulously at him. "Faolan, it's spectacular. I love it. I love you." She leaned down to kiss the magnificent man kneeling in front of her.

The kiss was gentle, tender, and when Faolan climbed into bed with her, they clung together, rejoicing in their love.

Chapter Twenty-seven

Faolan was right. Elena was sore, in more spots than one, and she relished the chance to lie around and have him wait on her. She took a long afternoon nap curled up on the couch in the library, Shadow cuddled up tight next to her stomach. When she woke, Faolan was seated on the opposite end of the couch and had her feet in his lap while he was reading. She watched him for a long time, loving him.

Without looking up from the book, Faolan smiled, "I love you too, lass."

Elena gasped. *How did he know what I was thinking?*

Faolan laughed and looked at her. "Well, you were thinking it rather loudly, my love. I usually canna read you, lass, unless you want me to. Today, sitting here next to you, I could sense when you woke. Then you started thinking how much you loved me, and well, I thought I should say something before you started thinking about something else. Although it would be verra enjoyable to hear your thoughts on our lovemaking the last two days, if you care to share," he laughed.

Of course, as soon as he'd said that, Elena's mind jumped to him slamming into her from behind while they were trapped in the chamber. She heard his quick intake of breath and veered quickly away from that mental picture and made sure she wasn't accidentally projecting. There was no way she could make love tonight. Even walking was uncomfortable.

Faolan resumed reading after readjusting the crotch of his jeans, an act that Elena pretended not to notice. *It was a very good thing I wasn't thinking about laying in the tub with the oil and the way his fingers—*

"Goddammit, Elena, are you trying to kill me?"

"You heard that too?" she asked, completely mortified by her thoughts.

"Aye, lass, I not only heard it, I saw it," he said tightly. "I think I'll go take a shower now." He stalked from the room.

Elena thought about things for a minute, and then decided to follow him. He had a towel wrapped around his waist, and was still stalking, heading for the shower in the hallway bathroom. There was a very visible rise under his towel. Elena's heart was pounding. She seemed to have become totally obsessed with sex and Faolan.

*

"Not right now, lass," Faolan said, keeping his voice gentle, as he tried to side step Elena.

When she put her hand on him, he froze. She spread her fingers wide and gently scraped her nails over his hard chest, stroking the bronze curls covering his pecs. "Faolan, I can't make love today. I really am too sore."

"I know, lass, I really do. I doona ever want to hurt you that way. Och, Elena, you have got to stop touching me though. I canna stand here next to you like this, 'tis fair driving me to distraction." He knew she was new to this, but could she not see how aroused he was?

She slipped her hand to his erection. "You're so hard."

He groaned and tried to step back, only to bump into the hallway wall.

"Elena," he tried again, but his voice came out harsh, guttural.

She reached under the towel and squeezed his cock, blushed clear to the roots of her hair, and asked, "Are you um, you know, going to do something about this?"

So that is what this was about. She wanted to watch! Christ the woman turned him on. Her innocence and curiosity were a verra sexy combination. He was going to lose it here in the hallway if she didn't let go of him.

"Come, lass. Come watch me, and let me look at you."

After adjusting the shower temperature just right, Faolan dropped his towel and stepped under the spray. He took his time, created a lot of lather and soaped his chest, but only paid cursory attention to his hard-on, before moving down to his legs. Once his body was clean he shampooed his hair; then he reached for the crème rinse. He filled his hand with a fair amount, turned the showerhead to the side, so it wasn't spraying directly on him, and leaned his back against the side of the stall.

He'd never done this with someone watching before. Elena had been sitting on the counter, but now she got up and came closer. She leaned against the wall so that she was directly across from him. Only the glass of the shower door separated them. His cock was rock hard, and he wrapped his slippery hand around it.

He slid his hand slowly up and down the length. He lifted his eyes to look at Elena and found her watching his hand hungrily. She looked as though she was jealous of his hand and would like nothing better than to slap it away and replace his hand with her mouth. She licked her lips and he moaned, moving his hand faster.

His testicles tightened, his leg muscles tensed. Christ, she had him hot! When she had flashed on him taking her from behind in the cell... Oh, and she liked the massage oil. She had relived that orgasm and wanted him to do that again... She was watching him, in his private pleasure... It wouldna be long, he couldna hold back. This was one of the most erotic things he had ever done. He didna have to imagine her face, her lips, her breasts. They were here in front of him, and he knew she wanted him. He heard her moan, and she reached forward to open the shower door. Elena knelt, watching him, but made no move toward him. Then she used his own words back at him.

"Tell me, Faolan, does it feel good? Tell me."

"Christ, Elena, you make me so fucking hard. I canna hold back." He shortened his stroke, going even faster. "Now, Elena, now."

Elena looked up to his face and back to his shaft and licked her lips again. He shot out in spurts, rocking him hard against the wall as his body jerked with the force of his orgasm. He continued to stroke until he was spent. He leaned back against the shower wall and looked at Elena. She looked back at him, and he heard her one-word thought.

Wow.

****

The following day, everyone agreed it made sense to try to find the island from their visions. Both she and Faolan had travelled west, and Faolan was sure it was northwest. That's where they would start, but they needed new maps and nautical charts. Faolan and Red had one of their conversations within a conversation when Faolan asked Red to explain his new needs to a boat broker. Later, when Elena asked him about it, Faolan answered cryptically that he and Red had done a wee bit of fishing before and Red knew what he meant.

Red and Lilly went to Inverness to buy supplies from several long lists. Elena and Faolan would be alone for hours, and she thought it was finally time to share what she had learned in the chamber and had pieced together since.

"Come with me," Elena said, pulling him by the hand to the library. She showed him the books in her backpack.

"Elena, my love," he said, his voice a hoarse whisper. "You are correct, this does look like a book of spells. Let me have a closer look," he said and pulled out a chair at the desk.

"Let's go see what other things are down in the chamber, first." She tried to sound enthusiastic, but truth be told, she was uncomfortable entering any more underground chambers. She'd had enough of them to last a lifetime.

They took her pack, flashlights, and an empty box to the steading. "Open it, lass. I want to see how it works for you."

After telling him the story of how she found the panels, Elena placed both hands on the metal plates and pushed. They opened as before and Elena shuddered and stepped back to let Faolan go first.

"Och, Elena, what was I thinking? I canna ask you to go in here with me. I will meet you back in the house when I am finished."

"No, Faolan, I need to go back in. I need to face this. It's just, well, would you mind if we put something in the doorways we enter? Just to make sure they don't close."

He swept her up into a protective hug and held her close. "Aye, lass, do not fash yourself over much. I will be puttin' something in each doorway, and I will be by your side, never fear."

"God, Faolan, I know I'm safe to go in, but I don't want to be lost like that ever again."

"Elena, love, I am not sure we can ever be separated that way. I feel you in here." He pressed his hand to his heart. "We are connected now. I think I will always sense how to find you." He gently pressed his lips to the top of her head.

As they entered the chamber, Faolan propped a book in the doorway. Elena gave him a tour of the main vestibule and showed him how she had opened each of the three walls. They examined the walls again for any other hidden secrets. After looking through both of the smaller closets, it was time to face Elena's fears, and walk down the long passageway.

Faolan took her hand, and they walked together. Since Elena had yet to try the door on the left, they chose that one first. He pushed it open, and they were surprised to see the little room outside the cell where Faolan and Elena had been held captive by Worthington. They were facing the open door to the cell and the stairway that led to the clearing.

"I wonder how Worthington knew about the cell, but not about the rest of the chamber? Why he didna break down this door?" Faolan asked.

"Maybe he couldn't see it," Elena answered. "Faolan, you stay in the passageway and close the door, I'll wait out here and see if I can see the room."

"Are you sure, lass?"

"I'm sure. I know I can go up the stairs if I get stuck."

"Aye, and I have the key, so you willna be there long," and he closed the door.

As soon as Faolan closed the door, Elena was faced with a complete wall of stone. No sign of the giant oak door remained. She ran her hand over the surface and though she could detect a slight warmth where she knew the door to be, no amount of pressure from her hands caused the door to be revealed, let alone open. Faolan opened the door from the other side and looked a question.

"Not a sign of the door once you closed it. Let me try," Elena said. They swapped places, and she closed the door on Faolan.

Less than a minute later, Faolan opened it from the outside. "The door never disappeared for me, lass. I could see it the whole time."

"It must be a legacy spell from your father, Faolan! It probably only appears for members of your family. I must have been able to see it the other day because I was with you."

Faolan looked at her for a long moment before answering slowly, "Aye, lass, 'tis what I think as well. Worthington knew a lot about my family and their…gifts. Likely, more that I myself knew. His ancestors always thought they would find treasures and Druid spells on this farm. 'Tis why his family stole it, why my father was killed."

"Worthington must have thought he found the secret chamber when he found the cell, and been upset when it was empty," Elena said. "Let's go look in the other room."

"Are you sure, lass?"

"Aye." She smiled.

It was hard to go into the chamber where she'd spent so much time trapped and alone. Faolan propped the door open and kept his eyes on her. She looked around the room with interest, seeing it through fresh eyes. She'd lost a lot of hours in here, but she was also changed. For the better.

She was sure the women she saw in her vision had somehow been much more than a dream. They had kept her safe and gifted her with the ability to project. She looked around the room for signs the women had been corporeal.

Faolan showed her the two chairs that had been pushed together, "Tis where I found you asleep, lass."

Elena showed him the marks on the door where she'd scraped it with the dagger. In the glow of the strong flashlight, and in full possession of her wits, she could see her attempt at removing the metal doorplate had been feeble. She looked up at Faolan to find him watching her, giving her whatever space she needed to process what had happened.

"Thank you, Faolan," she said, tears making her throat tight.

He answered by sweeping her up into a hug so tight it took her breath away. His lips were on her hair, and she felt him shudder. When she looked up, she saw the raw fear on his face at the idea of losing her.

With her hands on either side of Faolan's face, Elena filled them both with the healing light gifted to her by the sisterhood. They stood that way for several minutes, Faolan holding her while she held his face, looking deeply into each other's eyes.

"Elena, I doona' know what I would do without you." Then he smiled, taking some of the edge off the words. "Your life has been a right fankle since you met me,"

"It has been our destiny, Faolan," Elena answered him, smiling as well. "Let's see what we can find, what your father left for you."

They spent the next several hours, as if in their own private museum, examining the books and treasures throughout the chamber and its rooms. They decided to leave everything as it was, still in the chamber where it was safe, until they could make other arrangements. The Worthingtons hadn't been able to find it for hundreds of years, and they both believed it was still the most secure place to leave the treasures they'd discovered.

When they returned to the house, they called Red on his cell phone and asked him to get a small copy machine while he was purchasing supplies. It would be far easier to take copies of the pages they wanted, rather than entire books. Faolan and Red spoke a bit longer about arrangements, while Elena busied herself in the kitchen. Business taken care of, they ate lunch and then napped recreationally.

Faolan was especially tender, touching Elena with reverence, as though she was the most precious gift he could ever receive. He kissed her slowly and tenderly, touching her face, stroking her hair. As he kissed her, he murmured her name, then spoke in Gaelic, before translating them to English. He spoke of love and how she was now his life. It was exquisitely gentle, with an undercurrent of desperation borne from the thought of almost losing her.

Elena's throat grew tight. His gentleness was bringing fresh tears to her eyes. Suddenly, gentle was not enough. She needed to know she was alive, needed to affirm that they had survived much, and were still here, to live, to love another day.

Elena pushed Faolan back and straddled his chest. She pulled her sweater off and reached to pull Faolan's off as well. He seemed to catch her fever, and then they were both ripping off their clothes in a frenzy to be naked, to touch as much of each other as possible. They wrestled for the dominant position, each rolling from the other after only a few minutes on the bottom.

Their kisses bruised, teeth bumped, their desire entwined with the relief of survivors, creating a volatile cocktail. They would both walk away sore from this one.

****

By the time Red and Lilly finally returned, Elena and Faolan had scoured the books they brought up from the chamber and marked many pages for copying. They wanted to get the copies made and then put the books back in the chamber, as soon as possible.

After unpacking the truck, they all returned to the library and pinned the marine charts Red purchased to the wall. They each had different references and whenever anyone came across a likely island, a colored pin would mark the spot.

Unable to read another word, Elena leaned back and rubbed her eyes. "I wonder what Worthington did with the mirror," she asked no one in particular.

All activity in the room stopped, and everyone looked at her. Then Red and Faolan rose as one and ran out to look in Worthington's Land Rover. To no one's surprise and everyone's disappointment, it wasn't there.

"Show me where you had it hidden, lass," Faolan asked.

They all traipsed to the bedroom where the state of the rumpled covers testified to their afternoon activities. Elena pressed her hand to the stone, and it swung open to reveal the hidden cubbyhole. Nestled inside, just as she'd left it, was the mirror!

Chapter Twenty-eight

Everyone stared at the mirror, and the fear for what it could mean for all of them permeated the room. Elena remembered their previous conversation, when she'd asked Faolan what would happen once he got his true heart, the spell, and the mirror. Would he grow old and die in front of her?

Oh God, not now, please, not now. The curse was already lifted, wasn't it? Nothing else would change when Faolan held the mirror. It couldn't. Surely now that the moon didn't change them, it meant the curse was completely over.

"Elena, you pick it up." The tension was evident in Faolan's voice.

Elena looked at Faolan, and she knew what he was thinking. She took a deep breath but before she reached out to pick the mirror up, a phrase entered her mind and gentled her fear of losing Faolan. Elena projected the memory to everyone in the room.

"Reflect...you will see and you will be seen. Then without hesitation, you must follow the path of learning, 'tis important to our world." They all looked at each other with hope-filled eyes. Red and Lilly held hands, and Elena was reminded they were victims of the curse as well. Reflect had to mean the mirror, the mirror would tell them something, not cause the curse to kill them.

"We will not lose each other," Elena said firmly. She picked up the mirror and looked at her reflection, and as before, she saw Faolan's face in place of her own, but nothing more.

Elena took Faolan's hand and said, "We must do this together, I know we must. They looked in each other's eyes, memorizing, loving, then he reached for the silver handle, closed his big hand over her small one, and together they looked. The reflection of Faolan in the mirror was joined by another. *Elena's.*

As they watched, the scene changed, and an old man's face appeared in a swirling mist. She had a moment to wonder about how her life had changed. Once, she would have considered magick mirrors just another of her Grandda's fanciful stories. Now Elena trusted in the image, knew instantly that he was the one they were supposed to find, the one who would teach them.

The man in the mirror spoke, "Faolan of the Gailtry, it is time for you to come home. Bring your light. Care for her well on the journey, she is with child. The mirror will guide your way. Do not tarry, the time is nigh. Others will follow. You must be first.

"Red and Lilly, you have discharged your duties well and faithfully. The order thanks you for your service. You are released from your vows, and are rewarded richly." Then the mirror faded to a plain silver finish once again.

Everyone spoke at once. Red said, "Your boat is moored at a small fishing village on the coast. I will get you a map. 'Tis already prepared for your journey."

Elena said, "We need to pack right now. I'll get the list we made earlier."

Lilly said, "I'll gather food for you to take in the car. The boat has supplies, as well."

Faolan shouted, "You're pregnant?"

Okay, that one shut everybody else up.

Faolan picked Elena up around the waist and danced her around the room, yelling, "I am going to be a father. My beautiful wife is pregnant!" Elena was laughing and crying and filled with joy.

Red and Lilly were grinning like the proud grandparents they would be to the child. Elena reminded everyone that she could hardly be confirmed as pregnant after only a few days. "By the way," she added as an aside to Faolan, "I am not your wife!" She could see the desire in his eyes. He wanted the old man to be right.

"Put me down, you big buffoon." Elena slapped playfully at Faolan's chest.

"I'll make you my wife first thing on the morrow if you will be having me, Elena. Now, a boon for a boon. If you want down, you must kiss me first."

The things I must do.

Once they'd recovered from the big news that Elena might be pregnant and the bigger news that none of them was going to be swept back in time or die suddenly, it was time to get ready. It didn't seem to make sense to put off leaving even for one extra day. If someone was still watching them they might get a head start by driving at night.

Red left to run the farm while everyone else packed. When he returned, he told Faolan no one was about. So as long as there was not a bug on the car, they could leave without being followed.

Faolan and Elena decided not to bring the spell book; it

was safer back in the underground chamber than on a boat. They did want a few of the other books with them, and it made sense to bring the mirror. They would know soon enough if it was spelled to stay at the farm. They packed warm clothes, hats, gloves, and plenty of sweaters. Faolan said it would be cold on an island off the coast, and Elena believed him. She was from Phoenix, and so far, everything about Scotland was cold. Except for Faolan, she thought with a smile.

While the others finished loading, Elena stood looking out the library window, thinking how sad she was to be leaving, even if only for a while. She had grown to love the farm. It was difficult to believe how much and how quickly her life had changed. Marty and Phoenix were so far behind her now that she couldn't even remember why she'd thought she'd wanted to marry him in the first place.

She'd felt unloved and unlovable when she'd arrived, and had reconciled herself to a life of living alone. She certainly hadn't believed in nonsense like magick, Druids, or visions. She believed in Elena, in what she could do with her own mind and her will to survive. Her plan had been to live here at the farm for two years before returning to Phoenix to start her own law firm. Now Scotland was in her blood, it lived in her.

Elena put her hands to her flat stomach, wondering if it could be true. Was she really going to have Faolan's baby? Technically, it would still be in the cell dividing stage. How could the old man know? Still, she thought it must be true, not because of anything she knew, but because the old man in the mirror said so.

The island, the wren, the message. Faolan had seen the same vision. Whatever it is we're facing, we must face it together. Worthington terrifies me. He covets Faolan's power. He definitely knows who Faolan is, he kept calling him "Wolf" when he held us captive. What would

Worthington do if he knew I was pregnant with a MacGailtry? She shivered as a wave of fear passed over her.

****

Faolan entered the room behind Elena and stood watching her. She was so beautiful, he thought. He smiled as he watched her cradle her stomach, he knew she was thinking of their child. God, how he hoped the old man was right, but if he wasn't right yet, he would be soon.

He marveled that after more than three hundred years, he was free of the curse, and Elena was the one responsible for freeing him. He knew he was only just beginning to sense his own power, but what of *her* power?

When Faolan had first heard Worthington was selling her the farm, he'd been sure it was a ruse to place a spy. To see if there was still a MacGailtry somewhere. He'd followed Elena, and when he thought of the look on her face as she watched him from across the waiting area, it made him smile. It was clear she thought him an arrogant bastard.

When their gazes had locked from across the room, he'd been shaken by the strength of the attraction. What a disaster, he had thought. The woman Worthington had sent to destroy him was a woman he was unsure he could resist.

Then on the plane, he'd laughed when he'd realized she felt the attraction too. He was sure Worthington hadna counted on that. When he questioned Elena, though, he began to suspect she was exactly what she said she was. A woman scorned. How could any man turn away from such beauty? From such fire?

The thought of someone trying to kill her made his blood run cold. He believed she was still in danger from Worthington and his men. He knew Worthington had wanted Elena dead because of what happened in Phoenix. Somehow, though, while Worthington's men were chasing Elena, they had discovered Faolan, and his connection to the farm. What he couldna figure out was whether Worthington would continue to hunt them. If Worthington knew that Elena was pregnant—

That simply couldn't happen. He would take Elena far away from here... he would keep her safe. He stepped close to Elena and wrapped his arms around hers, both of them hugging her waist. Resting his head on top of hers, he said, "You have come to love this land as much as I do, haven't you, lass?"

"I really have, Faolan. I know we have to travel now, but I will always think of this as home, always long to come back here."

"Aye, lass, I have always felt the same. 'Tis time for us to leave for the now."

****

They finished packing, retrieved the map, and were ready to go shortly after midnight. They would get married at the first vicarage they found that was open in the morning. Faolan leaned against the Rover and looked back at the farm, then at Red and Lilly.

Red put his arm around his wife, but Lilly positively bristled.

"Doona' even be thinkin' to say good-bye, yet. If you think there is any way I would be missin' this wedding, Faolan MacGailtry, you are sadly mistaken! We will be goin' as far as the boat. I have already packed."

"Red, Lilly," Faolan said stepping toward them. "I canna thank you enough. I know the old man said you are released from whatever service bound you." He paused, both to search for the right words and to clear his tight throat. "No son could ask for better parents than you two. I would be pleased to have you in my life forever."

Lilly began to cry, and Faolan hugged the two of them. He looked over the tops of their heads at Elena, their gazes locking and they smiled at each other.

Elena silently mouthed "I love you."

Red followed Faolan's gaze and broke the hug to put his arm around Elena's shoulders and drew her into the little group hug, "We are proud to be your parents, Faolan, and—" he looked at Elena "—couldna be happier to be welcomin' your bride to our family."

Chapter Twenty-nine

The vicarage they found was in a tiny, out-of-the-way village. They were trying to cover their tracks a bit. The vicar was delighted to perform the ceremony with Red and Lilly as the witnesses. As far as weddings go, none could have been simpler. They hadn't worried about what they would wear or a guest list. The only decorations needed were the smiles on the faces of those gathered. Red and Lilly's love for Faolan was plain on their faces, and when they turned their gazes to Elena, she knew she was included in that love, part of their small family forever. She knew she would always be fiercely protected.

The vicar met with Faolan and Elena separately to ask if they were entering this union of free will and with love in their hearts. They were. The standard ceremony took no more than ten minutes, but when Faolan looked at Elena, time stood still. They held each other's hands, stood facing each other, and vowed to love each other for richer or poorer, through sickness and health, for better or worse, 'til death did they part.

The love in Faolan's eyes took Elena's breath away. With one arm cradling her waist, his other hand cupping her face, he bent Elena back and sealed their vows with a kiss that curled her toes, and the Earth shifted again.

The vicar wiped his brow. "Oh my."

****

They were starting on the northwest coast near the town of Uban, and they had several possible islands mapped. The little marina was brightly lit against the cold gray day. The sleek, modern yacht looked incongruous tied up at the small wooden pier, leaving the smaller fishing boats appearing shabby.

Both Faolan and Elena had restrained their hair in long braids in an attempt to keep from being blinded as their hair was whipped around their faces by the bitter wind. The gusts cut right through them as they carried boxes and suitcases from the Rover and stacked them on the pier near the boat. Lilly started taking bags onto the boat, but Elena wasn't in too much of a hurry to get aboard.

"Have any of you been to this island before?" Elena asked, already knowing the answer, and looking uncertainly toward the stormy sea.

Three "Nays" did nothing to build her shaky confidence, but Faolan swept Elena up in his massive arms and kissed her, until she forgot why she was so worried.

A side benefit of having Lilly and Red follow them all the way to the boat was Red could drive the Rover back to the farm after they helped to stow their belongings. It would be too easy to track them if they left their car at the marina, especially since they had no idea how long they would be gone.

Everyone had disposable cell phones, and the boat had a satellite phone, all in an effort to cover their tracks. They assumed Worthington was still looking for them, though they'd seen no sign of him since he'd escaped the cell. Despite Elena's misgivings, Red and Lilly were going to stay at the farm.

Once all the bags and supplies were loaded, Elena really couldn't avoid going aboard any longer. The boat was much larger than she'd thought it would be, but Faolan assured her the two of them would be able to handle it. Most of the time, they would be near land and could navigate to a safe harbor whenever necessary. The plan was to depart through the Sound of Mull, stay in protective waters for the first few days, and let Elena get her sea legs and learn about the boat. Red seemed to find that amusing. Elena was finding nothing at all funny about living on a boat.

It was time to say good-bye to Red and Lilly before they got underway. Lilly hugged Elena and patted her flat tummy, "'Twill be a beautiful baby."

Red hugged Elena next as Lilly moved on to Faolan. Whispering something too low for Elena to hear, Lilly and Faolan said their farewells. Red got a hug from Faolan too, and then they boarded the boat. Elena and Faolan called out good-byes as they stood on the deck, and watched Red and Lilly drive away.

Faolan turned to Elena and took her face in his hands, "I love you, Elena MacGailtry," and then he slanted his mouth possessively over hers. They stood on the deck of their boat, the wind whipping at them and kissed, alone for the first time as husband and wife. Never taking his lips from hers, Faolan swept Elena up into his arms and carried her below deck to the master suite.

Elena wrapped her arms around his neck and met his tongue as he thrust it into her mouth. His kisses dominated her, claimed her, owned her. They left Elena hungering for more. She held his tongue in her mouth, before releasing it. He pulled on her lower lip with his teeth then ran his tongue over her lips.

Faolan gently lowered Elena, pulling her sweater over her head, and laying her back on the bed. Her legs were draped over the side of the mattress, and he stood between them. "Och, Elena, 'tis taking all my strength to keep from making love to you right here, but we just doona' have time," he said before he kissed his way down her stomach.

Her mind was having problems connecting his words to his actions. He unbuttoned her fly, and then lifted her hips to slide her jeans and panties off. "Umm-humm," Elena responded.

"We canna take time right now. We must be getting out of here, so that we canna be tracked," he said, dragging his velvet tongue across the sensitive skin near where her hips joined her legs.

She tried again, "Uhhh…"

His fingers separated her folds, and his tongue found the nub at the center of her heat. "We must get underway," he continued to talk as though they were having a perfectly normal conversation. "Doona' fash yourself. We can stop early tonight to make anchor; then we will have all night to make love."

Elena began to pant. Licking faster, Faolan slipped his finger inside her, stoking her fire.

"When we stop for the night we can make love until dawn if you like, but we just doona' have time right now," he murmured with his lips against her womanhood. He rubbed the pad of his thumb against her sensitive nub increasing the pressure until she was moaning, on the precipice, ready to fall over the edge.

Elena grabbed for his head, holding it in place, encouraging him.

He slipped a second finger inside her, gliding in the slick heat, "Come for me, wife. Let me feel you, taste your sweetness." He put his mouth on her clitoris, kissing her, lightly flicking with his tongue. He curled his fingers, stroking a sensitive spot deep inside as he increased the pressure with his mouth.

"Ohhh, aahhh, Faolan!" Elena exploded, bucking against his mouth, her muscles squeezing his fingers inside, as spasm after spasm passed through her.

After her muscles released him, Faolan slid up, giving her a wicked grin. "No matter how much you beg, Elena, I canna take time to make love to you now." Then he laughed as he kissed her forehead and got up from the bed.

"Come on, love, get yourself up. I need to give you a tour so we can get underway."

"Faolan," she protested,

"Nay, no time to argue. Never fear, love, I will seek revenge tonight for the shameful way you have treated me this afternoon."

He was grinning, excited, electric. *Magnificent.*

Two can play at this game.

"We'll see, Faolan," Elena said, feigning a yawn. "I'm pretty tired, it's been a very long couple of days, and we were up all night. Maybe I should just go to sleep now. We'll see how I'm feeling tomorrow."

Then Elena really played dirty, knowing his penchant for winding his fingers in her hair and taking her from behind. Completely naked, she turned her back to him and rose to her knees, and pulled her hair out of its braid, mussing it with her fingers. It spilled in cascades of raven curls down her back. Then with her ass up in the air, she crawled on her hands and knees to the top of the bed. She was making a show out of fluffing her pillows and pulling back the covers.

Elena never even heard him move, but suddenly he tackled her from behind, flattening her under his hard body. He growled low in his throat, and placed open mouth kisses along her neck and shoulder, before biting down on her neck.

Elena yelped. Faolan unbuttoned his fly and tugged his pants down. In one smooth motion, he snaked his arm around her waist, lifting her so her ass was back in the air. He rubbed his erection against her wet opening, and then entered in one fierce stroke. With one hand fisted in her hair and the other holding tight to her hip, he slid into Elena. The sound of their breath was harsh, and she rocked her hips back to meet his, thrust for thrust. His heavy testicles slapped against her and his shaft filled her to the mouth of her womb, sliding back, and slamming in again. It was pure passion.

Elena looked back over her shoulder at him, "Come in me, Faolan. Fill me now."

His hand tightened in her hair as he pulled her head slightly back so he could lean down and kiss her; then he put both hands on her hips and drove them both to orgasm.

Chapter Thirty

"So you already have a sense of the master suite," Faolan said dryly "Let me show you the rest of the boat before we get underway."

Elena looked around their room. In addition to the king-size bed they'd already mussed, there was a built-in closet, a dresser with a mirror, a flat screen television, and large and small portholes that would let in light on a sunny day. A doorway led to a luxurious bathroom, including a shower big enough for two with a lovely bench against the back wall.

As they explored, Elena found there were actually two master suites on the lower deck, and the second bathroom included a Jacuzzi tub for two! There was one other room, which had been set up as a library, and even though they didn't have many of their books, their meager supply was already on the shelves and Elena's laptop was set up on the teak desk. Lilly had been busy in her brief time aboard.

The main deck was where Faolan would drive the boat, seated on something that looked more like a love seat than a captain's chair. It was cream-colored leather and faced an impressive array of screens and gadgets, fit for the bridge of a starship.

Directly behind the captain's area was the galley, a sleek gourmet kitchen that had more amenities than any kitchen Elena had ever seen. She was itching to look through the cabinets, but there would be plenty of time. The floor plan was open, and the space was large and inviting. There was a bar between the galley and the lounge.

The lounge included an area with a dining table, couches, and the latest in entertainment technology. The teak floor was covered in plush lambskin rugs. French doors led out to the deck, which had more chairs, another table for outdoor dining, and a grill.

They briefly braved the flybridge where Faolan could drive the boat from the top deck should the weather ever get warm enough. When they returned to the main deck their cheeks were flushed from the wind, and Elena's unbound hair was wild.

At first, Elena asked endless questions. Where was this? How did that work? What was that? By the time they got to the top, she'd gotten increasingly pensive. When the tour was finished, Faolan looked at her, his unease at her quietness apparent on his face.

"Tis a part of my wedding gift to you. What's wrong, love? Is it not to your liking?"

She could hardly speak. "Faolan, I married you today, and I don't know a thing about you."

He went very still, his eyes guarded, and hardly breathing, he asked, "Do you regret becoming my wife?" It came out in a choked whisper.

She realized he'd misunderstood. She placed her hands on either side of his face and looked deep in his eyes, Elena said, "I love you, Faolan. I have no regrets about marrying you. I never want to be separated from you. Don't ever doubt my love." She spoke the words firmly, sending light along with them, so he would hear and see the depth of her feelings.

"Then what is it, love? What troubles you?"

Elena knew her insecurities were part of the baggage she brought. She struggled to put her feelings into words. *How could a man like Faolan love me? Surely, there were other women he had loved in all his lifetimes. Had he loved one more than me?*

Elena glanced away, but she was still holding his face, and her thoughts were visible to him. Placing his hands on top of hers, he moved them to cover his heart, as he had done when he'd pledged his love.

"Och, lass, there is much we doona' know about each other, but know this. I was not an innocent when I met you. I am naught but a man and aye, I experienced sexual intimacy with women before you. You knew that." He looked at Elena until she finally nodded in agreement. "Elena, I told you this before, but I see you were not yet ready to believe it. Listen to me with your power. Feel what I am telling you, take it from my heart to yours." He put more pressure on their hands, where they covered his heart.

"I have never loved a woman before you, and for as long as we live, I will never love another. When I learn the ways of Druidry, I will find a way to bind us together for all eternity. What is mine is yours. You are my life."

They kissed long and tenderly, and promised each other a night of loving. For now, they needed to get underway.

Faolan taught Elena how to untie the boat and throw the ropes back on to the deck before climbing back aboard. He promised that this boat, with all of its power, was perfectly capable of waiting for her to walk back across the little gangplank, and jumping was not necessary. Once back onboard, all she had to do was pull a lever, the gangplank retracted, and they were unfettered by land. Elena was terrified of leaving the solid ground behind but tried not to show it.

****

Elena. She was his light and his life. She thought he didna know how afraid she was on the boat. She, who was fearless when fighting street punks, invading Worthington's head, and loving a wolf. She who faced death head on and won. She was afraid of being on the water. It made him love her all the more.

When Elena joined Faolan on the captain's bench, she gripped the arm of the seat so tightly that her knuckles were white. It was positively endearing. He wrapped an arm around her and spoke through each of his actions, letting her become familiar with the operation of the boat. For the next hour, they cruised slowly, within easy sight of the coastline, while he pointed out the little villages that lined the Sound of Mull. Although there weren't many, he was able to tell her stories of the boat and of the land, and that distracted her sufficiently so he could see her visibly begin to relax.

He had told Elena the truth. In all the years he had been living, he had never loved a woman before. This was as new to him as it was to her, not the sex, but the loving. He had taken a lover occasionally when the isolation of his lifestyle had been too much, but it had never eased the loneliness in his heart. Other than Red and Lilly, he had not even been able to have friends. How do you explain not aging, disappearing every full moon, and a tendency to growl?

His love for the sea had been a balm to his soul. No one was in danger while he waited out the effects of the full moon when on his boat. Red and Lilly had never loved the ocean as he had, but they would take two or three extended trips a year with him. He had found that people in marinas all over seemed to enjoy an easy camaraderie, becoming instant friends without long-term obligations. He could travel from port to port, making casual acquaintances, knowing there would always be someone to greet him, and share a draught.

The powerful engines were underused at this slow speed, but he had no desire to scare Elena. This slow, leisurely pace gave them time to talk. He told her a little of his love for the sea.

When they had put enough distance between themselves and Uban, Faolan felt it was safe to anchor. He found a small inlet that was out of direct sight of any villages, and he couldna detect any houses on the cliffs surrounding the cove. It was perfect for the night, absolutely calm and very private.

"Come, Elena, let's explore." Since they had already had fierce sex upon arrival, he thought they could wait a while before returning to the bedroom. He wanted to romance his bride tonight.

He pulled out a wine bucket and put the champagne on ice. Then he got out two Baccarat crystal rocks glasses and started to pour each of them a glass of single malt whisky. Smiling, she asked for a sparkling water instead.

Elena started opening each of the cabinets in the galley, looking in earnest. "What have you done, Faolan? Where did all this come from?"

He just smiled at her. "Help me with the table, lass, so I can show you all of it."

Faolan handed her a linen tablecloth and napkins. He snuck up behind her as she bent over the table, and reached around her with a vase of roses that had been hidden in the refrigerator. Elena sucked in a shallow breath, and turned around. Her eyes were bright with unshed tears, and full of love.

He placed the vase on the table behind her, took her face in his hands and kissed her gently. Just as she was ready to deepen the kiss, he backed away. He would not lose control early tonight. He had gifts and surprises planned for the entire evening. He had not had much time to plan, but it had been enough.

With a smile, he returned to the kitchen, leaving her standing by the table with her mouth open. He removed tonight's dinner from the refrigerator. It only needed to be heated.

"Elena, love, take a seat, start on your drink. I will be back in a few minutes."

Faolan went below deck to shower and change for dinner. He laid a black sequined gown on the bed that he had ordered for her, along with shoes, and new lingerie, that reminded him of the night they had finally made love. He hid a small velvet box under the mattress, where he could reach it when he was ready. He put two more velvet boxes in his jacket pockets and prepared to treat his bride like a queen for the night.

****

Elena took up her drink of sparkling water, just in case she really was pregnant, and sat on one of the soft leather couches. She wondered what he was planning, for it was apparent he was up to something. As she sipped her drink, she curled her legs up, and looked around the room. It was decorated in a masculine manner, but it was not unpleasant.

The wood was teak, and there were lambskin rugs tossed around in various parts of the room. The couches were white leather and the tables were ebony. All of the accessories were black or white. It would be easy to add a few touches of color. It was well lit with overhead lights, spot lighting, and lamps near the couches for reading.

She got up and played with the controls until the room was dimly lit. She walked over to examine the built-in entertainment center, under another flat screen television. She quickly gave up on the idea of playing music; the system was too complicated for her to tackle tonight.

Before she sat back down, Faolan called from below deck, "Elena, come down here, love."

Elena grinned. She suspected as much. He had gotten down into the bedroom and decided it was time to make love. She went quickly down the stairs, a smile on her face. When she saw Faolan, she lost her breath in a whoosh.

Six and a half feet of glorious man in an Armani tuxedo, white shirt, black bow tie. His hair was pulled back with a leather thong, face freshly shaved. He held his hand out to Elena, and she placed her hand in his. He pulled her close.

"I thought you might enjoy a real date tonight, my love. I hope you will forgive my presumptuousness, but I bought you a dress and laid it out on the bed. I will await you upstairs."

Her jaw was having a dropping problem. Elena couldn't decide which was more surprising, that he bought her a dress or that he went upstairs while she was taking her clothes off.

They'd been up all night and all day, driving, packing, and loading. There was no way she was going to go back upstairs before she cleaned up. She hurried through a shower, partially dried her hair with a blow dryer she'd found in the bathroom, and then pinned it into a simple twist on the back of her head. A quick swipe of mascara and lip gloss, and she was finished with the bathroom.

The bra and thong were made of the softest black silk. The dress was actually a gown and it was spectacular. Black and sequined, the bodice was a halter with a low-cut front, and the back was bare to the bottom of her spine. The skirt clung to her hips, before flaring out and sweeping the floor. Everything was a perfect fit. She dressed quickly, anxious to get back to Faolan.

At the top of the stairs, she saw Faolan before he knew she was there. *Or not.* With his wolf senses, he would know Elena was there, but he didn't turn around. He was standing at the large glass doors at the rear of the lounge, looking out at the star-filled night. He had placed candles around the room, and dimmed the lights even more. Diana Krall was singing about flying to the moon and playing among the stars. Faolan looked as though he knew exactly what she meant.

Elena walked up behind him and slipped her arms around his waist. Pressing her face to his back, she inhaled the scent of him. It was the part of him she'd met first, and it still called to her soul. He placed his hands over hers and leaned back into her embrace.

"Look up, Elena. Look at the stars. You'll never be seeing them brighter."

Elena laughed. "From where I stand, the whole night is one broad expanse of your back."

They changed places, Elena leaning back against his chest, and he wrapped his arms around her as they looked up to the stars together. He pointed out constellations and planets to the south, before turning them around to face the north. Elena gasped. The northern horizon was filled with colors. The Northern Lights.

They stood and watched for a long time. Somehow, while she was watching the sky, cradled in Faolan's arms, some pieces of a puzzle were falling into place. When she had met Faolan, they had been on the move. Shortly after, she'd moved to the farm and was busy making it hers. She'd commented once regarding his home, but he had deflected the conversation, saying he would leave once she was out of danger.

With all the things that had happened over the last month, she'd not given much thought to his home, his life before her. She finally realized that although this was a new boat, purchased for the two of them, his life must have revolved around the sea. She told him what she was thinking. Taking her shoulders, he turned her around, his tawny eyes glowing in the candlelight.

"Aye, Elena, I lived much of the time on my boat. I hope someday you will come to love it as much as I do. I felt my other boat was too small for the two of us to spend a great deal of time on, so I purchased this one. I can get another if this is too small," he added hastily.

She laughed at his offer. "I think I'll get used to this one first, but there is so much to learn about you."

"Aye, lass, and I will start telling you tonight, but first, let me look at you." Then he stepped back.

His breath came fast as he started at the top, and scorched her with his eyes as they raked down her body. His gaze lingered on her breasts on the return trip. He brushed his fingertips down the exposed length of her neck to her cleavage, and back up again. He stepped back, shaking his head, his brows furrowed.

"What's wrong, Faolan? I think the dress is beautiful. I can't believe you would buy me something like this. Don't you like it?"

Still shaking his head, he said, "'Tis not complete. The

neckline is missing something." Then he pulled a box out of his pocket and flipped it open with a flourish. There was a stunning emerald pendant in a platinum setting accented with diamonds. Her eyes flew to his, and she caught him watching her hungrily.

"Faolan, it's spectacular. I don't know what to say. The boat, the dress, the necklace." Elena was sputtering. He placed a finger to her lips to silence her, and then followed with his mouth, before turning her around again.

"Let me see it on you, lass." He took the necklace and fastened it for her. It nestled between her breasts at the perfect height. "Christ, Elena. You are breathtaking. The color of the emerald made me think of your eyes, but where it settles on you makes me think of other things."

He followed that thought by tracing the chain with his finger, then gently brushing the top of her breasts. He kissed her neck, before biting the sensitive cord that connected to her shoulder. She shivered with anticipation.

The song changed just then and Krall was singing "Look of Love." Faolan took Elena in his arms and danced her around the lounge, looking deeply into her eyes. He stroked her cheek with a finger, caressed her back, nuzzled her neck. She melted from the heat of his love.

With a visible effort, he pulled himself back when the song ended and led her to the table. Popping the cork on the champagne, he poured them each a glass and then offered a toast.

"To my wife. We begin our journey together this day. You loved me for who I was, and you made me into who I am. Your inner radiance lights my way and completes me. Separately, we were just two people; together, we are a force of nature. I love you, Elena, more than life itself. To an eternity of our love." They drank to their future.

The rest of the evening was filled with love. While they took turns feeding each other chunks of lobster dipped in butter, he told her stories of growing up with his family and later of Red and Lilly. He explained he had continued to age normally until he was about thirty, and then nothing had changed for hundreds of years. He told her of how he had discovered boats and the kindred transients he met at small villages and marinas around Scotland. It had started as a safe haven and developed into a passion.

Elena needed to put the concern she'd hidden earlier to rest. *Who'd paid for all this?* Coming at it sideways, she tentatively asked about working once their lives settled down.

Faolan laughed gently, "Is that what has been concerning you, lass? Who paid for all this?" he swept his arm, gesturing at the room. "My clan had money enough, and you can make a lot of money in three hundred years, if you live simply. Neither of us e'er needs to work." Then he was quick to reassure Elena that she could work if she so chose, he didna mean to dictate.

Elena thought about that for a minute. She had never imagined herself in a life where work was an option. She thought she might like to try a life of leisure. Or rather a life of raising a family, with him by her side.

She placed her hands on her stomach, thinking about children. "Do you think I could really be pregnant?"

"Aye, lass, I think it's a good possibility. I am sure the old man would know from his Druid ways, and they'll not be wrong."

"And you're okay with that? With us having a baby so soon?"

"Aye, Elena, 'tis a dream come true to be having children with you. I would like a lot of children. Maybe a dozen or more."

Elena's head shot up in shock, until she realized he was teasing her. "Maybe three or four, if I have anything to say about it," she countered, laughing. Smiling into each other's eyes, they knew they would have plenty of time to continue making their respective cases.

He ran his fingers down her exposed neck and pulled another jewelry box out of his pocket. "'Tis just another little something."

Astonished, Elena opened the box to find emerald earrings to match the necklace he had already given her. She put them on and they hung gracefully, accenting her long neck perfectly, especially with her hair worn up as it was.

They finished dinner and cuddled together on the couch. Elena had never experienced such luxury. She was sure the gifts tonight must have totaled in the tens of thousands of dollars. She was speechless. She did the only thing she could think of, and kissed him. He pulled her onto his lap, and they finally let nature take her course.

Later in bed, after they were both replete in their loving, Faolan pulled out one more gift, this one was tucked under the mattress. Elena started to protest, but he covered her mouth with his until she quit trying to talk.

"A mere boon, lass. Doona' fash yourself over it, 'tis but a trinket, one to be worn for fun."

When she opened it, she found a charm bracelet, already containing three charms: a boat, a heart engraved with their wedding date, and a wolf, with amber gems for eyes.

"I will add our babe's to it when 'tis time, love."

Elena would treasure this gift the most. It was the loveliest of wedding nights.

Chapter Thirty-one

Liam was standing in front of Worthington's desk at the Edinburgh office of Worthington, Tyler, and Walters. The office was starkly furnished in a modern motif with black slate, black leather, and chrome. As a corner office of a five-story building, two walls were floor-to-ceiling windows. The third wall contained a wet bar and bookcases, and behind them, secrets.

"What do you mean they lost them?" snarled Worthington. Shaking his head, the older man took a deep breath, pulled himself up to his full height, and said, "This is well out of hand. There is nothing that we need them for now, Liam. Let it go. I have other, more important jobs for you." Worthington led the way over to a seating area and invited Liam to sit while he turned to the bar to pour drinks.

"Some on the council have begun to question your activities."

Liam sucked in his breath and waited.

"Fear not, Liam. I have laid the blame on a young author who heard rumors of magick and secrets at the farm. These rumors have survived for a millennium; it was not hard to imagine some enterprising journalist uncovered them. We are both safe; however, I am convinced it is time to distance ourselves from any connection with the wolf for now."

"I don't like that the...Master," Liam sneered the title, "feels the need to concern himself with our business."

"I agree. It is time to end this most ignoble period in the history of the Bresal Etarlam, the rightful Druid sect. Next month, the high council will meet on Beltane, then we shall bring forward our most important...proposal. We have much to do to prepare, and I need you to focus your energies."

Liam looked at his uncle for a very long time, before replying, "Aye, 'tis good to move forward, at last." Both men sipped their drinks, each lost in thought.

Liam was relieved his uncle would move on from his obsession with the little bitch his stupid cousin had been mixed up with. He'd insisted that they follow Steve's plan to make her murder appear to be random street violence, which was not Liam's forte. However, Steve was the most senior of Uncle Martin's personal inner circle, and a trusted associate. It left Liam feeling inept, and he'd performed poorly in his tasks related to Elena and the farm. Magick would have been so much easier. Ordering Martin IV to clean up his own mess would have been even better.

Liam was careful not to think about his cousin, young Martin, when he was around his uncle, so he would put those thoughts away for now. It was time for him to concentrate on the plans for Beltane, the night of the welcome feast for the first day of summer. He knew how long Uncle Martin had been planning for the day he would assume his rightful place as Master of the order of the Etarlam. Liam would do everything in his power to make that happen. He understood the need for power, for taking one's rightful place. He also understood lines of succession.

****

What a monumental waste of time the search for the mirror had turned out to be. It was never intended to be used by anyone other than a MacGailtry. Martin studied Liam and realized he'd made a tactical error in restricting the methods he could use to kill the woman. Liam was an incredibly talented apprentice; the potential for great power was there, just barely under control. It had cost Liam much to use conventional methods and outsiders to correct the mess created by the boy. Perhaps it would soon be time to claim Liam as his own.

The girl. Elena. Who would have thought she was made of such magick? He was sure she hadn't known. His son certainly hadn't known; he didn't know much of anything and certainly nothing about the Order. Yet here she was. Not only did she survive the three attacks, she'd fooled him in the cell. How had she survived? How had she lifted the curse? He had no doubt now that it was she who had lifted the curse, and not the wolf, although he had untapped power as well. He would figure out how to harness their power. Using power intended for others was his specialty.

Worthington cleared his throat, bringing them both back to the present. He flipped the switch on a small box on the table, which sent unseen and unheard waves into the room and began speaking a strange mix of Gaelic, Scots, and some other tongue. He wanted to make sure his words remained secure and that no one at the firm could eavesdrop. He was not expecting others to be around on this Sunday afternoon, but you could never be too careful.

They put their heads together and spoke of unspeakable

acts. They had spent the last five years collecting the right spells and potions. Certain artifacts had been imbued with false power. At the feast of Beltane when the council next met, the power would recognize its true master, and Worthington would finally hold the exalted position of Master. As he always should have.

****

Elena awoke to another morning nestled in Faolan's arms and thought life couldn't get any better. They'd been on the boat for more than a week now and each day passed in a happy glow. The concerns that had plagued them at the farm had fallen away. It was beautiful, peaceful, and private. So far, neither the maps nor the mirror had provided any insight as to their destination.

They spent their days and nights finding ways to pleasure each other. They stayed to themselves, rarely stopping at the marinas and villages that dotted the small islands, because they needed to keep their location private if someone were looking for them.

After a week at sea, Elena had become quite the sailor, in her opinion. She was learning to read the night sky and the nautical maps. She even drove the boat while Faolan continued his research. They checked the mirror several times each day, always seeing their images. On the eighth day at sea, the mirror showed clouds instead of their reflection.

"It must mean we're getting closer. Come help me look at the maps again." Examining the charts, they saw an area of the map that showed several small islands that formed a crescent shape, going from largest to smallest, north to south. At the farthest end of the crescent the islands faded away to a series of marks on the map. The entire section of the chart was covered with symbols indicating previous shipwrecks and submerged rocks, and nothing remotely resembling an island. *Oh God, I just know that's where we have to go.*

The weather raged around them for the next two days, pitching the boat violently, cresting the waves, slamming them brutally into the troughs. The navigation alarm sounded continuously, increasing Elena's tension a hundred-fold. She imagined jagged rocks beneath the boat, reaching for them, calling them to share the fate of the hundreds of shipwrecked sailors who had come before and died. In truth, there was not much imagination necessary, since the black rocks poked up on either side of the boat in the trough of the waves.

Faolan didn't attempt to persuade her everything was all right. His jaw was tense, his forearms corded with the strain of maintaining their course. The mirror clearly showed their path, a light gray trail, surrounded by a darker mist. They sat together on the captain's chair, drawing strength from each other.

By the afternoon of the second day, they were both exhausted. Elena had been constantly sick, unable to keep down any food. Sleep had been impossible; they couldn't set anchor, and neither was willing to leave the other to navigate alone. Elena checked the mirror again, monitoring their progress, when she noticed the gray pathway through the mist had changed. It was getting progressively lighter than the surrounding darkness.

Despite the lighter path reflected in the glass, the dense fog in front of them was the worst they'd yet encountered. Although the clock said it was mid-afternoon, the darkness settled around them. Slowing the engines even further, they inched through the near total darkness. It was eerie. No sounds penetrated the air, not even the water against the sides of the boat. The silence was unnerving.

Without warning, all power on the boat died, and Faolan desperately tried to restart the engine and regain control. Without the navigation system and engines, they would be tossed around and killed against the rocks.

"Faolan, look!"

"I canna just now, Elena," Faolan gritted through clenched teeth.

"No, Faolan, look at the mirror," Elena said urgently, as she held it out to him. The mirror had changed to a near blinding light, with no discernible image.

The boat jerked forward as though someone was tugging a string attached to the bow, pulling them through the clouds that surrounded them. They rushed up to the flybridge, straining to see through the fog. The air was not the bone-chilling dampness Elena had expected, the balminess made her think of the monsoon season back home. Faolan put his arm around her protectively, and Elena circled her arm around his waist. Side-by-side they stood, watching, and waiting.

Chapter Thirty-two

Breaking through the mists was a lot like what Elena pictured arriving at heaven might be like. She wouldn't have been surprised to hear celestial trumpets in the background while an angelic choir heralded their arrival. The clouds that had surrounded their boat for days suddenly separated and the sun shone down on them, the warmth caressing her skin. She looked out at a land that was green and fertile, a valley surround by gentle hills, with a backdrop of a soaring mountain.

"It's lovely," Elena breathed.

"Aye, lass. I canna begin to describe the feelings it causes to arise in me." His brogue thickened with the depth of his emotions. She looked at him, moved to see the sheen of unshed tears in his eyes. His big hand clasped tightly around Elena's, and she could feel tremors from the strength of his emotions.

A small wren, like the one from their visions, landed on the railing near them. It peered curiously at Elena and Faolan before flying off. As the boat drew inexorably closer to the dock, there was a man standing there, where previously it had been empty. He was dressed in flowing cornflower blue robes with long white hair and a rather wispy long beard. It was their man from the mirror.

Where did he come from?

The boat glided to a stop at the dock, and Elena tugged Faolan's hand towards the stairs. He pulled her close, kissed the top of her head, and whispered, "Stay behind me for now. I doona' believe there is any danger, but I willna take a chance with you."

They climbed down to the main deck, and Faolan called a greeting, just as he had at every marina, "Good day to you. May we join you ashore?"

"Aye, lad, and bring your lass. Welcome home."

They crossed the small gangplank to the dock, and Faolan thrust his hand forward, saying, "Faolan MacGailtry."

The older man looked surprised for a moment, and then reached with his own hand, saying, "I am Earnan." The men shook hands; then Earnan peeked around Faolan and grinned impishly, "Welcome, Elena. It seems you are well protected from the danger I present."

Elena stepped around Faolan, and Earnan took her proffered hand, kissing it with a grand sweeping gesture. His eyes were a vibrant shade of cornflower blue that matched his robes. He appeared to be in his mid-sixties, tall and slight, with a bookish air about him.

The sounds of yipping and yapping filled the air as a tiny ball of fur barreled down the hill until she reached Faolan, where she promptly rolled over on her back, feet in the air, tongue lolling.

"Hussy?" Faolan asked wonderingly. Bending down to rub the dog's belly, he scanned the shore, obviously looking for Brigid. Although the scenery was lovely, there was no indication from where the dog might have come.

"Come, Elena and Faolan. We know you have many questions. We will answer them over the course of the evening. Let me take you to the castle." Faolan and Elena exchanged glances, before turning as one to look at Earnan. With another dramatic gesture, he swept his arm toward the gently rolling hills, and a majestic castle was revealed.

The castle appeared to rise from the base of the mountain, nestled in its protective embrace. It was white stone, with turrets and towers, and a massive wall protecting against invasion from the sea. From their position, it towered above the shoreline, visible for miles on a clear day. Yet they'd not seen it, even from the dock, until Earnan waved his arm.

Elena gasped. "It's lovely! Where did it come from? How many rooms does it have? How many people live here?" She would have gone on, but Faolan interrupted with a question of his own.

"How is it you kept it hidden from our view?"

"'Tis but a parlor trick, my young friend. I am surprised that with the skills of your wee wife you need ask. 'Tis naught more than her power used on a grander scale. Look behind you. See you the horizon?" He waited to continue until they both nodded.

"How many days since you last saw the sun from your boat? Did you see any sign of a navigable waterway? 'Tis but one way we protect ourselves. A Druid skill of imagery. Come now, we have prepared your welcome."

Faolan and Elena again exchanged a long look, and Elena sensed they both felt comfortable in following the old man. They followed Earnan with Hussy announcing their arrival. Elena struggled to keep pace with the men, their long legs making short work of the hill. Of course, much of her lagging behind was simply due to the fact she wanted to see everything. Her head swung this way and that, trying to take it all in.

The castle was two stories on the outer wings, three stories for the keep, and the turrets on each corner rose to the equivalent of a five or six story building. It had been hewn from the lightest colored stone and bleached by time to a soft white, the color of clouds against a summer's day. If it had ever been surrounded by a second outer wall or moat there was no sign of either now. The inner wall was intact, but the gateway between the two unmanned guard towers was open and didn't look as though it was ever raised to close the castle walls.

They followed a smooth pathway that snaked up the hillside, the switchbacks reducing the rate of incline needed to reach the castle at the top of the hill. Elena noticed that there was a small metal track similar to those used in mines that ran straight up the hill from the dock to the castle. That must be how they brought in supplies, she thought, relieved she wouldn't have to carry the luggage up the hill on her back like a pack mule.

As they quickly paced through the courtyard, Elena barely had time to take in the large garden plots of vegetables and a rose garden with stone benches and a fountain. She was giving herself whiplash, trying to see everything at once. She couldn't wait to explore every inch of the extensive gardens and stables.

The massive oak door to the castle was designed to open from the top, swinging down and outward to create a twenty-foot entry ramp. Earnan walked directly to the door, which would surely have crushed him if the door swung down. Nearly invisible until you were right up against it was a smaller, more traditional doorway cut into the original oak slab.

They entered the keep through the great hall and came to a

stop. Earnan had provided little in the way of commentary as they'd walked. Elena had wanted to keep up a steady stream of questions as they climbed the hill, but she was worried about Faolan. He was becoming increasingly withdrawn; she could scarcely sense him. She felt the wolf very close to the surface, and placed a comforting hand against his back.

Apparently, she was not the only one who sensed his unease, because Earnan turned around and looked at Faolan, saying "Peace, brother."

Faolan shivered, his eyes were wild, nostrils flared, as though scenting nearby danger. Or prey. It was as close as Elena had ever seen him come to losing control. She needed to bring him back. Speaking softly, Elena reached up to cradle his face in her hands, urging him to look at her, to look into her eyes. He came back by degrees; slowly his eyes regained their focus, his breathing slowed, and his muscles began to relax.

Finally, with a great shuddering breath, his eyes locked with Elena's, and she felt him return, sensed his feelings again. He was overwhelmed by his emotions, his fear rolled off him in waves, the worry that his wolf still might not be controllable. As if seeking answers to the question of Elena's safety, Faolan looked at Earnan.

Without turning away from Faolan, Elena asked Earnan, "I wonder if it would be possible for us to go to our room for a while, if you plan for us to stay here in the castle, that is."

Earnan spoke directly to Faolan, ignoring Elena's question.

"Doona' fear, Faolan. You wouldna have hurt her. You must trust me on that. You must trust yourself. There are two things you need to see now before I can leave you alone."

Faolan gave Earnan a long, searching look, glanced at Elena, then back at Earnan and gave a curt nod.

Earnan led the way across the great hall, which Elena

belatedly realized was covered with portraits. He came to a section of the back wall, and Faolan's quick intake of breath was audible as he looked up at a portrait of himself.

No, that wasn't right, Elena thought. At first glance, she thought it was Faolan before she noticed the slight differences, the eye color, the shape of his jaw were not the same.

"'Tis my father," he said, his voice unsteady. "Why would there be a portrait of my—"

"Faolan…." A woman's voice came from behind them.

Faolan's head whipped around to look at the beautiful woman. She was wearing emerald colored robes, and looked to be in her mid-fifties. She had tawny gold eyes with reddish-blonde hair, streaked with white and pulled into a chignon on the back of her head. She was regal, and Elena realized with the coloring and the way they held themselves that the woman and Faolan could be related.

Faolan followed a different train of thought, his eyes widened, breath quickened, and his voice was raspy as he croaked out, "Brigid?"

The woman held a hand out to him, and he slipped his into hers and let her lead him away from the portrait. She took Faolan toward the stairs, speaking softly, never releasing his hand.

"'Tis sorry I am we had to tell you this way, Faolan, but we need you to know you are safe now. The old woman you have known was also me, just with the imagery applied. You know me. You can tell by the portrait that your father was known here." She stopped outside a door and turned to face a very stunned looking Faolan. "This is a place for you, a home for you. I wouldna put you in danger; you are safe here."

She turned to look at Elena then. "Elena, dear, I know we doona' know each other well, but you have seen my image in your visions. We saw the sisterhood together; this is the start of your journey. Tonight is for the two of you; some time to accept you are here. We willna give you more tonight, we will start on the morrow. Know that you both are safe.

"We have had your bags brought to your room, and we will have food sent up, so there is no need to leave unless you want to. Earnan and I will be in the drawing room tonight if you decide to join us after dinner."

As Brigid turned to walk away, Elena again noticed the similarities between her and Faolan, in the eyes, and the way they moved. She wondered how they were related, and wondered if Faolan knew. She jumped slightly as Brigid's voice spoke softly in her head, "Please doona' tell him that tonight. I will tell him on the morrow."

Faolan, completely unaware of the mental exchange said, "Let's go inside," and opened the door to the most luxurious suite either of them had ever seen. They stepped into a sitting room fit for royalty with brocaded chairs and a settee, a large hearth, and a museum quality tapestry hanging on the wall. There were fresh flowers in a crystal vase, and a basket with fruit and snacks, and a tray with glasses and decanters. Everything you might find in a five-star hotel. *Not that I'd ever been in a five-star hotel.*

A king-size four-poster bed dominated the bedroom, and the bathroom had an even larger claw-footed tub than the one at the farm. *Yummy.* Someone had brought their belongings from the boat; their clothes and toiletries were all here, ready for them to use.

Faolan had been strangely quiet since he had nearly lost control earlier, but he was in control now. He wrapped her in his arms, pressing his front to her back, holding her close. With one hand, he pulled her hair aside, so he could kiss and bite her neck. He placed his other hand between her legs and pulled her back tight against his erection. Without a word passing between them, they made love, finding comfort in the familiarity of each other.

Much later that night, Elena woke as she felt Faolan leave the bed.

"What's wrong?"

"Och, lass, I need to run. I believe we are safe, but today the wolf was close to appearing without my intention. I need to stretch, to taste the air. Fear not, love, I will return anon."

"I'll be waiting," she said and kissed him.

Chapter Thirty-three

Faolan and Elena felt completely refreshed after their long night together in the castle. She'd been waiting for him when he returned from his run around the grounds. While sharing a late snack from the food sent up earlier in the evening, he'd described the grounds and surrounding hillsides. He was electric, cheeks flushed, hair wind-blown, eyes sparkling. He needed to run as his wolf more often, it was still a necessary part of him, even without the curse.

When they'd joined Earnan and Brigid for breakfast in the great hall, they'd found them both dressed far less dramatically than they had been the previous day. The robes had been replaced by jeans; Brigid's topped by a jade green silk tee, while Earnan favored a faded denim button-down. A banquet of food was set to the side of the large table, raising questions of who had prepared all of it. For that matter, who had brought the luggage and left the tray of food outside the room?

The large dining hall echoed with an uncomfortable silence. Elena started to throw out inane questions, hoping that eventually one of the other three would pick up the conversation in a more meaningful way. "Are there servants here?"

"Aye, lass," Earnan answered, "'Tis the MacMartin family who stays here on the island, except for occasional trips to the mainland." It was actually seventeen MacMartin's, Elena found out later.

"How is it so much warmer here than it was in Scotland or on the boat?" she asked next, giving voice to another thing that had her curious.

Eyes sparkling, Brigid said, "It could be because we are in the middle of the Gulf Stream," she said, "The west coast of Scotia has long been renowned for its more temperate climes." Then turning her head regally to look at Earnan, "Or it could be because Earnan likes to muck about with the weather." An unmistakable laugh in her rich voice. "What do you think, dear Earnan?"

Earnan grinned his impish grin again and said, "Aye, maybe a wee bit. I doona' like my bones cold."

Faolan, who had been loading his plate during this exchange, joined those seated at the table. Before beginning to eat, he looked back and forth between Earnan and Brigid, before locking his gaze on Brigid. "You first. You have a lot of explaining to do, woman."

Brigid turned a brilliant smile on Faolan, "Aye, Faolan, I do owe you a story or two. I have been knowing you, since you were born," which caused Elena to gasp, considering he was over three hundred years old!

"Aye, 'tis true. I used a spell of imagery to change my appearance to stay near you all this time. You have known me as Brianna, Brigit, Brenda, Brighde, and now Brigid, which is my true name. The face you see before you now is my true form. Like you, I have aged very well over the years." She laughed delightedly before continuing.

"It was my role to read the signs and to guide you. I am Druid born and trained, with a special talent for prophecy. When I wasn't needed near you I would come here to the island. Lilly and Red were your caretakers, and they did an excellent job. You have grown into a fine man, and now that you are here for your training, you will make an exceptionally strong Druid.

"We could not train you while you were cursed. It would have been far too dangerous. Now we need you to begin your training immediately, there are skills you must have before this Beltane."

"Why?" Faolan asked between bites. He must have been famished; Elena had never seen him eat like this.

"Och, lad," Earnan answered him, "There is a prophecy about this Beltane and the return of the Druids. Know ye the stories of the Druids who were scattered by the Tuatha Dé Danann?"

"Aye, but Elena may not," he answered, looking at Elena.

"I've read a lot of different stories about the Druids recently. I'd rather hear it from you," she told Earnan.

"Well, neither of you know all of it, so I will be tellin' you some of it now, and more will come out during your training. I'll not be keeping secrets, just some of the information will only make sense after you know certain other things."

Earnan looked at Elena and said, "The Tuatha Dé Danann, the Fae," he paused and Elena nodded for him to continue. She knew those were other names for fairies.

"The Tuatha Dé Danann and the Druids occupied Scotia thousands of years ago. There are many legends surrounding both groups. We will be telling you what we know about their histories, but for now, you need to know they were both verra powerful in different ways. They were also verra fascinated with each other, and began to form alliances, liaisons.

Earnan continued, his voice somber, "There were a handful of men and women that formed the Druid council, and they were kept secret from the world to protect the magick. It was their job to sit in judgment should any Druid abuse his or her power. The council became complacent and went from visiting the outside world every year, to only venturing from their hidden spot every four or five years.

"The members of the Tuatha Dé royal court, along with their Druid consorts grew completely out of control, corrupted by power, and the Druid council was not there to see it happening. There was much coveting, and each side taught the other secrets that should ne'er have been shared. Through their unholy alliances, wars, disease, and famines were used to control vast parts of the land, to try to prove superiority. Mankind and the very fabric of our world was at risk."

Earnan stopped, apparently to make sure Elena and Faolan were following his story. He need not have worried about her, she was mesmerized.

"By the time the Druid Council heard of the crimes against nature and man that were being committed, the problem was too wide-spread for them to handle on their own. They petitioned the Fae Queen of the Seelie Court for help, and together they formed the last Fae-Druid alliance. They secured away the Druid writings and magick, and then the Queen scattered the Druids throughout the world. Without their magick, the Druids lost their influence, and nature was left to her own."

Cornflower blue eyes met theirs, steady and calm, but Elena felt the power of the gaze reach into her soul. Elena glanced at Faolan, who appeared as fascinated as she was by the tale. Everyone sat there looking at each other, waiting for Earnan to tell what happened next, because clearly, not all the Druids died.

"So go on, what happened?" Faolan prodded.

"The Council returned to their…hiding place and held a summit to decide how to keep the Druid knowledge from becoming extinct. During this summit, a great Druid prophetess saw that the Druids would again be needed, that their powers must not be lost for all time. It was decided that the council members would return to the land of Scotia, to their clans, forsaking the influence other Druids had sought. These remaining Druids would continue their clan, training only their direct decedents, serving only that which their eye could behold.

"From what we know of the prophecy, it is more important than ever that those with the potential for power, like yourself, receive their training. We are reaching out to the other known clans, but time has diminished our numbers and our skills. Few have kept to the old ways, most have moved on, their lines extinct or no longer producing offspring capable of power. We have feared for a while now that there may not be enough left of the council descendants to meet the needs of the prophecy."

Brigid, who had been listening quietly, sat forward, ready to take up the tale. "This is where you come in, my dear," she said looking directly at Elena.

"Me?" Elena squeaked.

"Aye. Faolan told me about Worthington turning the land over to you. Like him, I was suspicious of you, and I encouraged him to follow you. However, when he brought you to my shop, I knew right away there was something he didn't know. There was light pouring from you. It was blindingly bright. It took me aback. I read your tea leaves, just to be sure, but there was no mistaking."

Faolan, finally finished with his breakfast, pushed his chair over next to Elena, and draped his arm over her shoulders. "That was the day you first called her my light, Brigid. The day you realized she would help break the curse of the wolf."

"Aye, lad, but that was not all I thought I saw. I came here to consult with Earnan and the books. We never thought it was possible, but it was hard to argue with my vision."

She turned back to Elena. "Then you were lost, and the sisterhood visited you. I visited you. I didna know how 'twas possible, but it was and you are." She finished by looking at Elena as though Elena could possibly have a clue what Brigid was talking about.

"I don't understand. What are you saying?" Elena looked from Brigid to Earnan and finally to Faolan, who looked stunned.

"Really, you all seem to know something I don't. What in the world is going on?"

Faolan looked at her with something new in his eyes.

Brigid almost whispering said, "Reach out, Elena, taste the air."

Sitting there, wondering why everyone was looking at her so expectantly made Elena feel cranky. She set her feelings to the side and tried to taste it, as Brigid had said. At first, she just felt stupid, as if they had already finished the test, and she was the only one still working. Then there was a bit of a whooshing sound in her head and she could hear three voices as clear as anything, all saying "Druid."

Elena whipped her head around to face Brigid, who answered in her head, before she could ask, "Aye, lass, you were born of the Druid power."

How could this be? I am Druid? Did that mean my Grandda— and what does that mean for Faolan and me?

Then they all spoke at once, excitement filling the air. Faolan and Elena were asking questions, Earnan and Brigid were trying to answer them as best they could.

"It seems likely now that some of the original bloodlines survived in those who no longer held the sacred knowledge," Earnan explained. We doona' ken how many more are out there. We do know that with the coming of this year's Beltane, there is to be a new time of Druidry, a rebirth. Brigid has seen that the time of the prophecy is now."

"The journey you will take is along the path to become fully trained in the art of Druidry. You are not to be alone on this journey. There are others waiting to have the path open to them. 'Tis our duty to find them and bring them home."

****

Faolan and Elena spent the rest of the day together outdoors in the surprisingly warm sunshine that they now knew was thanks to Earnan. Although there was much to learn, everyone agreed it wouldn't hurt for Faolan and Elena to rest after their trip. They needed the time to explore their new home and to come to terms with what they'd learned.

They walked hand in hand, exploring the castle and grounds. In the inner courtyard, they wandered through gardens. Even in the coldest of winters, the courtyard would capture the sun and warmth of the day, so at the very least there would be fresh salad year-round. There were three plots currently filled with vegetables, and two lying fallow.

The heavenly smell of the rose garden reached them long before they actually entered the formal paths through one of the arbor-covered entryways. Each path led toward the fountain at the center of the garden. They found a bench under a white wooden trellis covered with an abundance of miniature climbing roses. They sat for a while on the bench and watched the water trickle down the tiers of the fountain.

Plucking a peach colored rose from a nearby bush, Faolan brushed Elena's face with its soft petals then lightly pressed his lips to hers. "Lass, one night verra soon, I am going to bring you down here and cover your naked body with rose petals. Though the splendor of these roses will surround us, 'twill fade when compared to the beauty of you. I will make love to you here, my sweet Elena, under the stars." Elena got lost in that idea for a while, and Faolan led her from the garden by the hand.

They walked over to the small paddock that was in front of the stables. Faolan's arm was gentle around her waist as they watched a new colt wobble around on shaky legs while his mother nuzzled him. Faolan surrounded Elena with his arms, her back to his, his chin on her head, as they spoke softly of the joy of creating a new life.

The main paddock was visible through the open stalls, and extended beyond the castle walls. There were a dozen horses in the stables, and chickens running everywhere. In fact, there was an entire barnyard of animals, all tended to by various MacMartin's.

They entered the tack room; the walls were covered with the paraphernalia found in any stable: ropes, bridles, whips, and various tools all hanging from sturdy hooks. Horse blankets and saddles covered the sawhorses and the air was an intoxicating mixture of smells, of leather, sawdust, and hay.

"Do you see that saddle over there?" Faolan whispered to Elena, his breath hot against her ear. "I am going to carry you down here one night verra soon, and tear your lacy night gown from your beautiful body. Then I am going to bend you over that saddle and bury myself in you. I will love you until you scream for me to let you come. And lass, if you doona' please me, I might just take down one of those small leather whips, and punish you," he growled, his voice rough with desire. Elena shivered, and was lost in that image even longer than the last one.

Faolan led Elena on shaky legs to a large clearing that held a circle of standing stones behind the castle. Faolan told Elena the ring would have to be at least three thousand years old, and maybe, if it was from the Neolithic period it could be nearly nine thousand years old.

"What are they for, Faolan? I mean, I've seen the specials about Stonehenge on the Discovery Channel. I know there are many controversial theories, but are they really for time travel? Did they come from outer space?"

Smiling down at her, Faolan said, "I believe we will find out soon enough, but aye, lass, I expect they can move people through dimensions of some sort. Either time or space, or maybe both. Druids have many special talents and much knowledge.

"I could show you some of my Druid knowledge, if you would only follow me over there to that lovely copse of trees. There we will be out of sight of the castle."

Then he kissed her so thoroughly, he left no doubt what type of knowledge he wanted to share.

Chapter Thirty-four

Brigid and Earnan were waiting for them when they entered the keep, so they'd quickly made themselves presentable and headed to the drawing room for cocktails. There were several bottles of fifty-year old Macallan, only the best for these Druids. Elena chose to stay with the sparkling water, Brigid had a glass of merlot, and the men enjoyed their single malt.

They kept the conversation casual, speaking of the grounds, recounting the details of the boat trip, and wondering how things were at the farm.

Then Faolan asked, "Will we be starting our training on the morrow, then?"

Earnan and Brigid exchanged looks.

"What's wrong?" Elena asked.

With a sigh, Brigid looked at Elena, "Although I have seen you with child, I canna see everything. I doona' think it will be wise for you to train while you are pregnant. We Druid women always refrained from doing much magick while with child."

Brigid's heart lurched with an emotion so sharp it bruised Elena's own heart, their gazes locked, and Elena was suddenly certain.

"Tell him," Elena thought into the older woman's mind. Brigid continued to look at Elena for a long time, her thoughts colored with uncertainty, and some other strong emotion Elena couldn't fathom. Faolan, who seemed to be waiting for Elena to say something about not being allowed to train, suddenly became aware of the incredible tension between the two women.

Seeking to be a peacemaker he soothed, "Elena, fear not, you will have time to train after the baby is born. Canna she at least read the books, gather the history?" he asked Brigid.

"Tell him…"

With a deep sigh, Brigid said, "Tis not the problem, Faolan. There is aught I must tell you. Your Elena is a clever lass. She knew right away." Sighing again, she glanced at Elena who nodded encouragement.

Brigid began, "Before your Da married your mother, he was here on the island, receiving his Druid training. I was also here in training, and we did everything together. He challenged me, and I challenged him. We were well matched. We became lovers and made plans to spend our lives together. He returned home before I did, only to discover his betrothal had been announced in an arranged marriage."

Faolan went very still and watched Brigid through narrowed eyes.

"Your grandfather was a poor estate manager. He was an even weaker Druid and promised his son's title and marriage in exchange for some much needed gold. Your father was a man of honor and accepted his father's obligations. He was married before I returned home.

"When next we spoke, he learned I was pregnant with his child. He spoke to his wife. They agreed to raise the child as their own, and so it was. Their first-born son grew to be a fine man, and no one ever doubted the love his parents felt for him."

Brigid paused and put her hand on Faolan's arm. "When they came to kill your father for the Druid secrets he protected, he did everything he could to keep you safe. He didna mistakenly reveal any information. Nay, he revealed what he had to in order to keep them from learning about you, Faolan."

The room was silent, everyone was breathless listening to Brigid's story. She paused, looking at Faolan, her face a mixture of love and pain. "After your father died, I nearly lost my will to live, I loved him so much. Looking after his first-born son, making sure you found your path, making sure you finally take your rightful place as your legacy foretells. This has kept me going. It keeps me going still."

Faolan looked at her and whispered, "You loved my father? You are my mother?"

"Aye, lad, you are my son, my one and only." A sheen of tears filmed Brigid's eyes, and her face wore an expression of love and pride. She'd been waiting over three hundred years to tell Faolan of their relationship. Centuries of watching, caring, guiding, protecting. Elena thought there was nothing so pure as the love of a mother for her child.

****

Worthington was nearly finished with his preparations; however, he needed to bring Liam fully into the plan before it was finalized. It was time he knew the truth. They were in the sitting room of the Edinburgh manse and Worthington was about to tell a story.

"My ancestor, the one who founded the Etarlam, was

named Oswald. It means divinely powerful, and near as I can tell he was. There are few of his writings in our vault, but those that exist paint the portrait of a man who felt power running in his veins, but unsure of why or of what to do with it. Men sought his opinion, followed him into battle, deferred to his wishes.

"Knowing he was not of royalty, Oswald began to research other men of power throughout history, looking for others on whom power had been bestowed. He discovered the Sorcerers and Druids, and began to believe he was descended from one or the other. There was very little lore about either that he could find, but what he did manage to locate led him to believe he was a Druid."

Worthington stopped and looked at Liam for a minute, as if assessing him, his reaction. "Am I boring you with this old family tale?" he asked.

"Not at all. I always wondered how—"

Worthington continued to look at him, so Liam went on, "I always wondered how the Etarlam started...who had first noticed the power."

Worthington leaned forward then and asked very quietly, "Do you feel the power?"

"Aye, ever since I was a lad."

Worthington nodded and then continued, "You know the story of the Fae and the Druids? It explained why everyone believed that Druidry was only an oral tradition, since the Queen destroyed all of their books. Oswald believed that some of the Druids must have survived. Certain he must be a descendant, he began to look for others like him and for places that their elders might have hidden some of their books and treasures.

"He found that even without spells, he could bend the will

of others, he could direct attention toward other objects, and he could draw people of power to him. He formed the Order of the Breslan Etarlam and they began a worldwide search for books and writings that had escaped the Queen's wrath.

"This was how Oswald gathered those to him to form the initial members of the order. From that time forward, whenever a person of power was located, a member of the Order would get close to determine if that person knew of Druidry or had artifacts. An attempt would be made to bring the person to the Order, but if it was unsuccessful—"

Worthington paused. This was it; this was where he would know whether Liam had what it took to go forward.

Watching Liam carefully, he continued, "If the person could not be recruited for the Order, he was considered an enemy, and he was killed, and his artifacts added to the collection."

Liam never even flinched. Not physically, not mentally.

Worthington was pleased. He continued, "My father and his father before him were weak men. They wanted nothing to do with the Etarlam, so the leadership passed to other members, lest the work be lost. I felt the power, and sought to participate from an early age. I was always suspect, because of the weakness of my father," he said bitterly.

"Some of what I have told you tonight you already knew, but some of this information is only to be known by the council and the Master. You must guard against Symington. He is a talented reader. However, he has not been able to read me, and he does not seem to be able to read you, for you have guarded my secrets well.

"You know that I desire to be the Master of the Order. The rules of our Order allow any member of the Council to present a challenge to the leadership, should he suspect the Master is weakening. Symington has made his plan for succession, and has chosen his own son over me, that way should any ever choose to challenge him, his son can step forward, and the family retains the power.

"His plan will fail, and come this Beltane, I will do more than challenge him. You have been working toward helping me as you gathered artifacts and learned certain spells—an offense punishable by death should the challenge fail. Are you ready to go further to ensure that the leadership of the Order is returned to the rightful heir? Returned to me?"

Liam looked directly at Worthington and opened himself, allowing his thoughts to be examined. "Read me," he said simply. "You have my word that I will do anything in my power to help you."

Worthington looked into his eyes, probed deeply, then said, "You have been loyal, and loyalty is rewarded. There is more I must tell you." Worthington stood and refilled their glasses, ordering his thoughts. Liam waited.

Handing Liam his drink, Worthington said, "Your mother was a lovely woman." Liam's head jerked back and he looked at Worthington in surprise. Whatever he expected, it wasn't this.

"My wife is a lesbian. She has been since long before I met her. Her father was a very wealthy man, who was unwilling to indulge her lifestyle. He arranged for us to meet and offered me a large settlement if I married her. I knew nothing of her...preference until our wedding night.

"Her father was pleased with our marriage. However, when we did not present him with a grandchild in a timely fashion, he withheld the remainder of his money until we produced a child, and provided proof via DNA that the child was ours. We'd traveled to Switzerland for one of our annual excursions, and while there, she had in vitro fertilization. Her father was satisfied and left his fortune to us upon his death. In truth, we have never consummated our marriage.

"When I was in London establishing our branch office there, my life was changed forever when I met your mother, Katarina. She was wild, exotic, and full of power. It was she who first recognized the full power in me, and it was she who encouraged me to pursue my rightful place among the Order. She was skilled at prophecy and at reading people. She had deep magick. She found more documents and artifacts than any other ten members of the Order, combined.

"I know you are aware of our relationship; after all you have known me since you were a child. She told you I was an uncle. From the moment I met her, I begged her to come with me, to live near me in Phoenix, but she always refused. She wanted to move closer to her spiritual home, she said. Your mother was fiercely independent.

"She told you we met when you were four. It was the only lie I knew her to tell you. When she became pregnant with you, I told her I was buying a house for her, and if she wanted to have a say about where it was located, she'd better decide quickly. She chose Scotland, this house, and she chose to raise you alone.

"Although I was here and part of your life, there is more I would have done had she allowed it. I would have proclaimed the truth, but she was afraid it would place you in danger. As a powerful prophetess, she sensed extreme danger should some discover that she and I had produced a child. Together our power was formidable, and there are those on the council who would seek to destroy a child of our making."

Standing, Worthington walked over to Liam and held out his hand. "I would claim you as my son. My firstborn son. The son I will acknowledge to the council this Beltane, once I am proclaimed the Master, and then I will name you as my successor."

Liam stood and put his hand out, stunned. Worthington grasped his hand and pulled him into a hug, slapping him on the back, before releasing him and turning quickly away, his throat working.

Liam had wondered, of course, if Worthington was his father, but Katarina had been so very firm in her denial of that fact that Liam had believed her. Not only was Worthington admitting he was Liam's father, but he was going to acknowledge it before the council and name him as his successor. He did not underestimate the significance of that declaration. Worthington's...no, *his father's* plan must involve permanently removing Symington and his son, as well as his supporters from the council, and it must be foolproof.

"I am honored to be your son," Liam said rather formally.

His father smiled at him, and said, "Although this is news to you, it is not to me. I have always been proud to be your father."

Chapter Thirty-five

Elena was not particularly happy. While everyone else was at the castle practicing spells and getting ready for Beltane, she was back on the boat. Matt, one of the many MacMartins, was taking her to the mainland so she could return to the farm and gather certain books they needed. Matt was a big, strapping lad with orders to watch over Elena, get her to the farm, and back, no later than the day of the Beltane ceremonies.

She thought that task would be impossible, since it had taken them so many weeks to find the island. Matt assured her that it was only a day's boat ride, if you knew where you were going. A fast trip was preferable to Elena, since she was not anxious to be separated from Faolan for long.

The copies from the spell book and the other books Elena had discovered had stunned Brigid and Earnan. Neither had known the Gailtrys had such books in their possession, and Earnan thought it sounded as though some of the original Druid council's library might be intact. He was desperate to get his hands on it and secure it on the island.

Unfortunately, no one else could leave because of the necessary preparations that must occur before Beltane, just under two weeks away now. So Elena had volunteered because it seemed petty not to, and there were good reasons for her to go. Faolan was finally convinced that she needed to leave, not only for the sake of the Druid's, but also for her self-esteem. She needed to be needed, to feel useful. Of course, now she really had no one to blame but herself. *Sigh.*

Aside from getting the books, there were other good points to returning, and Elena tried to focus on those. She would get to see Lilly and Red, her beloved farm, and Shadow. In fact, she'd already decided the boat was big enough, she was going to bring Shadow with her when she returned.

She had plenty of errands to keep her busy. They needed more clothes than they'd brought the first time, preferably clothes more suited to Earnan's preferred mild climate. Best of all, she was going to visit a doctor to confirm her pregnancy. Since she could determine that with a home pregnancy test, the doctor's visit had an ulterior motive.

Dr. Gabhran MacLachlan was an obstetrician in Edinburgh. Brigid had come across the name multiple times over several generations. She wasn't positive it was the same man. It could have been a family name, but something about it resonated with her. The time had come to seek those of possible power, to draw them close and train them in the ways of Druidry. They would need every Druid they could find in order to fight for their side, the side of the light.

Elena had researched the doctor using the Internet. There were a few references to someone with that same name over the past one hundred years. The sources and locations changed with each reference, and only one had a picture accompanying the article. It was grainy, and the subject was half-hidden behind a tree.

They'd spent a pleasant evening speculating whether

MacLachlan might be someone like Faolan, Druid-born, cursed, and long-lived, or more like Elena, blissfully ignorant of powers lurking below the surface. It was up to Elena to try to figure out that conundrum and bring him to the fold, if she could.

Matt had been right, the trip to the mainland had taken just about a full day. After sleeping on the boat, they set off early the next morning in the MacMartins' old truck they kept near the marina. They made a quick stop to buy three large waterproof trunks for the books, then headed towards Inverness. With Matt's willingness to defy the laws of physics as well as the laws of the land, they made it to the farm safely.

It was so nice to see Red and Lilly, and of course Shadow, who took his name so seriously he even needed to follow Elena into the bathroom. Lilly fussed over her and wanted to hear all about the island and everything they'd done since they'd been gone. Red had given Elena a gruff hug as soon as she emerged from the truck and then let Lilly talk herself out. When Lilly went to start the water for tea, Red took his chance and asked about the boat and finding the island. Elena felt as though she'd talked for hours by the time she'd answered all their questions.

Exhausted by all the travel over the last two days, Elena took her cat and went to bed. When the morning sunlight streamed in her bedroom window, she woke rested, feeling strong and anxious to get started. It was too early to call the doctor's office for an appointment, so she went to the barn to start packing the books.

When they took a break for breakfast, it was time to call for her appointment. Elena was disappointed that she couldn't be seen until the following week. That would leave a scant few days to get back to the island before Beltane. It couldn't be helped; they needed the information, and she needed to see this particular doctor.

The rest of the day was spent packing the books and selecting the next round to pick up after the first batch was transported. After dinner, Elena used all her skills of persuasion to convince Matt and Red to leave in the morning and take the trunks to the island.

The books were needed to prepare for Beltane, and she would not be arriving until the day before, if her schedule held true. There was plenty of time for them to make a round trip and return to reload more of the books when they came to get her.

Elena would spend the week taking care of a few errands, getting her shopping done, and continuing her research into Dr. MacLachlan.

****

All he ever felt anymore was darkness inside, and it had been that way for as long as he could remember. He'd always felt like an old soul. It was as though he'd climbed out of a peat bog, fully-grown, full of shadows. Christ, had he ever even laughed?

He was actually relieved that he was about to get some answers. Now that he'd found his new acquaintances, it seemed there might be a reason behind all that darkness. According to them, he had a power the world needed. A power that wasn't being utilized.

That thought was almost enough to make him want to laugh. Save the world? Then, when he'd thought about it, wasn't that the reason he'd gone into medicine in the first place? To ease his own darkness by bringing new life into the world, to see how all people started, before the world had a chance to wear them down? He sighed and thought about what was coming.

This all began because he'd changed his route between office and home, gone down a nearby street, and saw that restaurant, The Saucy Sorcerer. He'd made a last minute decision and went there for dinner instead of returning directly home. His new friends told him later that was how they'd found him. They told him of spells, wards, and compulsions. They spoke of destiny.

At first, he hadn't wanted to believe them, but his nights had become filled with disturbing dreams, and the things they said resonated. He'd had a hard time shaking off their stories, and eventually he'd called them back, asking to learn more, fearing what he might learn.

The truth was, he hadn't learned much more after those first few meetings. He wasn't stupid; he knew they were withholding serious amounts of information until they were sure they could trust him. Just as he was holding back something from them. Something that might put his life in danger if they knew he had it. Trust went both ways, and until he knew for certain what they wanted and why, he would keep it close to his chest, no matter how much he hated it.

Chapter Thirty-six

Faolan's mind was quick and his power immense. There was only one spell he'd tried so far whose power had eluded him. He'd tried manipulating the weather at the island until the temperature dropped twenty degrees in one hour and Earnan had hastily reclaimed that duty. That one was going to take a little more practice.

He'd spent the day mastering scrying, a more difficult spell, used to communicate with others across a distance. The object was to use a reflective surface to "see" what was happening some distance from the spell caster. The "somewhere" could be another room, another part of the country, or even another time, depending on the power of the Druid.

Faolan used the mirror that had brought Elena and he together and ultimately led them to the island as his reflective surface. Although it was rather ornate for his preference, it had obviously been imbued with magickal properties hundreds of years ago, and was still capable of holding a spell. He and Brigid had started with small distances within the castle, continuing to increase the space between them throughout the grounds. Late in the afternoon, she'd declared he'd mastered the skill, and would now need to practice over even longer distances, to further improve.

Faolan had been released from lessons until the dinner hour. With some time on his hands, he thought he would try to encase a spell of his own into the mirror, and cast the scrying spell, feeling the power transfer from his mind to the mirror. He placed the mirror on the mantle, not hidden but not obvious either, and left the drawing room. He knew Earnan and Brigid would meet there for drinks before dinner; he was expected to join them. He would join them, but not in a corporeal sense.

When they entered the drawing room, Faolan clearly heard Earnan and Brigid speaking of plans for dinner. He spoke to them after only a few minutes and made himself known, before he inadvertently invaded their privacy.

"Pour my whisky, Earnan, for I will be there in a moment," Faolan's disembodied voice filled the room.

Brigid gasped loudly and looked around until she located the mirror.

Earnan said quietly, "Faolan, I think you better come down here."

When Faolan entered the drawing room, he was grinning broadly, clearly pleased with himself. His grin faded when he saw Earnan's serious face. "Is something wrong, Earnan?"

"What gave you the idea to try distant scrying, Faolan?"

"I doona' know. It just seemed like a good idea. Since my mirror has held spells cast by others, I wanted to see if I could cast one into it myself. T'was the first spell I thought of. Why? Is something wrong?" he asked again, feeling a little annoyed at the questioning.

"Faolan, when you want to talk to someone using the scry spell, it is customary that both parties have a scrying surface, such as a mirror or a pool or water and the spell. Otherwise, if only one has the scrying surface and performs the spell, that person can watch unobserved, but the ones on the other end have no way of knowing they are being watched and the spell caster cannot hear or be heard," Brigid explained.

Earnan, still speaking very quietly, asked, "'Tis not about manners, Faolan. We don't mean to lecture. You have surprised us. What were you looking at, to be able to see and hear us if you left your mirror in here?"

Faolan grew very still. "I wasna looking at anything. I saw it in my head. I saw you and heard you, as if I was standing right here in the room with you. It didna even occur to me that I would need another scrying surface. Is it the magick of this mirror?"

"I doona' know, lad. End the scry, and I will try the same thing with your mirror."

For the next little while both Earnan and Brigid tried remote scrying with the mirror without success. They could each cast the scry spell using the mirror, but only if they held it, and they could not see anything if they left it in the room, as Faolan had.

"I want to try one more thing, lad, and then I will tell you what I think. I want you to cast the spell as you did the first time, then leave the mirror here and go run the island. Shift to your wolf shape in several different locations, try to get as far away from the castle as possible. Let us test the limits of this power. If you canna hear us, if you lose the scry, return. Otherwise, just speak to us whenever you take your human form."

Faolan was gone nearly three hours and never once lost the thread of the conversation between Brigid and Earnan. He spoke to them from the opposite side of the island, as though he were in the room with them. Earnan tested him further, holding up notes for him to read, speaking with his back turned, and taking the mirror into other rooms with him.

Faolan grew more confident in his abilities with each of Earnan's tests. Finally, he informed them he was returning to the castle, and to please have some food brought to the drawing room, or plan to meet in the dining hall.

As Faolan wolfed down his dinner, Earnan told him some Druid history. Earnan had only heard of two other Druids with the power of remote scrying, the High Priest and Priestess of the ancient Druid Council. It was always assumed that the power came with the position, for each new Druid High Priest.

It was powerful magick because the person who could cast that spell could listen unobserved to any conversation, as long as he had placed a scrying surface in the room ahead of time. Not only could he listen, he could speak, and needed no corresponding scrying surface because the spell caster could hear within his own mind. And if Faolan could hear the words of others across great distances even while he was in his wolf form, well it was an unprecedented amount of power.

Faolan grinned. "I sent you my last words, the ones when I told you I was hungry while I was still in my wolf form. I didna change back."

Earnan just stared at him. "I have ne'er had a student with such magick, Faolan.

Magick was not his only strength; Brigid also sensed a strong power of healing. She had never told Faolan or Elena just how close to death Elena had been that day they found her. She would not have made it to the hospital in Inverness. Faolan had called upon his spirits and gave her the gift of his heartbeat. Elena would have died had they been but a few minutes longer in finding her. Och, my son is powerful, she thought with pride.

****

As the time to prepare for the feast of Beltane grew nigh, Earnan wanted to introduce two other areas of magick. Although some sorcerers could master a spell that mimicked shape shifting, it was temporary, and the caster retained little power once he or she was wearing the spell. True shape shifters were born not made, and their power remained intact within their incarnation. The shape was passed from parent to child, along patriarchal lines, and most commonly involved wolves, cats, or birds. Very few Druids had ever possessed sufficient power to master shifting into multiple forms; that took a tremendous amount of concentration and strength. Earnan suspected Faolan was well up to the task.

First, Faolan would use the mirror to hold the spell of the shape he wanted to become, and then through a form of scrying, he would see the shape, and then become it. Since he had long ago mastered the art of returning to his real form from wolf, Earnan thought he would be able to use those same skills to return to his true form anytime. Once he mastered shifting to a different form using the mirror, he would learn to perform it without the mirror.

They started with a dog, a task so easy that Faolan hadn't needed to use the mirror after his first attempt. Next, Faolan tried a cat, which was quite a bit trickier. He discovered that the mind of a cat was more complex than the mind of a dog, and that made a difference when shape shifting. Even with the added complexity, Faolan mastered that spell after just a few attempts, as well.

Earnan wanted him to try a winged animal, one of the most

complex forms for a human to undertake. It was just not natural for man to be untethered from the Earth.

After some research, Faolan selected the Peregrine Falcon as his bird of choice. The bird could soar to incredible heights, reached speeds over 200 mph, and mated for life. He liked the sound of that.

Shifting to a bird was an incredibly difficult bit of magick, and Faolan struggled with the complexity of the transformation. After several hours of practice, he had finally mastered the task of shifting shape, but had been unable to fly. He would continue his practice on the morrow.

Although it was nigh on gloaming, Earnan could not rest until he walked with Faolan to the standing stones. Only the most powerful of Druids had e'er been shown the truth about traversing dimensions. Earnan had never before trained an apprentice with such power.

He knew he was pushing Faolan hard and fast, trying to cover in two weeks what took years to learn through a normal apprenticeship. Faolan was not a normal apprentice, though. Although Faolan's skills had been dormant over the course of three hundred years while he'd been trapped within the curse, it seemed his innate Druid power had matured.

With the Druid prophecy nearly upon them, there was no time to waste. Faolan's barely suppressed power sizzled just under his skin, electric, and alive. Faolan was about to learn the truth of the standing stones.

****

Red was becoming increasingly uneasy, caught halfway between the mainland and the island. He was unable to go further until the weather and seas settled. He'd not liked the idea of leaving Elena and Lilly alone at the farm, but he also knew it was important that the trunks full of books, plus a few artifacts reach the island well before the ceremony at Beltane. The women had agreed to stay at a hotel in Edinburgh, rather than at the farm. Red was sure no one had been watching the farm for quite some time, but he'd felt better about leaving the women behind knowing they would be in a big city and not isolated in the countryside.

He looked down at the 'no signal' message on the display screen of the satellite phone. "Faolan is going to kill me," he said to the empty cabin.

Chapter Thirty-seven

Elena entered the doctor's office and filled out the masses of paperwork necessary to be examined and treated. She sensed no Druid powers emanating from within the building. The office seemed perfectly normal, not fortified with wards and there weren't any suspicious pictures showing human sacrifices hanging from the walls. On the other hand, she was surrounded by women, children, and babies. She snorted to herself. *I'm getting more fanciful by the minute.*

An hour later, she was walking back out the door, not much wiser. She had provided blood and urine samples, been weighed and charted, and after a brief meeting with the doctor, been invited to return the following week for her results.

She'd worked at maintaining her cover as an anxious, possibly pregnant young woman and tried to schedule something sooner, like tomorrow, but the appointment clerk held firm. "Doctor said not until next Tuesday." Taking what she could get, Elena wondered where she would be, come the next week.

When she'd entered the small examination room, the nurse told her to hop up on the table, "Doctor will be with you shortly."

The bright blue tape that held the white gauze to her arm where the nurse had drawn blood felt tight and she was just picking at the ends of it when the door swung open and the doctor rushed in.

"How do you do? Mrs. Thomas, is it?" he asked holding his hand out to shake. She'd used Lilly's last name as a precaution.

Wow! When he'd entered the room, it was with the same force of being hit by a train. There was nothing subtle about this man.

His face was chiseled, with strong, aquiline features, cleft chin, and his jaw was brushed with a blue-black shadow of a beard. He had wavy black hair that fell silkily to his shoulders and gorgeous blue-gray eyes the color of steel.

She'd had to look way up to see those eyes; he was nearly as tall as her husband, which probably accounted for that feeling of déjà vu. Their body types were similar, too; the build of a professional athlete, tall, broad shouldered, narrow waist, and thick, powerful legs.

He took up every ounce of space in the room not already occupied. What he didn't fill with size, he filled with magnetism. Elena was willing to bet that more than a few women had transferred to his practice to just to look at this gorgeous man.

"Please, call me Elena," she invited, taking his proffered hand.

Smiling, but not deeply, he'd replied easily, "Then you must call me Gabhran."

Puzzled, Elena looked at the spelling on his diploma hanging from the wall, but repeated the name as she'd heard him pronounce it, "GAV-run?"

"Aye, 'tis pronounced G-A-V-R-U-N." He spelled out each

letter. "And don't worry about the spelling until it comes time to pay for my services! Then I'll want you to get it right. Are you American?"

"That obvious, huh?"

"Don't fash yourself about the spellings over here, or you'll make yourself crazy. Where else but a Gaelic country would you pronounce D-U-B-H as Doo?" He laughed.

This exchange took place while they were shaking hands and as he pulled up his leather stool near the table. Elena had known from the moment he'd entered the room there was a barely suppressed energy within him. Elena kept her own power carefully shielded, and tried just listening to him and his intentions.

As the exam began, what she sensed was a man absorbed with his job, listening to her health history, asking questions, making small talk. However, the whole time they spoke, she was aware of something else, something coiled within him, a beast not quite tame.

Despite a sense of something a little bit dangerous, she did like him and was a little disappointed that he wouldn't be her doctor for long. Elena knew her time with him was short. She expected the nurse would return with the results from her lab work any minute, and then the conversation would shift. She decided to go out on a limb and see if he knew of any special powers.

"Doctor," she said, instantly correcting herself, "Gabhran, I wonder if I might talk to you about an unrelated issue?" She let a bit of her power out, not enough to project or shield, just enough to nudge him if he was able to sense power. His quick intake of breath was sufficient to let her know he'd felt it.

"Who are you?" he demanded, his previously pleasant demeanor vanishing instantly, edges suddenly sharp.

"I'm a woman who believes she is pregnant and came to you to find out for sure. I'm also a woman who recently found out about certain elements in this world, powers I'd never even suspected existed. It seems I have some of those powers, and you might too. I can sense it in you. I know you can sense it in me."

Fighting her increasing unease at the waves of suspicion rolling off him, Elena continued. "I'm preparing to learn more about myself and my power, and thought maybe you should be learning about power too. It seems it might be dangerous out there for people like us. Some might wish to use us in a way that's against our true nature."

He looked at Elena a very long time. She could sense his inner power uncoiling, but in an unexpected fashion. It was as though there were two sources of power in front of her, or maybe not two sources, but two sides of the same coin. Like the Greek god, Janus, he was perched in a doorway, facing both inward and outward, presenting both darkness and light. Elena shivered.

"I doona' know what you mean," Gabhran finally said, his brogue much thicker than it had been previously. "I will think about what you have said. Come back next week, and I will have the results of your pregnancy test. Perhaps I will hear more of which you speak then, as well."

Although she had tried to further engage him in conversation, he'd been firm in his dismissal, opening the exam room door and calling for the nurse to escort Elena to the appointment desk. She got in one final warning before the nurse joined them, "Guard yourself this Beltane, Gabhran."

Elena hoped it was enough. She sensed something coming toward this man, something dark, predatory, and powerful. Something that was going to force him to choose.

****

Gabhran's heart was pounding when the woman left his office. His hands shaking, he swallowed a couple of aspirin, and told the nurse he was taking a short break. He stepped out the back door of the clinic just in time to see her head down the street, walking in the direction of the Saucy Sorcerer. Had she come from there? Was she a test sent by his new *friends*? Somehow, he didn't think so.

She was right, he could sense the power within her. A lightness that was strong and true. He could have told her she was pregnant, even without the results from the urine specimen. However, he'd needed time to think about what she'd said, time to think about the others who were seeking his power.

For years, he'd thought he was a freak, perhaps bordering on some form of mental illness or depression. There were times when he thought he could hear people's intentions; times when he was positive he could heal with more than his medical skills. He'd thought he was going mad.

Recently he had felt a darkness descending, threatening to overwhelm him. He thought he might have felt that way before, and then...nothing. After the darkness, the memories just seemed to be lost. He wished he knew what he meant by that, what he'd meant about being lost.

When he'd met with the two men who had sought him out, they seemed to understand his darkness. They'd found him, they'd told him he was someone special, and they were ready to guide him along the way as he learned about himself. They promised he could learn to control his power.

Gabhran had tasted their intentions. They wanted him. They wanted him badly for their Order, as they'd called it. It was really quite simple, they'd explained. He could come to the feast at Beltane, meet others like himself, ask all the questions he wanted. Those questions that could be answered, would be. Once everything was explained, he and the other invitees would be given the chance to join the Order, and all who were not interested could leave. Simple, really, the older man had insisted.

If he chose to stay, he would be sworn into the order and then the ceremony of the Beltane would begin. It was a time of new beginnings for their Order, and the men felt Gabhran was a perfect fit.

As they'd prepared to take their leave, and Gabhran had agreed to come, they'd casually mentioned that if there were any family heirlooms, special artifacts he thought might be related to power or magick, he should bring them along. They planned to have an appraiser at this particular meeting who specialized in such things, merely as a courtesy to their members.

It was well done, he'd realized. The men had played well off each other and off his own need to belong, his need for answers. They'd also managed to make the invitation to bring any artifacts sound like a complete afterthought. Completely casual. Except later when he'd thought back over the exchange, he realized he'd sensed an increase in the heart rates of both men. They thought he had something they needed, and they wanted it badly. Interesting. Well, he would find out soon enough, he supposed.

****

"Goddammit, man, you must get back to them now," Faolan roared.

Belying his own inner tension, Red said calmly, "Aye, young pup. 'Tis on my way I am, as soon as we empty these trunks. Your woman would not be too happy with me if I returned without them. 'Twas the reason behind her ordering me away in the first place.

"Besides, I just spoke with Lilly, and Elena is at the doctor's office as we speak. They will stay the night in Edinburgh, leave early on the morrow to stop by the farm to pick up the supplies. They should be at the marina when we arrive.

"The storm put us a few days behind, so I'll not have time to drive to the farm myself to have this set of trunks repacked until after Beltane. 'Twill mean one more trip to mainland, unless you'd like for us to return to the farm to wait out Beltane, since the time draws nigh."

After consulting with Earnan, it was decided it would be best for Red, Lilly, and Elena to all return to the island for Beltane and then they could travel together afterwards to retrieve the rest of the books from the farm.

The boat would head back out as soon as the empty trunks were reloaded. The weather would be clear, and they would make shore midday on the morrow and return to the island the morning after. They would return in time for the evening feast and for the ceremonies held at midnight.

Chapter Thirty-eight

Lilly and Elena decided to go to dinner at a restaurant Elena had noticed earlier near the doctor's office. The name was catchy and the ambiance was elegant old Scotland. Large burgundy leather booths lined the walls and the tables were spaced far apart. Everything was designed for maximum privacy, with high sides on the booths, walls that were covered with heavy gold fabric, and sound dampening carpeted floors. When they'd first come inside and Lilly had gotten a good look at the place, she suggested they go somewhere else. She was afraid it might be too pricey, but something about the place made Elena want to try it, so they stayed.

Their charming server appeared to be nearly a centenarian and flirted with both women shamelessly. He clearly felt it was his special mission to make their evening memorable. Although he recommended a bottle of wine, both women declined and ordered sparkling water, which arrived in elegant stemware. He asked if they had any questions about the menu, reviewed the evening's special, and offered to return in a moment.

As Elena watched him speak, her attention was caught by

someone across the room. She thought the back looked familiar, but before she could think any more about it, her eyes were drawn to the menu. She must have been hungrier than she thought; she couldn't seem to keep her mind off the delicious assortment of meals from which to choose. She'd figure out the mystery man later, after she made her dinner selection.

Elena kept paging through the menu, her mouth practically watering at all the options, she just couldn't make up her mind. Glancing back over to the familiar back, she was surprised to see he was gone. She was even more surprised to recognize the person he'd been sitting with. Dr. Gabhran MacLachlan.

Before Elena had a chance to tell Lilly about the doctor, their server returned. Lilly was having the special, lamb chops, medium rare. Elena was still dithering and finally looked up at the server. "I can't make up my mind. Do you have any other specials, maybe something not on the menu?"

****

Gabhran was deeply disturbed by the woman's visit to his office. He'd been sufficiently concerned that he'd returned home and opened the vault, reassuring himself that the artifacts were still secured. He hadn't visited the vault in a year and now he'd been there twice in two weeks. When he'd opened it the last time, he'd been irresistibly drawn to the Talisman of Cycles, an ancient pendent of gold and amber stone that seemed to pulse when he held it in his hand. He'd removed the talisman and slipped it around his neck, but whether as a protective ward or invocation, he wasn't sure.

The talisman was one of several relics left to him by mysterious relatives, without explanation. On his thirtieth birthday, he'd received a letter from a previously unknown attorney, about previously unknown relatives, directing him to a previously unknown vault behind the bookcase in his study. It was enough to make a man roll his eyes. He'd inherited his home in a similarly mysterious fashion when he'd turned twenty-five. It was one more thing that needed answering. *Who was he really?*

For the past week, he'd been wearing the Talisman under his shirt, thinking he might just show it to his new acquaintances on Beltane. He discovered that wearing the Talisman was unpleasant, that he was even more aware of the darkness he felt inside. When he'd stepped into the restaurant tonight, he could have sworn the pendant jumped against his skin.

He brooded over his drink. Just what had he gotten himself into, he wondered. The Beltane Feast was tomorrow night and he still wasn't sure what his answer would be when asked to join the Order. He wished he could know more about it before the time to choose arrived.

What about the woman's warning? "Guard yourself this Beltane." Was that a coincidence? Could she know he was being recruited and tomorrow night was his deadline to choose? He'd left the office that night without consciously knowing his destination, yet his feet led him here, back to the restaurant where it had all started.

The maître'd had recognized him as soon as he entered. He was called by name, ushered over to a booth and a single malt whisky arrived while he and the headwaiter were still making small talk.

"I hope you don't mind. I ordered your drink when I saw you arrive, sir. If you would prefer something different tonight, I would be pleased to replace that with your pleasure."

"Not at all, thank you, and thank you for remembering."

Smiling rather smugly, the man gave way to the server, and went back to his station at the front door.

The server asked if he would like to see a menu, or if he would prefer the member's special tonight. Gabhran knew he would order the member's special as soon as it was offered, which troubled him. It was an irresistible urge and he realized it was part of the compulsion woven around this restaurant.

As soon as the server left his table, Liam approached and asked if he could join him for a drink. Liam was one of the two men who had explained the Order to him, and Gabhran was anxious to ask more questions. The men enjoyed a pleasant conversation over their cocktails, and neither revealed any new information to the other.

Once Gabhran's food was served, Liam excused himself and exited the dining room. It was only then that Gabhran noticed the woman. Damn. He had come here tonight hoping to find more answers about the Order or maybe more about what they wanted from him. He'd been stone-walled by Liam, and now here was the woman from his office sitting in a booth across the restaurant. Had she been working with the Order all along? Maybe she'd been sent as a test, to see if he would reveal the Order. If so, he'd passed with flying colors, he thought.

She was sitting with an older woman, perhaps her mother, and kept paging through her menu. He continued to watch her as he ate his dinner, and although he was seated across the room, he clearly heard her dinner order, "I can't make up my mind. Do you have any other specials, maybe something not on the menu?"

Chapter Thirty-nine

Elena was sitting on the floor, unable to move her hands, and completely disoriented when she woke. She could hear men speaking nearby, and she wisely kept her head down and eyes closed until she could figure out what was happening. She was tied to something, maybe a pillar or a pole? The last thing she remembered was having dinner with Lilly. *Lilly! Where was Lilly?*

"She's caused us a lot of trouble; why don't I just get rid of her? Throw in a memory spell and dump her somewhere."

A voice she would recognize anywhere said, "Patience, Liam. I wish to have her here for the ceremony. You may kill her tonight, when her sacrifice will do us the most good. Kill them both."

Dear God, that was Worthington talking.

The men's voices faded, a metal door clanged in the distance, and then silence. There was a scraping sound nearby, so Elena waited a few more minutes, trying to decide if she was alone. Cracking her eyelids infinitesimally, she peeked, trying to see if anyone was watching. She was in a large, basement-like room, with high ceilings, exposed ductwork against brick walls, no windows, with a rectangular table at the far end.

Other than the table and the pole she felt pressing into her back, the room was completely empty. She twisted her head as far as she was able and could see Lilly. They were secured to the pole by rope, back-to-back, and both of them had their legs splayed out in front of them. Lilly's head was slumped to the side. "Lilly? Can you hear me?"

Nothing. Either Lilly was still unconscious or…well, Elena didn't want to think about what else might be making her quiet. She tried reaching out with her mind but she received no response in return.

Elena could sense nothing at all; her brain felt sluggish. Try as she might, she was unable to make her thoughts go where she wanted them to go. Her eyes started to glaze over; she was so tired. Her head sank to her chest, and she drifted between half-remembered thoughts and dreams.

"Elena," whispered Lilly. "Elena, wake up."

Elena's head shot up, and she bumped it sharply against the pole behind her. "Lilly, are you okay?" she whispered urgently.

"Aye, but I can't get loose."

"Me either. Do you know where we are? Or how we got here?"

Sighing, Lilly said, "I think we were drugged at dinner. 'Tis the last thing I remember, we had just finished eating and then that old codger of a waiter brought over a special dessert. I canna remember anything after we ate dessert."

Dinner had been delicious and elegant, the service extraordinary. Elena had settled on the member's special without even knowing what it was. Shortly after, the manager came by to visit with them, promising a meal they would never forget. It turned out that the member's special had been angel hair pasta with shrimp and a salad. Although it was nothing she would have selected from the menu, when Elena tasted it, it was as though she had taken a bite of heaven. Try as she might, she couldn't remember eating dessert.

What Elena did remember was waking earlier and hearing Worthington and Liam talking about killing them as part of a ceremony. They needed help. She tried to reach out with her power again, but her thoughts jerked uncontrollably. Pick something familiar, she told herself.

"Lilly, I'm trying to make a projection of Faolan in front of you, tell me if you see it."

"Nay, lass, there's nothing here," Lilly said after a moment.

"Oh, help," Elena whispered quietly, "I can't remember what he looks like." She wanted to cry. She felt no more special, no more powerful than when she'd arrived in Scotland all those months ago.

"Lilly, I can't control my thoughts. Whatever drug they gave us, it's messing with my projection. Listen, we have to get away at all costs. If someone comes in, we better fake being unconsciousness but be ready for anything. We have to get free."

Just then, the door opened and both women dropped their heads. A man walked over to the pole where they were tied and approached Lilly first.

He grabbed Lilly by her hair and yanked her head back violently, exposing her neck. He laughed at her sharp intake of breath.

"Do not try to fool me, you fucking old woman. I know you're awake, I can smell your stench. You smell like the dying," Liam said.

Elena heard some movement, then the snap of plastic. "Just a little pinch now," Liam murmured. He moved to Elena, squatting next to her and resting on his powerful haunches. He stroked her cheek and whispered as though they were lovers engaged in an intimate moment. "Open your eyes and look at me, or I will kill the old woman."

Elena opened her eyes and met the gaze of her would-be-killer. He removed a syringe from his pocket, uncapped it, and then held it up for Elena to see. She realized the source of the sound she'd heard a moment earlier was when he'd removed the cap from before he'd injected Lily with something.

"I am just going to give you a wee bit of this, not enough to knock you out, like your friend here, just enough to protect me from the power of your thoughts."

As he was speaking, he leaned forward and depressed the plunger on the syringe, and Elena had the sensation of warmth spreading through her veins. She was suddenly very glad he liked her and would take special care of her. She smiled at him, thinking he was a good-looking man. How had she not noticed before that he reminded her a bit of Marty?

"You are a very powerful woman, Elena MacFarland. When did that happen? You didna have such power when I met you in Fairth. Aye, there was a wee bit of interesting in you, but nothing like I sense now. Worthington told me what you did the last time he held you captive. Would that I could keep you for myself, but it's not to be, for you have an important role to play here tonight."

Elena felt bitter disappointment flood her, and then realized he was projecting his feelings into her. He wanted her to know how he felt, and without her shields, she was helpless to protect herself.

*

Liam found everything about Elena fascinating. He pushed his desired at her, easily overpowering the shields he felt her try to erect. He might not have a lot of choice in how things were going to work out, but he needed her to sense his desire, to taste his power. "Tonight we'll celebrate the Beltane, and the coming of the Druids. It's the biggest night in the history of our order. We will regain all that was lost. You should be honored to be such an important part of the ceremony. The greater the sacrifice, the more pleased the gods, and the greater the reward.

"Once the order is rid of the unworthy, those who remain will lay you upon the altar. There we will offer you to the gods, first through the flesh, then through the blood." He substituted his lips for the blade of the knife he'd held against her throat. He inhaled her scent before sucking hard on her neck, tasting her. The minute his lips tasted her flesh he was overwhelmed with desire for her. Her power thrummed through him, hot and demanding in his veins. A fierce jealousy twisted inside and his hatred for the bastard that claimed her flared.

Liam threaded his fingers through her hair, and he pulled her head even further back. "Did you know a life force grows within you? I can feel it. You are carrying the wolf's pup. This will add immeasurably to the power we will receive through your sacrifice. Or should I say sacrifices, since you will be giving your flesh in the mating ceremony before you give life force in the blood sacrifice. We will worship you. No woman has ever been the object of such desire, such reverence." Again, he let his feelings of desire flood her.

"Fear not, sweet Elena. I shall work an enchantment for you before we begin. You will participate willingly and you will be pleasured many times by your sacrifice. I only wish I could keep you for myself."

Although unable to speak, Liam could sense Elena's terror,

feel the horror grow, spreading a fear so palpable it threatened to strangle her.

"Don't let the fear overwhelm you, Elena. Act afraid, so no one will know of the enchantment, but I will not let you suffer." Liam lowered her head to her chest by her hair, then leaning over her, Liam whispered the words to an ancient spell, and Elena slept. He would need to get her alone for a few minutes before the ceremony to work the second spell.

Liam smoothed her hair back from her face, "Would that I could keep you for myself," he whispered again. He kissed the top of her head before walking slowly away.

Chapter Forty

A few minutes, or maybe it was hours later, Elena woke as the room started to fill with black robed figures. They entered slowly and the conversations were subdued as each person took a place around the room, forming a loose circle. Two men stood behind the table and laid out a book, a chalice, and a purple cloth.

A screen was now propped in front the women, and although Elena could see through, it appeared no one in the room could see in from the other side. No one spared them a glance. The hooded robes prevented Elena from recognizing anyone. Except for one man, standing directly in front of the screen, and wearing street clothes. Gabhran MacLachlan. She vaguely wondered why he didn't merit a robe.

Voices, chanting, incense. Elena's drug-addled brain clicked: this was a ceremony of some sort! *Brilliant, eh? B— B, something with a B. What was important about B? She was supposed to be somewhere for B.... Oh God, am I drooling?*

The man presiding over the circle raised his arms and called to the gods, to ask their blessings upon the gathering. Elena recognized him, even though she'd never actually seen him in person. It was Symington; the man Worthington had called Master.

Symington led the group in a responsive chant, one that continued for many minutes before the members all fell silent. Then a robed and hooded person joined Symington at the table. The second man carried a scepter and presented it to Symington, but before handing it over, he turned toward the room and made an announcement. Elena recognized him immediately... it was Worthington.

She focused hard trying to make sense of his words.

"I am making this presentation to the Order of Etarlam," Worthington said, and he pulled a staff from the folds of his robes. The surprise rippled around the room. "I ask that the Master and you the Council accept this gift of the Scepter of Entitlement, a relic of the Royal Court of the Tuatha Dé Danann. With this Scepter, the Tuatha Dé could bestow immense power to the Druids, and with this Scepter the ungrateful Fae Queen stripped the power from the Druids before she scattered us about the Earth.

"The Tuatha Dé came to our Earth and expected to rule with impunity, and they destroyed the Druid Priests that opposed them. We honor our ancestors. We, who have brought forth their genes through the ages are gathered together this Beltane to enter the epoch of the Druid. The prophecy will be fulfilled, the power of Druids fully restored, and we will wield our power in that which was our way."

The group responded with shouts and fist pumping. He continued, "When those with power choose our ways, the Scepter of Entitlement will show us whose heart is truly Druid. Tonight we have one who sought us out and has expressed his desire to join us."

Worthington bowed formally, and appearing completely

submissive, he presented his plea. "Council of the Etarlam, please accept this gift of the Scepter, and allow it to test our newest potential apprentice before we begin the ceremony of Beltane."

Again the robed figures cheered, the Master nodded, as did several others standing near the front. Symington reached for the Scepter, and the members erupted.

Whatever Liam had done to Elena, it had paralyzed her vocal cords, but some sound must have escaped. She gasped with her effort to call out. Gabhran was directly in front of her now, and he turned his head slightly at the sound she made. He looked at the screen, his eyes sliding unseeingly over the women before he turned back to watch the ceremony. "No," Elena shouted with her mind. Again, he turned his head slightly in her direction, and she tried the mental shouting again, "Yes!"

It was like some bizarre game of Hot and Cold, trying to get him to look beyond the screen. Elena knew who he was, but she didn't know if he was a good guy or a bad guy. What she did know was that if she and Lilly were still here at the end of the ceremony, someone would kill them.

Gabhran's posture changed slightly, and he shifted to the right, which let him look toward the bound women without it being obvious to the others in the room. His attention appeared focused on the leader, but his eyes kept returning to the screen.

Master Symington was lighting candles, calling on fire to light the way. The faceless voices in the room replied, chanting again. Placing the candle in the center of the human circle, Symington returned to the table for stones and placed them around the circle. Someone else brought a large tub of water and placed it near the candle. Symington turned to

Worthington and nodded for him to continue. The ceremony was getting ready to start.

Worthington stepped forward and raised his hands. Looking in the direction of the ceiling, he called out and a breeze began to blow through the room, although there were no open windows or doors, and no visible vents. The air seemed to swirl just because Worthington had commanded it so.

In all the pomp of the ceremony, Elena had nearly forgotten about Gabhran, and she looked up to find him staring directly at her. Not at the screen that had been shielding her, but through the screen, directly at Elena, their eyes connected. She silently pleaded, "Help!"

His eyes, took on a faraway look again and he turned back to the ceremony. "Nooooooo," Elena thought desperately, but he didn't turn around again.

Symington was speaking loudly in order to be heard over the wind as it continued to gather strength. He called on the spirits to bless this convocation, to open the assembled minds to the ways of the Order, to bless the leader of the Bresal Etarlam.

"We, the true and rightful heirs to the Druidic nature, have been called together from beyond the borders of Scotia. We knowingly enter into this time of prophecy, call to the spirits of our ancestors, show us the way, summon the intended heirs to come home, turn away our enemies."

Symington raised the scepter high in the air. "We call on your power to make our Order sacrosanct, to keep those from us who are not the true believers, to bless our council with wisdom!" He finished on a shout over the now howling wind.

Symington glanced at Worthington, and his look held a measure of uncertainty as though the increase in the wind was unexpected. Symington was still holding the Scepter in the air when his eyes bulged in their sockets and the wind began to turn dark.

There was no other way to describe it; the wind became visible as black wispy strands began to reach around the room. The tendrils curled, testing, tasting each person before moving on to the next. Elena watched in horror as the darkness encircled Symington in a lover's caress before tightening around him, constricting until he screamed in agony. Soon one voice was joined by many, as more members of the council were wrapped in the tentacles of the spell.

Dear God what's happening? Elena's panic found a voice. "Don't look," she managed to shout as the tendrils reached lovingly for Gabhran. Elena didn't know if he heard her or if either he or Lilly could understand what she'd shouted. In truth, she didn't know if Lilly was even conscious.

The temperature around them plummeted as the icy black tendrils passed over Elena, surrounded her, caressed her for a moment before moving on. She felt as though she might never be warm again, bile crept up her throat, and she struggled to keep it down.

Gabhran was yelling, but Elena kept her eyes squeezed tightly shut. She knew he must be surrounded by the same black ice that had passed over her. She could not look, she was not going to open her eyes until she was sure the icy black tendrils had gone. Their end of the room began to warm slightly, but the wind was still howling, the black seeking others.

Worthington's voice boomed over the roar of the wind, reverberating, unnaturally loud, "The ancestors are calling judgment upon us! There are those on the council deemed unworthy. Stand tall, make your heart pure lest you be found lacking in your heart of hearts."

Someone grabbed Elena roughly and tried to pull her up. Her arms were jerked tight against the ropes and then she dropped hard back against the pole. The rope was pulled tight and then fell as it was sliced away. She heard a muttered, "Shit! Can you walk?"

The screams in the room continued and she was afraid to open her eyes. Who ever had her shook her so hard her teeth rattled.

"Goddammit, woman, look at me! We've got to get out of here. Your friend is unconscious, so if you want me to bring her along, you have to walk! Can you?"

Elena managed a feeble nod and took her weight on her own feet moving them experimentally. She thought they might work. *They have to work!*

Gabhran let go of Elena and picked Lilly up, before whispering urgent instructions. "Do not look to the center of the room. Keep your eyes on my back or on the wall to your left. I am going to take us out through the door near the front. Keep your head down."

With that warning, they were off, and he was moving fast. Elena had expected stealth, but he was practically running, Lilly was cradled in front of him, and Elena desperately tried to hang on to his jacket. Her feet were clumsy from the effects of the drug, her body uncoordinated from being tied in one position for so long.

When Gabhran stopped suddenly, Elena crashed into his back, and he grabbed her before she could fall. Shifting Lilly over his shoulder, he wrapped an arm around Elena. Supporting all of Lilly's weight and most of Elena's, he dragged the three of them to the door.

People were still screaming, and the icy fingers slid over

them once again, bypassing Elena, seeking the man. She felt the cold as it surrounded her would-be savior. He stiffened, his feet jerked practically to a stop, and his grip tightened painfully on her arm.

Elena could not summon a projection to protect him and she still couldn't properly form words, so she thought loudly and with all her heart and soul. *Fight it.* She used her feeble legs to try to force them forward, shouting with her mind, *fight it, fight it.* Her mouth tried to form the words too, and she whispered, "Fight."

Gabhran shuddered, shook himself, and propelled them through the door, and out of the building. The darkness was within him, fighting for control of his soul, coming with them into the night. The cold air hit Elena like a tonic, slapping her awake, but she still couldn't completely control her body.

He half dragged, half carried the women, until they reached the street near the front of the restaurant. He was trying to get to the black BMW a few cars away.

Elena thought she might be sick, whether from the drugs, the fear, or the blackness she knew not. Their lives were in Gabhran's hands, and blackness was in his soul. *God help us all.* He was fighting the black, Elena could feel the struggle within him, but she had no idea which was stronger, his own soul or the darkness seeking to claim him. He leaned her against the car for balance while he opened the door, to lower Lilly into the back seat.

A sound so unexpected in the middle of Edinburgh reverberated into the night... a feral growl so menacing it brought him to an abrupt stop.

Gabhran grabbed Elena again, trying to push her into the car. Instinctively she pulled back and said, "Wait," but the word that emerged was unintelligible. Elena tried to turn toward the growl and lost her balance, falling towards Gabhran.

Then everything slowed, time shattered, each event became its own shard of glass, splintering into the night. Lilly slumped against the back seat, still unconscious. Elena fell forward and her sluggish muscles prevented her from catching herself. Blood splattered over Gabhran's chest. The sound of a shot exploded, echoing off the empty storefronts.

Chapter Forty-one

Three months later...

Alone Again, Naturally. The world's most depressing song played over and over in her head. Her Grandda used to play that song on the jukebox in his bar. The poor singer, left at the altar, his parents dead, thinking of suicide...all sung to a bizarre, poppy little beat.

Now she understood why her Grandda would listen to that song, pouring himself shots, and wiping his eyes. His heart had been broken so completely he would never be able to love again. Elena knew how he'd felt. Her heart was broken beyond all possible repair. She'd been back on the farm for nearly three months now and she could never have imagined being so alone. She let her mind drift back, deliberately cloaking herself in pain. It was an exercise in grief that she'd performed every day for the last twelve weeks.

****

"Elena, can you hear me? It's time to wake up now, Elena."

Elena had tried to look around, but the tubes restrained her, tubes in her mouth, in her nostrils, in her arms. Dear God, what happened to me?

The doctor was speaking to her, but Elena had panicked, her throat working at trying to expel the invasive tube.

"Elena, stop fighting now. I am going to remove the breathing tube, but you have to stop fighting first. Do you hear me?"

Elena had fought to control her panic, looked the doctor in her eyes, and nodded, as much as she could. Once the breathing tube was removed, Elena had tried to ask questions, but her throat wouldn't work.

"Don't try to talk yet. You're in the hospital. There's been an accident, but you're going to be fine now. I'll talk to you more when you wake up again." The doctor had nodded to the nurse on the other side of the bed, and he injected something into the IV line. The warm feeling took effect immediately and sleep had become inevitable, despite her desperate need for answers.

The next time she'd woken, she'd been more coherent. Elena had needed to know what happened. She'd found the call button and pressed it, desperately needing to talk to the doctor.

The lovely young doctor had offered her a tissue and held her hand as she told her what had happened. Elena and her husband had been mugged, and both of them had been shot. The bullet had pierced her lung and nicked an artery.

"You lost a lot of blood. It was touch and go for a while. If that doctor hadn't found you and called for an ambulance, it would have been much worse. He tried to stop your bleeding while he waited with you for the ambulance. Don't worry, Elena, you're a fighter. You'll be all right now."

A roaring started in Elena's ears, and the world began to shrink until it was no bigger than a pinpoint on the doctor's face. Elena stared at her as if her last hope depended on the answer to her next question.

"Faolan?"

"No, dear, I had my hands full with you, but I checked when I was

finished with your surgery. I am sorry, he didn't make it. He jumped in front of you and was shot through the heart. He died at the scene. There was nothing that could be done. He must have loved you very much; the police said he died trying to save you."

The black around her edges had threatened to overtake her. She'd had to know the final piece. She'd tried to reach her stomach, but her arms were restrained by tubes and probes, but the doctor knew what she was hoping for and delivered the news Elena had dreaded.

"No, you lost too much blood. Your body just couldn't sustain the stress of the pregnancy, too."

Elena had stayed in the hospital for nearly two weeks recovering while mourning the loss of Faolan, their baby, her happily ever after. She'd asked about Lilly, but the doctor knew of no one else found at the scene. What had happened to Lilly? Red and Lilly were the closest thing left she had to relatives, and yet she'd heard nothing of them since the day she'd been shot. Was Lilly okay?

She had no family, no friends. No one called. She was alone in her grief. The social worker tried to get her to talk about her support system and who would care for her once she returned home. In a dead voice, Elena had told her there was no one.

When the police had visited her, she'd had no information to give them. She didn't know how she had come to be shot, she never saw her assailant, and she didn't remember any events leading up to the shooting. The doctor was sympathetic and told the officers it was trauma-induced amnesia, and she would call them if Elena remembered anything.

Elena actually had remembered some of what had happened, at least that which she'd seen. None of it made sense and it just wasn't information anyone would believe. It was information that needed to be protected.

Upon being released from the hospital, Elena had rented a car and driven directly to Fairth to Brigid's shop. Brigid was now her mother-in-law; surely they could share their grief. The store was empty, and the grocer next door, sensing an opportunity to tell a juicy story approached Elena.

"Aye, old Brigid up and died last week. Her niece or summat came to pack up her things, and they buried her behind the church."

All signs of her happy life were gone, wiped away by the cruel hand of fate. Numbly, she'd turned the car toward home.

Her heart rate sped up on the drive, hoping against logic that when she got there, everything would be back to normal. She would find Faolan. Red and Lilly would be there waiting for her, Shadow would be crying for her attention.

Opening the door to the kitchen, Elena braced herself as she entered. She was driven to her knees by overwhelming loss. Howling to the fates, she raged, shaking her fists, screaming in the emptiness that was now her world. How could she have found her love, her destiny, only to lose him so cruelly? How could any God have taken him and the baby they had made, the evidence of their love?

Faolan had spoken to her soul from the very first, and she had wasted precious time fighting it. Why hadn't she turned around the moment she smelled him that first day and claimed him as hers? Why had they spent one minute outside each other's arms?

It didn't matter if you believed in the gods and goddesses or the one great God, Elena knew it was all a lie. There was no God. No all-caring, all-powerful being would be as hateful and cruel as to take her love. To rip her body apart rather than let a baby form and grow. No God could have left her so barren and bereft.

Then as suddenly as it had come, the rage had left her, replaced by tears that seared her eyes and closed her throat. Great wracking sobs had wrenched her body, consumed her, ripped from her throat in an agony of the soul. Elena had collapsed on the floor in her overwhelming grief, and stayed there.

She'd awakened the next morning still on the kitchen floor, and struggled to get to her feet. Her body was weak from the injuries and the cold, hard floor had offered no comfort. She couldn't face another day; she *needed protection from the realities of her life. She taken her pain medication with a large glass of water and found her bed.*

It still smelled like Faolan. Dear God, what was she going to do? Before a fresh wave of tears overtook her, she lay on his side of the bed, buried her face under his pillow, and breathed the scent of him, waiting for the drugs to take her to oblivion. It was how she had spent her first week at home, drugged, in bed, barely drinking and eating enough to stay alive.

It had taken another week before she'd discovered the rest of it. She'd woken one morning to find Shadow lying on the bed with her. Shadow? How had he gotten there? She'd jumped out of bed and run through the house calling for Red and Lilly, her voice cracked from disuse. Shadow's meow was the only reply as he followed her from room-to-room.

She'd run across the yard in her pajamas and bare feet and raced up the stairs to their flat. She hadn't even thought of looking in the flat since she'd returned. They must have returned from wherever Red had taken Lilly to heal. Lilly must be all right now!

Elena banged on the door with all her might. Her knock echoed back, the flat was silent. When she tried the handle, the door swung open. It was as though Elena had gone back in time. All of Red and Lilly's things were gone. The only sign they'd ever been there was a note propped on the counter in Lilly's neat handwriting.

Elena,

We packed while you were in the hospital. We are glad you will be all right in time. We waited to bring Shadow until you were well enough. We won't be returning. It's too painful.

Forgive us,

Lilly and Red

Returning to the house, Elena realized they must have

checked on her while she was in the hospital. They'd known how long she was there and they'd known she'd lost the baby. Yet they hadn't come to visit. Instead, they made sure they never had to look at her again. Faolan's death was her fault. Losing the baby was her fault. It was all her fault, she should have returned the farm to Worthington from the very beginning. Now she had paid for trying to get the best of him, with the loss of everything dear to her.

She'd wondered if Lilly and Red had returned to Beauly, the island, or somewhere different. Somewhere without such painful reminders of the past.

****

The days had turned into weeks, and Elena realized the awful truth was she didn't have the courage to die. She would live with her grief, afraid all the while that if it lessened in time, she would no longer be able to see Faolan. She never wanted to feel better; she would always want to keep Faolan in her heart.

As the months passed, Elena realized that having Shadow to care for had probably saved her life. He depended on her to feed him, to give him water. He followed her incessantly, never leaving her side. They engaged in those silly conversations between cat and human that left no doubt which one was smarter. He gave her unconditional love at a time she thought she would never know love again. Of course, it wasn't the same as her feelings for those she'd lost, but it was love, it was returned, and it kept her sane.

She'd tried to track Martin III down not too long ago. Not to talk to him, just to see if he'd made it out of that ceremony alive. To see if she still needed to worry he would come after her. After a few useless Internet searches, she'd finally just called the firm. She'd posed as a potential client. Yes, Mr. Worthington was still the senior partner, and of course, he was still alive. However, when she'd asked to make an appointment with him, she was told he was currently on a leave of absence due to a medical condition, and could someone else help? *No, thank you!*

If he was still around, then she was still in danger. Somehow, her life had become important to her again, and she was not willing to have Worthington steal anything else from her. Not her life and not her farm.

Tonight at midnight, the farm would become officially hers. No more strings attached. She'd once vowed to Faolan that Worthington was not going to kill her before the six months was up. So now, here she was, three months after losing everything, ready to think about saving herself.

At least she could give Faolan that much. She was a MacGailtry now, and the farm would return to the MacGailtry hands. By God, it would not go to Worthington.

Elena had been expecting him or one of his underlings all week. She believed he would send someone tonight. He would make one last effort to reacquire his land. If so, Elena was ready.

Chapter Forty-two

Elena. Liam had been trying to get her out of his head for the last three months. Something had happened at Beltane. Something he couldn't explain, and something he'd worked hard to keep hidden. He'd let Elena sense just a little of his feelings, but he knew it hadn't been the time, nor the place.

When he'd put his hands in her hair, his lips to her neck, everything had changed. He'd wanted to pick her up and carry her off to his house, to keep her, to make her love him, and to claim her as his. Nothing about Elena ever went smooth for the Worthingtons, he thought wryly.

Liam had been trying to get at her for the past week. He'd tried everything he could think of, and still he couldn't get near her. His father had understood. He'd tried too. That didn't make it any easier to take. They would give it one last try tonight, in order to take advantage of the legal loophole his father had left. If she died before midnight, the land reverted to his father.

Actually, it didn't matter much when she died, the land would always come back to them. He was confident that his father could make whatever necessary paperwork appear in the appropriate land office. Killing her tonight would be more expedient. Now that Martin was in charge of the Order, they had nearly unlimited resources at their hands. There were people from judges to clerks who would be happy to do a favor for the Master. Still, it would be better if no one else knew about the farm.

Liam had decided that if it didn't work tonight, all bets were off. He would approach his father, tell him of his feelings for Elena, and seek permission to take her for his own. His father was the most powerful Druid alive, and if they worked together, it was well within their power to make Elena care for Liam. If he were her husband, what was hers would be his. Either way, the Worthingtons would have this farm.

Someone had placed protective wards around the farm shortly after Beltane. The wards were one of the things that kept them from getting too close to Elena. Neither of them had been able to approach the perimeter of the farmhouse without bumping into an invisible field that turned them away despite their own intentions. Each time he'd tried to cross the boundary, he found himself suddenly facing the opposite direction, momentarily forgetting where he'd been going. He had walked the entire perimeter last week, looking for a weakness. There was none.

The wards weren't the only things causing problems for him. After confirming that the wards were actually in place around the entire farmhouse, Liam had returned with a rifle. Last night he'd come up close to the boundary, hidden behind some bushes and sighted his weapon. He was able to aim it through the window, but she wasn't in the room. He would wait. Then two of those fucking wolves had jumped him. He'd been lucky to get out alive.

He was going to try once more tonight, but he had an extra

weapon tonight that should take care of the wolf infestation. He'd brought a tranquilizer pistol. He'd have preferred something larger, but the small handgun version was all he could find on such short notice. He'd broken into the zoo and stolen it from the keeper's office. He knew he would be lucky to get a dart into each of them, but it was worth a chance. He didn't want to kill them. They could be valuable bargaining chips, if he got to keep Elena.

****

Elena wasn't exactly sure she was right in her head, but sometimes there's a lot to be said for being a little crazy. She had arranged everything so that her library window offered the only clear view of her in the house, just in case one of Worthington's men was out there trying to kill her tonight. She closed all the shutters except for those on the library windows. She turned on timers for the lamps, so lights came on and went off in different rooms of the house at different times. The goal was to make it appear from the outside that she was moving through the house as she made dinner, ate, and then finally ended the day, as she did every day, in the library.

Elena pulled a chair in front of the windows with the front of the chair facing away from any prying eyes. Her final step was to put a wig on top of a pillow in the chair, so it would look like someone was sitting there reading. She had been putting the pillow there every night this past week. Someone was coming. She could feel him.

It wouldn't be an easy shot, not with the way she had angled the chair. She knew exactly where the killer would have to set up in order to take his shot. Only Elena wouldn't be in the library as he would expect. She would be right behind him, in a spot between an outcropping of rocks and hidden by bushes.

In Great Britain, acquiring a gun is a lot more difficult than it was in the Wild West state of Arizona. Unless you're a hunter, of course. Elena had bought a shotgun shortly after returning to the farm. She didn't want to have to aim, and she wanted the bad guys to know she didn't have to aim.

Her backpack was filled with a few essentials like food and water, and she bundled it and the shotgun into her arms along with a light blanket and crossed the yard to the south end of the steading. If anyone were watching, she hoped the assumption would be she was carrying out a bundle of trash. Once inside the steading, she added the blanket to her provisions.

Heading through the barn, Elena went to the north wing, carefully slipped behind the pile of boxes that still concealed the panels, and entered the chamber. It was the first time she'd been back in here since they'd packed up the books to send to the island. It made her heart ache. She lit the lantern and closed the doors. Picking up the keys from the table, she opened the doorway leading to the two chambers and entered the long passageway.

She went first to the room on the right, keeping her gaze straight ahead. This room would always cause problems for her, she'd nearly lost her life in it. She took two of the dirks from the shelf, put them in her pack, and left quickly. Entering the other room, she made sure she had all of her supplies before she let the door shut behind her. Once the door shut, it would become invisible, only the MacGailtry could see it, and the only way out would be up the stairs, into the clearing.

The vestibule looked just as she remembered, with stairs leading out. There was the door to the chamber where

Worthington had held Elena and Faolan. Turning, she saw the door that led back to the farm. She could see it now! Whatever the magick was that had kept it concealed had died with Faolan. Or the magick now recognized Elena as a MacGailtry.

Her hand trembled as she opened the door to the chamber where she and Faolan had been held. The memories came flooding back.

"Love me, Faolan."

"Elena, you know I do."

"I am in you love, you have all of me."

"I doona' think you understand, lass. We have mated for life now. I willna be leaving you, and you willna be leaving me."

Oh God, he'd left her in the most permanent way possible. Elena lay down on the tapestry where they first made love and cried for her lost life. Eventually, she pulled herself together, for Faolan, for herself. Worthington was not going to get the Gailtry farm. It was the last gift she could give to Faolan.

She waited for the sun to go down before she left the chamber. She dressed in black, including a lightweight jacket, because it got cool out there after dark. After giving herself a good once over, she was sure she'd be nearly invisible against the night. She left her backpack in the vestibule and brought a bottle of water, the blanket, and her shotgun.

Stepping into the clearing for the first time since she'd been there with Faolan she was startled by a sense of motion. She froze, pressed against the wall of the building, and waited. Nothing moved. Yet she couldn't shake the feeling that something was different, just outside her peripheral vision. *What is it?*

She skirted the clearing, shielding herself with magick, masking any signs of movement by staying to the trees, moving silently. Although she suspected that whoever might be coming for her would wait a little longer before coming out here, she knew her life depended on her stealth. She'd spent the last week establishing a pattern of going to the library for at least two hours after dinner. She wanted to make sure the killer would know where to look for her and when.

Once ensconced in her hiding spot, Elena propped her rifle on the rock in front of her, ready for anything, prepared to wait. The leaves in the trees moved restlessly, the gentle breeze caressing her face. As the sounds of the night began to settle in, she fought the urge to think every noise was the killer. Eventually, she heard the sound she'd been waiting for... a car door. She was expecting no visitors, the only reason to hear a car out here tonight was if someone was coming with bad intentions.

It took forever for him to get there. She could hear him moving carefully through the brush, coming from the east, just as she had predicted. He positioned himself in place, unzipped a long bag at his side, and removed two weapons, a rifle with a scope, and some kind of a smaller gun. He placed them by his side, fished out a cigarette and smoked while he waited. The light turned off in the kitchen, and then came on in her bedroom, and then the bathroom. It was bizarre to watch her house from out here, and she fought an urge to run to see if someone was really inside, despite knowing that the timers were working as planned. Twenty minutes later, the light in the library came on, and he picked up his rifle. She followed his lead and picked up her shotgun, aiming it straight at his back.

A noise to his right caught his attention, and he swiftly picked up the smaller gun instead, and dug something out of his pocket. More noise to the right, then a low growl filled the night. *Red? Lilly?*

"Where the fuck are you?" he said aloud, and Elena knew

that voice—it was Liam. Another growl, coming from the other side this time. *They were both here.* Liam had the gun in one hand and picked his rifle up in the other. "I can kill the bitch before you can stop me," he taunted.

Something about that wasn't right, Elena thought. A split second too late, Elena realized what it was. Liam had made it sound as though he was ready to pull the trigger and shoot Elena, but he wasn't aiming at the library now. He had the small pistol in his hand. Red stalked slowly forward, close enough to jump if Liam started to raise his rifle. Liam's hand rose swiftly. *Pffft.*

Red went down on his side with a thud, a dart protruding from his chest. Liam dropped his rifle and stuck another dart on the end of the pistol and was ready when Lilly got there.

Pffft. She was down too.

"Stupid mutts," Liam said with evident satisfaction. "Now if I miss with the rifle, she'll still come out to save you."

He raised his rifle and took aim at Elena's library silhouette; Elena raised her shotgun again and took aim at his back. She'd planned to wait until he'd taken the shot and then turned around, so she could see his face, but she hadn't expected Red and Lilly. *Dear God, let them be all right.*

She was afraid now; afraid he might kill one of them after he'd taken his shot at her, so that he'd only have to concern himself with one wolf. Liam wouldn't know for sure Elena was dead until he went to the farmhouse and checked, and he wouldn't want to risk leaving both of them here while he did that.

Elena decided she would pull the trigger as soon as Liam did, and then she would call the local police to surrender. It would be up to them to decide whether to prosecute. She just needed to know that Red and Lilly were safe.

Liam adjusted his rifle so it sat more securely on his shoulder. Elena took aim and held her breath. He fired. Without any hesitation and less than half a second later, Elena fired, too.

It all happened so quickly. *Something was wrong.* Her finger pulled the trigger at the sound of his weapon firing, before she could process the sight of another large wolf leaping from the bushes, slamming into Liam.

Liam's screams mingled with the growls of the wolf, and then he was silent. The wolf ran, or rather limped away, whimpering deep in his throat.

Another wolf! Where had Lilly and Red found him? Was he a relative of Faolan's? At least some of her shotgun pellets would have hit him. Was he hurt badly? Before following him, Elena stopped briefly to check on Red and Lilly. They both appeared peacefully asleep. She pulled the darts from their fur and promised to return soon.

Elena ran after the other wolf—she needed to help him. He'd taken off toward the clearing and she followed as fast as she could run. As she drew closer, she heard the gently trickling stream change until it sounded as though there was a roaring river just ahead. The wind began to whip, blowing leaves and debris, making it hard to see. Lightning streaked across the sky; it was centered over the clearing. Thunder rumbled. It looked like the quiet Scottish evening was turning into a sudden squall.

This was magick, and Elena needed to see who was behind it. She raced to the clearing, following the trail of blood. She was running so fast, the changes to the clearing didn't completely register. There were giant standing stones where before there'd only been a circle of trees surrounding a grassy field, and the lightning was crackling between the stones. Like stone henge under an electrical storm.

The wolf ran into the circle to the center of the stones. The storm strengthened around him. Elena's breath was coming in gasps, the pain sharp in her side. She ran faster. Branches whipped across her face, her hair swirled with the leaves. She was running as fast as she could, trying to catch him. Elena dove toward the center of the clearing, surrounded by the stones she'd never seen there before, and was sucked into a vortex of light.

Chapter Forty-three

Bright lights swirled all around Elena, flashing past her with lightning speed. Or maybe she was the lightning, splitting the air at the speed of light. She tried to scream, but her lungs felt compressed. Her limbs were being pulled apart, and she thought her head would be crushed. She was tossed from side to side, her head snapping, wind whipping her face. There was no up or down, no way to tell where she was headed.

It was over in an instant. One minute she was hurtling through space, the next she was unceremoniously dumped on the ground and all signs of the storm were gone. She quickly shrouded herself with a projection, to be invisible to anyone looking her way, while she tried to figure this out. Looking around, she was astonished to see the castle she'd last stayed in months ago. *With Faolan. She was on the island!*

She followed the wolf with her eyes as it made its way unsteadily toward the castle steps. The doors to the castle opened and Brigid rushed out to the wolf, just as it collapsed on the ground in front of the doorway.

Brigid? Oh my God! Could that mean…. Her knees buckled, and she hit the ground. Her mind screamed Faolan's name, and Brigid looked up sharply. Elena didn't know if Brigid could see beyond her projection, but she felt the compulsion that Brigid sent her way. *Come help Faolan.*

Dropping her projection, Elena ran for the castle toward her destiny. She was trying to keep from sobbing, her side had a stitch, and she couldn't breathe. It was him.

Elena wanted to scream at him, shake him, ask him how he could have done such a thing to her. How could he have let her mourn his death? Elena followed the trail of his blood, not knowing if his lie would become her truth.

Brigid was reciting words over him. She didn't look up as she said, "Elena, he must shift back, I canna do it for him. You must call to him, whisper in his ear, call his name, tell him to change, I will get Earnan. Doona' let Faolan see you if you can help it."

Her words cut Elena to the quick, but she knelt next to him and softly crooned in his ear, "Faolan, you must change back. You must shift back now."

Elena wasn't prepared when it happened. He rippled, like he was under water and she was looking down through the surface waves trying to keep him in focus. One minute, wolf, the next minute, man. A very bloody man.

Keeping Brigid's words in mind, Elena stayed to the side, in case his eyes opened, while she tried to see where the worst of the bleeding was coming from. Tearing off her jacket, Elena stuffed it against the gaping hole in his lower rib cage. *Oh God, she'd done this to him. He was alive, and now she might have killed him.*

Brigid returned with Earnan and Matt. Together, the men carried Faolan into the house, followed by Brigid, who directed them to carry him to his room. The housekeeping staff scurried in search of hot water and sheets. Elena stood watching the activity. Everyone focused on helping the injured man and Elena didn't know her role.

When Brigid got to the top of the stairs, she turned around and looked at Elena. Her gaze was so penetrating, it felt as if Brigid was looking into her soul, but she kept her shield around her heart.

"Get up here and help. Now."

Brigid must have realized Elena had shot Faolan, and she would blame her if he died. Then a much more important thought slammed into Elena. *Faolan was alive!*

When she'd left this castle all those months ago, she was Faolan's wife, mother to his future child, daughter-in-law to Brigid. Twenty minutes ago, she was Faolan's widow, and Brigid, Lilly, and Red were gone. Now they were all back, and she didn't know where to put that knowledge. They had obviously known she was alive, that she'd lost her baby. What kind of monsters were they to leave her to grieve, to rip her heart out, believing the love of her life, her soul mate had left this life? They all let her think he was dead. Brigid, Red, Lilly. Faolan. *All of them*. She was hurt, furious.

Put it away for now.

Elena slowly followed Brigid up the stairs, her heart in her throat. *Please be alive, Faolan.* She went into his room. *Our room*, she thought with a stifled sob. Helping Brigid pull the covers down on the bed, Elena was struck by the scent of the sheets. They smelled like him, earthy and elemental, essential man. She experienced a memory of mornings wrapped in his arms. Loved and loving, igniting a fire in the heart she thought had died with him. She never thought to capture those feelings again.

Brigid and Elena worked together to heal Faolan's wounds; Brigid chanted and used potions, Elena cleaned and used warm water. Together they wrapped the wounds securely in bandages of torn sheets, although he wasn't bleeding much anymore. Whether that was his wolfish healing powers at work or because he'd already lost so much blood, Elena didn't know.

"Brigi—"

Brigid cut Elena off, "He'll be alright for a few minutes. Go clean yourself up lass, then return straightaway. Hurry."

Elena couldn't understand Brigid's tone, and snapped back at her, "I don't have anything to change into," as if that were relevant.

Brigid stood up to her full height, which was considerably taller than when she was the ancient shopkeeper. She looked at Elena then with the same piercing look she'd used outside. Elena deliberately lowered her defenses and let Brigid search her heart.

"By the gods and goddesses, it was all a lie!" Brigid exclaimed. She rushed across the room and pulled Elena into her arms, crooning in Gaelic.

Elena pulled away stiffly, not trying to see into Brigid, holding herself tightly together lest she lose her threadbare control.

"Och, lassie, put your back down and change now. Your clothes are still here. Faolan never cleaned them out. I thought he was being maudlin, not getting rid of them, but he refused, said he wasna ready yet."

Brigid opened a drawer and handed Elena a pair of her own jeans, then reached into another drawer and grabbed a t-shirt. Without waiting for a response or providing any explanation, she shoved Elena toward the bathroom and returned to Faolan's side. "Hurry, lass!"

When Elena saw her reflection in the bathroom mirror, she understood Brigid's desire to have her in clean clothes. She was covered in blood. Faolan's blood. Washing herself quickly, she put on the clean clothes and tried to piece this all together. *Too much had happened, too many truths were lies. What had Brigid meant when she'd said it had all been lies?*

Brigid was waiting when she came out of the bathroom. "Elena, forgive me. We have much to talk about, but not right now. Faolan needs you the way you needed him when you'd been lost in the chamber. Can you do it? Will you do it?"

Looking at her strangely, Elena replied, "Of course, tell me what you need me to do."

"He has lost a lot of blood. We have stopped the bleeding, and he heals remarkably quickly. However, I fear he does not want to heal; that he willna come back unless he believes there is a reason. I can feel him giving up, even now. He is very nearly gone. You must bring him back, Elena."

"What do I do, tell me how," Elena demanded, desperate to start before he gave up completely.

"Lay next to him, lass. Let him feel you. I know you are untrained, but you must call to the sisterhood. They are deep within you, waiting for you to ask for their help. Feel his heartbeat and join yours to it. Use your voice inside his head and in his ears. Project your love, your healing light. Hurry, lass. Och, I doona' know what it is with the two of you, but it worked once for you. Perhaps there is hope for him."

Elena climbed on the bed and got under the covers with Faolan, jumped back out slipped off her jeans and then climbed back in again. She lay on her side, with her arm carefully draped over a part of his chest. She placed her hand over his heart and felt a very faint beat. Once, twice, and then nothing. His heart gave up the good fight, and he slipped into the void.

Elena gave a howl, refusing to accept that he was really gone. "Help him, help me," she beseeched, not knowing to whom she cried.

She pressed her legs to his, skin to skin, "Faolan, you come back to me right now!" She felt the light of the sisterhood join hers, and peace filled her heart. Elena spoke quietly to Faolan, using both her voice and her heart to reach into his inner place, sending the white light that had joined them the first time they'd made love.

"Come back to me, Faolan. Come back, my love. I need you. Your clan needs you. Come, Faolan, please come home." Elena crooned to him in a singsong voice. Her hands stroked his arms and shoulders.

She'd already mourned his death once, she couldn't bear it if it happened again, if she was the cause of it a second time. She pushed away all the negative energy and focused on their love, on the time she'd known he'd been happy, and replayed her memories for him.

Elena felt a small bump under her hand, impossibly faint. She pressed her chest hard against his back and concentrated on her own heartbeats, seeking to join his heartbeat to hers. There was another beat, stronger this time, then another, and another, until Faolan's heartbeat joined hers and became stronger, a steady rhythm beneath her hand.

Chapter Forty-four

"Is there something else I should do? His heartbeat is steady now," Elena looked up at Brigid, seeking further guidance.

Brigid's face was pale, and she was holding herself together every bit as tightly as Elena had been. "He stepped into the void, I felt him go."

"Yes, I felt his heart stop just after I lay down. But it started back up almost immediately, I'm sure he's going to be okay."

Brigid was a powerful Druid, skilled in healing and when she felt Faolan step into the void, her grief knew no bounds. A Druid healer could start a stalled heart, cure fevers, and heal many wounds. Once someone stepped into the void, however, there was no power on earth that could bring him back.

As Elena was getting into place under the covers with Faolan, Brigid had felt him go. His spirit gave up on this world, the world he believed he would have to endure without Elena. When Elena put her arms around him, she may have felt the last of his heartbeats, but his spirit had already gone.

"Help him, help me," Elena had cried. Brigid felt a power such as she had never known surge through the room, carried on Elena's cries. This was not a Druid power, it was the pure

energy of light, to the degree that it cleansed all emotions and consumed every shadow.

The sisterhood appeared to help Elena, responding to her pleas, but Brigid knew it was not their light that called Faolan. Their light was feeble compared to the illumination Elena had called forth with her pleas. Brigid had long known Elena was Faolan's light. She had read it in the tealeaves, sensed it whene'r they were together. However, the light Brigid had sensed then was pale compared to the radiance Elena had called forth to bring Faolan back from the void. Brigid had to turn her eyes away, lest she be blinded by the brightness.

It appeared from her comment, Elena did not realize his spirit had gone, nor that it was she who had brought his spirit back. She knew only that his heart had restarted.

What was the lass? They had thought she was of Druid descent; mayhap there was more to her story. She needed to find Earnan, as soon as he returned from getting Red and Lilly. For now, 'twas important that Elena stay with Faolan. Brigid needed to think.

"Aye, lass, I believe he will recover in time now."

"Brigid, I don't understand, how are all of you alive?"

"Lass, I doona' understand why you thought we were dead, we will talk it out when Faolan recovers, however, 'tis important you know, he never stopped loving you. Not for one moment. I need to go help Earnan when he returns with Lilly and Red. Will it be all right to leave you here with Faolan? You willna leave him?"

"I won't leave him," Elena replied through gritted teeth, as Brigid left the room.

Elena rolled Faolan onto his back and checked his wounds. The largest wound now appeared as pink scar tissue, still healing, but no longer a danger to his life. Brigid had sent up a meal so Faolan could eat and drink when he woke. Elena poured a little of the water into his unresponsive mouth. Even if his skin was healing, he'd lost a lot of blood; he needed liquid.

His mind felt very far away to her, not like when she felt him leaving earlier, but like he was hiding, not quite ready to come out. She wondered if she had felt that way to him when she was recovering from her dehydration. She needed him to come back to her, needed him to explain how he was alive, to make everything okay again.

Emptying the bowl of fruit on the tray, Elena filled it with warm water and began to clean Faolan's body. Although she'd cleaned the wounds previously, she cleaned them again, before moving on to the other parts of his body with the dried flecks of blood. She refilled the bowl of water frequently and kept working until the water remained clear. Once the water was clear, she started again.

It was impossible not to think about the magnificence of the naked man, or of the ways he'd made love to her. As she gently wiped his face, she touched her lips to his, softly, lovingly, tasting him. She moved to his chest, running the warm, damp sponge over every chiseled muscle, remembering how he had jumped when she'd scraped her nails over his nipples. She washed the broad expanse of his pectorals and followed the washboard ripples of his stomach.

She tore her eyes away from his flaccid manhood, knowing he was well and truly far from her, she had never seen him when he wasn't at least semi-erect. Ceding his privacy, she draped the towel across his hips, feeling a little bit dirty from having such thoughts while he was unconscious.

She moved to his legs, working first on his calves and feet before moving up to his thighs. She began to feel his consciousness, it fluttered against hers, fragile. He was much farther away from the void now, and beginning to make his way back. She sensed despair, loneliness, heartbreak. And she sensed the beginnings of desire. Glancing up to his towel, she saw the telltale signs of his returning arousal.

Desperate to bring him back to her, she reached under the towel, knowing she was violating him, yet positive he needed her. He swelled at her touch, his breathing changed, but still he didn't waken. Fighting a losing battle with her morality, Elena began to stroke him, murmuring his name with her mind, while her lips wrapped around him. Faolan threaded his fingers into her hair and moaned.

When she had taken all he had to give, she looked up, fearful of what she would see. She had violated him, taken advantage while he was unconscious. He had wanted her to believe he was dead. *Dear God what did I do?*

His hands slipped from her hair, and fell to his sides, and he lay there, breathing fast, but otherwise motionless. She looked at his face, his eyes were closed tight, and Elena was stunned to see a single tear, slip out, and disappear into his hair. Then he gave an anguished moan, his chest heaved as he fought the urge to sob, and more tears spilled from his eyes.

Elena was scared. She had never seen Faolan lose control of his emotions like this. This was an anguish equivalent to hers on the floor of the kitchen, when she'd finally accepted his death. His grief was overwhelming him and threatened to pull Elena with it. She didn't know the source of this heartache, but if her being here caused him this pain, she needed to get away, to leave him in peace.

Shielding her heart, she crawled up alongside of him, cradled him in her arms, and crooned nonsense words, promising to go, telling him everything was okay. When he calmed, she climbed from the bed, pulling the covers over him, and slipped on her jeans. She turned to find him staring at her, an unfathomable expression on his face.

"Elena?" he croaked.

"Yes, Faolan, I'm here, but don't worry, once you're healed—" Elena's face twisted, and she couldn't say the words. She would leave. It was what he wanted.

At her words, he turned his head away. A knock sounded at the door and Elena opened it to find Brigid and Earnan. Stepping back to let them in, she reinforced her shield. With so many powerful Druids in the room, she felt inadequate and vulnerable. These three had lied to her in the worst possible way imaginable.

She had felt the loss of Faolan with the intensity of losing a limb. In her dreams, she was whole. Every morning she would wake, and just for a minute, he was still alive. Then reality would wash over her, cover her with devastating pain. The grief, the sense of loss, they were her constant companions. All of them had let her mourn. No, she would not be putting her shield down in here. She used her anger to make herself strong.

Brigid went to Faolan, and pulled his covers back far enough to check on the wound in his side. Satisfying herself that he was nearly healed, she reached with a mother's loving touch to brush his hair back from his face.

"How are you feeling, lad?"

He turned his head toward the wall, and didn't answer.

Brigid's nostrils flared, and she turned toward Elena.

Elena braced herself for the recriminations and armed herself with righteous anger. Yes, she had fired the weapon that injured Faolan. She shouldn't have been out there trying to kill a man. She wouldn't have been out there if they had told her Faolan lived. She knew they must have thought she would never let him go, but she would rather have watched him walk away, than ever think he was dead.

In the time since she'd followed the unknown wolf through the stones until this moment, she had realized the truth of the matter. No one could have kept him from her if he had wanted to be there. Faolan had made the decision to let Elena believe he'd died.

Brigid said, "You brought him around much more quickly than I anticipated, lass, thank you."

"I'll wait downstairs, while you all visit. Then one of you can return me."

Faolan started to shake, and Brigid spoke softly to him, a calming spell. Earnan gave a rather dramatic sigh, cleared his throat, and began to speak.

"It is clear to me that we are all operating on differing levels of understanding here. No one leaves," he looked pointedly at Elena, "until we talk and clear the air. Now bring a chair over and sit."

Earnan pulled a chair to the side of the bed, and looked at Elena expectantly. She knew she was being childish, but she didn't move, debating whether to wait downstairs despite Earnan's words. He pulled a chair over next to his and exchanged a glance with Brigid.

"Elena, sit in this chair so we can talk," he said, adding a touch of Druid compulsion.

Elena turned away, and walked toward the bathroom, then leaned against the door jam.

"I will hear you out. Or, let me rephrase that, I'll listen, as long as I can stand it, but I can't take much more right now. I'm warning you... don't lie to me. My senses are stronger than they used to be. While I'm in this room with you, I'll know if you lie."

She didn't miss the look that passed between Brigid and Earnan. Faolan covered his eyes with his arm, but still said nothing.

"Are you sure this is the best time? He's been through a lot," Elena asked Brigid.

"You and he both need to hear this, and we must talk it out now. Your lives may depend upon it. You have each saved the other, but some force is working to keep you apart. Nay, not some force, someone, and we must have the answers."

Elena blinked, but said nothing, Faolan kept his eyes hidden, so Earnan took up the tale.

"Since I expect it is useless to ask you to go first, my dear," he inclined his head to Elena, "I will start, but this is mostly Faolan's tale. We'll go over it briefly at first and come back to answer questions later, since I expect you will need time to digest what I am about to say.

"On the eve of Beltane, Red was in a right panic when he got to the marina and you and Lilly weren't there. He hoped it might only be car trouble, but he couldna reach either of you by cell phone. He tried to reach us here, but we were out gathering and preparing for the ceremony, we did not bring a phone.

"Red drove as fast as he could to the farm, and discovered you hadna been there. The hotel said you checked out the previous evening, but Red had spoken to Lilly the previous evening and knew you had not. He drove to Edinburgh, went to the hotel, and insisted they check the rooms, but they were empty.

"He called the satellite phone and let it ring until it was answered and demanded to speak to Faolan. Old Sheila, the housekeeper, had been told under no circumstances was she to interrupt the ceremony, and Red fought with her for all he was worth. He told Sheila that your life was in danger and you would die if he didna speak to Faolan, right away."

He looked at Elena apologetically, "Although we were expecting all of you to arrive by boat earlier in the day, we had no reason to think something was wrong, and so we had gone ahead and started the ceremony. Someone would have had to start even if we had known you were in trouble. Sheila took a big chance and came out to the stones to find us.

"Brigid and I were performing the ritual, and Faolan was watching, when he sensed Sheila's approach. He left the circle and she told him of Red's threats and handed him the phone. Red was outside a restaurant called The Saucy Sorcerer, because that was the last place Lilly had called him from to say you and she were going out for dinner.

"Red could sense a compulsion enchantment, although it didna call to him, and after walking around the building, he believed there was a Ceremony of Beltane happening in the basement."

Earnan rose from his seat and poured himself a glass of water from the tray. He seemed to be waiting for something, and Elena noticed his eyes stray to Faolan. Faolan had uncovered his eyes, and was looking at Earnan with a pleading expression. Elena sensed their wordless conversation. Whatever was coming next was what Faolan had been dreading.

Brigid looked at Faolan lovingly, patted his shoulder, and said, "You must tell her, son." Then she moved from the bed to the other chair.

Elena crossed her arms, as if she could protect herself from whatever it was Faolan feared.

Without meeting Elena's eyes, Faolan took up the tale, his voice low and bleak. "I had learned some new magick while you were gone. I can shape shift into a falcon and fly. I can use the standing stones here to travel to the standing stones on the farm. I know you didna know of the stones before tonight. They have an enchantment, much like the door in the chamber. Only some can see them or sense them.

"I dared not tell you about them because I am bound to keep them hidden, and I was afraid Worthington had somehow learned of them. I thought perhaps 'twas why he wanted the farm so badly." His voice grew faint and lost all inflection as he continued. "I used the stones and the falcon to reach Red, and arrived in time to see you being dragged from the building by a man, and he had Lilly over his shoulder. The compulsion of the building was strong upon me; I struggled to return to my human form, but only managed the wolf at first. A man followed you out the door, and was taking aim. I couldna shift. God forgive me, I leapt at him, just as he fired."

His voice changed to a harsh whisper, "I saw you collapse, your blood was everywhere."

"By the time I got far enough away from the building that I could shift back to human, the ambulance had already taken you to the hospital. Red had gotten Lilly out of the man's car, put her in the truck, and was looking for me. I helped him get Lilly into a nearby hotel and left for the hospital.

"The doctor who came out to meet me was shaking, she was so angry. She told me that you were on a ventilator with a breathing tube, that you had lost enough blood it would be touch and go for the next few days, and that you had lost the baby. I begged to see you, but she said you were in critical care, and needed to be left in peace. The doctor said the police told her you had been shot when a large dog jumped at the man with the gun, and caused it to fire.

"She said you couldna have visitors for at least two days

and to go home, she would call me as soon as I could visit you. I didna leave, I stayed waiting for you to wake, for any sign you could forgive me. After the third day, the doctor came to me and said you had been moved to a new facility and were being placed under a protective order at your own request. You didna want to see me or anyone else. The doctor knew things only you could have told her. She said ever since you had known me, someone was always trying to kill you. You told her you'd nearly died three times, and now this last one had cost you your baby. She said you didna want to see me again.

"At first I thought she was being sympathetic, she said sometimes these feelings of blame lessened over time. I left a number, in case you changed your mind. The doctor said it sometimes took six months or more for the emotional healing necessary, but it would be very dangerous for your mental health if I tried to see you.

"A week later, the doctor called me to come to the hospital, she had your note." He stopped, as though he thought he'd reached the end of the story.

Elena waited for him to continue, and when he didn't, she prompted him, "What note?"

"You said you never wanted to see me again, that you blamed me for the loss of our baby. I was to get whatever items I needed from the farm before you were released from the hospital.

"The doctor was very clear that you had written the note and were of sound thought. She said you had told her I was responsible for your getting shot, and in her opinion, I should be arrested, but that you just wanted me gone." The last part came out in a rush, delivered without inflection while he looked out the window.

Faolan had directed Lilly, Red, and Brigid to help him

secure the farm. They packed up all the belongings, the books, even the cats and taken most of it to Beauly. Then he and Brigid had placed the protective wards around the land and they all returned to the island.

"Och, lass, I realize you are better off without me in your life, you had nearly been murdered twice before this, and now by my own hand, I nearly took your life. It cost us our child, it cost us everything. I understand why you couldna' look at me, I canna even look at myself."

Chapter Forty-five

Elena kept her shield tight around her, she couldn't go through the grief of losing him again, and she didn't yet know whether to trust what she was being told. It didn't make any sense. Could Brigid or Earnan have something to do with all of this?

Then Brigid spoke, "Lass, you have the most powerful shield I have ever encountered. You must lower it a bit so you can sense Faolan... sense all of us. I know you must wish to protect yourself, 'tis plain you have been hurt badly, but we doona' yet know how. You have heard Faolan's story, and you sensed my anger at you when you arrived. Does it not make sense to you lass, that I would be angry? You have my word we will not intrude, but you canna know if we tell you the truth unless you lower your shield."

Elena looked Brigid then Earnan in the eye, before turning to Faolan. He would not meet her gaze. She lowered her shield slightly, trying to taste the atmosphere, sense the lies. Faolan's despair washed over her, a flood of emotion, of loss. His grief was palpable, his self-loathing knew no bounds. Elena gasped with the pain of it.

She turned to Brigid and Earnan again, and sensed their

love for Faolan, for her. Brigid said, "He has been that way since he returned to the island without you. Is it any wonder he turned toward the void today?"

"Turned toward the void, what do you mean?"

"Aye, lass, just before you lay with him, I felt him slip into the void. When you put your hand on his chest you felt his last heartbeat, but his spirit had already gone. Before I could warn you, you cried out with such power as I had never heard before. I know of no Druid power that can bring a man back from the void. Lass, I doona' know exactly what you are, aye, we have all sensed Druid, but there is more to you than that.

"You saved his life today, you brought him back from the void. Can you bring him back from his despair? Will your story ease his heart?"

Elena went to Faolan, sat on the edge of the bed, and took his large hand in her small ones. She lowered her shield, not all the way, but further so the others could sense her story, as well as hear it. With a sigh, she began.

"I went to the doctor's office, and met Gabhran MacLachlan. You were right, Brigid, he is powerful, but I sensed more. There were two sources of power, a duality about him, and a sense of impending struggle. I let him sense a little of my power and he responded right away. I am sure he is untrained. Or rather, he *was* untrained. I don't know about now. He refused to give me any more information once I warned him about his power. I tried to get him to come with me, but he said I needed to return the following week and perhaps we could speak more of it then. He didn't even confirm I was p—pregnant." She swallowed hard and waited a moment before she could continue.

"That night, I insisted Lilly and I go to a restaurant near his office, The Saucy Sorcerer. I realize now there must have been some type of enchantment on it that drew me in. Ordering felt like a tremendous burden and I finally asked the waiter if there were any unlisted specials. He acted as though I had won the grand prize. Other staff visited us throughout the meal and they fussed over us, or maybe it was just me. Lilly said they brought a special dessert, although I have no memory of that.

"The next thing I knew, I was on the floor, tied back-to-back with Lilly. Worthington and Liam were there, and Worthington said he would have us killed as part of the ceremony. Later, Liam returned by himself and injected Lilly with something to make her sleep. He injected just a little into me, he said it was so I couldn't invade his thoughts. He said I was powerful."

Faolan still wasn't looking at her, but he hadn't pulled his hand back. She knew the ending would be painful, but maybe this next part would make him angry. Anger would be preferable to the despair that poured from him.

"Liam kissed my neck, and said he wished he could keep me for himself, but that I was to play an important role at Beltane." Faolan's hand jerked in hers. "He said I would be a sexual sacrifice, but that he would cast an enchantment so I would enjoy it, and then I would be a blood sacrifice. When he kissed my neck, he said I was carrying your child, that he could feel it. He said it would make my sacrifice that much more potent."

Faolan finally made eye contact with her, and she could sense his fury. *Good, it's a start.* "Then he put me to sleep, and the next time I woke there was a ceremony and people were in the room. Almost everyone had on dark robes, but I figured out which one was Worthington and which was Symington. Gabhran was there too, but he wasn't in a robe. I tried to call out to Gabhran, but my voice felt paralyzed. He heard me a couple of times with his mind, but kept getting drawn back into the ceremony.

"Worthington said Gabhran was there to be inducted, and then he gave Symington a scepter called the Scepter of Entitlement to test Gabhran with. He said they were entering a new era of Druidry and he was presenting the Scepter to the Order.

Earnan and Brigid gasped, and Faolan and Elena looked at them. "'Tis a powerful and ancient artifact. Go on Elena," Earnan said.

"Worthington handed the Scepter to the Master on behalf of the Order. He held it high in the air and Worthington called on the wind as part of the ceremony I think. Only it seemed the wind was much stronger than Symington had expected. Symington asked the Scepter to judge the worthy, or something like that, and then the wind turned dark. Tendrils crept through the room, tasting us," she shivered.

"I yelled at Gabhran not to look, and he must have heard me. The next thing I knew he was cutting us loose, and helping us escape. We almost made it out, and I felt the dark find him again. It passed right over me and I felt it slide into him. He fought it, somehow; he still got us out, even though I could feel the darkness entering him. We kind of pushed each other onto the street. He was trying to put us in his car, but the dark came with him. The dark liked him; it felt like... I don't know, like it was home?"

She went on, very quickly now, her voice a whisper, "Anyway, I heard a growl, I tried to turn and lost my balance, I fell, I heard a gunshot, and I woke up in the hospital. The doctor took out my breathing tube, and I wanted to ask questions but I couldn't, all I could do was sleep. The next time I woke up, she told me my husband and I had been mugged and we'd both been shot. She said you had been killed trying to save me, and I lost our baby because I lost so much blood."

Elena had been trying to keep her shield low enough to sense them, but high enough to protect herself. The shield crashed down around her with those words. Her tenuous grip on control slipped and she wailed, "You were dead, I'd lost our baby, I couldn't sense you anymore, I wanted to die!"

And she did what she'd wanted to do since the moment she realized he was alive, she buried her face against his chest and sobbed. Such was the power of her emotion that it threatened to carry all of them away on a wave of grief.

Brigid quickly came to Elena's side, worried that the strength of her feelings was too much for Faolan in his condition. She spoke urgently "Elena, you must pull it back, it's too much, you're hurting Faolan. He's not recovered enough yet. Elena, pull it back!"

Wave after wave crashed through Elena, each bringing its own tide of emotion. Her anger at Faolan for not trusting their love was blazing, searing into her, flames scarring her soul. A sense of blood-thirsty revenge for Liam, for tasting her soul without permission, for all he would do to her, for the obsessive love she knew he felt. Betrayal stabbed at her heart, Lilly and Red, people she had felt would come to be the parents she'd never had, and the knowledge they would always choose Faolan over her.

Finally, her rage settled where it belonged, on herself. If she hadn't insisted on sending Red back, on staying one more night in Edinburgh, ongoing to that restaurant. If she hadn't fallen over when she did, her baby would still be alive, physical proof that Faolan had once loved her, that she had been lovable.

*

Faolan brushed Brigid's hands aside and took Elena in his arms, pulling her fully onto his lap so that he could cradle her, rock her while she cried. He looked over Elena's head at Earnan, and said one word. "Go." They did, locking the door behind them.

Faolan held Elena against his chest, and mourned with her. He felt her white-hot anger at him, and winced. Could she ever forgive him? Would he forgive himself? Och, Red, and Lilly had raged at him, swore at him for leaving Elena. He'd used the Druid compulsion to make them listen, they hadna wanted to leave her. It was only his promise they could return as wolves to watch over her that made them finally agree. He swore an oath to kill Liam, if he hadn't already died. He'd touched Elena, wanted her, would have sacrificed her. Aye, he and Worthington were dead men.

As Elena wept, a raw power hit Faolan with the force of a nuclear shockwave. The energy that exploded from Elena pushed outward, rippling through the air. The solid objects around him began to shimmer, as though the force of her rage was changing their molecular structure. She was incensed, placing the blame for the loss of their baby on herself, as proof of her unworthiness.

Christ, what was she? His mind was assaulted, nay his very cells were contracting with the force of her fury. The edges of his vision began to darken, a roaring in his ears told him he would be conscious only a minute longer.

With great effort, as though he were moving his arms against hurricane force winds, he placed his hands on Elena's face. He had but moments of willful determination left before his mind was forced to blackness by the strength of her emotions. He gasped her name with his last breath.

"Elena MacGailtry."

*

Elena heard her name from very far away, as though from a dream. She fought the turmoil she suddenly felt around her. *Dear God, what's happening, who's attacking us?* She raised her shield quickly around both of them. As soon as her shield rose, she felt the turmoil cease. Whatever the threat, it had retreated; they would be safe for now.

She turned to Faolan and saw his face had turned gray, he was barely conscious. She tried to jump from his lap, to make him lie down, but he only held her more tightly to him.

"Kiss me, lass," he gasped.

"Faolan, what happened? You need t—"

"Kiss me now!"

His hands were still pressed to her cheeks and he turned her head up for access to her mouth, and pressed his lips lightly to hers. He kissed her gently, almost lazily, as if they had all the time in the world. *Or as if he were nearly unconscious.*

Elena leaned away from his kisses and examined his face carefully. Some of the color had returned, but there were lines of pain etched around his mouth. She realized Brigid had been speaking to her before she left the room, telling her to pull them back. It was her own feelings that had caused the storm. No matter how upset she was, she would never intentionally hurt Faolan. He needed to heal; they needed to talk.

She felt stronger now, different. A force within her had awakened; it was both exhilarating and frightening. It was the light, only changed, more potent. She tentatively placed her hand against Faolan's chest, and sent a small pulse of energy.

He inhaled audibly, shivering against the heat of her hand.

"Elena," and then his lips were on hers, insistent, hungry. His fingers traced her jaw line, and he put his thumbs on either side of her mouth, opening her lips wider. His tongue thrust in, only to be met by hers, he plunged and plundered, claiming her.

She felt him stiffen beneath her, and she squirmed against his erection, causing a moan to escape. With an unexpected swiftness, she was on her back and he was pressing himself to her side, his fingers lacing into her tangle of hair, and holding her head so that his mouth could move to her neck.

"Faolan," she sighed, unsure if this was a dream, and unwilling to wake if it was.

He traced her neck with his velvet tongue, planting open-mouthed kisses below her ear, along her collarbone. He returned to ply her mouth with more kisses, running his tongue along her teeth, the roof of her mouth, her lips.

"I need you, Elena, my only love. I want you. Och, I know we didna finish talking, but we have talked enough for the now. Let me love you, I need to taste you, hold your desire against my tongue. I want to feel you come against my lips and around my fingers. And then my love, I will fill you, take you the way I need you."

"Yes," was all she could manage, as the fire built low in her belly, and aching, empty muscles clenched in anticipation.

He helped her undress, not slow or gentle, but frantic to feel her skin against his. She sat on the bed, her black hair curling down her back and over her shoulders, hiding her breasts from his view. He pushed her back, and cupped her breasts in his hands, pushing them together, and buried his face in the cleavage. His tongue raked over her nipples, he nibbled and kissed every inch of first one breast, and then the other.

She arched her back, pushing the breast he was kissing against his mouth, pulled his head close, "Harder, Faolan, harder."

With a groan, Faolan pulled her nipple into his mouth, taking the whole areola and more into his mouth, sucking and kneading with his hands. He switched to the other breast, and she pressed her head back into the pillow and arched her back even further, pulled his head tighter against her breast, seeking the pain with the pleasure. He bit down, and her moan told him she was nearly ready to come.

"Och, not yet Elena, my love. You must wait for your pleasure until I am ready to give it to you." He left her breasts, and ran his tongue slowly down her stomach. He pushed her legs apart and he poised between them in perfect position to give her what she wanted.

"Please, Faolan, now."

"Oh, 'tis asking you are doing now? You must be punished for seeking your pleasure while I was unable to join you." He licked and nibbled her thighs.

"Wh— what?" She couldn't bring her mind to understand his words.

He continued to lick and nip all around her thighs and lower belly, but never quite reaching that spot where she wanted him. "Do you think I doona' realize that you woke me with your mouth? I was having a most explicit fantasy of you, a wet dream as they call it. I could feel your sweet lips, your hot mouth. You pulled me in deeper, sliding your hand along in rhythm, and you clutched my sac in your wee hand."

Elena arched her back again, and thrust her hips toward his mouth. "Please."

"Nay, lass, you need to know, 'twas one of the most

beautiful moments. I am only sorry I was not believing 'twas real, else I'd have turned you over and returned the favor. 'Tis what I am going to do now."

"Yes," she panted, her hands went to his head and again she tried to position him between her thighs, but he laughed.

"I know you, lass, you will come the minute I put my lips to you, which is hardly a sufficient torture. So I will do it a second time, only much more slowly than this first time, and I willna let you come until I believe you have been punished enough."

She started to move her hand to between her legs, gasping, "Been months, can't wait."

He actually growled as he pushed her hand aside, "Mine." Then he pressed his lips to her hard nub and she shuddered beneath him, coming, but feeling empty as her muscles contracted around nothing. He barely let her recover before he began his delicious torture, his fingers gliding, his tongue lapping, he brought her to the edge repeatedly, before backing off. She was strung tight, but so was he. She could feel the restraint in the hard press of his muscles.

"Sit up a bit, lass," and he placed a second pillow under her shoulders. Soon, I am going to give you your release, but then I am going to fill you. I am going to fuck you; I am going to take what I need."

He pumped his fingers, and flicked her with his tongue, and the sight of his mouth placed so intimately was intoxicating. He removed his fingers and she whimpered a little, which caused him to laugh against her in a most interesting place. He looked up at her and their gazes locked, as his tongue lapped at her wetness. He pushed his long fingers back inside her hot tunnel, pumping fast and closed his mouth over her clitoris and kissed hard. She threw her head back as muscles clenched around his fingers, and her orgasm swept over her.

Elena was still shuddering when he drove his cock inside, stretching her, filling her. She gasped with the feel of him, she'd forgotten how large he was, and little huffs of breath escaped with each thrust. Then he went quite still.

"Faolan, are you okay?" Elena asked, frantic that he had hurt himself. He was just recovering from a very serious injury. What was she thinking?

"Aye," he said through clenched teeth. "Doona' move, lass."

Elena realized he wasn't in pain, or at least not in pain from his wounds. The knowledge that she did this to him, brought him to the brink of losing his self-restraint was heady. She held very still waiting for him to get his control back.

He cupped her face in his hands, his cock buried deep inside her. "Elena, my love, I will spend my life making up for these last few months. It seems we have much to forgive, from each other and from ourselves."

"I forgi—"

"Nay, lass, not now," he interrupted. "These are feelings deep within us that will take time to heal. Any words of forgiveness spoken now wouldna heal the heart."

Elena knew he was right, and as much as she longed to take him in her arms and declare all forgiven, she knew they each harbored deep emotional scars that could only be healed by time and love.

He kissed her slowly, possessively, until she rocked her hips beneath him in a silent plea. His hips moved languidly, in a shallow, circular motion that brought new intense feelings, bringing her close to the edge again.

"Elena, my love, tell me that this willna be the last time we make love, that you willna ever leave me," his voice broke on the question.

They'd made promises before, could the promises last this time? He hadn't even heard the rest of her story yet. She had questions for him. Elena hesitated, hedged in her answer, "This will not be the last time we make love."

He buried his face in her hair, but not before she'd seen the sheen of tears in his tawny eyes.

Her own eyes filled with tears, and she wrapped her legs around him, her body responding despite her emotions. His rocking brought her ever closer to the edge, "I'm so close, come with me, Faolan."

He continued with the short, quick strokes, circling his hips, his breathing fast. He lifted himself on his hands to gaze into her face, she looked back, her face filled with love. Her lips parted on a sigh, and she felt her climax build from the inside, slowly, rolling over her, one gentle spasm giving away to another.

"Now," she sighed.

Chapter Forty-six

The six of them were to meet in the drawing room after breakfast the next morning. Elena was uncomfortable and had again pulled her shield up tightly around herself. She stood at the window and looked out, not turning when she sensed others arrive. When Faolan entered, he walked behind her, slipped his arms around her, and kissed the top of her head. His face lingered in her hair and he inhaled sharply.

"I'll be on the couch should you care to sit next to me, lass," he gave her a squeeze and went to sit.

Of all the things she knew she faced this day, facing Lilly was by far the hardest. Elena simply didn't know how to feel. She'd loved Lilly like a mother; they shared the last normal week of Elena's life. They'd laughed and talked. They'd dreamed of the baby. Elena had feared for Lilly's life when they'd been tied in that chamber. She would have done anything, bargained with the devil to secure Lilly's freedom. So much had been lies.

The protective barriers Elena had placed around her heart began to weaken. Elena realized Lilly's pain had been great, too. She'd lost Elena, had lost her future grandchild. She had believed Elena no longer cared for Faolan and never wanted to see any of them again.

Elena heard a muffled sob behind her, and turned slowly, eyes seeking Lilly.

They met in the middle, hugging and crying, speaking over each other, apologizing, each seeking forgiveness. Lilly wiped the tears from Elena's face, "Och, Elena, shh, no more crying now. I have something to tell you and you are going to be listening to me.

"Someone did magick or an enchantment to keep us apart, just like that night we went to dinner in that damned restaurant. I am sure as I live and breathe that someone is Worthington. Nevertheless, he's not the only someone that kept us apart. You needed me and I wasna there for you. 'Twill not happen again." Lilly thrust her chin in Faolan's direction, "He has found his own mother, he willna be needing me to take care of him, but you do. He didna listen to me anyway! I love you as much as any mother could love a daughter, and I am claiming you as mine. Anyone who tries to hurt you again will have to come through me."

Elena was wrapped in Lilly's loving hug and the final barriers protecting her heart fell away. *Lilly thinks of me as a daughter.* It wasn't the people in this room, it was someone else that had done this to them, and they needed to forgive each other.

"I love you, too, Lilly, I would be proud to have you as my mother." Both women hugged and cried some more. Then Lilly looked fiercely over Elena's shoulder at Faolan. "I doona' know why I listened to that big ugly brute of a wolf!"

Faolan's hurt emanated from across the room, and Elena swiftly stole a glance at him. *Was he pouting? He was!* Elena laughed and Brigid, who had been watching from across the room laughed right along with her. Lilly was standing with her hands on her hips, glaring at Faolan, and Faolan had his lower lip poked out. Red looked like he wanted to melt into his chair, but Earnan's eyes sparkled.

Elena grabbed Lilly's hand from her hip and dragged her over to the couch were Faolan sat. "In America, we have this custom, where daughters have to introduce their parents to their boyfriends. I don't know what to call him any more—"

Faolan's pained intake of breath interrupted Elena.

"Because, he was my husband, and then I was his widow, but now he's not really dead..." She fought hard against the giggles that were threatening to overtake her.

"So, my wonderful new Mom," she looked at Lilly, who practically melted on the spot, "Allow me to present to you the man I love with all my heart and with whom I promise to spend the rest of my days."

"And nights, lass, doona' be forgetting the nights," Faolan added, as he jumped from his seat and swept both of the women into his arms.

It was much easier to talk after that. Brigid had already filled Red and Lilly in on what she knew, and now it was time for Elena to finish. She told of her call to Worthington's office and discovering he was still alive. She'd expected him to try to kill her once more as the deadline approached. She had set up the timers and shutters to make sure any shooter would have to approach the house from only one direction, she knew just where to hide.

"I planned to shoot him with buckshot and then call the police. I didn't care what happened to me. I just wanted to make sure the farm stayed in MacGailtry hands, even if I was the last one.

"I was stunned to see you," she nodded at Red, and turning

to Faolan, "I never really did see you, I fired as soon as Liam took his shot."

Speaking slowly now, processing the thoughts as she spoke them aloud, "It was the same as when I was shot. Everything happened at once. There wasn't anything either Faolan or I did on purpose to hurt the other. When we work together, it seems that nothing is stronger than we are, but it's when we allow ourselves to be separated that other forces interfere. Fate forces us back together when we're apart, but always under near impossible circumstances. It seems each of us is always depending on the other in order to survive."

Earnan stood suddenly and looked at Brigid, "Finally, they have gotten there!"

"Yes, but we needed to let them discover on their own."

"I doona' ken what you are talking about. Explain." Faolan looked irritated at the older man's interruption.

Earnan answered, "Aye, lad, I will explain, and ask a few questions along the way. Elena, lass, you are positive it was Worthington and Liam? In the ceremony? And Liam who tried to shoot you?"

"Positive."

"Did the darkness, as you called it, kill anyone? Or does the whole sect remain intact?"

"There were many who died. It crushed Symington. I could hear others screaming, but it left Worthington alone. He seemed to…swell? He was taking back the sect that night. Don't ask me how I know, I either heard it or just know it." She gave a gasp, "Liam is Worthington's son. I don't know how I know that either, but I am certain."

Earnan nodded, "That makes a fair amount of sense, else he would not have trusted him. Do you know the names of any other survivors, is that Gabhran one of them?"

Elena replied slowly, feeling a terrible sense of foreboding as she answered. "I don't know. I want to tell you no. There is something about him...I can't put my finger on it...."

"You willna be putting your finger or anything else on that man," Faolan growled.

She gave him a small strained smile. "I'm serious, I told you of the sense of duality I felt in him, but there was much more. When I met him in his office he felt...I don't know, lost? Like he needed answers and had hopes of getting them soon. I saw him at dinner that night, he was sitting with Liam, and I was worried for him.

"He was at the ceremony, but apart, not yet theirs. Worthington wanted him, and wanted Gabhran to see what a powerful master of the Etarlam he was going to be, it was part of the seduction. Part of all of the show was to impress Gabhran. But, Gabhran helped us, he saved our lives that night, of that I am certain.

"There is dark in him now that wasn't there before. He got us out, but when he started to put us in his car, the dark was calling for him to complete the sacrifices, and I don't know if he would or could have resisted. I can't help but feel he is important and we need to find him."

"All right, lass, we will need to consider that. Now a last question and then some answers," he smiled at Elena gently. "Tell me about your shield. How does it feel to you, how have you used it?"

"My shield? I don't know. I can make people see things sometimes, things that aren't really there. I used it to keep people from knowing I was hiding nearby, hiding my thoughts. I haven't needed it these last months, except maybe to protect me from my own thoughts," she laughed.

Earnan did not laugh with her. "You shielded your heart

from the pain. Elena, I think we may have only been half right when we told you there was Druid about you."

"Nay!" Faolan shouted and jumped to his feet.

"Aye, lad, now sit." Brigid and Earnan exchanged looks, before Brigid picked up the explanation.

"Elena dear, we believe your heritage is both Druid and Fae, you are a changeling. There were a very few of the most powerful Druids who became consorts of members of the Fae Royal Court. It was believed they could mate and successfully produce an offspring, but these changelings never actually appeared. I believe you are proof that it must have been successful at least once, thousands of years ago. The power must have been deep within you, and how or why it came to the surface is something we may never know." She waited, but Elena said nothing, just pulled her shield tight again.

"When I first met you I sensed the light, but I thought 'twas the light of the Druid Sisterhood, and aye, that is present. I have seen evidence of a much stronger light since you returned. A light powerful enough to bring Faolan back from the void. 'Tis not just your light but your shield that has changed.

"When you have yourself surrounded by your shield, like now, 'tis impossible for any of us to penetrate. You have the most powerful shield I have ever encountered. Yesterday, you let us in by degrees, and you were able to sense our emotions. When your grief overwhelmed you, your shield fell, and you very nearly made Faolan pass out with the power of your feelings. Although he bade us go, I suspect it got stronger after we left. I could feel the energy throughout the castle.

"Tell me, lass, do you sense the truth of what I am saying? That you are both Druid and Fae?"

"Yes," Elena whispered, and then she was hit by a wave of

overwhelming sadness coming from Faolan. "Is this really important? What do we do now?" Elena asked, reaching for Faolan's hand offering comfort.

"Aye, lass, 'tis important. We have told you about the prophecy, the one that foretold of a time when Druids would again be needed on this earth. That is why Faolan's family has been protected, why others have been in hiding. Obviously, Worthington also knows of such a prophecy."

Elena gasped with the memory, "He called it the Epoch of Druidry, and said it started with this Beltane!"

They all exchanged looks before Brigid continued. "I have seen a vision, though 'tis not complete. It continues to visit me in stages, in parts, as though even now events are changing things." Her eyes grew distant and her voice took on a dreamy quality, "It has been revealed that man as dark Druid will shift the balance of power on Earth and mankind will suffer greatly. A child who was lost twiceover, of nature and light, joins one who was hidden, a child of the night.

"Others are lost, some will be found, which path to follow? Light can exist in darkness, darkness can never exist in the light. The past revealed. The journey for darkness and light, from Beltane to Beltane has begun, they are called for great purpose," Brigid finished on a sigh.

****

They all stood at the little dock where Faolan and Elena's boat was tied. Brigid and Lilly had spent the day making the boat ready for an extended journey.

Faolan seemed to be struggling with something, and wasn't yet willing to tell Elena what was bothering him. She felt him give himself a sort of mental shake before he walked over to where she was speaking quietly with Lilly.

"Lilly, I doona' know what to say. You were right and I should have listened to you," Faolan said.

"Aye, you should have," she answered a bit, sharply. Then she softened, and hugged him.

Faolan said, "You knew 'twas all a lie, but Elena and I were both unable to see the truth. It must have been done with magick. I wonder if the doctor at the hospital was a willing participant?"

"Aye, Faolan, I believe she is a member of Worthington's order," Earnan spoke up. "She disappeared after Elena was discharged, and no one remembers where she came from or how long she worked at that hospital."

"And you are fair certain Elena and I should leave today? We have not even begun Elena's training yet."

"Will you quit worrying about that," Brigid asked, clearly frustrated with him. "The wards have been cast upon your boat, none can find you by tracking it. There are books that you both must read onboard. You know which spells she needs to learn first, and you will be a fine teacher. She must explore certain parts of her shield alone. The prophecy is still unfinished, but 'twas clear from what we know that you and Elena belong together; you will be instrumental in whatever battles we face.

"Before you can do that, you both must come to terms with what happened. Intentions are not enough. You must build your trust again; your lives depend on it. You must make yourselves strong so that no enchantment can e'er again tear you asunder. What is it that fashes you, lad?"

"Och, I should have come to you sooner and asked. I wished to learn the Eternal Vow spell. I wish to be bound through time to Elena, if she will have me," he smiled at Elena.

"Will you prepare it for our return?"

"By all that's sacred, Brigid, did you not tell them?" Earnan roared.

Unperturbed, Brigid smiled. Instead of answering, she asked a question.

"Tell me, Faolan, what was it like the first time you kissed the lass?" She went on without waiting for an answer. "How about the first time you made love? Did you ever offer your life for hers? What happened then?"

Elena's eyes grew wide and she turned to Faolan, but he stared at Brigid.

"Aye, lad," she continued softly. "I doona' know the where or the how of it, but she is already your mate, you have already spoken the vows in some life.

He turned to look at Elena, "'Twas the shift, lass," he said wonderingly.

"Aye," Elena replied leaping into his arms and wrapping her arms and legs around him.

He cupped her head reverently in his hands and looked deep into her eyes, before capturing her mouth with his. The first time he'd kissed her, Elena had felt the earth shift around them at the magick of their connection. This time the shift started on a shiver and ended on a sigh. It was the in-between that had Lilly sitting on the deck, and everyone else staggering.

****

Elena leaned back into Faolan's embrace, as they stood together on the rear deck of the boat. The black velvet sky hung heavy with a thick blanket of stars, the Milky Way low over their heads. It was quiet out here, the only sounds the gentle lapping of the water against the hull, and Faolan's breath near her ear.

"Tell me why you were sad, Faolan, when you found out I might have Fae blood. You know I don't know the legends. Does that mean something is wrong with me?"

He pulled her hips back and she inhaled sharply at the feel of his erection pressing against her back. He was quiet so long that she thought maybe he wasn't going to answer, but he was merely gathering his thoughts.

"'Tis said the Fae have a special power and a beauty so compelling that if a man is touched by a Fae princess his soul will be lost to her forever. If 'tis a male Fae, the woman is ruined for any other man, for none can match the attraction and sexual prowess."

Elena leaned away from him slightly and looked back over her shoulder, trying to see his face. He smiled at her, and she felt no trace of the earlier sadness. He leaned down and covered her mouth with his, kissing her gently for long slow minutes. When he straightened, she pressed her back against him once more, and waited.

"I was sad because I thought Brigid was telling me that I had these feelings because you were part Fae. I didna want my love to be part of a Fae enchantment. I have been irresistibly drawn to you from the moment we met. Loving you is like breathing, something I canna live without.

"I am not sad about it anymore. If your being part Fae was the only reason I loved you, then I would still be a lucky man, because you love me back. We know 'tis much more than that, now. We know we found each other and we canna resist each other because we have been bound through eternity. You are my destiny, and I know I will love you, and you will love me through the end of time."

Faolan scooped her up and carried her to the flybridge, and

they made love under the stars. Their hearts were healing. They were beginning their life journey together. They were off to see new lands, learn magick, and someday, they would make babies. Elena marveled that this magnificent Highlander loved her. They made the very earth shift with the power of their love. She knew that whatever adventures awaited, they would face them together.

Eternity. That was a concept she could live with.

~~The Beginning~~

About the Author

Raised in California, Laura likes it hot, which explains why she ended up in Arizona via such diverse places as Japan, Maine, and Florida, and many more places in between. After retiring from the US Navy, she found a niche working for land management agencies, including the National Park Service and the Bureau of Land Management. Though she has held many jobs around the world, her favorite was working and living in Grand Canyon National Park. Working (and eating) in New Orleans was a close second. You will find many of her books are set against the rich backdrops provided by coastal Louisiana and northern Arizona.

When asked how she started writing, Laura tells of waking on Boxing Day a few years ago, with a woman named Elena MacFarland yammering in her dreams, demanding her story be told. Despite never attempting to write fiction before that morning, Laura ignored all of the holiday visitors and the Highland Destiny series was born. She doesn't believe it was a coincidence that the great grandmother who died when Laura was just a baby was named Elena MacFarland. Destiny does play a hand.

Laura became a full-time writer in 2012, and now she spends her time writing, watching her Arizona Diamondbacks, and working on her very own version of the Willow Springs Ranch in northwestern Arizona. She is a multi-published author of erotic romance, mystery, and urban fantasy and her books can be found at all major online retailers.

Connect with Laura at:

Twitter: @LauraHarner

Facebook: facebook.com/lauraharner

Or even better…check out the website at:

http://LauraHarner.com

Also Available from Laura Harner

Highland Pull,

Highland Destiny Book Two

Waking up next to a dead woman was a good indication that Dr. Gabhran MacLachlan was in bigger trouble than he'd realized. Recognizing this as another trap set by the dark Druid Master, Gav races from Edinburgh to New Orleans to find Alysone, a mental patient who claims to have awakened in a reality that isn't hers. Her story, so close to his own, may be the necessary key to unlock his Druid memories and prevent him from shifting realities once again.

When Alysone disappears, Detective Miranda Close is less than thrilled to discover her new landlord and would-be lover is the missing woman's doctor. Raised in the magick of New Orleans and already familiar with the darkness coiled within Gav, Randi's belief in the supernatural may be all that saves her life when they are pulled hundreds of years into his past, and only one of them remembers the truth. When realities shift once again, Randi realizes they may be pawns in a much larger game.

Highland Push,

Highland Destiny Book Three

The Highland Destiny saga continues in Highland Push, a tale of betrayal, murder, and magick spanning two continents and hundreds of years.

Using the spell of time shifting, Alexander MacLachlan says good-bye to his beloved brother, his brother's wife, and his own darling Alysone--necessary sacrifices for the survival of Druidry. With his family far in the future preparing for battle, Alex must fulfill his destiny: find the Worthington heir, then kill and be killed.

Thrust forward to a time not her own, Alysone and the others discover precious few light Druids remain to offer their protection to Scotia and the world. As the time for the prophesied battle grows nearer, past meets present, and they realize someone besides Alexander is manipulating events. In a race against time, they must discover the lost secrets of Druidry, even as the members of the dark Bresal Etarlam work to destroy all that is light and claim the Druid legacy as their own.

Highland Destiny,

Highland Destiny Book Four

Although Professor Andi Cunningham knows Druidry and magick are real, her dream to recreate a twelfth century Scottish castle is destroyed when the Druid who claimed her heart wards her from the land. Now Andi's deeply hidden Druid powers have been awakened by her new husband, Liam—Ian's descendant and the son of the Master of the Bresal Etarlam, who wants her untapped power as his own.

Ian Worthington, the ancient warrior displaced by time, knows sacrifices must be made for the good of the order, including his own heart. However, as prophesies are revealed, he discovers sending Andi away for her protection may prove too costly for them all. When Ian convinces her to return to finish her work on the castle, both sides in the Druid conflict are pleased.

With both Ian and Liam keeping secrets, Andi must uncover the darkest secrets of her Druid heritage and the connection to the past, before the upcoming battle destroys the balance of power forever. All that's at stake is the fate of the world.

Honey House

Former con artist Katherine "KC" Carmichael inherits the Honey House, a Bed and Breakfast located in the tiny town of Juniper Springs, AZ, a hot bed of the paranormal tourism industry. It doesn't take her long to discover that both the town and the House are keeping secrets. The town entices thrill-seekers with special photo-safaris at "The Way They Were" Ranch, to take advantage of the rumors that werewolves have been spotted in the area.

KC realizes something doesn't add up when the local sheriff throws her in jail for breaking the town's full moon curfew. She soon discovers werewolves and witches are real, and she wonders what other fairy tales might be waiting to come to life. With multiple murders and men to distract her, KC needs to discover her own hidden magick in order to survive.

Forbidden Love

Detective Danielle Delacroiux is one kick-ass detective with the Généreux PD, and she's got a murder on her hands. By all accounts, Crease Martin was nothing but a homeless drunk and a lousy informant, but Dani counted him as one of hers. Now she'll stop at nothing to find his murderer. With a red silk handkerchief under the body as her first clue, Dani wants a quick break. When a handsome stranger practically strolls up to the crime scene, Dani can't help but notice his expensive Italian suit, red silk tie, and empty breast pocket. Could he be who she's looking for?

Dani is less than impressed when Mr. tall, dark, and yummy is introduced as the newest lawyer in town, and even worse, he's another of the Charbonnet offspring. The deadly feud between the Delacroiux and Charbonnet families goes way back, and there is one thing she knows without a doubt. If Hawk Charbonnet committed this crime, she'll be damned if his connections will do him any good. She'll happily lock his arrogant ass in jail for the rest of his life. Which would be a shame, because she had to admit, it was a fine-looking ass.

Altered States, free prologue for the

Altered States Series

New Orleans Police Detective Sam Garrett can't believe his bad luck when he's assigned to investigate a string of gay-bashings turned deadly in the French Quarter. Especially when he realizes Travis Boudreaux, his new, hot, and most-likely-straight partner, plans to use him as bait. The worst part? They've got no back-up because the rest of the city is preoccupied by another series of killings — the victims drained of blood.

Deep Blues Goodbye, Book One of the

Altered States Series

The world might not have been ready for vampires when NOPD Detective Travis Boudreaux had the bad taste to sit up at his own funeral, but two years later, the new cause célèbre is civil rights for preternatural beings and most humans are on the bandwagon. Except whoever is killing vampires and wannabes.

Detective Sam Garrett hates all things preternatural. Having your undead partner try to make you his first meal will do that to a guy. One final screw-up gets Sam banished to the Paranormal Criminal Investigations Unit—the Odd Squad—under the oversight of Detective Danny Burkette.

Now it's up to Burkette to work with Garrett by day and Boudreaux by night as they follow a trail of clues that leads from the historic cemeteries of New Orleans to the bayous of southern Louisiana. Under the all-too-interested gaze of a Master vampire and the local werewolf pack Alpha, they discover some lessons in life—and death—take longer to learn...and not all second chances are created equal.

Warning: In this series the vampires don't sparkle, werewolves kill, and sometimes the men have sex. With each other.

Ty Hard, Book One of the

Willow Springs Ranch Series

Tyler has used Don't Ask, Don't Tell as a shield against the truth since he was seventeen. Now, Ty finds himself cut loose from his Navy career after months of rehab from a debilitating head injury. At a loss as to what to do with his life, he travels to Willow Springs Ranch in Arizona to visit his surrogate father, only to arrive minutes after his oldest friend's death. Ty must come to terms with the loss while he fights to keep the PTSD from pulling him under. The last thing he's ready to think about is his growing attraction for another man.

Rancher Cass Cartwright's relationships never last more than a few hours, and that's just the way he likes it. Now he's in danger of doing the one thing he swore never to do: fall in love. Can Cass convince Ty to let go of his past or will sabotage at the ranch kill their love before it has a chance to grow?

Hold Tight, Book Two of the

Willow Spring Ranch Series

Sheriff Holden Titus had organized his fresh start down to the last detail. Except for the part about the bomb that blew his plans all to hell. Now he's running out of time, without a job, without a home, and struggling to get back on his feet. Literally.

Despite the impolite rejection, Drew knows he didn't have the wrong impression months ago when he asked the sheriff to dance, but he never expected to have Holden's life in his hands. Literally.

Thanks to some meddlesome matchmaking, the two men are now temporary housemates at the Willow Springs Ranch and Drew is determined to help Holden heal, both physically and emotionally. Even if it means he has to drag the other man kicking and screaming to physical therapy...and out of the closet. In fact, that might be kind of fun.

The problem is, Holden doesn't consider himself in the closet...but not all secrets are created equal.

Rescued, Book Two of the

Three's Allowed Series

Elizabeth Ashford runs into the wilderness near a highway rest area, trying to escape her abusive husband before he kills her. Self-made millionaire and expert in high tech security, Michael Enwright is at the first rest stop of his long overdue sabbatical when he sees the fleeing woman and intervenes, saving Elizabeth's life, while nearly losing his own. When Michael's help is misinterpreted, he ends up handcuffed and face down in the dirt before Elizabeth can set her former lover, Sheriff Graeme Kennedy, straight. In order to protect Lizzie, Graeme is forced to work with Michael and brings both of them to his cabin for protection.

Now Graeme finally has Elizabeth under his roof, right where he's always wanted her. So why is he jacking off to visions of the drop dead gorgeous and take-charge Michael? Some things never change.

Part of Me

Jason's life hasn't been easy. Feeling responsible for the death of his twin the night they graduated from high school, Jason commits emotional suicide by revealing he's gay after his brother's funeral, permanently severing all ties with his ultra-conservative parents. But when he runs to Hunter Dane for comfort, all he can see is the same rejection mirrored on his best friend's face.

Twelve years later, Jason needs all the support he can get to beat back the cancer invading his body. When Hunter unexpectedly shows up to shift from former friend to caregiver, Jason must battle his attraction even while he's waging the biggest fight of his life.

Oceans Apart,

Book Two of the Separate Ways Series

It's been two years since Lord Jamie Mainwaring and Detective Remy Remington worked and loved their way through their one and only case before going their separate ways.

Now Jamie is once again mixing agency business with pleasure as he and his partner, Agent Ryan Whiteside, are assigned to a case involving piracy in the Caribbean.

Remy and his old friend Miggy are still detectives, but they've gone private in Phoenix. When their biggest client sends them to supervise an unusual diamond transfer, they think their toughest challenge will be maintaining their cover as a gay couple on a barefoot-style cruise.

When murder connects the dots between the two cases, the four men must learn to work together as relationships and loyalties are tested amid misunderstandings and memories on the high seas.

For preview and purchase details
and news of exciting new releases. visit:

http://LauraHarner.com